Alison Roberts has bee~~n~~ ~~able to~~
live in the South of Fran~~ce for a while~~
recently, but is now back ~~in her native~~
New Zealand. She is also lucky enough to write
for the Mills & Boon Medical line. A primary
school teacher in a former life, she later became
a qualified paramedic. She loves to travel and
dance, drink champagne and spend time with her
daughter and her friends. Alison is the author of
over one hundred books!

FALLING FOR HER FORBIDDEN FLATMATE

ALISON ROBERTS

MIRACLE TWINS TO HEAL THEM

ALISON ROBERTS

MILLS & BOON

First published in Great Britain 2024
by Mills & Boon, an imprint of HarperCollins*Publishers* Ltd,
1 London Bridge Street, London, SE1 9GF

www.harpercollins.co.uk

HarperCollins*Publishers* Macken House, 39/40 Mayor Street Upper, Dublin 1, D01 C9W8, Ireland

Falling for Her Forbidden Flatmate © 2024 Alison Roberts

Miracle Twins to Heal Them © 2024 Alison Roberts

ISBN: 978-0-263-32170-8

09/24

This book contains FSC™ certified paper
and other controlled sources to ensure responsible forest management.

For more information visit www.harpercollins.co.uk/green.

Printed and Bound in the UK using 100% Renewable Electricity
at CPI Group (UK) Ltd, Croydon, CR0 4YY

FALLING FOR
HER FORBIDDEN
FLATMATE

ALISON ROBERTS

MILLS & BOON

PROLOGUE

IT WAS THE noise that made her turn her head, but it was what she thought she could see that made the chill run down Grace's spine like a trickle of ice-cold water—so shocking it made her gasp.

'What's wrong, Grace?'

'Did you see that?'

'What?'

'I think someone was looking in our window.'

'You're not sure?'

Grace frowned. It had almost been more of a feeling than anything visual. 'I just saw something out of the corner of my eye and then it was gone...'

As if someone had moved fast because they didn't want to be seen?

'It was probably just a branch on that tree in the street moving. This storm's moving in fast. Listen to the wind and rain—who'd be mad enough to go out in this just to look through people's windows?' Jenni smiled. 'And how good is it that we've both had the day off and we can stay warm and dry?'

But then Jenni's brow creased with concern.

'You've been jumpy ever since we heard that gossip about your ex. News that comes through any hospital grapevine should always be taken with a grain of salt, you know.'

'I know. And you're right. I'm just on edge.' Grace blew out a steadying breath as she got up from the couch. Perhaps physically moving would quell the upside-down sensation in her stomach? 'Why should it bother me anyway? I'm not surprised wife number two has walked out on him.'

She knew exactly why it would have happened and it was too hard to not have memories trying to escape the place where she'd done her best to lock them away. That could well be the reason she'd imagined something menacing lurking in the shadows.

Grace moved swiftly to the windows and pulled the curtains closed, shutting out the darkness. It was only late afternoon but the days were short and could be bleak in the tail end of a Scottish winter.

The small gas fire was providing welcome warmth indoors but Jenni, her flatmate, who was curled up on one end of the couch with a laptop open on her knees, still had a blanket draped around her shoulders.

'Come and look at this, Grace. Jock's sent some more photos.'

A distraction was exactly what was needed. Grace sat beside her friend, picking up a corner of the blanket so it was around both of them. Maybe this was what she really needed—to remind herself that moving all the way from London to Glasgow to do her midwifery training had been the best thing she'd ever done, because she'd met Jenni, who was her best friend ever and now they lived together and worked at the same maternity hospital and…

…and Grace was finally starting to feel genuinely safe for the first time in far too long.

'Oh…'

The sound was one of longing because what Grace was

seeing on the screen was so idyllic. A deep blue sea that was calm enough to be reflecting the rugged-looking hills of the nearby tree-covered islands. A sky that was as blue as the sea with not a cloud to be seen. The photo had been taken looking over the stern of a small boat.

'And look at this…' Jenni clicked on the arrow.

The next image had a pod of dolphins following the boat, leaping over the foam of the wake. It made Grace smile.

'They look *so* happy, don't they? I love dolphins.'

'Jock's just as happy. He says it's paradise. Mostly…'

'Only mostly? Just how fussy is your brother?'

'Apparently they're so short of midwives that he's having to do some perfectly normal deliveries himself and he says he didn't train to be an obstetrician for so many years just to catch babies.' Jenni shook her head. 'He says it's messing with his love life and his fishing, and that wasn't part of the plan when he moved to New Zealand.' She closed the laptop. 'I think he's sending me all these postcard pictures to try and entice me to go and join him. He even took photos of all the spare bedrooms in the house that's available for hospital staff.'

'And you're not tempted?' Grace could hear the wind rattling the window in this tiny living room of the terraced house they shared. At least, she *hoped* it was the wind…

'It's a tiny little town at the top of the South Island. Almost a village, and I'm never going to live in a place that small again. You couldn't have a night out without the entire town knowing about it, and where's the fun if you can't meet anyone new, anyway?'

Grace shook her head. 'Didn't you say that Jock seems to find a new girlfriend every other week or so?'

'True. The only long-term commitment he's going to

make won't be to any woman. It'll be to that boat he's bought. Going out fishing is his favourite thing to do.' Jenni shuddered. 'I hate boats. I fell out of one once, when I was about seven or eight. Jock will deny it, but he totally pushed me.'

'I thought twins were supposed to be lifelong soul mates?'

'He thought it was funny.' Jenni was smiling now. 'It kind of was, I guess. It was summer and we were living in a place that had a huge pond. One of the better foster homes we got sent to because we got to stay together.' Her tone was overly bright. 'Want to get something delivered for dinner? Like a pizza with the crust that's stuffed full of cheese?'

'Sounds good.' Grace knew when a subject needed to be changed. She pulled out her phone. 'What's the name of the town where Jock works?'

'Picton. It's where the ferries go in and out, getting from the North Island to the South Island. They have to go through the Marlborough Sounds, which have hundreds of islands which are apparently the tops of an ancient mountain range that sank into the sea.'

'And it's got a hospital big enough to need an obstetrician and midwives?'

'I think it covers quite a big population but it's spread out. Some of the islands are inhabited. Jock says that sometimes the midwives have to go to home visits or deliveries by boat.'

Grace was scrolling through more images on her phone. 'It looks amazing.'

'It's totally on the other side of the world. Who on earth would want to go there? Unless you were really into boats, of course.'

Grace glanced up—towards the windows, where a draught was making the curtains billow gently. 'I can think of other reasons the other side of the world might be a good place to live,' she said quietly. 'It would make it a lot harder for someone to find you, wouldn't it?'

Jenni was silent for a moment. 'Well, Jock would be thrilled if you wanted to apply for a job there. I'd miss you like crazy, but—'

'But you'd *have* to come and visit, wouldn't you?' Grace interrupted. 'You've been saying for ages that you must go and visit Jock one of these days.'

Jenni blinked. 'You really *like* the idea, don't you?'

'I wouldn't want to live with your brother, mind you. He sounds like he thinks any single woman is fair game.'

'Hey...if I told him you were out of bounds you'd be as safe as houses. Apart from you, Jock is the only person on earth that I would trust with my life.'

There was a much longer silence this time. One that was full of things that hadn't been spoken about since a night of wine-fuelled confessions between two new best friends. Stories of children who had never been wanted and a woman who'd been trapped in a desperately unhappy situation. The bonding of two women who'd learned that courage and determination could get them where they wanted to go.

But they both knew, all too well, that it was dangerous to assume nothing else could go wrong.

'You know I'll support you whatever you want to do,' Jenni said quietly. 'But do you really think he would come looking for you? Just because he's single again?'

Grace didn't answer because her phone was vibrating in her hand. She closed the webpage but didn't answer the call. Instead, she held the screen so that Jenni could see the message that said *No caller ID*.

It was most likely one of those automated calls from a

scammer but Grace felt another one of those shivers run down her spine as she caught Jenni's gaze. Her fingers moving to find the setting that would block the caller.

'Probably not,' she said softly. 'But the real problem is that I'm thinking about it again. I'm not going to let that happen. And if making a fresh start on the other side of the planet is what it takes, then that's what I'll do.'

CHAPTER ONE

IT FELT AS if Grace Collins had stepped into one of those postcard images that Jock had sent to his twin sister on that stormy night in Glasgow.

Good grief...was it only five or six weeks ago?

Picton Hospital had clearly been desperate enough for a new midwife to arrive that they'd accelerated the online interview process and all the paperwork needed for her to be able to work in a new country.

And here she was, in the early hours of the first day in her new life, sailing between the islands towards the pretty seaside town that was going to be her new home. It still didn't feel real but part of that had to be jetlag, despite getting a decent amount of sleep on the long haul from Glasgow to Wellington. It was good that she'd chosen a ferry trip rather than a quick flight on a small plane to cross the strait between the islands because it was giving her a bit of breathing space to get used to the speed with which her life was changing.

Passengers who didn't have a vehicle to take off the ferry were allowed to disembark first. Grace rolled her suitcase along the wharf, found a taxi with a friendly driver who even took a bit of a detour to show her where the hospital was and, in no time at all, she was bumping her case up the concrete steps of an old villa. She took a deep breath at the top of the steps, looked over her shoulder to a stunning view of a marina with a forest of yacht masts and a backdrop of the sea and islands and found she was smiling as she reached for an old iron door knocker to announce her arrival.

Her smile began to fade, however, as the door was opened a few seconds later by a woman with tousled blonde hair. She had a piece of toast in one hand with a large bite taken out of a corner and she was wearing a man's shirt that only had the lowest buttons fastened. It was quite clear that she wasn't wearing anything at all underneath the shirt.

Grace blinked. 'Um… I'm Grace,' she said. 'This is the hospital accommodation, isn't it?'

'Yeah…' The woman's smile was as friendly as the taxi driver's had been. 'Jock said someone might be arriving this morning. Come in.' She pulled the door open wider, turning to look down the long hallway. 'Jock? Are you out of bed yet?'

'No need to shout, Greta.'

The man who came through one of the doors opening onto the hallway was, thankfully, wearing more clothes than Greta. He might have bare feet and spiky, unbrushed hair but his faded denim jeans and tee shirt were perfectly respectable for a late Sunday morning and she would have recognised Jock McKay anywhere. With his red hair, bright blue eyes and freckled pale skin he was the male equivalent of Jenni and that made it feel as if she knew him already. His smile was far cheekier than Jenni's, however, and he had the confidence of a man who never had the slightest difficulty charming any woman he chose to.

Even Grace, who was immune to any male charm being directed at her, found herself smiling back at him.

'You're just in time for breakfast,' he told her. Then his

smile widened. 'Or maybe that should be brunch? Can I tempt you to one of my famous bacon butties?'

His accent was just as familiar as his looks and the warmth of that smile just as welcoming as the offer of food. Grace had to blink back a sudden prickle behind her eyes that threatened—embarrassingly—to turn into tears.

She was tired, that was all. Jetlagged and displaced and suddenly on the wrong side of the world and winter had become summer but...

...but it felt, astonishingly, like she'd finally arrived home.

Wow...

Jock McKay had seen pictures of Grace Collins with his sister over the last few years but they hadn't done justice at all to the woman now sitting on one of the wicker chairs in the shade of the veranda which was one of the best features of this old house. Grace was eating the bacon sandwich he'd made for her after she'd had a chance to put her suitcase in her bedroom and freshen up.

His date from last night, Greta, had gone to start her day's work in one of the town's popular pubs and it was no hardship for Jock to spend a bit of time to make his sister's best friend feel welcome.

'Is that good?'

'Best buttie ever.' Grace licked a drop of smoky barbecue sauce from her fingers. 'Jenni didn't tell me you could cook.'

'It's a recently acquired splinter skill.' Jock grinned. 'I had to learn to do something with the fish I was catching so I made friends with a frying pan.'

'Ah... I saw photos of your boat. It's cute. Wooden?'

'Her name's *Lassie*. And aye, she's a clinker cabin cruiser.'

'Did you name her?'

'No. She was already a Scottish boat. That was how I knew it was meant to be.'

'Does she have sails or a motor?'

'Both, but I tend to use the motor more. It's one with a propellor so she's not as fast as a jet boat, but who wants to hurry when you're out in the Sounds? It's the most beautiful place on earth.'

Grace was nodding. 'I loved coming in on the ferry but it has to be even better to have a boat of your own. There must be a thousand secluded little bays to choose from around those islands.'

'There are. And I've got a mate at work—Dan, who's one of our anaesthetists, and he likes fishing as much as I do. It's not flash inside *Lassie*, but there's enough room for us to sleep in her and we can get started at the crack of dawn. There's nothing that tastes as good as a fresh snapper fillet buttie for breakfast.'

'You've got a frying pan on board, then?'

'I do. And thanks for the reminder—I need to replenish some supplies in her galley, like the olive oil I use in the pan. If you fancy a bit of a walk down the hill, you could come to the marina with me and have a look at her. I could give you a quick tour of the hospital too, if you like. Unless you need to sleep for a while? I remember how much harder it is doing a long-haul trip in this direction than it is going back home.'

Grace shook her head. 'I've been told the best cure for jetlag is to stay awake until it's bedtime in your new time zone. And I'm feeling good. The taxi driver showed me where the hospital is, but it would be really helpful to know where to go when I turn up for work tomorrow. I'd love to see the marina too. It's so pretty, even from this distance.'

Jock took advantage of the way Grace was staring out at the view to let his own gaze rest on *her*.

She really was the perfect English rose, wasn't she? With skin that looked like porcelain, golden hair that was glowing in this bright light and eyes that were the colour of a summer sky. Or, even better, the colour the sea was today, which would normally be an irresistible invitation to get on his boat and get out there on a day off—to bask in the kind of serenity that never failed to make him feel a level of happiness he'd spent his whole life trying to find.

Jock found he had to drag his gaze away from Grace. It was probably just as well that Jenni had read him the riot act about hitting on her best friend.

Not that she'd needed to spell it out quite that clearly. Jock would never try it on with someone he was going to be sharing a house with. He'd discovered long ago how awkward it could become working with women he'd dated, even after they'd happily accepted that hooking up with him was just a bit of fun.

'Do not lay a single finger on her,' Jenni had said. *'She hasn't even been on one date since she escaped a really awful marriage and that was five years ago. She might look tough, Jock, but...she needs looking after, okay? Be the kind of brother you always were for me...'*

He might be on the opposite side of the globe but nothing would ever break the bond Jock had with his twin sister. Or how protective he'd always been of her. Looking out for her best friend was like an echo of the way he'd looked out for Jenni during the kind of childhood he wouldn't wish on anyone. It was a form of love and it required complete trust—on both sides. Trust that needed to be built, starting now.

So, no... Grace Collins had nothing to worry about as

far as he was concerned. Disappointing Jenni was the last thing he'd want to do.

Jock got to his feet and held his hand out for Grace's empty plate. 'I'll look after that. Why don't you find some comfortable walking shoes and we'll head off?'

The small town had a rather delightful holiday destination feel to it.

Relaxed-looking people wearing sunhats and shorts were drinking coffee at outdoor cafés or browsing in shops. There were grassy areas with children's playgrounds, a caravan selling ice creams, seagulls drifting overhead and private boats of all shapes and sizes bobbing gently against their moorings at the marina.

'Half the fun of owning a boat is pottering around on days like this, doing stuff that needs doing,' Jock told Grace.

'I can see that.' Grace shook her head at the hand Jock was holding out to help her onto the boat. 'I'm good, thanks. Oh...' She looked around as she climbed on board. 'This is lovely...'

The boat was obviously well cared for and its wooden ship's wheel, panelling and brass fittings were gleaming. Jock opened cupboards to stow the canned food and other supplies he'd brought with him and showed Grace how neatly all the cooking utensils and other necessities were tucked into tiny spaces around the sink and cooktop. In the low space that was at the front of the boat were cushioned benches with more storage space. Rays of sunlight came in through small portholes.

'Is that a first aid kit?'

'Yes. Not that I can leave any drugs out here, but I'd hate

to not have the basics if I find someone in trouble in some isolated spot.'

'Me too. I used to be a paramedic before I became a midwife.'

'Really? I didn't know that. What made you change direction?'

'I got sent to my first case of a woman in labour,' she said simply. 'She ended up giving birth in the back of the ambulance on the way to hospital and... I guess I fell in love with catching babies.'

It had been a call-out that had changed her entire life, not just her career. An experience that had given Grace a strength she'd never known she had and a way forward from the life she had thought she was trapped in for ever.

'It's magic, isn't it?' There was a soft smile in Jock's voice. 'When you hear that first cry and see them looking at the world for the very first time.'

'Mmm.' For Grace, it was the moment the mother got to hold her safely delivered baby in her arms. To feel that wash of relief that was always mixed in with the wonder of new life. Because it never, ever went away completely, did it? Knowing what it was like to have held her own baby, who had never had the chance to take her first breath...

This cabin space suddenly felt too closed in and she turned away to step out into the sunshine again. She saw a small dinghy heading towards the end of the marina. A man threw a rope around a bollard and jumped out onto the pier.

'What's going on?' Jock came out as the man came rapidly towards them. 'Hey...mate? You okay?'

'Have you got a phone? My battery's dead and I need to call an ambulance.'

'I'm a doctor. What's happened? Has someone had an accident?'

The man shook his head. 'It's my wife. I can't get her out of the boat and I think the baby's coming…'

Jock's startled gaze caught Grace's. 'Could you grab that first aid kit?'

As Grace ducked back into the cabin to get the kit, she could hear him telling the man he'd come past the right boat because he was an obstetrician and had a midwife with him. He had already made a phone call by the time she came out again.

'Ambulance is on its way,' Jock said. He took the kit from Grace but opened a side pocket to give her some gloves to shove in her pocket. 'But I think we should go and see what's happening before it gets here.'

'*Please*…' the man begged. 'And I need to get back to Suzie. We're moored to an anchor buoy further out. My name's Oliver, by the way.'

Jock introduced himself and Grace as they followed Oliver.

'When's the baby due?' Grace asked.

'Not for another couple of weeks. We thought we could get one last weekend in. We came over from Nelson yesterday and we were going to go out for a nice lunch and then head back home this afternoon.' He was leading the way at a jog. 'We got told that first babies are usually late. And there's always lots of warning that labour's really started, isn't there?'

'Not always,' Grace said.

Jock was right behind her as she reached the ladder close to the dinghy. 'Any problems with Suzie's pregnancy?'

'No. Maybe because it's been so easy we thought we had

this bit under control as well.' Oliver started the outboard motor. 'Suzie thought she'd just wet her pants but then the pains started and there was no way she could climb down to the dinghy.' He looked over his shoulder. 'I'll have to go back to get the ambulance crew, yeah?'

'They'll need to come out on a boat that can cope with a stretcher if it's needed. Don't worry—the coastguard head-quarters is just down the road from the marina and they'll be able to sort out the logistics as soon as I can update them on the situation.' Jock was shading his eyes against the sun as they sped out to where boats were moored in open water. 'Our job is to get to Suzie and give her whatever support she needs.'

Grace took another glance at Jock's profile. How different was this version of her new colleague to the laidback, charming playboy she'd met only a few hours ago. This was Jock McKay the surgeon she was seeing now. Focused.

In charge.

This might be the last thing Grace could have expected as her first clinical experience in her new job but she couldn't be in better company, could she?

Her heart sank, however, as they got close to the sleek yacht that belonged to Oliver and Suzie. They could all hear the agonised cry coming from within the cabin.

'*Ollie*...where are you? I can't *do* this...'

Oliver looked as white as a ghost. He cut the motor but then looked as if he had no idea what he should do next. Jock stood up to steady the dinghy against the back of the yacht. 'You okay to climb up?' he asked Grace. 'It might be best if you go in first. I'll have a wee chat with Oliver and bring the kit in just a sec.'

A flash of a glance told Grace that he would prefer that

Suzie didn't see her husband looking quite this terrified and she sent back a nod that was agreeing with more than her going in first. If this labour was already advanced enough to make it impossible to move the mother, hopefully, it would only be the skills of a midwife that would be needed. And if Oliver could be reassured enough to find the strength to support his wife, it could make a huge difference for everybody involved.

The interior cabin of a small yacht was not the ideal space for any kind of medical intervention. The ceiling was too low to be able to stand up straight and the gap between the cushioned bench seats that doubled as beds was barely enough at the pointy end for a person to turn around, let alone to set out any gear that might be needed.

Grace didn't seem perturbed, though, and Jock realised that her previous experience as a paramedic had to be a huge bonus. She was used to facing any kind of challenge in every kind of environment. She had her ponytail looped up into its fastening to keep her hair completely out of the way and her face was still enough to suggest utter concentration as she was giving Suzie an internal examination. Oliver had squeezed onto the cushion on the other side of the boat and was holding his wife's hand. They both had their heads on the widest part of the cushion in the bow.

Grace looked up at Jock.

'So the baby is in a longitudinal lie with a cephalic presentation. Suzie's fully dilated and in second stage of labour. She's not feeling the urge to push yet but I can feel baby's head. Foetal station one, possibly two...'

Jock nodded. A foetal station of one to two meant that

the baby's head was already well into the birth canal. It also meant they wouldn't be moving Suzie.

'Oliver, could you find as many clean towels as you can?'

'Why?'

'I think your baby's pretty keen to get born on a boat.'

Oliver gulped and then wriggled backwards to go hunting for linen.

'You don't have a portable Doppler or a fetoscope in that kit of yours, do you, Jock?' Grace was pulling off her gloves and reaching for a clean pair. 'It would be good to get a heart rate.'

'No.' And Jock knew that what was even more important was to be able to detect changes in the heart rate, which could be a warning that the baby was in distress. 'But I do have a stethoscope.' He pulled open the zip on the kit.

'Oh...' Suzie groaned loudly.

'Another contraction?' Grace asked. She checked her watch. 'That's only two minutes since the last one finished.'

'I need to push...' Suzie sounded like she was speaking through gritted teeth. 'Oh... *God... No...*'

'You're doing great,' Oliver told her. 'Remember to breathe...'

Suzie swore at him.

Jock had the stethoscope in his ears. He had to squeeze against Grace to get close enough to put the disc of the stethoscope against the stretched skin of Suzie's abdomen that felt as solid as concrete right now. The contraction made it harder to locate the best position to hear the baby's heart and Suzie's cries made it difficult to hear anything at all.

'I feel sick,' she said between loud groans. 'I need to go to the loo... Oh...it *hurts...*'

'Save your breath for pushing,' Oliver suggested.

Suzie swore at him again.

'Heart rate's one thirty,' Jock told Grace. Normal. They shared a glance that was relieved.

And Grace's calm voice had an ability to cut through the rising tension. 'You're doing so well, Suzie. I can see baby's head now… He's going to be here very soon…'

Jock could see the baby's head appearing as well.

And then it went backwards far enough for the chin to vanish in what appeared to be a classic 'turtle sign' that was an indication of the baby's shoulders being stuck.

A warning of a potential obstetric emergency.

This time, the glance he shared with Grace was intense but Jock kept his voice as calm as hers had been.

'Swap places?'

It was awkward because there was not enough space for two people to pass without considerable body contact, but again Grace managed to make it seem easy. Perhaps that was because she was just as focused on their patient as he was.

'Suzie…? We're going to put you in a different position to see if we can make your next contraction more effective, okay?' Jock was about to ask Grace to help move Suzie to abduct and hyperflex her thighs onto her abdomen but she was already moving.

'McRobert's?' she murmured.

'Yes. Thanks… Okay, Suzie, we're going to shift your position to make a bit more room to help things along.'

The wall of the boat made it trickier for Jock to get one leg into position but Grace was ahead of him on the other side, lifting and squeezing the leg into the position that could rotate her pelvis and widen the opening to release the baby's shoulder.

'I can't do this,' Suzie wailed. 'It hurts…'

'What's going on?' Oliver demanded. 'Why are you doing that?'

Suzie was beginning her next contraction and Jock found he was holding his breath. He'd taken note of the time when the baby's head had first appeared and the countdown was on to deliver this baby. They only had a few minutes before they could run into real trouble.

'Sometimes the baby can get a bit stuck for a moment,' Grace told him. 'This is the best way to get past that.'

'You could help hold Suzie's legs, Oliver,' Jock suggested.

'Climb past me on the other side and get near her head,' Grace added.

Suzie's cry of pain was sharp. Oliver scrambled to get to her.

'Hold your legs behind your knees,' Grace instructed Suzie as she leaned back against her husband. 'Oliver can put his hands over yours and help you pull your legs as close as possible to your chest. And don't push, Suzie... Just blow...' Grace was demonstrating the breathing to remind Suzie how to help quell the urge to push.

'Grace? Can you give me some suprapubic pressure, please?'

Jock was pleased to see her locate where the anterior shoulder of the baby was and then link her hands in a CPR position directly behind the shoulder and apply pressure in a rocking motion. She knew exactly what she was doing, didn't she? Jock could let himself think ahead in case this technique wasn't successful.

He had a scalpel in his kit so he could perform an episiotomy to make it easier to perform the internal manoeuvres of slipping his hand in to get hold of the posterior arm and get this baby out. The clock was ticking. The tension was increasing rapidly.

The whole boat started rocking as more people climbed on board. There was no hope of any extra rescuers fitting into this cabin space, but they didn't need to.

'I can feel baby moving…' Grace said. 'I think we're almost there, Suzie…'

And, just as suddenly as it had begun, the potential emergency evaporated as the baby slithered out into Jock's hands.

Even better, this baby boy, who was big enough that his size had probably caused the worrying hiccup in his arrival, began crying instantly and, in this confined space under the deck of the boat, the sound was so loud it made his parents laugh.

And then cry.

It looked like Grace had tears in her own eyes.

'Apgar at one minute is eight,' Jock announced.

'Is that good?' Oliver asked.

'It's great,' Grace assured them. 'Let's get baby onto Mum's skin to keep him warm. Do you want to cut the cord in a minute when we're ready, Dad?'

Oliver sounded a lot more confident now. 'Absolutely.'

Grace hesitated before picking the baby up, however, because she could see what Jock was checking as he carefully felt around the baby's shoulders.

'All good,' he said quietly. 'No fractures of either clavicle.'

Yes…they were tears, but she was smiling. Not at him, but at the baby she gathered into her hands to transfer him to his mother's skin. He could see the joy in her face and he could sense the extraordinary satisfaction she got from her profession.

He could *feel* her passion.

Jock loved meeting people who felt the same way he did about the job he'd chosen to devote his life to. He appreciated working with people who were intelligent and capable and exceptionally good at what they did.

And, okay…he couldn't deny that he liked being around very beautiful women.

Like the one who seemed to be waiting to catch his gaze as she rested her hand on Suzie's abdomen.

Suzie was so entranced with her baby she didn't seem to be noticing the new contraction she was experiencing, but Jock shifted his attention to the last stage of labour and the delivery of the placenta.

Most of his attention, anyway.

A part of his brain was still collating all the positive attributes he was discovering about his new colleague, who was also—at least for the moment—his new flatmate.

Grace Collins might be out of bounds, but she was, quite possibly, his perfect woman.

No…on second thoughts, maybe the fact that she was out of bounds was exactly *why* she was his perfect woman.

No matter how attractive she was, if Jock even thought of responding to that he would see his sister in the back of his mind, wagging her finger at him, and that would be more than enough to remind him to back off. On the other side of that coin, however, that meant he wouldn't have to walk away as soon as an uncomfortable level of closeness was reached.

He could follow Jenni's edict and look after her like a big brother. Which meant he could have fun with Grace. Tease her like he would tease Jenni. Enjoy a conversation or going out somewhere together without being on alert for any hidden agenda.

Aye…this was as safe as it got.

And that made it perfect.

CHAPTER TWO

WAKING UP THE next morning, Grace had a very disconcerting few seconds wondering, quite literally, where on earth she was.

And then she heard the faint sound of someone whistling.

A male person whistling, and that was far more disconcerting than not knowing where she was.

Grace froze in her new bed, looking up at a high ceiling with an ornate plaster centrepiece that the light was dangling from. The plaster flowers were creating shadows because there was sunlight filtering through curtains that she hadn't pulled shut properly last night, when jetlag had rendered her incoherent enough to crash into unconsciousness by seven p.m.

Remembering where she was made her suck in a huge breath.

The reality of being alone in a house with a male person made that breath catch in her chest. Had she really thought she would be okay with this?

She found herself letting that breath out slowly enough for it to be soothing. Reassuring.

That was Jock McKay whistling.

Her best friend's brother.

The man with the twinkle in his eyes and the cheeky grin, who couldn't have made her feel more welcome when she'd arrived yesterday. Good grief…his first words had been to offer her something to eat, as if he'd just been waiting for the opportunity to look after her. How could she possibly feel nervous about being in this house with a man like that?

This was a man who'd looked positively misty when he'd told her that he thought there was magic involved in bringing babies into the world, but had then demonstrated his scientific skill and absolute focus by doing exactly that.

Above all, he was Jenni's brother and she'd told her that she'd be as safe as houses.

And wasn't being able to take a huge leap of faith underpinning everything about this enormous change she was making in her life?

That didn't stop the nerves kicking in, of course, as Grace threw her clothes on before heading for the bathroom and then the kitchen, where she found Jock rinsing some dishes.

'Morning, Sleeping Beauty,' he said. 'How did you sleep?'

'Like the dead,' Grace told him. 'I'm not sure I'm quite awake yet, to be honest. It feels like I'm still dreaming.'

There was that grin again. And the gleam of warmth that made his eyes the most remarkable shade of blue. Grace felt herself releasing another slow breath.

This was okay. She *could* cope.

'You need coffee,' Jock told her. 'I'd offer to make it, but I need to see all my patients before my Theatre list starts at eight.'

'You don't need to look after me, Jock.'

'Oh, I think I do. Jenni will have my guts for garters if I don't.'

Grace laughed. 'I'm more than capable of making my own coffee.'

'There's plenty of bread for toast. You'll find jam and Vegemite in the same cupboard as the coffee.'

'Vegemite?'

'Like Marmite, but not nearly as intense. I love it.' Jock was heading out of the kitchen. 'You're coming into the hospital today?'

'Yes. I'm getting the grand tour and induction process so I'll be ready to hit the ground running when I officially start on Wednesday.'

'Might see you round. If you want to go exploring later, you're welcome to use my car. The keys are on my bedside table.'

'Thank you. But I won't need a car.'

One of Jock's eyebrows rose. 'You do drive, don't you?'

'Of course I do. I used to drive an ambulance, remember? But the hospital's an easy walk from here.'

'Yes, but your home visits won't be. They could be an hour or more's drive away. You might want to start getting to know the roads.'

'I think I get to use a hospital car for home visits, but you're right—I will need to get a car of my own soon so I can get out and see as much of New Zealand as possible.'

'Now, that's something I *could* help you with. I know a guy at one of the local car yards. Best I come with you, though, and make sure you get the best price.'

'What time is it for you?'

'Just coming up to five p.m. What about you?' Jenni seemed to be peering into her phone screen. 'Looks like you're having breakfast. Ooh...what's that black stuff on your toast? Marmite?'

'Vegemite. My new fave. With toasted wholegrain bread.

You let it get a bit cold and put lots of butter on first. I hear it's even better with some avocado on top, but I haven't tried that yet.'

'Yuck…'

Grace ignored the face Jenni was making. 'And it's six a.m. here. It's going to be a glorious day. Look at that…' She turned her phone around. 'Can you see how blue that sky is already?'

'I don't want to know,' Jenni grumbled. 'It's been snowing here again today. Well…sleeting, which means that there's slush everywhere. And it's *freezing*…'

'Tell me more.' Grace was grinning as she reached for her mug of coffee.

'No. You're too happy as it is. I'm dead jealous.'

'Have you booked some tickets to come and visit yet?'

'Working on it. It's not cheap travelling that far. And Fergus wants me to go to Portugal with him for a weekend.'

'Isn't Fergus the guy you hooked up with before I left Glasgow?'

'That's the one.'

Grace laughed. 'I wouldn't book Portugal then.'

'Why not?'

'It's been nearly three weeks. You'll be breaking your own record if it lasts longer than a month.'

'That's a bit harsh.'

'You're as bad as Jock. He's got a bit of a reputation of being a playboy here, although nobody seems to think any less of him for it. He's a popular lad, your brother.'

'That's why it's good to keep things casual. If it's clear it's never going to get serious, nobody's going to get hurt and you can just enjoy it.'

Grace used taking a bite of toast as a reason to avoid

having to respond to that statement. Maybe she was out of sync with the majority of her generation but casual sex had never appealed to her.

And now…well, it was the stuff of nightmares, wasn't it?

'But you're right,' Jenni added. 'I won't book Portugal. I'll put the money towards that ticket to New Zealand instead. If that's a deal breaker for Fergus, so be it. What are you up to today?'

'I've got an almost forty-two weeker who's coming in for an induction first thing, so she could well deliver later today. And then I've got an antenatal clinic this afternoon. If it's anything like almost every shift I've had here so far it'll be full-on, but at least I'm starting to get used to where everything is now and I can find my way around. That nervousness and how tiring it is to be the new girl at school is finally wearing off.'

'But you're loving this job, aren't you?'

'Yeah…' Grace glanced at her watch. 'Speaking of which, I'd better go and get myself ready. I can't keep sitting here and looking at all the boats in the harbour and the sunshine glistening on the sea. Did I tell you that Jock said I could come out on his boat next time he and his friend Dan go fishing? If I'm lucky, I might be able to go swimming with some dolphins.'

'Oh, *stop*…' But Jenni was laughing. 'Is he around? I could annoy him for a wee while until Fergus gets here to take me out on the town.'

'No…he's out for a run. Or was it a game of squash? I can't keep up with his fitness regime. Maybe it's a bit like his love life. Endless variety and always something on the go.'

Jenni laughed. 'You haven't come across any more semi-naked women in the house, have you?'

'No. I think he's gone underground while I'm settling in. There has been a night or two when he's been very late home.' Grace picked up the last corner of her toast as she got to her feet.

'Is it as bad as you thought it would be, having to live with a guy? Are you still planning to find a place of your own?'

Grace gestured that she couldn't say anything because her mouth was full, but that gave her a moment to consider her friend's question and, to her surprise, she realised she'd almost forgotten that had been her original plan. That, even on a temporary basis, the idea of living with a man—if he hadn't been Jenni's brother—could easily have been a deal-breaker for coming here in the first place at all.

Maybe that tension had been defused by the fact that Greta had been here when she'd first arrived. Or that Jock had been so laid back and welcoming, with that 'it's no big deal' and 'the more the merrier' kind of vibe that had somehow sneaked past her defences—possibly due to being dazed by jetlag.

Or maybe it had been that totally unexpected introduction to working with one of her new colleagues when they'd delivered that baby in the bottom of that yacht. It could have been the jokes on the way home about the water birth where nobody had even got wet because, later that evening, before she'd crashed into the deepest sleep ever, Grace realised that Jock was the first man who had made her laugh since…well…since her life had slipped towards the cliff she had inevitably fallen over.

But it was more likely to have been the way she'd felt working with Jock like that, being thrown into the deep end and having nothing to rely on other than each other. The focus that felt like she was looking into a professional mirror. The need for the arrival of a new life to be, above all, *safe*...

That was it, in a nutshell.

It wasn't just because the rent was subsidised in this hospital-provided accommodation. Grace was letting go of the idea of moving out because *she* felt safe.

And why would she want to fix something if it wasn't broken?

Okay, there had been the odd moment in the first few days when she'd frozen, like she had when she'd woken up that first day, wondering where on earth she was. It had happened again a day or two later, when she'd come out of her room to see Jock emerging from the bathroom with only a towel around his waist and she'd been hit with a curl of sensation in her gut that took her breath away. And the time she'd been in the kitchen and heard the click of the front door opening as he'd arrived home and she'd felt a familiar chill trickle down her spine.

But, now on her way to the same kitchen as she swallowed her last mouthful of breakfast, Grace had the distinct feeling she wasn't ever going to overreact like that again. It felt like she was moving on in bigger ways than changing her location and lifestyle so convincingly.

'He's been brilliant,' she told Jenni. 'He got me such a good deal on the car I bought last week. He came with me for a test drive and then drove the hardest bargain with the car salesman.'

And that had been a test for something more than how the car handled, hadn't it? She'd been beside Jock in a small hatchback car. Close enough that it would have been so easy for him to touch her and…she'd still felt safe.

She'd seen the envious look the receptionist in the car yard had given her when she was signing the sales agreement for the little blue car—the one that told her how lucky she was that she had a super cute boyfriend to help her buy a car and, if she was honest, Grace had rather liked the assumption being made.

Not that she would ever confess that to Jenni.

'He's a really good cook,' she added hurriedly. 'He makes the best bacon butties in the world and sometimes he even remembers to put the loo seat down.'

Grace tried not to let her smile stretch too far across her face. She didn't want to make Jenni feel bad that she was settling in so easily to her new life. That she felt so much safer than she had, thanks to living so far away from the UK—and her past. That she was feeling happier than she had in…possibly for ever?

'I always wanted a brother when I was growing up and now it feels like I've got one,' she finished with genuine sincerity. 'And he looks so much like you that it helps me to not miss you so much.'

'Aww…' Jenni made a sad face. 'Now I feel really left out. And I'm missing *you* heaps. Say hi to Jock for me.'

The first time Grace saw Jock at work later that morning certainly wasn't the time to pass on any greeting from his sister.

Her patient, Melissa, who had gone well past her estimated date of delivery with her first child, had been scheduled to have an induction this morning but had, instead, come into hospital in active labour and four centimetres dilated at almost the same time Grace had arrived to start her shift. Her birth plan included an epidural for pain relief and it was Jock's fishing buddy, Dan, who arrived to give Melissa the spinal anaesthetic. A tall, serious man, he said very little after asking for current vital signs for the mother and whether the foetal monitoring was giving any cause for concern. Grace helped him position Melissa, sitting on the edge of the bed with her spine curved, and supported her shoulders as Dan did his work swiftly and efficiently, inserting a fine catheter to allow release of medication that could be topped up as needed by the patient-controlled button on the infusion.

Hours later, however, the contractions were slowing down, her dilation hadn't progressed at all, Melissa's anxiety was increasing and, even more concerning, the baby was beginning to show signs of being distressed, with the heart rate slowing during contractions and then taking a little longer each time to go back up. When Melissa's waters broke and there were signs of meconium in the fluid, Grace paged Jock, as the obstetrician on call, to come down to the labour suite, where she introduced him to Melissa and her partner Jason.

'Mel's a thirty-four-year-old primigravida,' she added. 'No complications with the pregnancy but she's at forty-one weeks, five days from her EDD, and was due to have an induction this morning because of reduced foetal movements yesterday.'

'Hey, Mel.' Jock was wearing pale blue scrubs and had a stethoscope slung around his neck. He was quickly scanning the patient's notes as Grace was speaking and would have noted both the presence of meconium in the amniotic fluid and the decelerations of the baby's heart rate during contractions, but his smile as he looked up at Melissa was more than reassuring. He looked impressed, even.

'I see you decided to jump the gun and go into labour all by yourself this morning,' he said. 'Good for you, getting a head start like that.'

It was the first time Grace had seen Melissa smile since she'd arrived that morning and she could understand why. She'd feel reassured herself if Jock was standing beside her bed, looking as if he was proud of the effort she was making to have her baby and that he was ready to help her in any way she needed. As if nothing was a problem and the only person that mattered in this moment was the person he was focused on. For an exhausted, frightened first-time mother—and her husband, who was hovering nervously beside her—he was the medical equivalent of a knight in shining armour.

He represented hope that the worst was over.

And he brought a new level of safety to an increasingly tense situation. Grace could see both Melissa and Jason almost breathing a sigh of relief. It wasn't that they didn't have faith in their midwife, it was more that they were being reminded that they were in the right place, with the best people and resources they could have around them.

And who wouldn't trust Jock McKay?

That quintessential boy-next-door friendliness and dependability was so obviously genuine. Melissa and her partner couldn't know the level of professional competence that Jock possessed but perhaps they could sense the respect with which other staff members regarded him. They would certainly be able to feel that he was more than interested in his patients—that he cared about both his mothers and their babies. As deeply as Grace cared about each and every mother she worked with to help bring their babies safely into the world.

She really liked that about him.

His examination of Melissa was gentle but thorough. He watched her go into another contraction and they could all hear the ominous dip in the baby's heart rate on the CTG machine that was monitoring her through the flat discs strapped to her abdomen. A new section of graph paper began emerging as part of the automatic recording when acceptable parameters were being breached. Grace had silenced the alarms to prevent the additional anxiety they would cause.

Jock perched his hip on the edge of the bed, which made his eye level much closer to Melissa's as she took a bunch of tissues from her husband and wiped tears from her face. Grace was on the other side of the bed and took hold of the hand Melissa stretched out towards her.

'You're doing a great job,' Jock told her quietly. 'But it's been a wee bit too long without any progress and I think your baby's getting tired too. The safest option for both of you would be for you to have a Caesarean section.'

Melissa nodded. Grace had already discussed this possibility with them. 'I just want this to be over,' she said. 'To have her out so that we know she's okay...'

'Which is exactly what we want too,' Jock said. 'Grace is going to get you ready and I'll see you up in Theatre. You've already got an epidural so you're good to go. And you've met Dan, our anaesthetist on duty today. He'll be in Theatre with us too, to help look after you.' His smile included Jason now. 'You guys will be meeting your baby very soon. Have you got any questions you'd like to ask?'

Melissa stifled a sob. 'Is Jason allowed to be there the whole time?'

'Of course. Grace, are you okay to organise the theatre gear for Jason?'

'Yes. I'll find everything he needs.'

'You'll be right beside Melissa at the head of the bed,' Jock told Jason. 'You won't be able to see the actual surgery because we put a screen up, but you'll be able to talk to her and hold her hand. Dan will be able to answer any questions you might have.'

'But Grace will be there too?'

'She's your midwife.' Jock's smile was for Grace this time. 'I might be doing the actual delivery this time but I'm quite sure she wouldn't want to be anywhere else.'

'He's not wrong,' Grace said. 'We're all going to be there to take the very best care of you and baby, Mel.'

Jock *hadn't* been wrong. Grace had always enjoyed every part of being in the surgical team performing a Caesarean section. She loved being in Theatre during the preparation, where her job was to check that the resuscitation unit was turned on to pre-warm and the settings were correct for delivering the suction and oxygen functions. She loved getting both herself and the father-to-be ready to enter Theatre with the clothing and hats, masks and shoe covers, along with plenty of encouragement and reassurance for what was a frightening prospect for someone who hadn't expected to end up being rushed into an operating theatre.

She loved waiting to one side of the sterile area as the surgeon and their assistants worked, ready to receive the baby in a sterile towel—as long as the delivery was uncomplicated—show the infant to the parents and then take it to the warming unit to do the initial examination. Because this surgical delivery was happening urgently due to foetal distress, there would be a paediatrician standing by for possible resuscitation but, for the moment, Grace could stand alone and watch the first minutes of the operation.

She could watch Jock engaged in one of the most dramatic ways to help bring a baby into the world and she held her breath as she saw him start a procedure she'd observed countless times, but it was always a little bit different.

The steps were familiar. The horizontal incision low on the abdomen that exposed the layer of fat, followed by muscle and then the gleaming globe of the uterus. The smell of blood vessels being cauterised and the sound of the suction unit clearing amniotic fluid were also familiar enough to be welcomed and Grace wasn't surprised by the frown of concentration she could see on Jock's face as he reached in to free the baby, who was probably well engaged in the pelvis after the hours of Melissa's labour.

'I can feel something…' Melissa's cry was alarmed.

'You should be able to feel pressure.' Jock's voice was calm. 'But it shouldn't hurt.'

'It's not hurting, is it?' The anaesthetist, Dan, leaned forward so that Melissa could see his face.

'No…it just feels…weird…'

'Not long now. Hang in there,' Jock said.

The baby's head was out and the theatre nurse quickly suctioned the tiny nose and mouth. Grace stepped closer, a sterile towel in her gloved hands, as Jock wriggled the shoulders free.

'And here we are…' He held the baby up between both hands, with a secure grip under her arms and supporting her head, high enough to be seen by the parents over the drape that was clipped to a frame to provide a screen. The tiny legs were still curled up and the rope of the umbilical cord hung beneath her.

'She's gorgeous,' he pronounced.

Then, before the cord was clamped and cut, Jock turned his head to look at the baby himself, holding her in front of his own face—for just a heartbeat—as if he was making eye contact to reassure himself that everything was all right. The baby's eyes were open and she seemed to be looking right back at him, too startled to move.

And there it was again.

That moment that never quite went away for Grace.

The echo of that awful silence when you just knew that everything wasn't okay. That it would never be okay ever again. When your future—and the world as you knew it—had just been derailed into complete catastrophe.

The memory was no more than a ghost. So fleeting it almost wasn't there these days, but it was what happened next that was almost Grace's undoing on this occasion.

Jock smiled at the baby.

Grace couldn't see his mouth under his mask but she could see the way his eyes crinkled and his body language softened in a glow that was like a telepathic welcome to this new little human.

It felt a lot like love and that gave Grace a squeeze on her heart that was so painful it almost made her gasp. Jock would probably smile at his own baby like that as it took its first breath, wouldn't he?

The way she had once, for a nanosecond, after her baby was born. Before she'd remembered what the silence around her meant. That there wasn't going to be a first breath…

The ghost evaporated in the same moment that she remembered something that Jenni had said that day the direction of her life had begun to change—that the only long-term commitment Jock McKay was ever going to make would be to the boat he'd fallen in love with and purchased. It was unlikely he would ever be having telepathic conversations in his own baby's first moments of life but, oddly, that only made it feel as if there was more of a bond between herself and Jock.

The baby didn't seem too impressed by Jock's attention. She scrunched up her little face and was crying vigorously as she got her umbilical cord clamped and cut and was then laid onto the towel Grace had over her hands. She could take her to the parents for a closer, brief peek before the first, more thorough assessment of the tiny girl's condition was done in the warmth of the resuscitation unit.

Given the all-clear from the paediatrician, Grace could then swaddle the baby in towels to keep her warm and put her into her father's arms as he sat beside Melissa while the longer part of the surgery happened, with the removal of the placenta and the painstaking closure of all the layers of the abdomen.

And that gave Grace another chance to watch Jock.

To remember that conversation with Jenni early this morning that had made her realise how happy she was that she'd made the decision to leave her old life behind. Because it really did feel as if it was a long way behind her now.

It almost felt as if the brush of that ghost, when she'd seen Jock holding Melissa's baby girl in the air to make eye contact with the newborn, might have been the last time it was going to hurt quite that much.

Grace didn't realise that her lips had curved into a hint

of a smile that must have shown in her eyes until she turned back to Melissa and caught a glance from Dan on the way.

Oh, help…did he think she was smiling at *him*?

Her heart skipped a beat and sped up, and not in the good way of being attracted to someone—it was more like a faint touch of panic. That embryonic smile evaporated instantly.

Grace wasn't trying to attract the attention of any man. She had, in fact, perfected more than one or two techniques to make sure she *didn't*.

Clearly, there were still some parts of her past that weren't far enough behind her yet.

Maybe they never would be.

As if he sensed something untoward, Jock lifted his head from his stitching to glance at Grace.

Just a glance, nothing more. But it was enough.

Whatever was threatening her peace of mind and joy in this particular moment was gone. It felt like Grace's feet were back on solid ground.

Yeah… Jock was here and…it felt safe again.

CHAPTER THREE

'STELLA WATSON?'

The woman who was sitting quietly in the corner of the outpatient department waiting room, staring out of the window, jumped visibly as Grace called her name.

'I'm so sorry to have kept you waiting for so long, Stella. Antenatal clinics can get a bit hectic. I'm Grace, one of the midwives here. Come with me...'

Hectic was the word for it today, that was for sure. The departmental staff had been very helpful but this was the first antenatal clinic Grace had run by herself in what was not simply a new work environment but a new country with slightly different protocols, and she was still familiarising herself with what was offered during pregnancy in the way of appointment schedules, tests, vaccinations and birthing options.

Fortunately, the basics of the monitoring that needed to be done at all stages of a woman's countdown to giving birth were familiar enough to be automatic and Grace had been busy all afternoon meeting her patients, taking blood pressures and doing urine dipstick analyses and physical examinations to check the position of the baby and fundal height and listening to heart sounds. She'd booked ultrasound scans, ordered blood tests, discussed any symptoms or worries, offered advice and made plans for any follow-up needed before the next scheduled visit. She'd picked up toys thrown around her consulting room by pre-schoolers who had accompanied their mothers and recorded every measurement, along with scribbling copious notes so that she could complete her paperwork later and not keep people waiting too long as appointment slots invariably ran over time and it was frustrating not to have had more time to get to know these women she was meeting for the first time.

Like Maureen Petersen, a forty-year-old primigravida who had just passed the halfway point of her pregnancy and was carrying a recent ultrasound image of her baby in her wallet. She took that out to show Grace as she got up to leave an appointment where every check had been reassuringly normal.

'I keep looking at it,' she'd confided in Grace. 'Because it seems too good to be true. My friends think I'm crazy to choose to become a single mother at my age but…it felt like my last chance, you know? And I thought, why should I have to miss out on being a mum just because I haven't found a partner? I know it won't be easy but I'm not scared to do it by myself. Except for the birth bit… I am a bit scared of that.'

'You won't be doing that by yourself,' Grace promised. 'We'll be taking care of you through the rest of your pregnancy and the birth, and for the first six weeks of you being at home with your baby.'

'Will it be you there for the birth?'

'That might depend on whether baby wants to play ball,' Grace said. 'But I really hope so. And I'll be looking forward to seeing you at your next appointment. In the meantime, call any time if you're worried about anything.'

At least the pressure was off for the last appointment for

this clinic. Stella Watson had been put at the end of the list because this was a first antenatal visit and would need more time, especially when the patient file was empty apart from a GP's very brief referral form. Grace needed to know about any significant health issues and current medications or allergies and past medical history for both the mother-to-be and her family. She would also be gathering any impression that extra care might be needed due to any individual physical, social or emotional needs.

Grace shifted the chairs so that they were both on the same side of the desk.

'So I understand that this is your second pregnancy, Stella?'

'Yes.'

'How old is your first child?'

'He's…six.'

Grace made a quick note. There could be all sorts of reasons for a longer than normal gap between children. Commonly, it was as simple as a relationship break-up and a new baby with a new partner. It could be due to fertility issues and it might be the result of Stella losing a child before or after birth. It was definitely a subject that Grace needed to approach with sensitivity.

'And you didn't have your first baby here?'

'No, I was living up north. We only moved here recently. My husband got a job down on the wharf.'

Stella glanced over her shoulder as if she half-expected someone to come into the room. Or was she looking for a way out?

Something didn't feel right.

'Are you okay for childcare today?' Grace checked.

'You're not in a rush to get back home to…what's your son's name?'

'Scott. No, it's okay—I'm not in a hurry.'

Grace wasn't convinced. She glanced again at the referral note to request the antenatal appointment.

'So you're not sure when your last period was?'

Stella shook her head. 'There's been a lot going on, what with finding a new place to live and shifting and getting Scott started at his new school and everything.'

'I totally get it,' Grace sympathised. 'I've only moved to Picton very recently myself. It's such a big upheaval in your life, isn't it? And it's not a problem.' She made another note. 'I might see if they can fit you in for a quick ultrasound, which will be able to give us an estimated date of delivery. What we'll do in the meantime is just have a chat so I can ask you about your medical history and your last pregnancy and so on. I'll take some baseline recordings like your blood pressure and weight. We'll do a blood and urine test, if that's okay, but today's appointment is mainly a chance for us to meet each other.' She made eye contact with Stella as she smiled warmly. 'I'm really looking forward to helping you in whatever way I can so you can really enjoy this pregnancy.'

Stella was staring at Grace, her eyes wide. 'But…but I don't *want* to enjoy this pregnancy,' she whispered. 'I don't want to be pregnant at all…' She burst into tears. '*Sorry*,' she sobbed. 'I'm really sorry…'

'You've got nothing to be sorry about…' Grace leaned closer and put her hand over Stella's. 'It's okay,' she said. 'Talk to me…please?'

But Stella shook her head. She grabbed her bag from the floor beside her chair and stood up so fast she knocked her chair over as she turned. Before Grace could even say anything else, Stella had wrenched the door to the room open and she was gone.

Jock had no chance to avoid the woman, who walked straight into him as he came out of the coffee shop in the hospital foyer, probably because she was almost running. She had her head down, which meant she hadn't seen him.

And she was crying…

It was totally instinctive to catch the woman's shoulders and steady her, but Jock didn't let go straight away. It wasn't that it was unusual to see upset people coming and going in a hospital environment, when they could be visiting seriously ill family members or might have just lost a loved one. Perhaps this woman had been given bad news about her own health, given that she seemed to be running from the direction of the outpatient department.

'Hey…' Jock tried to catch her gaze. 'Is everything okay?'

Stupid question when it was clear that something was very wrong, but Jock could sense the panic this woman was experiencing and he needed to say something to let her know that he was there. That he was willing to help if he could.

'You might hurt yourself if you're not watching where you're going,' he added.

'Sorry… Oh, God…' She looked up, finally. 'Did I hurt *you*?'

'Not at all.' Jock smiled at her. 'Made of steel, I am.' He was about to let go of her shoulders as he felt her relax a little, but then he saw someone else coming out of the outpatient department's entrance.

And the concern on Grace's face as she approached them let him connect the dots instantly.

'I think someone might be looking for you,' he said.

'Stella?' Grace was close enough to call without attracting attention. 'Oh, thank goodness you're still here.' She lowered her voice even more. 'Please don't run away—we can talk about anything.'

Jock could feel how tense Stella was again. Something was very wrong and if she had run from an appointment with a midwife it was very likely that there was some kind of problem with a pregnancy.

'I was heading home,' he said casually, 'but I'm not in any hurry if there's anything I can help with.' It wasn't strictly true. Jock hadn't got near his boat in days and he had been planning to make the most of a long summer's evening and head out for a spot of fishing.

'Jock's one of our obstetricians,' Grace told Stella.

Stella pulled away from him as if his hands were burning her shoulders.

'I can't do it.' Her whisper was terrified. 'I can't have this baby.' She was turning towards the main entrance. 'I've got to get out of here.'

'No problem.' Jock caught Grace's startled look as he agreed with Stella. 'We can't make you stay. But could you do something for me first?'

Stella also looked startled. 'What?'

'At least talk to Grace. Please…even if it's only for a few minutes.'

'Why?'

'Because she's new here and it was her first antenatal clinic today and I don't think she's used to having one of her mums running away from her.'

'Oh…' Stella bit her lip. 'Sorry…'

'So you'll talk to her?'

Stella nodded slowly. 'Okay… I guess I owe her that much…'

Grace caught Jock's gaze and he could see her lips moving in a silent 'thank you' as she led Stella back into Outpatients.

It made him feel surprisingly good that he might have done something that Grace really appreciated. Jenni would be happy too. Jock could already imagine making a joke of it and telling his sister that he'd stopped one of her friend's patients escaping.

Except that it wasn't anything to joke about, was it?

And he'd inadvertently become involved in Stella's case. He wanted to know the story behind what had happened and what was going to happen next.

Jock gave up on his plan to go fishing. He'd go to the supermarket instead and find something to cook for Grace when she got home.

'That smells *so* good.' The aroma had been making Grace's stomach rumble, in fact, even before she'd walked through the gate of her new home.

'It's nothing fancy. I'm doing bangers and mash for dinner—just to make sure you don't start feeling homesick.'

'It smells a lot fancier than the bangers and mash I used to get at the local pub.' Grace dropped her bag and stepped closer to the small barbecue Jock was using at the end of the veranda.

'These ones are traditional British beef sausages, but they do come from a gourmet butcher in town and they do fancy snarlers too. Like wild venison and fennel. Or pork and parsley. I wasn't sure what you'd like so I played it safe.'

'Snarlers?'

'It's Kiwi for bangers. I believe it comes from the sound they make when they're trapped in a frying pan.'

Grace laughed. 'I like it. Can I do anything to help?'

'No. It's all good.'

Grace sank onto the chair with a sigh. 'Jenni says hi, by the way. I've been trying to find a moment to tell you that all day, but things kept happening.'

'They have a habit of doing that, don't they? When were you talking to Jenni?'

'This morning, while I was having breakfast.' Grace leaned her head back and closed her eyes. Had it only been this morning that she'd been sitting here eating her Vegemite toast? She blew out a breath. 'It's been quite a day.'

'It has,' Jock agreed. 'A great one for Melissa. It was a good call on your part, not leaving her in labour any longer.'

Grace liked that Jock remembered their patient's name and hadn't just referred to her as a case, like 'this morning's C-section'.

He was using tongs to turn the sausages on the grill as they got licked by flames. 'How did you get on with Stella after I left?' he asked.

'We talked for an hour or more. That's why I'm late. Poor thing, she's got… Oh, what's it called again? That extreme fear of pregnancy and labour?'

'Tokophobia.' Jock was nodding. 'Did you find any obvious cause?'

'Yes.' Grace sat up straighter. 'She had one of the more traumatic birth stories I've ever heard. Not from here,' she added hastily, as she saw Jock's shocked expression. 'It was in a small hospital up north somewhere. Six years ago.'

'What happened?'

'First pregnancy. Went into labour at forty weeks and seemed to be doing well but, twenty-three hours later, the baby was in distress. Two failed attempts with a vacuum cup, an episiotomy with inadequate analgesia and a forceps delivery that sounds like it was a struggle. There was probably a bit of shoulder dystocia going on as well.'

'Good grief...sounds like something out of the Middle Ages.'

'She's lucky her son survived. He had the cord wrapped around his neck as well. And, just to add insult to injury, they did a manual extraction of the placenta without waiting for an effective anaesthetic. Stella said that was the worst of the whole experience. The pain was unbelievable.'

Jock shook his head. 'No wonder she's terrified. What was the reason for such an urgent removal of the placenta? Did she have a post-partum haemorrhage?'

'I don't know. I've requested to have her hospital notes forwarded.'

'Good thinking. It might help if there are some medical explanations to what went on, even if they don't excuse the result. Has she talked to anyone about it?'

'I don't think she's ever talked about it. She thought it would be better to put it all behind her. She's done everything she can to avoid getting pregnant again, but her husband's desperate for another child so she thought she could force herself to go through it for his sake. She hasn't even told him she's pregnant though, because...' Grace had to take a breath to try and stop the wobble in her voice. 'She thinks she wants a termination—without him having to know anything about it.'

'What did *you* say?' The encouraging glance from Jock told Grace that he understood that it could have been distressing for her to hear that.

'I managed to get a dating scan done for her and she's only around eight to nine weeks along, so I said she didn't need to make any big decisions urgently. I suggested an obstetric referral and she said she'd only do that if it was you she could talk to.' Grace's smile felt almost shy. 'She's terrified of obstetricians but you certainly won her over.'

Jock's shrug was modest. 'Sometimes it pays to look like an overgrown, scruffy teenager instead of a consultant surgeon, I guess. Did you talk about an elective Caesarean to avoid any repeat trauma like the first time?'

'I did. She'd done some research herself and found some online chat that said it was really hard to find an obstetrician that would agree to it. That you either had to be diagnosed with mental illness to qualify or you'd be branded as "too posh to push".'

'Not true,' Jock said. 'I'll be happy to see her. Mark it as needing an urgent consult and they'll squeeze her into my next outpatient clinic. I'd be happy to do the C-section myself if that's the best choice for her and I'd do my absolute best to make sure she gets a birth experience that won't end up giving her nightmares.'

'Like Melissa did this morning,' Grace said. 'I popped in to see her before I came home and she's so happy. Over-the-moon happy. It was a joy to be there.'

Grace was smiling properly this time. It hadn't been only the patients that Jock had impressed today. Not that she was about to tell him how much she'd been won over by the heart-melting moment when this obstetrician had welcomed the arrival of Melissa's baby. And—even more—by the way he hadn't hesitated to stop and help someone in distress, as he had with Stella. He wasn't simply an excellent surgeon, was he? He was a really, really nice guy.

Quite possibly the nicest guy she'd ever met.

And that made sense, seeing as his twin sister was the best friend she'd ever made.

Jock didn't see her smile because he hadn't turned around from tending to the sausages.

He shrugged off the compliment too. 'Good to hear. I hope we get to share many more success stories like that. Now…are you ready to eat?'

'I'm starving.'

'Excellent. Come with me.'

Grace chose Dijon mustard as a condiment to go with her sausages rather than the tomato sauce Jock preferred.

Classy…

'I think you cook sausages even better than fish,' Grace said.

'I'll put that on my CV.' Jock grinned. 'It might be useful one day.'

'What for?'

'Oh, I dunno. A dating site profile?'

Grace simply shook her head as she took another bite of her dinner.

'That reminds me,' he said. 'I got a text to say that there's a few people from work going to the pub later tonight. I thought I might go along. Why don't you come too? It'd be a good chance to meet some more people.'

'Is it a work thing?'

'No. Just social. You'll know a few of them by now, like Mandy—she probably did Stella's ultrasound today.'

'Yes, she did.'

'And Dan might come.' Jock kept his tone casual. 'You met him this morning when he did Melissa's epidural.'

'Mmm.' The sound was noncommittal.

'He's single,' Jock added.

His observation was met with a raised eyebrow.

'And...?'

He held up his hands, excusing himself. 'Hey... I was the teenager with ginger hair and freckles. I thought all women were automatically attracted to the tall, dark and brooding type of guy.'

'Been there, done that.' Grace's tone was light but dismissive. 'Have no intention of ever doing it again.' She got up to take her plate to the kitchen sink. 'Thank you for that. It was delicious.'

Well...that squashed any thought that there might have been a spark between his new flatmate and his fishing buddy. It also reminded Jock that Jenni had told him Grace hadn't dated anyone since she'd escaped a bad marriage some years ago. Thinking of his sister also reminded him of her decree not to even think about hitting on Grace.

As if he would...

Having her here was almost like having Jenni here. Another sister. He should be making sure she *didn't* hook up with anyone in a hurry instead of pushing her towards his single friends. Especially if she was still vulnerable in the wake of a failed relationship. But that had been years ago, hadn't it? Wouldn't it be a lot healthier for her if she moved on?

Jock scraped his plate clean and got up to take it to the bench, where Jenni was now washing up.

'Here you go.' He put the plate down on the side of the bench with the other dirty dishes. Without thinking, he touched Grace's shoulder with his other hand in something between a gentle squeeze and an appreciative pat. 'Thanks...'

He felt the jerk beneath his hand but what was more shocking was that the clean plate Grace was lifting from the hot, soapy water got dropped—almost thrown—to the floor, where it shattered into sharp fragments.

'Oh, *no*...' Grace put her hand to her mouth. 'I'm so sorry...'

She barely glanced up at Jock but that split second of time was still long enough to make Jock freeze. Because he could see the same kind of flash that he'd seen earlier today—in Stella's eyes.

Fear...

'Hey... It's okay.' Jock wanted to offer Grace a hug, but that would obviously be completely the wrong thing to do when it had been touching her in the first place that had caused this. 'It's me that should apologise. I gave you a fright.'

Grace peeled off some paper towels from the roll and crouched to start picking up pieces of broken crockery.

'It's not your fault. It's...'

Oh, God... Was that a tear he could see rolling down Grace's cheek?

Jock crouched beside her. 'It's okay, Grace,' he said softly. 'You're perfectly safe...'

She stopped picking up the shards. She stopped moving at all.

'You know, don't you?' she whispered. 'Did Jenni tell you?'

'Jenni didn't tell me anything,' Jock said. 'Only that you got out of what she said was an awful marriage a long time ago.'

Grace didn't say anything.

'Did he hit you, Grace?' Jock asked very quietly. 'That bastard that you were married to?

Very slowly, Grace lifted her chin, just enough to be able to raise her gaze to meet his. She didn't have to say anything at all because he could see the answer to his question in her eyes.

And something cracked in his chest. He hadn't felt this angry on someone else's behalf—or so determined to protect them—since…since some bullies had had a go at Jenni on their very first day at primary school. He'd only been five years old but he'd been fast and fierce enough to fight for his sister.

'You're safe,' he told Grace again. 'You'll always be safe with me.'

And this time it was a promise.

CHAPTER FOUR

JOCK DIDN'T REPEAT the suggestion that Grace went to the pub with him.

He didn't even go himself. Instead, he unearthed a bottle of wine from a kitchen cupboard, as Grace finished clearing up in the slightly awkward aftermath of her hurling that plate onto the floor.

'You're not on call tonight, are you?'

'No.' Grace picked up the cutlery to dry.

'Neither am I.' Jock held up the bottle. 'Do you like red wine?'

'Sometimes.'

'Would now be one of those times, do you think?'

Grace could feel her lips curving into a smile, which was really surprising given how discombobulated she was feeling right now. How mortifying was it that she'd overreacted to that casual male touch like that? How vulnerable had it made her feel that Jock had guessed one of her darker secrets?

But how much more vulnerable was she feeling in the wake of him telling her that she was safe?

Because she really, really wanted to believe him.

She *did* believe him—as far as being in his company was concerned, anyway.

Grace caught her lip between her teeth, catching the smile

that was trying to wobble free as she dried her hands on the tea towel and turned towards Jock.

'Now would definitely be one of those times,' she said.

They went outside to sit on the wicker chairs and watch the sky take on enough of a pretty pink tinge for it to reflect on the sea. The day seemed to be taking a breath and releasing it in a sigh of relief that Grace could feel right down to her bones. She let out her own soft sigh as she sank into the cocoon of old cushions and for a quiet minute or two they simply sat there watching the colours deepen before they began to fade. It was Grace who finally broke the silence.

'Can you tell which boat is *Lassie* from this distance?'

'I can. There aren't that many clinker-built boats in the marina. Most people prefer flashy fibreglass hulls because they're much easier to maintain.'

'Does clinker mean it's made out of wood?'

'It's a type of building with wood. The planks in the hull overlap each other. It's probably the oldest and best-known technique of boat building.' Jock made an appreciative sound. 'I fell in love with it when I was a kid. When I got to play on a pond in this ancient dinghy with peeling paint and a seat that gave you splinters. I learned to row in that boat, which was quite an achievement given that the water was only about knee-deep.'

'Was that the boat you pushed Jenni out of?'

Jock paused as he was reaching for the wine bottle to top up their glasses. 'She told you about that?'

Grace nodded.

'It's not true,' Jock growled. 'She was leaning over the side of the boat because she thought she could see a fish. I was actually trying to catch hold of her before she fell in.'

That seemed perfectly believable, coming from a man

who could look at you as if he was prepared to fight dragons to protect you.

A man who could tell you that you would always be safe as long as you were with him.

A man whose smile—like the one Grace was getting now—seemed to make everything a bit brighter. Shiny, even...

The tendril of sensation flickering through her body could have been misinterpreted as attraction but it was easy to reassure herself that it was nothing more than the warmth of a developing friendship.

If it was anything else she wouldn't feel this safe, would she?

'But then she stood up and I knew she was okay,' Jock said, 'but she looked like a drowned rat and she was so cross that it was funny. I think she decided I'd pushed her because that was less embarrassing than her just falling out. She's never forgiven me for laughing at her so much.'

'Oh, I think she has. She adores you.' Grace took a slow sip of her wine. Of course she did. Who wouldn't?

'I was an only child,' she confessed. 'I would have given anything to have had a brother—even if they did push me out of a boat.'

Jock laughed. 'Be careful what you wish for,' he said. 'I could arrange for that to happen, you know.'

This silence that fell as dusk deepened around them felt even more companionable. Grace could even forget the embarrassment of someone knowing that she'd been in an abusive relationship. At least he didn't know that she'd been weak enough to stay in it for far too long. Or why...

'Did Jenni tell you that the boat incident happened when we were in a foster home? Just for the long school break in summer. Our mother couldn't cope with school holidays when she had to work and social services didn't seem to like a pair of twins being left to fend for themselves for weeks on end.'

Had Jock sensed the direction her thoughts were straying? Or did he want to make her feel less exposed by sharing something of his own that was personal?

Grace's nod was hesitant. She would never have pushed him into talking about a childhood she knew had been a lot less than ideal, but perhaps this was a chance to let him know that the safety he'd offered her went both ways. And that it was something that felt very unexpected. And very special.

'We only spoke about it once. I'm pretty sure there might have been some wine involved on that occasion as well. Jen said it was one of the better foster homes you had to spend time in. Because you got to be there together...' Grace needed to wash away the lump in her throat with another mouthful of wine. 'I'm so sorry you guys had things to deal with that no kids should have to, but you must be so proud of each other and how far you've come since then.'

Jock's gaze was steady. 'It leaves scars,' he said quietly.

'Of course it does.' Grace offered Jock a smile. 'And it's so much worse when you get those scars when you're too young. Most of us collect a few scars along the way later in life, but when you're a kid you should be protected. Wrapped in the kind of love that can kiss so many things better.'

Jock's breath came out in a huff that told her he'd never been wrapped in that kind of love.

'I learned two things,' he said. 'That broken promises can feel like the end of the world. Like the promises our mother would make that we kept believing, even when we knew we shouldn't. Like the one about never having to go somewhere else in the holidays. Or that her new relationship would make us a real family because she was *in love* and he loved her back and that everything was going to be perfect from now on...' Jock cleared his throat. 'I decided when I was about ten years old that I would never, ever make a promise I couldn't keep. And I never will.'

'I knew you could be trusted before I even met you,' Grace said. 'Jenni said you're the only person on earth that she would trust with her life.'

Jock smiled. 'Siblings and friends.' He nodded. 'The only kind of love that can be trusted. That was the other thing I decided. Jenni and I saw our mother lurching from one disaster to another and we gave up hoping that everything would ever be perfect. When we were about thirteen we both made a solemn vow that we would never get married. I don't know about Jenni, but I also decided that I was never going to fall in love because that was how the worst disasters always started.'

'That explains a lot,' Grace said. 'I thought Jenni was just super fussy when it came to boyfriends. That she'd find "the one" if she kissed enough frogs. But I wasn't really joking this morning when I said that the current model might be getting near his expiry date, so she shouldn't waste her money on a weekend with him in Portugal.'

'And she accuses me of breaking hearts?' Jock let his breath out in a huff. 'I'm very careful that I don't do that. I make it absolutely clear right from the start that it's never going to be anything serious. To be honest, I don't think I'm capable of falling in love.'

'Really?'

'The risk is way too big.' Jock shrugged. 'If you build

your whole world around trusting that someone else feels the same way you do, you give them the power to destroy everything.'

'That is true,' Grace said softly. She knew that, so how could she disagree?

'At least it's safe enough to love your friends and siblings. Much harder to break those bonds—even if you live on opposite sides of the world.'

'I don't think Jenni really believes that you go around breaking hearts. She did, however, suggest that the only long-term commitment you were likely to make was to your boat.'

The sound from Jock was one of amusement now. 'And she told me that you were so out of bounds she'd never speak to me again if I even thought about breaking the rules.'

Grace didn't have to confess that Jenni knew she couldn't handle being touched by men since she'd escaped her marriage. Jock had already found that out the hard way, hadn't he?

'There was another part of that vow we made to never get married,' Jock added. 'We both said we never wanted to have kids. In case they ended up like us. Living with those broken promises and catching the fallout of the disastrous new relationships.' He held Grace's gaze. 'We were hiding out down by the canal at the time. Keeping out of the way of a stepfather who liked to hit us.'

The look Grace was receiving from Jock was telling her that he got it. That he knew what it was like to have someone that hurt you physically, but she could sense the undercurrent of empathy that went deeper. That advertised an understanding of how deep the emotional scars that got left behind could be.

And then his face lightened and that cheeky grin emerged again. Clearly, it was time to step out of the shadows that dark memories caused. Grace suspected this was a defence mechanism that Jock had learned to apply at a very early age.

'So…when are you going to come out fishing with me? We can talk about how we're going to lure Jenni out here. If she just came for a visit, I'm sure we could persuade her to emigrate. Let's make it the next day off we have that co-incides.' His grin widened. 'That should give me enough time to plan my strategy for pushing you overboard when you least expect it…'

If Grace was bothered by the prospect of being pushed off his boat, she certainly wasn't showing it. She was look-ing a lot more relaxed about life in general, in fact, as the days following his teasing threat ticked past. Even better, she hadn't tried to revisit any part of what they'd discussed that evening.

Jock had been a bit shocked at himself, to be honest, for having discussed his childhood at all. There was only one other person on the planet that he'd ever talked to about it and it had to be a good ten years or more since it had come up in any conversation with Jenni. By tacit agreement, they were moving forward with their lives and neither of them wanted to revisit a past they'd worked so hard to deal with and leave behind.

And he hadn't told Grace everything. He'd let her assume that he and Jenni had vowed not to have children because of physical abuse they'd had to face, but that hadn't been the worst of it. The deepest wounds hadn't been inflicted by a stepfather or any 'uncles' that joined their family for any length of time. No...those scars had been left by the twins' mother.

Being told so often that their arrival in the world—and their continued existence—had ruined her life.

The shame of feeling unwanted had seeped into every cell before they'd been old enough to know that it wasn't their fault. On some level they believed they weren't good enough to be loved by anyone other than each other, but that had been enough to survive and nobody else ever had to know. It was just another part of the past that was never talked about and never would be.

Jock was happy enough with his life now that he wouldn't want to change anything. So happy, he had moments when the past might have never even existed, but he didn't regret what he *had* said to Grace.

Especially that she was safe.

It felt like he was protecting Jenni all over again, but with the wisdom and strength that all his life experiences had given him it was not only easy—automatic, almost—it was a genuine pleasure.

And somehow, what had happened that evening had created a connection with Grace that Jock had never had with anyone other than his sister and that was...

It was nice, that's what it was.

He had promised that Grace was safe with him, but he hadn't expected to start feeling that *he* was safe with *her*.

And why wouldn't he?

The person *he* trusted the most in the world trusted Grace and Jenni's instincts about people had always been spot on.

But it was also partly due to her not raising the subject of their conversation again—respecting his privacy in the same way he was guarding hers. No one should ever intrude on a space like that without an invitation.

Maybe she'd forgotten all about the threat of being pushed overboard from *Lassie*'s deck—or even the promised fishing trip, given that it was proving difficult to find a day they were both off work and not on call.

But that was okay.

He had a fishing trip lined up with Dan for his next day off, a job he loved every minute of and a flatmate who was as easy to be around as his own sister and had the promise of becoming one of those friendships that could last a lifetime.

And life didn't really get much better than this, did it?

CHAPTER FIVE

ONE BUSY DAY led into another and Grace didn't mind juggling her rosters and postponing her scheduled days off to fill gaps left by the ongoing staff shortages in the maternity department of Picton Hospital, even if it meant she still hadn't been out on Jock's boat.

The jigsaw puzzle pieces of her new life were coming together to form a picture that was reminiscent of the dreams that had been sparked by Jenni's suggestion that Grace came to work in a small country at the very bottom of the world.

She wasn't a stranger here any longer. She was making new friends at work and the kind of connections that were created by cases that were shared. Grace worked with other midwives, obstetricians, anaesthetists and technicians during births and liaised with GPs, practice nurses and others in her antenatal and postnatal care of mothers.

Some of those connections were going to become stronger as time went on. Like the one she had with Jock that Stella Watson had created. Grace was delighted to hear that she'd been added to an outpatient clinic within days of her running away from her first midwife appointment.

'I told her that a planned C-section was not only possible but, in her case, advisable,' Jock reported. 'Her physical and mental health—maybe even her marriage—could be at risk if she felt unable to continue with the pregnancy, when she *and* her husband really want another child. But they could be at greater risk if she goes through a pregnancy with the level of anxiety she has about giving birth again and that, in my opinion, outweighed any increased risk of having surgery.'

'What did she say?'

'She was so relieved it took about half a box of tissues before we could plan the next steps, and we didn't get very far because all she wanted to do was go and find her husband and tell him everything.'

Grace hadn't realised how worried she'd been about Stella until she felt a wash of relief that morphed into happiness. She wrapped her arms around herself as if she needed to hug someone. 'You're a bit of a star, Jock, you know that, don't you?'

Jock shrugged in what was becoming a familiar gesture to dismiss a compliment. 'I've made an appointment for them both to come in next week and we'll discuss everything.'

'Brilliant. I'll get in touch with Stella and see if I can catch her at the same time to arrange our first proper antenatal visit.'

It had been her turn to add a new strand to another connection between them a day or two after that.

'I did a postnatal home visit to see Melissa today,' she told him. 'I took her stitches out.'

'How's the wound looking?'

'Really clean. Her temperature, blood pressure and heart rate were all normal too, and she's feeling well so there's no sign of any infection.'

'How's her PV bleeding? She still had a bit of ongoing loss when I saw her just prior to discharging her.'

'It's slowed down a lot. She's keeping mobile to lower any risk of thrombosis. As much as she's allowed to, anyway. Jason's taken a few weeks' paternity leave and he's not letting her do any housework. He was hanging out the washing when I arrived.'

'And the baby?'

'Oh, she's gorgeous. They've named her Charlotte but are calling her Charlie. She's doing really well—just a touch of nappy rash. I'll visit again when Jason's gone back to work and make sure she's managing by herself. She might feel a bit isolated then. They live down a windy shingle road at the bottom of a huge hill. The house is hidden by trees and they have a tiny private beach that's even got a jetty for their boat.'

'Nice… Just the kind of property I'd love to have one day.'

Grace could imagine him there, happily pottering around with his boat or fishing off the jetty. With a couple of cute kids playing on the beach who had curly red hair and were shrieking with laughter.

Oh, no…wait… There wouldn't be any children. There wouldn't be a wife either. Because he—and Jenni—had convinced each other that was the best idea.

She could understand why they'd made that vow. Of course she could. Their mother had given them appalling evidence of how bad things could be when they went wrong. But surely they'd seen evidence of how amazing it could be when it *didn't* go wrong? Were Jock and Jenni really so sure they wanted to keep such a solid barrier in place they weren't even going to try?

If she told either of them what she thought, they would just say it was a case of the pot calling the kettle black, wouldn't they? At least she'd dreamt of a family of her own, though. And she'd done her best to make it happen. Maybe she hadn't quite given up hope that it *could* happen for herself one day. Maybe that was partly why she'd found the courage to start a completely new life.

Whatever. What was in her own past wasn't something Grace wanted to think about, much less start talking about again. So she found a smile as she raised her eyebrows.

'This is so you and *Lassie* can live happily ever after together?'

'Exactly.'

The laughter was shared but Grace felt a squeeze on her heart that was poignant enough to be almost painful.

No matter how beautiful the setting, living alone without even another house in sight would have to be heartbreakingly lonely at times. And Jock McKay was someone who really, really didn't deserve to end up being that lonely.

But he was smiling and shaking his head now, as if he'd read her thoughts and wanted to reassure her.

'Never going to happen,' he said. 'I'd never stay in one place long enough to own my own jetty.' His smile widened. 'It's much more likely that *Lassie* and I will just sail off into the sunset together.'

It had been a throwaway comment.

A joke.

Judging by the expression on her face, the prospect of sailing off into the sunset with his beloved boat was clearly not something that Grace had deemed a future worth dreaming about. She almost looked as though it might be something to feel sad about.

Jock, however, heard the echo of her words in his head again a few days later when he took Dan out for an afternoon's fishing and the contented purr of the engine as they headed out into the Sounds to see if the snapper were biting made him think that *Lassie* was quite content with his newly forming plans for their shared future. And Grace was working today so she wasn't here to give him that look again.

'How long have you been living here now, Dan?' Jock handed his friend a cold bottle of lager from the tiny fridge in *Lassie*'s galley when they dropped the anchor in one of their favourite spots.

'Longer than you, mate. Why?'

'What made you choose Picton?'

'Job came up. I needed a change.'

Dan was a man of few words, which was a desirable attribute in a fishing companion but he was quite happy to talk if someone made the effort to engage him. He was also a friend whose opinion Jock respected.

'Do you still like it here?'

Dan took a long swallow from his beer, letting his gaze rest on the idyllic scenery around them. 'Are you kidding? What's not to like? I've got no plans to leave any time soon. That's why I've bought a house here.'

Jock nodded, his smile one of complete agreement. 'We've got the best work-life balance, that's for sure. A place that's got this to offer as a playground but the town's big enough to keep work interesting. And small enough to keep us on our toes on a good day.'

In a larger city, a specialist in maternal-foetal medicine would be consulted for the management of any pregnancies with a higher-than-normal risk of complications, but here Jock had the responsibility of monitoring cases in an area of obstetric medicine that provided the kind of challenges he loved the most. A low-lying placenta, perhaps, or a history of previous miscarriages or—his favourite—a multiple pregnancy.

It was comforting to have the backup of New Zealand's capital city's medical resources being only a short flight away across the short distance between the South and North islands, and that meant that more complex cases could also be managed, with Jock as part of a team of local specialists for pregnant women with existing medical conditions like congenital heart disease, high blood pressure, diabetes or a previous organ transplant.

Jock might grumble about the workload occasionally, like when he'd been trying to persuade Jenni to apply for one of the vacant midwife positions, but he got enough downtime to know exactly how lucky he was to be living here. It was paradise for anyone who loved the sea and this part of the South Island was also a mecca for people who loved good food and wine, picturesque towns, dramatic scenery and interesting company. People who loved life and wanted to make the most of it, in fact. Like Jock did.

Was that why Dan sounded so content to stay here? Was Grace right to think that never staying long enough in one place was the wrong approach to finding lasting happiness?

What real reason did Jock have not to try putting down roots and building a life that he'd never want to leave?

Jock took a swallow of his own beer. 'Maybe I should start looking for a house to buy too,' he said cautiously, testing his thought aloud. 'Might even see if I can get one with its own jetty.'

'Sounds like a plan.' Dan's nod was approving. 'So you're not tempted to go back to Scotland?'

Jock grinned. 'And leave this behind? Are *you* kidding?'

'Don't you have a sister still there?'

'I'm working on a cunning plan to persuade her to move here. Grace is helping.'

'Grace?'

'My new flatmate. The midwife who was at that last emergency C-section we did together.'

'Ah, yes… I remember her. Blonde. Cute. Seems quite shy.'

'Cute' wasn't quite the word Jock would have chosen to describe a woman who was not only gorgeous but intelligent and clever and…caring. 'Shy' wasn't exactly appropriate either. Grace was wary. And she had reason to be.

'Blonde and cute is way more your type than mine,' Dan said dryly. 'And, come to think of it, I did notice the way she was smiling at you when you were holding that baby. And you're living with her?' He gave Jock an incredulous glance. 'So how's *that* working out so far…?'

Oh, good grief…did Dan think he was incapable of keeping his hands off a gorgeous woman?

'She's my sister's best friend,' he said firmly. 'Which puts her completely off-limits as far as I'm concerned.'

'Why?'

'It just does. It could end up messing with their friendship and my sister might never speak to me again. It was Jenni who told her about the job going here, and she made it clear that nothing was allowed to happen between us. So that's that.'

Dan's grunt sounded almost impressed. 'Good for you.'

'Anyway, Grace is talking Jenni into a trip to come and visit. We're going to try and make sure she has such a good time she'll want to come back permanently.'

Dan smiled. 'That would definitely make life interesting. Does she like boats?'

'No. She hates them. But that's her only real flaw. She makes up for it in many other ways.'

'I'll look forward to meeting her,' Dan said. 'But I'm wondering how Picton would cope with having both the McKay twins in residence.'

'Double trouble.' Jock nodded. 'Oh—' he put his beer down hurriedly '—I've got a nibble...'

The conversation was forgotten as he began the tussle to land what felt like a big fish. A flash of colour as it came closer to the surface confirmed that it was a snapper, which was his favourite fish to eat. Fresh from the sea and cooked to perfection on the barbecue, Grace would be more than impressed with how delicious her dinner was going to be.

Maybe he'd flick Greta a text and see if she wanted to come and join them. She might have moved on because she was looking for more than he could offer but, as far as Jock knew, she hadn't found a new relationship yet. Maybe she'd like to keep their friendship going in the meantime? With those benefits they'd both enjoyed in the last couple of months?

That way, Jock would be able to end a perfect day with the perfect meal, in the company of good friends. Maybe even the bonus of overnight company?

No...

The idea was remarkably unappealing.

He didn't want Greta's company tonight, did he?

He wanted Grace's.

Not for sex, of course. But for everything else—like the companionship and conversation and...and that feeling of connection. With a frisson of foreboding, Jock realised that maybe Dan hadn't been so far off the mark when he'd given him the look that suggested he was very likely to fancy Grace.

No… He wasn't even going to think about that. That sense of connection was there because of the bond they both had with Jenni, that was all. She was another sister for Jock.

And he didn't have to think about it any longer. A distraction came in the form of a huge snapper that he managed to flip onto the deck.

'*Yes…*' Jock's shout was triumphant.

Life didn't get any better than this, did it? It wasn't perfect, but it was such a waste not to make the most of the best it had to offer when everyone knew how short life was. Moments like this. With good friends and good times. And, aye…sex *was* a part of some of the best moments Jock had ever found in life, but he wasn't going there with Grace.

He was perfectly capable of following rules when they made sense.

He did, however, feel sorry that Grace was missing what was an important part of life. As a brother, or even just as a friend, would it be possible to encourage her to be brave enough to try again?

Not with him, of course, but perhaps he could facilitate a friendship that she could trust enough to let it grow if they happened to find they liked each other? With someone who was thoughtful and patient and quite happily single, so there would be no reason to apply any pressure whatsoever for it to be more than a friendship.

Maybe that idea of setting her up with Dan shouldn't have been discarded so soon?

His mate was happily single. Jock knew he'd been married once but they'd never talked about past relationships. Or even present ones. They'd double-dated once or twice, and maybe part of their connection was due to respecting the privacy of each other's love lives. Jock certainly wasn't going to judge Dan on something as trivial as enjoying an occasional one-night stand.

But it was, in fact, possible that Dan was on the lookout for someone special to share the rest of his life with and he just hadn't met the right person yet.

And Grace Collins was certainly special…

Jock's gaze slid sideways. How easy would it be to suggest that Dan came for dinner tonight to share a meal of the fish they were catching? That way, they could meet each other properly.

No…

He didn't want to set Grace up with Dan.

He didn't want to set her up with anyone, in fact. Why would he risk putting her into a situation where she might feel uncomfortable—or worse, where she might end up getting hurt?

He'd promised she would always be safe if he was around.

And Jock never made a promise he couldn't keep.

CHAPTER SIX

ANTENATAL CLINICS WERE a favourite part of Grace's duties as a midwife. This was where she got to know the women under her care and built the relationship that was so important when it came time to play her part in the major life event that having a baby represented.

If a midwife did her job well, a mother would remember her for ever.

As a midwife, Grace could often recognise women she knew she was going to remember well before they gave birth.

Like Maureen Petersen, who hadn't given up on her dream to be a mother and had decided to do something about it on her own when she turned forty.

And Stella Watson—the first woman who had ever run away from Grace.

Stella had now entered her second trimester and, thanks to the reassurance that she would not have to go through another traumatic birth experience, was beginning to relax enough to start enjoying her pregnancy.

'I wish I'd spoken to someone a long time ago,' she confided as Grace wrapped the blood pressure cuff around her upper arm. 'Do you think six years is too big a gap between siblings?'

'I think Scott's going to be the best big brother.' Grace

fitted the stethoscope to her ears and smiled at the small boy who was going through the toy box in the corner of the consulting room. 'Is it school holidays at the moment?'

Stella nodded. 'And he came to the last appointment we had with Dr McKay so he wanted to come back again. Dr Jock, he calls him.' Stella was smiling. 'To be honest, I'm not sure that talking to anyone else *would* have helped this much. There's something about Dr McKay, isn't there?'

Grace let the rest of the air out of the cuff and pulled her pen from her pocket to record the blood pressure measurement.

'There certainly is,' she agreed. 'And luckily, he's not just a nice man—he's an excellent surgeon.'

It was no surprise that Stella was now feeling safe enough to be able to cope with this pregnancy. Being anywhere near Jock was enough to make Grace feel safer than she had in longer than she could remember.

More than that, even. Thanks to the boundaries that had been put in place so firmly by Jenni, there was no threat of anything getting out of control or for either of them to think of their relationship as anything more than friends or honorary siblings. Grace had something in her life now that she hadn't realised how much she was missing.

Male companionship.

And…okay…maybe there was an element of admiration there. On both sides. But it didn't have any sexual significance. Instead, it could be enjoyed. Grace could allow herself to feel more…feminine? Feeling desirable was a step too far, but she was definitely feeling better about herself.

And she had Jock McKay to thank for that. The brother of her bestie was becoming not only an equally good friend but someone she could be proud of knowing—as much for his compassion for others as any practical skills he had as a surgeon.

Did Jock realise what a gift it was to make a pregnant woman feel safe? Not just for Stella, but for her husband and her son and the baby whose birth she might be able to look forward to instead of being terrified about.

'Everything's looking great,' Grace told Stella. 'Now... it's a bit early, so it might not work, but would you like me to see if we can hear baby's heartbeat with the Doppler?'

'Ooh...yes, please.' Stella lay back on the bed and pulled up her top to expose her belly again.

'Just don't get worried if I can't find it, okay? It doesn't mean there's anything wrong, just that it's too early.'

'I won't,' Stella promised.

Scott had abandoned the toys. 'What's a Dop-er-la?'

'It's this little device.' Grace showed him the handset and attached transducer. 'It can send out high-frequency ultrasound waves that can go through the skin and then bounce back to tell us what they've found.'

'Like dolphins?' Scott's eyes widened. 'We learned about that at school. That's how they find their food.'

'Exactly like dolphins.' Grace nodded. She held the flat head of the small transducer against Stella's abdomen. 'And do you want to know something I learned about at midwife school?'

'You went to *school*?'

'I did.' Grace moved the transducer to another spot and pressed a little more firmly. 'And when we were learning to use Dopplers, the teacher told me that dolphins really love to be around pregnant women because they can hear the heartbeat of both the mother and the baby. They might even be able to *see* the baby.'

'Is that really true?' Stella asked.

'Apparently,' Grace said. She smiled. 'But even if it's exaggerated it's still another good reason to love dolphins, as far as I'm concerned.' Her smile widened at what she could hear from the speaker built into the handset of her device— the rapid beats that sounded like muffled horses galloping past. 'Can you hear that, Scott? That's your little brother or sister's heart that's making that sound.'

Stella had her fingers pressed to her mouth and tears in her eyes as she looked up at Grace. Things had just become even more real. But joy was winning over trepidation.

Jock would be just as delighted as she was at this development in a case that could have gone in a very different direction.

'Where's your phone?' she asked Stella. 'Shall we record this so you can take it home for Dad to listen to later?'

It was Scott who proudly took charge of the phone with its new audio clip as they left a short time later and Grace welcomed her last appointment for this clinic.

This was the second time Grace was seeing Tessa, who was nearly thirty weeks pregnant with twins. As it was a multiple birth, Tessa was already under the care of the obstetric department as a higher-risk pregnancy, but she had chosen to work with a midwife as well for antenatal visits that were more frequent than the normal routine but, because the twins were currently both in a breech position, Tessa was scheduled for an elective Caesarean at around thirty-seven weeks gestation as the safest option for delivery of her babies.

'Did you manage a urine sample?'

Tessa rolled her eyes. 'I need to pee constantly. Catching a bit of it is the least of my problems.'

She handed over the specimen jar and Grace unscrewed the bright yellow lid to put the dipstick into the liquid.

'Jump on the scales for me, Tessa, and then hop up on the bed and we'll do all our usual checks.'

'Jump?' Tessa laughed. 'And *hop*? Being able to do either of those things is becoming a distant memory.'

Grace smiled. Tessa's belly was certainly an impressive size. 'I'm not surprised you're feeling the need to pee frequently,' she said. 'Your uterus is the size of a full-term singleton pregnancy already and it will be putting a fair bit of pressure on your bladder.'

Grace noted a small increase in the level of protein in the urine sample but it wasn't enough to be a concern.

'Oh, my God...' Tessa was staring down at the numbers on the screen of the digital scales. 'I'm the size of a whale.' Tessa was pulling off her shoes. 'Look at that—I don't have ankles any longer. They've turned into *cankles*.'

'You have got a bit of swelling,' Grace agreed. 'But walking will help with that. Getting your feet up above the level of your heart for a decent stretch of time is good, and try and sleep on your left side at night.'

'What does that do?'

'It improves blood flow, which can reduce the swelling in the ankles and legs. You've got quite a lot more blood circulating in pregnancy and the pressure of the uterus doesn't just make the bladder overreactive, it can interfere with blood trying to get back from the legs to the heart and lungs.'

'Is it dangerous?'

'If it gets any worse, or you have symptoms like headaches or blurry vision, then you need to get checked as soon as possible because it can be a sign of pre-eclampsia. Have you had anything like that?'

'No. I just feel tired all the time. And a bit short of breath.' Tessa had managed to climb onto the bed without difficulty. She pulled the stretchy fabric of her maternity jeans down and then rubbed the enormous, pale mound with its dramatic, dark central line and the more randomly scattered red stretch marks. 'At least they've settled down today. They kept me awake half the night with what felt like a game of rugby going on.'

'Oh?' Grace placed the edge of one hand on the top of Tessa's belly to find the top of the uterus. 'Have the movements been what you're used to since then?'

'There still seems to be a lot of kicking.'

Grace used both hands on either side of the belly as she began to apply gentle pressure. She could feel the kick of a baby's foot against her hand almost instantly. 'What are you two up to in there, huh? Having a bit of a party?'

She moved her hands down slowly and systematically towards the lower uterus.

'Hmm…'

'What is it?' Tessa sounded anxious.

'I'm just going to check that again. Sometimes it's hard to tell the difference between a bottom and a head, especially when the space is getting more cramped and the babies are active.'

Grace had felt these two babies only a couple of weeks ago when there were two round, firm shapes of their heads in the upper uterus and the softer shapes of their buttocks pointing downwards. Yes…she could only find one head near the fundus now. One shape that she could 'ballot' by pushing gently from one side to the other between her fingers. She couldn't be entirely sure what she was feeling with the other twin, however, which could indicate a transverse position where it was lying more sideways than head down.

'I think one of your babies has turned around,' she told Tessa. 'That could well have been what the gymnastics you could feel last night were all about.'

'Really? Oh…' Tessa's eyes widened. 'Does that mean I might not have to have a Caesarean?'

'I'm not saying that.' Grace shook her head. 'It would be entirely up to your obstetrician to make that kind of call. What we need to do is to find out whether I'm right first and confirm which twin it is who's moved. In fact…' She glanced at her watch. 'We might go and see if we can find an ultrasound room and a technician who's not too busy.'

The radiography department which housed X-ray, MRI and ultrasound facilities was between the outpatient department and the emergency department and could also be accessed from the main reception area in the hospital foyer.

There was a pharmacy, gift shop, florist and a café adding to the busy ambience of the hospital's entrance. As Grace walked into the area with Tessa, she saw Stella and Scott coming out of the café to head towards the main doors. Coming from the opposite direction, she saw Jock coming from the emergency department.

'Jock McKay's the obstetrician you're under, isn't he?' Tessa nodded.

'Wait here for a tick. I'll just try and catch him and let him know what's happening today.'

Jock looked as though he was heading for the café. Grace was watching the delight on Scott's face as he noticed 'Dr Jock' approaching and stopped following his mother. To her astonishment, when Scott held his arm straight up like a 'stop' signal, Jock high-fived him and then they both made fists with their hands and bumped them together. As Grace arrived, they were doing a pretend 'explosion' where they jerked their hands back and wiggled their fingers.

Scott's grin stretched from ear to ear, ignoring Stella, who was looking embarrassed that Jock had been ambushed and signalling her son to catch up with her.

'Is that a secret handshake?' Grace's voice was a stage whisper.

Scott nodded importantly.

'Don't tell anyone,' Jock warned.

'I won't,' Grace promised. She bit back her smile but that small demonstration of how good Jock was with kids had been noted. When she had time later, she would add it to the list of reasons why he didn't deserve to be alone. Or lonely.

She might have to add a degree of perception as well. She saw the tiny frown that told her Jock could sense that she wanted a quiet word.

'Your mum's waiting for you,' Jock told Scott. 'See you next time.' His gaze caught Grace's. 'Got time for a café coffee? Or some cake? I missed lunch…'

She shook her head. 'I'm just finishing my antenatal clinic and I'm with Tessa Brownlee. One of your high-risk mums? Breech twins and on the list for an elective Caesarean?'

Jock's nod was terse. He was fully focused as he listened to why Grace was heading to the radiography department with Tessa.

'I'm just hoping there's a technician available,' she finished. 'Otherwise, I might wait with her. If you had time to call in an urgent request, that would probably help.'

Jock knew just as well as she did what the implications of this could be.

'We just need a machine that's free.' He had already turned his back on the café with its tempting coffee and cake. 'I can do the ultrasound.'

'So Twin A, who's closer to the cervix and most likely to be born first, is still breech, but Twin B has turned around to be cephalic?'

Jenni's face filled the screen of Jock's laptop that was open on the small table between the chairs on the veranda. She'd slept late on her day off and was still in bed when she answered this video call, a mug of breakfast coffee in hand.

'Yes. It was Grace that picked it up on palpation. I confirmed it with the ultrasound.'

'Told you she was good at her job, didn't I?'

'You did indeed. And you weren't wrong.'

Grace leaned in so that Jenni could see her as well as Jock. 'She thought it meant she wouldn't need to have an elective Caesarean and could at least try for a vaginal birth.'

'I guess it could.' Jenni seemed more than happy to be talking work on her day off. 'What are the odds that Twin B will be able to turn around as well?'

'There's still time for that to happen,' Jock said. 'But we're going to keep a close eye on them with frequent scans from now on.'

'Manual cephalic version's not a good idea with twins, is it?'

'It's feasible but there's not enough evidence of its efficacy or safety yet. We'll see what happens naturally in the next few weeks.'

'I'm going to be checking frequently for any signs that

she might be going into labour,' Grace added. 'She lives in a bay that's not far away from town but it can only be accessed by boat, which complicates things. She wasn't that happy when Jock told her she might need to be admitted for the last week or so, so she'd be close to definitive care.'

'Did you tell her about the risk of locked twins? Even though it's rare?'

'Jock did that so well,' Grace said. 'He managed to get the message across without terrifying the poor woman.'

Her smile told Jock she had appreciated the care he'd taken.

'It *is* terrifying.' Jenni took a sip of her coffee. 'Someone was telling me a horror story just the other day. Primigravida went into a precipitous labour, came into hospital with the body of the breech twin already delivered—legs hanging out and the classic chin lock with the second twin.'

'Worst-case scenario,' Jock muttered.

'They did an emergency C-section but it was too late.' Jenni was shaking her head sadly. 'They lost both babies…'

Jock turned his head to catch Grace's gaze. They were so close together, trying to stay visible to Jenni while they shared the chat that their heads were almost touching. Jock had never been quite this physically close to her.

He'd never noticed that the colour of her eyes changed so much in different lights. The last of the daylight was fading as they sat out here to get the best reception for the call, but it might have been anxiety that was making Grace's eyes appear such a dark shade of blue. So dark they made the gold of her hair look like a halo around her face.

If it was anxiety, he could help.

'We're not going to let that happen,' he said quietly.

'Which is why it's good that we're onto it now. We're going to be watching her like a hawk.'

'We are.' Grace was still holding his gaze. 'And she's got the best obstetrician in town, so it's all good.'

Jenni laughed. 'Look at you two, bonding over a high-risk case and telling each other how you're the best in the business.' She seemed to be leaning closer to her screen when Jock shifted his gaze. 'Is it my imagination or am I catching a vibe?'

'What sort of vibe?'

'Like there's something going on that I should know about?'

'I have no idea what you mean.' Jock's tone was deliberately puzzled but it didn't fool Jenni.

'You so do,' she told him. 'It's been obvious for weeks that you two like each other.'

'Of course we do. We're *friends*.' Grace sounded horrified. She straightened up, which increased the distance between herself and Jock. 'Flatmates. We work together—'

'As if I'd break the rules,' Jock put in before Grace could come up with any more personal reasons why the notion was so appalling. 'You know how scared I am of you, Jen.'

'Just checking.' Jenni seemed satisfied. 'It's none of my business, anyway. I'd just rather know in advance.' She made a face. 'I wouldn't want to discover I was getting in the way of the romance of the century between my brother and my bestie when I come and visit next month. That would be too weird.'

Jock ignored the teasing. 'You've booked tickets?'

'I have. Flying visit. Just for a week. I've got a friend in Australia I've promised to go and see on the way back.'

'Is Fergus coming with you?' Grace asked.

'Fergus?' Jenni laughed again. 'Who's Fergus?'

Jock shook his head. 'So that wasn't the romance of the century, then?'

'*Touché,*' Jenni conceded. 'Fine…let's talk travel dates instead of our love lives. You'll need to book some time off so you can come and get me from the airport. I'm flying into Christchurch. That's not too far away, is it?'

'Only a few hours' drive. Message me with all the details and I'll come down and get you if I can,' Jock promised. 'You'll love the trip back. You can do it by train or bus, but if I can get enough time off I'll drive you one way at least. Maybe we can stop in Kaikōura for a night. The mountains there drop straight down into the ocean and it's famous for whale-watching. And crayfish, which is even better than the lobster we get at home.'

'I can't wait.'

Grace tilted her head closer to Jock again. 'Neither can I,' she said. 'There's going to be so much we can do. I'll make sure I've got time off as well and we can take the ferry over to Wellington for the day and go sightseeing and shopping. It'll be a good time for vineyard tours too.'

'And fishing,' Jock suggested. 'You're going to love my new boat.'

'I'm not setting foot on your boat,' Jenni declared. 'You push people off.'

'He hasn't pushed me off yet,' Grace said. 'Oh, wait… I haven't been out on the boat. For some reason, our days off never seem to coincide.'

'I'd keep it that way if I was you. That brother of mine is not to be trusted on boats.' Jenni sighed theatrically. 'I should get up and get on with my day. And it's probably past time you two were in bed.' Her expression was pure mischief now. 'Oops. You know what I meant...'

'Bye, Jenni. Nice talking to you.' Jock slammed the laptop shut before she could say anything else. 'Sorry about that.' He made a wry face. 'She should know better than to make jokes like that. As *if...*'

Grace turned her head sharply enough to make him think he'd said too much. Was he breaking an unspoken promise that he wouldn't intrude on her privacy more than he already had?

But she was smiling at him. 'It's okay,' she said. 'Real friends never need to tread on eggshells. 'Night, Jock.'

'Night, Grace. Sleep well.'

He watched her walking towards the front door to go back inside the house. He was happy he hadn't upset her, but those two words were still hanging in the air.

As *if...*?

What had he meant by that, exactly? It wasn't as if he found Grace unattractive, was it? Far from it. She was the perfect woman.

It wasn't as if he wouldn't be delighted if she found the courage to get back into the dating game either. Grace deserved to find the very best of everything life had to offer.

It was just the idea of them being attracted to each other that had been so far out of the question he hadn't even considered it to be a possibility. If only he'd said something that had captured how he really felt instead of just dismissing it so blatantly. He could say something now but he hesitated, wondering if he might end up making things even more awkward, and the opportunity vanished.

Maybe they could just pretend it hadn't happened? Or that it was no big deal?

It didn't need to affect their friendship, did it?

Grace was about to disappear through the door but turned her head slightly at the last moment, as if she felt Jock watching her. It was no more than a fleeting glance that barely lasted longer than a heartbeat, but it left Jock with the impression that Grace knew exactly what he was thinking.

Because she was thinking about the same thing?

CHAPTER SEVEN

IT HADN'T BEEN INTENTIONAL, of course, but there was no denying that Jenni was responsible for this...

This...what was it?

Awkwardness?

Or maybe it was a different level of awareness. Of each other.

It *wasn't* attraction. Grace hadn't had even a frisson of sexual attraction to any man since her marriage had ended and if it ever happened—which was highly unlikely—her best friend's brother certainly wouldn't be a contender, no matter how highly she regarded him or how much she loved his company or even how safe she felt around him. Jenni had hit the nail on the head when she'd deemed that possibility simply 'too weird'.

But Jenni's light-hearted suggestion there might be a sexual undercurrent to their friendship had changed something. Eye contact was suddenly uncomfortable. Spending time alone together was something to be avoided. The fact that they were living together was starting to feel like it was becoming a problem.

The obvious solution was to talk about it. To share a private joke even, about how ridiculous it was. If anyone could make Grace laugh about how she'd practically thrown a plate at him when he'd barely touched her, it would be Jock

McKay. But the time to have done that easily had slipped away and, as one day morphed into the next, it was proving surprisingly difficult to find the right moment to say anything at all. Was that because she didn't want to make things any worse?

The way he'd said 'As *if...*'

As if he wouldn't be remotely interested in Grace even if she was the last woman on the planet?

It seemed as if they had somehow agreed it would be better to say nothing at all and pretend it hadn't happened. But that wasn't working, was it?

Even catching sight of Jock at the other end of the ward corridor took something off the shine Grace felt, leaving a very tired but ecstatic young couple to spend some time with the beautiful baby she'd just helped deliver just as dawn was breaking.

It was a relief to turn into the sluice room to deal with the dirty linen she'd taken out of the delivery room. She wouldn't have to avoid eye contact that was even a nano-second too long. Or find something to talk about that was purely professional—just in case it could be interpreted as being...*too* friendly?

Despite her assurance that their friendship was real enough for them to not worry about walking on eggshells, that seemed to be exactly what they were both doing and it was bothering Grace. Squeezing sanitiser onto her hands after putting the linen into the appropriate laundry bag, she came to the conclusion that something had to be done about this.

She was going to find Jock and talk to him.

Determined to do it before she could change her mind, Grace pulled open the sluice room door and walked out—

straight into the path of someone heading for the ward's reception area.

Someone she knew.

'Yvonne? Is everything all right?'

Grace had seen Yvonne at an antenatal clinic only days ago and she'd been filled with excitement because she'd felt the first movements of her baby, eighteen weeks into her pregnancy.

She wasn't looking excited right now, however. She looked pale and…frightened. The man walking beside her looked just as distressed.

'We didn't know where to go,' he said. 'Our GP's clinic doesn't open for hours and Evie's bleeding…'

'Come with me.' Grace led the young couple to a delivery suite that she knew was unoccupied. A private space.

'Tell me what's been happening,' she said.

'I woke up because of the cramps,' Yvonne said. 'And I thought I'd wet myself but…but then David turned on the light and…' She squeezed her eyes shut and stifled a sob.

David was perched on the side of the bed, his arm around his wife. 'It was blood,' he said. 'Watery blood.'

'Are you still getting the cramps?'

'No.'

'Still bleeding?'

'I don't think so.'

'We'll check. And I'll find a portable ultrasound. I think one of our obstetricians is on the ward at the moment too, so I'll have a word with him.' She took Yvonne's hand and gave it a squeeze. 'I know how scary this is but we're going to take very good care of you, okay?'

It wasn't enough but it was all Grace could promise.

She could see the fear in this first-time mother's eyes and instinct told her that it wasn't misplaced.

She recognised that fear.

Sometimes you just knew when something was terribly wrong.

He could tell something was wrong.

'What is it, Grace?'

'Are you busy?'

'I've got a theatre list starting in thirty minutes.' This felt like the first time Jock had looked at Grace properly in days and…her eyes were as dark as they'd been the other night, when he'd known she was worried for one of her mothers. He gave his head a tiny shake. 'How can I help?'

'I've just had to tell a couple that their baby's died in utero. She's eighteen weeks and it's their first pregnancy.'

'Oh, *no*…'

Late miscarriage and stillbirth were never easy cases. Jock could feel the cloak of sadness settling around his own shoulders—sadness for the baby and the family—but he had to stifle the urge to touch Grace, to put his arm around her even, and offer support for what was likely to be a very difficult day for her as well.

'I've talked about options with them. They're both distraught but they're quite certain they don't want to go home and wait for labour to start naturally. Her cervix is closed so I had to warn them it could take up to a couple of weeks. Yvonne says she couldn't even imagine doing that.'

Jock nodded. 'Let's go and see them.'

The lights in the room had been dimmed for using the portable ultrasound and clearly hadn't been turned up again. Jock found the grief-stricken mother in the arms of her husband, who was on the bed with her. Grace went to stand beside them and he saw the way Yvonne immediately reached out to hold her hand. He pulled up a chair and sat beside the bed as Grace introduced them.

'I'm so very sorry this has happened,' he said gently.

'*Why* has it happened?' Yvonne had tears streaming down her cheeks. 'What did I do wrong?'

'You haven't done anything wrong,' Jock said. 'This can happen for so many different reasons, but usually it's because of a problem with the baby's development, like a genetic abnormality or a serious problem like a heart defect. We can do tests but often a reason isn't found. I'm sorry...'

'What's going to happen now?' David's voice was raw.

'We'll give Yvonne some medication to soften the cervix and to induce labour. It might happen quite quickly or it could take a few hours. You'll stay here and you'll have someone with you at all times.'

'Me,' Grace said softly. 'I'll be here. I won't leave you.' She only came as far as the door with Jock as he went to chart and find the medications.

'Are you familiar with the local protocols and regulations?' he asked her quietly.

She nodded.

'Are you okay?'

She nodded again. 'The first postgraduate training I did was in bereavement midwifery. I know how important it is.'

'I'll come back as often as I can.'

'Thanks, Jock.' Her eyes were the darkest he'd ever seen them but there was a serenity in her body language that was reassuring. 'But don't worry. I've got this...'

* * *

From the corner of her eye, Grace saw the moment that Jock slipped quietly back into the room when he had finished in Theatre. She didn't turn around, however, because her attention was completely on Yvonne, who had given birth just a short time ago and then collapsed into her husband's arms, overwhelmed with grief.

Grace had been working quietly, taking care of what needed to be done. She had gently cleaned the baby girl and wrapped her in a soft blanket and she was standing with her back to the door, the baby in her arms, as Jock entered silently. She could actually feel the moment he sensed what was going on and went very still so that he didn't interrupt.

'Would you like to see her?'

Yvonne had her head buried against David's shoulder, her face hidden. He had his head bent over hers, his eyes closed.

Grace knew how scared they both were of this moment. 'It's okay,' she whispered. 'There's nothing to be afraid of.'

Yvonne's broken, muffled words were heartbreaking. 'But…does she look like a real baby…?'

'She looks perfect,' Grace said. She didn't have to force her smile and she knew they would be able to hear it in her tone. 'She's very tiny—just the length of my hand—but she's beautiful. She has all her fingers and toes and the sweetest little ears and nose.'

Yvonne's head was turning slowly as she listened to Grace. For a stunned moment, she stared at her daughter. And then she caught her breath in a half gasp, half sob.

'Oh…she *is* perfect…'

Grace was still smiling. 'Would you like to hold her?'

She had to blink back her own tears as she put the tiny bundle in Yvonne's arms.

'You can have as long as you want with her,' she said.

'Can we do some of the things you talked about?' David asked as Grace turned away. 'The handprints and the photos…?' He choked up and drew Yvonne closer into his arms, his gaze fixed on his daughter.

'I'll get everything ready,' Grace promised. 'I'll leave you alone for a little while but I won't be far away. If you need me back just ring the bell.'

Jock had already opened the door, slipping out as unobtrusively as he'd entered, leaving the door open for Grace. He was waiting outside and, for the first time in days, there was nothing awkward about the eye contact they made with each other.

If anything, it felt like a statement that anything that had been interfering with the bond they had—as colleagues and friends—was irrelevant. Apart from possibly making that bond even stronger, because this situation was making it obvious how much it was valued.

There were tears in Jock's eyes and a depth of emotion that totally mirrored her own. Without even thinking about it, Grace did what she could see he needed. She gave him a hug.

Just a quick, almost fierce squeeze, which she hadn't realised she needed as much as he did until he squeezed her back after a moment's stunned immobility.

And that was that. He dropped his arms the instant he felt her loosen her hold. They both wiped their eyes and got on with what needed to be done.

'How did the birth go?'

'As well as it could have gone.'

'Pain control?'

'A bit of gas and air was all she needed.'

Placenta?'

'Delivered. Intact.'

'Do you need me for anything?' Jock asked.

'Not at the moment, but I expect they'll have more questions later. About the tests or how likely it is to happen again, maybe.'

'I'll be here. Just page me.' Jock turned to leave, but then paused. He caught Grace's gaze again. 'You're brilliant at this,' he told her quietly. 'And you're doing something that will make a real difference.'

His voice dropped to no more than a whisper. This was a personal, rather than a professional comment. 'I just wanted you to know that.'

CHAPTER EIGHT

BY THE TIME Grace got home she was done.

So drained it felt like a marathon to keep putting one foot in front of the other to get through the gate and up the path towards the house.

Jock was sitting on the top step. Waiting for her?

Watching her carefully as she came closer.

She could feel the weight of his gaze as if it was a hug. A gesture of caring.

He didn't ask how she was but the tone of his odd words made it sound as if that was his intention. 'Get changed,' he told her. 'Into your oldest, comfiest clothes. I'm taking you out.'

Grace shook her head. All she wanted to do was have a shower and go to bed. She wasn't hungry and she was beyond exhausted.

'Thanks, Jock, but I really don't want to go anywhere.'

He was getting to his feet as she walked past him. 'You want to go where I'm taking you,' he said quietly. 'Trust me. *Please...?*'

Trust...

She did trust Jock. She'd felt safe with him from almost before she'd met him, thanks to him being Jenni's brother. The weirdness of the last few days, after Jenni's left-field comment, seemed to have evaporated in the intensity of today's events and…if there was ever a time that Grace needed to trust someone to make her feel safe—and cared for—surely it was right now?

'Okay,' she sighed. 'Whatever…'

She put on her oldest pair of jeans, a tee shirt and some well-worn sneakers. She picked up a cardigan, even though the day had been a late summer scorcher because she had no idea what time she might get home and the nights could get chilly.

Jock's nod was approving when she came out of her room. He was waiting near the door with a rucksack dangling on his back and a big box in his arms.

'Can you grab the bag in the kitchen?' he asked. 'It's got the bait in it, along with some other chilled stuff.'

'Bait?'

'Aye…' Jock's nod was satisfied. 'You're finally going to go fishing. Come on…we need to get to where we're going before it starts to get dark.'

Fishing…?

It was the last thing Grace would have ever thought she would want to do, but she was too bone-weary and drained to even summon a protest. She followed Jock down to the marina and along the pier and climbed onto his boat and just sat there as he got everything ready and then started the engine and took them out to sea.

The water was calm and the breeze a welcome relief from the heat of the day and there was nothing that Grace needed to do. She could just sit in the back of the boat on one of the wooden seats over the storage bins, her arms resting on the polished wooden side rail, watching the houses of Picton receding and the inviting inlets created by the complicated coastline around them.

If she turned her head she could see the solid shape of Jock's back as he stood nearby in the covered area of the boat with his hands on the wheel as he navigated their path, but it was more appealing to trust that he knew where he was going and simply watch the white foam of the wake the propellor was creating as it spread out in an endless V behind the boat.

Jock clearly did know where they were going because he slowed the boat and took them into a narrow channel that led to a small bay. Tall trees and the punga ferns that grew beneath them reached right down to the rocks at each end of the bay, but in the centre there was a tiny pebbled beach and when Jock had killed the engine and dropped the anchor it was so quiet Grace could hear the wash of almost non-existent waves rolling over the stones between the calls of the birds.

'Hear that?' Jock lifted one of the seats in the back of the boat to reveal fishing supplies. 'That's a bellbird.'

'It's beautiful.'

'You might even hear kiwis when it's dark.'

'Don't we need to go home before it's dark?'

Jock shook his head. 'We can go back any time you want, but we can also stay overnight and sleep on board. The best fishing is often at dusk and dawn. Fish are more active when it's dark.'

'But what about work?'

'We'll get up early enough to get some fishing in and get back in time for work. Or we can watch the sunrise on our way back.'

It sounded *so* peaceful.

'Okay...' Grace put her chin down on her arms and closed her eyes. She still wasn't excited at the thought of trying to catch a fish, but the serenity of this location was…exactly what her soul needed.

This was a gift. For her.

She opened her eyes. 'Thanks, Jock,' she said quietly. 'This is…perfect.'

He looked up from baiting a hook. 'It'll be even better when we catch a fish so we've got something to cook for dinner.'

Jock had only baited one fishing rod. Maybe the fishing part of this expedition was only a reason to be out here and that was fine. Jock sat on the seat across the back of the boat, at right angles to Grace, and flicked the hook into water that was as calm as the proverbial millpond. He didn't say anything else to break the sounds of the birds or the waves. One minute passed and then another and another and the peacefulness began seeping into Grace's bones.

She was the one who broke the silence in the end.

'They called her Luna,' she said, so quietly it was little more than a whisper.

Jock was still staring at where the fishing line disappeared into the water. 'I like that.'

'We got some lovely photos. And the little handprints and footprints. She'll never be forgotten.'

'Neither will you.' Jock put the handle of the fishing rod into an attachment on the back of the seat, putting the activity on autopilot as he turned towards her. 'What you did for Yvonne and David will make such a difference. They told me they couldn't have got through it without you. Yvonne said you just knew exactly the right things to say. And do…'

Grace could feel her eyes filling with tears as she held Jock's gaze. 'You never forget,' she said softly. 'What it's like.'

She saw the muscles move in Jock's neck as he swallowed. Hard.

'It happened to *you*?'

Grace blinked back her tears. 'My baby died a few days before her due date due to cord compression.'

'Oh, God, Grace... I didn't know...'

'Of course you didn't. It's not something I talk about.'

'But...'

'It was a long time ago, Jock. Nearly ten years.' She smiled at him. 'Her name was Isla and she's the one who made me want to be able to help other mothers if the worst thing imaginable happened to them.'

Jock was looking stunned. 'You're...amazing. You know that, don't you?'

Grace shook her head. 'I'm really not,' she said. 'I only got to the point of being able to be there for others very recently. I thought that becoming a midwife and trying to stop it happening for other mothers was the biggest step I would ever be able to take.'

'I can't imagine what that was like for you.' Jock shook his head. 'How long after losing Isla did you deliver that first baby as a paramedic?'

'Nearly five years. And yeah...it was a shock, but it was what I needed to shake me up enough to get my life back together. To find the courage I needed to get out of a bad... situation.'

'Five years...' Jock echoed. 'Had it been that bad for *that* long?' He sounded shocked.

Grace shook her head. 'It was great in the beginning. Barry was a police officer. I met him at an accident scene one night. Whirlwind romance—we got married three months after we met.' She shrugged. 'Stupid, I know, but all I ever wanted was to get married and have lots of kids so they'd have the siblings I never had. Barry wanted a family too. And for me to be a stay-at-home mum. The pregnancy was wonderful…·Until it wasn't…' She swallowed hard. 'People process grief in different ways. Barry was angry. He wanted to try again right away but… I couldn't. We drifted apart and things gradually got…difficult.' Grace took a deep breath and let her gaze catch Jock's. 'Things can happen slowly,' she added. 'Slowly enough for it to become… I don't know…acceptable on some level…'

'Abuse is never acceptable,' Jock said quietly. 'On any level.'

'No…'

But Grace broke the eye contact with Jock abruptly. She didn't want to talk about how abusive her marriage had become. Or how she'd believed that maybe she didn't deserve to escape. She didn't want to say anything more about losing her baby either. She wanted…

She didn't know what she wanted.

For a horrible moment, the emotions of her day and work and memories of the past threatened to destroy the peace of this place Jock had brought her to and Grace couldn't see a way out of a head space that she didn't want to fall into.

She could feel Jock watching her. It felt as though he was absorbing the struggle she suddenly found faced with.

When he spoke, his voice was serious enough to suggest he was saying something meaningful. His words were totally at the other end of the spectrum.

'Maybe this would be a good time…to push you off the boat?'

Oh, dear Lord…

What on earth had made those words come out of his mouth?

Desperation?

He'd seen how lost she was. As if she'd been hanging onto a rock to keep her from falling down an emotional cliff and she'd finally lost her grip. She was falling into some dark space he couldn't see but could imagine and...

And he had to try and catch her.

For a heartbeat he thought he'd made a terrible mistake. He saw Grace's eyes widen and her jaw drop. Then she made a stifled sound that could have been the start of laughter. Or crying.

It was laughter. Shoulder-shaking, tear-making laughter that made Jock's tentative smile become a fully-fledged grin.

But then the laughter morphed into sobbing.

Heartbreaking, soul-scraping distress.

This was *his* fault, dammit, and Jock had no idea what to do. Until Grace held out her arms. Or maybe he was reaching towards her and she responded.

It didn't matter.

Grace wanted—*needed*—to be held and Jock was only too happy to oblige. He slid into the corner of the seat, folded Grace into his arms and held her for as long as it took for her tears to dry up. The sky took on deepening shades of pink and orange as the sun sank below the horizon and the white navigation light for an anchored vessel came on automatically. He heard the reel on the fishing rod begin to spin as a fish was hooked and then he heard it snap as the line broke and the fish fled to safety. He couldn't have cared less. *This* was why he'd thought it might be a good idea to take Grace out on the boat and he'd sit here all night holding her if that was going to make her feel even a little bit better.

But it didn't seem to take very long at all. The sobs became hiccups and the tears became sniffing. Grace sat up and pulled up the neck of her tee shirt to mop her face.

'I'm so sorry,' she said. 'I have no idea where that came from… I haven't cried like that since…' She sniffed again. 'To be honest, I've *never* cried like that…'

'It was my fault,' Jock said apologetically. 'Offering to push you off the boat was a pretty stupid thing to say.'

But Grace shook her head. A smile began to play with the corners of her mouth. 'I've never laughed like that either,' she said. 'It feels like… I don't know…a dam burst or something.'

Jock nodded. 'It did feel like that.' He held her gaze. 'Which isn't necessarily a bad thing. How does it feel now?'

Grace's eyes might be red-rimmed and puffy but they were wide and clear and a midnight blue that was very like the darkening sea around them and Jock had never seen anything quite as lovely.

'It feels good,' Grace whispered. She looked out at the idyllic bay they were anchored in as the final tinge of colour from the sunset faded and took a deep breath. Then she smiled at Jock. 'What would you have done?' she asked. 'If I'd said yes when you offered to push me?'

'I wouldn't have pushed you,' he admitted. And then another grin finally emerged. 'Unless I was absolutely sure it was something you really wanted me to do.'

'I think you might be the best friend I've ever had,' Grace told him. 'Only don't tell Jenni that, will you?'

'I won't,' he promised.

Grace looked back at the bay. 'It would be too cold to go swimming, wouldn't it?'

Jock shook his head. 'Only for the first sixty seconds and

it would be worth it, believe me. It's almost dark, though. You'd need to stay close to the boat.'

'I can't. I don't have a swimsuit.'

'So go in your underwear. Or nothing at all. Have you ever gone skinny-dipping?

Grace looked shocked. *'No...'*

'Why not?'

'Because…it's not something I would ever do…'

'Why not?' Jock was grinning at her again. 'They say it's the things that you *don't* do that you end up regretting. What if you are sitting in a rest home when you're ninety-something and you think, *Oh... I do wish I'd gone skinny-dipping when I had the chance. Now I'll never know what it's like…'*

Grace was laughing again. 'Incorrigible,' she told him. 'That's the word for you.'

'I will if you will,' Jock said.

Grace stopped laughing. 'Can you imagine what Jenni would have to say about that?'

'I'm not going to tell her. Are you?'

Jock watched Grace biting her lip. If nothing else, at least this crazy suggestion had distracted her from any ghosts from the past. But then it was his turn to be shocked because Grace stood up. She gripped the hem of her tee shirt in both hands, ready to peel it off.

'I'm going to do it,' she said. 'Shut your eyes until I'm in the water, okay?'

Jock shut his eyes. 'Okay.'

He heard her squeak as she climbed down the ladder at the back of the boat and discovered how cold the water was when she put her foot into it. Then he heard the splash as

she went in completely. Seconds later, he was also naked.
He didn't bother climbing slowly down the ladder.

He just dived right in.

CHAPTER NINE

OH, MY...

The water felt like liquid crystal. Cold, clean and clear. Sharp enough to cut through anything after the initial shock of how cold it was began to wear off.

Then the feeling of the seawater touching intimate parts of her body was like nothing Grace had ever experienced in her life. She swam a little way from the boat and then stopped, treading water as she caught her breath that had been stolen by the chill. She turned to reassure herself she hadn't gone too far from the boat, just in time to see Jock poised to dive in, and her breath caught somewhere deep inside her chest all over again.

Who was this person who was swimming in the sea, completely naked—with a man? Alone with him. Nobody in the world knew where they were or what they might be doing.

Or why it was happening at all.

It felt...

It felt like exactly what Grace had wanted. She just wouldn't have been able to define it.

It felt like something brand-new. A new beginning. The real start of her new—*free*—life.

And it was amazing. Grace leaned backwards, waving her feet just enough to keep her floating. She knew her breasts were probably in full view from the glow of the white light on the back of *Lassie* but it didn't matter. Even when Jock surfaced from another dive and his head emerged right beside her.

'The stars are coming out,' she said. 'Look…'

Jock turned to float on his back as well and the silence folded itself around them for a long moment. The birdsong of dusk had ceased. Even the waves had softened enough to be inaudible as they lapped the shore.

'Did you know…' Jock said finally, his voice soft enough to not break the complete peacefulness of this moment. 'That when otters are sleeping, they hold hands so they don't float away from each other?'

'I love otters.' Grace could feel her lips curve into a smile. 'Almost as much as I love dolphins.'

'You came to live in the right place, then,' Jock said. 'You need to be near the sea. As long as you don't float away…'

Oh…

In another time and place, she could have fallen in love with someone who said something like that to her…

Grace felt his hand touching hers. A blink of time ago she would have jerked her hand away from a touch like this, as if it was hot enough to burn her skin, but…this hand belonged to a new Grace.

And the other hand belonged to Jock, who might very well be the best friend she was ever going to have.

She curled her fingers around his and for another long moment they floated together, linked like otters.

Grace couldn't think of anywhere she would rather be. Or anyone she would rather be with.

But then she suddenly shivered hard enough to make her teeth chatter.

'Time to get out,' Jock decreed. 'Or we'll get really cold.'

He twisted to get off his back, ready to swim, and the tug on her hand made Grace follow his example. They were even closer now and as she caught Jock's gaze Grace was suddenly overwhelmed with a wave of emotion.

Amazement—at where she was and how it felt as if she was finally turning a page in her life that represented a whole new beginning.

Gratitude—to Jock, for making her laugh. For making that dam burst. For…for simply being Jock.

'Thank you,' she said.

'What for?'

'This… Everything…' Words failed Grace at that point so she reached out to him instead. She was only intending to give him a quick hug, like she had in the ward earlier today when they'd left those grieving parents with their baby, but she hadn't allowed for how different it was to be in water and the way it made her whole body bump against his.

Her naked body.

Against his.

The spear of sensation that created was even more of a revelation than swimming naked had been. Maybe Jock was feeling it too, because he was looking down at Grace with an expression she couldn't read. As if words were failing him as well.

The old Grace would have turned and fled after that split second of contact.

New Grace wasn't going to make a big deal out of this.

'Thank you,' she said again. 'I'll never forget this. Being an otter…'

She let herself float just a little closer. Close enough to drop a kiss on his cheek. Or it would have been on his cheek, but Jock turned his head as she was moving and somehow her lips were brushing the corner of his mouth.

Just for a heartbeat, but that was enough.

Too much?

Grace let go, turned and swam back towards the boat.

The plan had been to catch a fish and cook fresh, beer-battered fillets for Grace. Jock had even messaged Dan to get the recipe he used for his batter and put the ingredients in the box of supplies he had carried down to the marina.

But the opportunity to catch a fish was long gone, thanks to the broken line and the time they'd spent getting thoroughly chilled by the impromptu swim. Jock had stayed in the water long enough to give Grace time to get dry and dressed in private so he was really cold by the time he clambered back on board and pulled his shorts on before he even went hunting for a towel to rub himself dry.

Grace had her cardigan on over her tee shirt but she had rolled her jeans up to her calves and her feet were still bare. She was in the galley, looking inside the box and the bag of chilled items she'd carried to the boat.

'You've got wine in here,' she said when she saw him. 'And cheese.'

'It was supposed to be an aperitif for you while I was cooking the fish I'd caught for dinner. It might have to be baked beans on toast. Or fried eggs. You can decide while we have a glass of wine. Do you want to sit outside and see the stars for a bit longer? I can find a blanket if you get cold.'

'Definitely outside.' Grace picked up the bottle of wine. 'Can you find some glasses?'

Jock might not be providing the dinner he'd wanted to

impress Grace with but she was more than happy with his choice of chilled white wine.

'This is gorgeous…like drinking velvet.'

'It's a local Pinot Gris. I'll take you to visit the vineyard one day soon. Maybe when Jenni's here.'

Grace's eyes widened.

'What's wrong? You don't like that idea?'

'We can't ever tell Jenni about tonight.' Grace took a larger gulp of her wine. 'I can't believe I even did that.'

'Don't worry. I'm not going to tell her you went skinny-dipping.' He held up his glass to touch hers. 'Cheers.'

'Cheers.'

They looked at each other over the rim of the glasses.

Jock raised an eyebrow. 'It was fun, wasn't it.'

'So much fun,' Grace agreed. 'But I still can't believe I did it. I never thought I'd ever be naked in male company again.'

Jock gave a huff of sound but couldn't find any words in response, so he refilled their glasses instead and Grace seemed just as happy to be quiet again as they sipped the wine. But, while words might have deserted him, Jock found his thoughts were as clear as the water below *Lassie*. He could remember wanting to somehow help Grace get past the barrier she had to being touched because she deserved to find the very best of what life had to offer. And he could remember saying 'As *if*…' and the look Grace had given him before she'd vanished through the door.

He was never going to get a better opportunity than this to make up for that, was he?

'Don't give up on men completely, Grace,' he said quietly. 'Don't give up on sex. Or your dream of a family. You just need to find the right person. Someone who can make you feel as special as you really are.'

Grace didn't look up immediately. She was looking down at her glass. Or maybe it was her toes? Jock looked down himself as he caught a hint of movement and the sight of those exposed toes having a bit of a wiggle sparked a strange spear of sensation deep in his gut.

Good grief, he'd been swimming naked with this woman, and she had—albeit by mistake—almost kissed him, and he hadn't felt any inappropriate sexual attraction. But there was something about those bare toes that made him realise, belatedly, the desire he felt for her.

Because he'd just thrown the word 'sex' into the air between them?

Or was it because he knew so much more about Grace now?

Cared more about her?

He had already known how vulnerable Grace was for having been in an abusive relationship. Now he knew that had only been a part of it. He'd already known that she was courageous too, but how far had he underestimated that now that he knew she was so good at helping parents deal with the trauma of miscarriage or stillbirth because she'd been through it herself?

Grace Collins was, quite simply, the most extraordinary woman he'd ever met and, dammit...that water they'd been swimming in was so clear that how perfect her body was hadn't been hidden at all. You'd have to be some sort of saint not to feel a level of physical attraction to her—especially when she was this close to him—with those *bare* feet.

It was just as well she still wasn't looking at him so she couldn't possibly know what he was thinking.

Jock cleared his throat. 'How 'bout I make us something to eat? Have you decided whether you prefer the beans or eggs on toast?'

Grace lifted her head. She was smiling.

'Let's live a little,' she said. 'And have an egg on top of the beans.'

Don't give up on sex...?

And did Jock really think she was special?

The galley was too small for two adults to be in at the same time but Grace was trying to help. She was using a board that went across the tiny sink to cut some toast-sized slices of bread from a loaf while Jock was trying to fit both a frying pan and a small pot on the tiny gas hob.

As long as you don't float away...

Grace had to stop cutting the bread because she needed to close her eyes for a moment.

Denial was real, wasn't it? Had she really believed she wasn't sexually attracted to Jock? Blocked it out because she was so afraid of being that close to someone?

And she had honestly thought that she could only fall in love in a very different time and place?

Well...she'd been wrong, hadn't she?

The realisation was hitting her like a ton of bricks.

She could quite easily fall in love with Jock McKay if she let herself. She wasn't going to let herself, of course, but she couldn't deny that she definitely fancied him...

''Scuse me...'

Grace opened her eyes to find Jock leaning in front of her.

'I just need to get into the drawer to find a can opener for the beans.'

His arm brushed hers but she didn't flinch. She wasn't

ALISON ROBERTS 117

about to drop what she was holding either. She didn't move a single muscle.

Jock's gaze flicked up to meet hers and Grace knew he was startled by what he could see in her face. Concerned, even?

'Are you okay?' he asked softly. The step back he took felt like it made the boat rock gently.

Grace swallowed. Was she brave enough to say anything? Maybe this newly emerging Grace was...

'I was just thinking about something you said.' She took another breath. 'About not giving up on sex...'

The flash in Jock's eyes revealed more than she'd expected. It also sparked a source of heat deep in her belly that Grace hadn't felt in so long she'd totally forgotten what it was like to feel this...desire, that was what it was.

It was a feeling she'd thought she would never, ever experience again and it was a flicker of something precious. She didn't want to let it go. She wanted...

She wanted to feel more.

To find out if it was even possible to go there when she'd given up the hope that she'd ever feel like this again.

Jock was watching her—as if he was waiting for her to say more.

'I couldn't do it if I didn't trust someone enough,' Grace said slowly.

'Of course not.'

'As much as I trust you,' she added.

Jock hadn't let go of their eye contact. 'I might not be the man you need, Grace,' he said gently. 'I can't give you what you need in your future. That family and all those kids. A place to call home. I can't be in a place for more than a year without getting itchy feet. And I run a mile if a relation-ship even looks like getting serious. It's only about the sex.'

'Maybe that's what I need it to be,' Grace whispered. 'Just a one-off kind of experiment. To know if it's possible, even... Or I might not believe that a future with that home and family could ever happen.'

She could see the play of emotion on Jock's face and body language. He was almost nodding, as if he totally agreed with her. As if he thought it was a good idea, even? But he was fighting something—the thought of how horrified Jenni might be probably. Or that it was the last thing he wanted to do?

As *if*...

Grace could feel the colour and heat of embarrassment flooding into her face. 'Sorry,' she said. 'This is a terrible idea. Forget I said anything. Please...'

She dropped the bread knife and would have turned away, but the space was too small and Jock was blocking the exit.

''Scuse me,' she muttered, keeping her head down. 'I need to—'

Escape—that was what she needed to do...

'Hey...'

Jock wasn't moving. He was a solid wall of man in front of Grace. Worse, he put his fingers under her chin and tilted her head so that she had to look up at him.

He wasn't saying anything and the look in his eyes was... Oh, *my*...

Grace had never been looked at like that by a man in her life. Not even on her wedding night when she was about to lose her virginity. As if she was something rare and pre-cious. As if Jock wanted nothing more than to touch her.

'Are you sure?' he asked, so quietly his words were al-most inaudible. 'Would it really help you? To know...?'

Grace hesitated and then gave a single nod, pressing her chin into his hand. 'But that doesn't mean you—'

She didn't get to finish giving him an excuse because Jock bent his head and touched his lips to hers. As softly as he'd just spoken to her. For a long, long moment, that was all it was. The softness. The warmth. The closeness. Movement that almost wasn't there but it still felt like a conversation. Questions being asked and answered.

The odd feeling that her whole body was being supported by the way his fingers were holding her chin.

When she'd burst into tears earlier this evening, it had been as violent as a dam bursting. Now, Grace could feel a softening that was like something uncurling deep inside her. Something growing rather than exploding. A delicious sensation that was a mix of feeling safe but in danger at the same time.

Excitement.

Anticipation.

A heat that was rapidly spreading throughout her body. Grace wanted to sink into it and she made a sound that could have been one of surrender. Her lips moved as she made it, but Jock's mouth followed hers and his hand slipped from her chin to cradle the back of her head instead.

It was the touch—and taste—of his tongue that was the point of no return for Grace. She heard herself make another sound.

One of pure need…?

Dear *Lord*…

Whatever Jock might have imagined doing as a way of helping Grace overcome the barriers she had to being physically touched, it would never have been this.

It would have been more like encouraging her to date someone else. Someone safe, like Dan, perhaps.

Never in a million years would he have imagined he would be having the most amazing sexual experience in his lifetime.

How could he have imagined something he didn't even know existed in quite this form?

Had the flame of attraction been fanned because this was something they really shouldn't be doing? Okay, they were two single, consenting adults, but Jock had been told in no uncertain terms that he was not to even *think* of doing this to his sister's best friend.

Or was there something completely different at play here?

The fact that he was being invited to try and help heal psychological, physical and emotional damage that had been done to the person who had given him the invitation. That he was being trusted with something that was…huge.

Sex was the only time that Jock allowed himself to feel really close to someone. For such a brief burst of time, he could feel as if the past didn't exist. Or the future. He could live in the present and enjoy the closest human touch it was possible to experience. He could feel as if someone wanted to be with him.

That, even if it was just for a few minutes, he was enough.

It never lasted, of course. He couldn't afford to allow it to. Far safer to move on before he could find out that it was no more than wishful thinking.

But that meant Jock had had a lot of practice at sex and he was confident he was pretty damn good at this. He'd never focused quite like this on the woman in his arms, mind you—reading the body language that the touch of his hands and tongue prompted, hearing every sound she made and the way she was breathing and celebrating every touch that *he* was receiving in return.

Aye…this was like nothing he'd ever had before or ever would again and every moment had to be as good as it possibly could be. Not for him, but for Grace. The fact that it *was* so astonishingly good for him as well was an unexpected bonus.

Jock took the cushions off the narrow beds in the front of the boat and put them on the floor. They were both naked by now and Grace's tumble of blonde hair was loose and wildly tousled as she lay there in front of him. Jock had found a condom in the first aid kit, of all places, but he hesitated for just a moment as he knelt there. He could stop, if he had to.

It might kill him but he could stop.

He leaned down. Holding his body away from hers but getting close enough to give her another lingering kiss.

'Are you sure, sweetheart?' he asked softly. 'Are you sure this is what you want?'

Grace's eyes were so dark they were black. She didn't say anything but the answer to his question couldn't have been any more obvious.

It felt like she was reaching up with her whole body to pull them together so closely he couldn't quite tell where his skin finished and hers began.

There was no need for Jock to find any more words either. He could say everything he needed to with *his* body.

CHAPTER TEN

'I CAN'T *DO* THIS...'

'You are doing it, Jodie. You're nearly there. I think you're close to being fully dilated, which means you'll be able to start pushing soon.'

'I don't *want* to start pushing. I want to go *home*...'

'I know... Moving might help. Let's get you out of the shower. You might like to try leaning against Alec.'

'No...' Jodie pushed at her husband's hands as he tried to help her out of the shower in the en suite bathroom of this labour suite. 'Get away from me. I don't want you touching me. You're never going to touch me again. *Ever...'*

Her reference to the conception of this baby made Grace hide a smile as she turned off the shower and draped a soft, dry towel over Jodie's shoulders. It wasn't uncommon for women at this stage of labour to swear they were never going to risk going through this again. The vast majority of them had completely forgotten any such threats of dis-continuing their sex life by the time they were holding their babies in their arms.

Even the thought of anybody having—or not having—sex was enough to give Grace a very unfamiliar curl of sensa-tion in her own gut that made that hidden smile even wider. It wasn't enough to be distracting her in any way from her care of Jodie but it was very...pleasant.

No, 'pleasant' was totally the wrong word for the discoveries Grace Collins had made regarding sex last night on Jock's boat. She had always dismissed the heights of passion she'd heard or seen in books and movies as being flights of fantasy that had no basis in reality, but now she knew it could really happen.

She had, miraculously, experienced it for herself and it had quite possibly been…life-changing.

Even if she was only ever going to experience it that one time, she was never going to regret it. And she was certainly never going to forget it because it was always going to make her smile. And give her that oh, so delicious frisson of a sensation that was just the faintest echo of what it felt like to get taken to the edge of paradise and then pushed over it into a space she'd never known existed.

That secret smile vanished a heartbeat later, however, as Grace caught Alec's horrified expression. Was he blaming himself in some way for the ordeal that Jodie was going through now?

'This is transition,' she told him. 'It's not you.'

Jodie was groaning as Grace helped her move. She walked towards the bed and held onto the side, her head down.

'I feel sick,' she said a moment later. And then, 'Maybe I *do* want to push.'

'Let's get you on the bed for a minute then, Jodie. I'd like to check your dilation before giving you the all-clear to start pushing and we can put the CTG on so we can check baby's heart rate during a contraction. You've been in labour for a while now and that's tiring for both of you.'

But Alec was looking a lot happier. 'It won't be long now.' He looked at Grace hopefully. 'Will it?'

'It's Jodie's first time,' Grace reminded him. 'And we know baby's in a slightly tricky position, being face up, but this is when most babies will rotate to get ready for delivery. I'm going to check that as well—if you're okay with another internal examination, Jodie?'

The young woman was climbing wearily onto the bed. 'You do whatever you need to do,' she sighed. 'I just want this baby *out*…'

She was saying exactly the same thing more than an hour later, but now Jodie was sobbing and begging for an epidural anaesthetic she had earlier declared she didn't want.

'I want it *now*,' she pleaded.

'It's a bit more complicated when you're fully dilated,' Grace told her. 'I'm going to get one of our obstetricians to come and see you, but I need to do a few things first. We need to monitor baby continuously, so you'll need to stay on the bed on your back, but first I need you to go and empty your bladder. If you do get an epidural, you'll have to have a catheter inserted as well.'

'I don't care.'

'Alec, can you go with Jodie while she goes to the loo and help her back to bed, please? Push the button on the wall if you're worried about anything at all in there. I've got a couple of very quick phone calls I need to make.'

'Sure.' The young soon-to-be father was looking as exhausted as his wife.

Grace put out a call to the obstetric team and another one for an anaesthetist, who would be the person to insert the epidural catheter. She also called the ultrasound department to request a portable machine. Jodie's baby had still been in an occipito-posterior position, or face up, when Grace had examined her at the beginning of the second stage of her labour, but now she was facing the possible need for an assisted or surgical delivery and the obstetrician would want to know exactly how the baby was presenting.

Was it unprofessional, she wondered, to be hoping *this* much that it would be Jock who was on his way to help with this delivery?

'So… I hear you've got a "sunny side up" baby.'

'Like an *egg*?'

Jock nodded solemnly. At least he'd got Jodie's husband, Alec, smiling. How much more anxious would they both be looking if he'd confirmed that their baby had a persistent occipito-posterior presentation and was about to need assistance to be delivered safely.

'Left occipito-posterior.' The ultrasound technician was finishing her urgent examination and this information was important. It would inform the direction of rotation to apply with either a hand or pair of forceps.

'Thanks, Mandy.' Jock perched on the end of Jodie's bed as Mandy moved the portable ultrasound machine, to bring himself to the same level as the young parents. Alec had his arm around Jodie as she lay back against the pillows and she was clinging to his hand with one of her own. Grace was busy securing an IV line she had put into the back of Jodie's other hand. Her head was bent and, with her hair pulled back in a ponytail, he could see the tiny whorls of hair just behind her ear.

Not that Jock was going to allow himself even a nanosecond to remember that he knew exactly how baby-soft that hair was or how delicious the equally soft skin felt and tasted, but it did require an effort.

It was just as well last night had been a 'one-off'. Personal distractions of any kind during working hours were totally unacceptable.

'Here's the thing,' Jock said. 'We were hoping your little one would decide to turn herself around.' He tilted his head to include Grace as part of this team. 'But she's being a wee bit stubborn and we can see that it could become a problem.' Jock picked up the CTG graph that Grace had recorded. 'The way the heart rate is dropping during contractions and taking a while to come back up is a sign that we need to do something. I know you're hoping for an epidural, Jodie, but I think it's too late for that.'

'Oh, *no*…'

'We're going to help you,' Jock added quickly. 'And you're going to see your baby very soon. Worst case scenario is that you'll need a Caesarean and we're going to move you into Theatre to be on the safe side but there are other procedures we can try first, to turn your baby so that she can be born without you needing surgery.'

'Like forceps?' Jodie was sobbing now. 'No… I don't want that… It's not on my plan…'

'Jock needs to do what's safest for you and baby,' Grace said. 'That's the only thing that matters right now.'

'What would *you* do?'

Jock wasn't surprised that both Alec and Jodie turned to Grace. He could feel the level of trust they had with their midwife.

Grace smiled at them and then turned her head to include Jock in the smile.

'I would trust Jock,' she said quietly. 'Absolutely.'

* * *

'What's it like?' Grace was in charge of the toasted sandwich maker in the kitchen as they ate a late meal that evening. 'I mean, I've put pressure on when a baby's crowning to slow down a precipitous birth or get the cord from around the neck. And once I had to keep the head elevated in a cord prolapse while they set up for the C-section, but you were holding the head enough to be able to turn it. That must feel astonishing...'

'Imagine this.' Jock made his hand into a fist and then took Grace's hand to put over it. 'My fist is the baby's head. You need to hold it like this, with your thumb over the right parietal bone, and you put enough pressure on to reduce the foetal head station and push it back far enough to give you the room for rotation, but not too far because that could precipitate a cord prolapse.'

He was pressing Grace's hand gently down on his. 'And then your turn the baby's head. If it's an LOP you use your right hand and turn counter clockwise. If it's ROP you use your left hand and do a clockwise rotation.'

He could feel Grace's hand moving beneath his palm.

'If you meet some resistance, a slight tilt of baby's head towards the chest will help.' He bent Grace's hand a little. 'And when it's turned, you hold it in the anterior position over the next two contractions while you get the mother to push down. That way, you bring the foetal head back down into the pelvic outlet and the occiput under the pubic bone.'

Jock was still holding Grace's hand. Her gaze was fixed on his face.

'And then you've got a natural delivery happening,' she said, 'and a baby with an APGAR score of eight and two parents who think you're the best obstetrician ever.'

Jock could smell the cheese that was bubbling out through the join in the sandwich maker. It was probably time to open the machine and check the bread wasn't getting burnt, but he couldn't take his eyes off Grace and he could see exactly what he was thinking being reflected in her eyes.

'I want to kiss you,' he admitted.

'I want you to,' she said.

Jock bent his head. Grace sucked in a breath.

'We can't,' she whispered.

'Why not?'

'You know why.'

Jock did know why. Because it was highly unlikely it would just be a kiss. There was no reason not to let his body remember just how incredible the sex with Grace had been last night and, when he did, it let him know in no uncertain terms just how much it would like to repeat the experience.

'It was only supposed to be once.'

'Would it be all that different if it happened to be twice?' Jock kept his tone deliberately casual. 'I mean, it was supposed to be an experiment, wasn't it?'

'Mmm…' Grace was staring at his mouth.

'And it worked…?' He was trying not to sound smug now. *'Mmm…'*

'Most scientists would say that the experiment would have to be repeated, just to check that the first results were trustworthy.'

Grace had closed her eyes. Because she didn't want him to know what she was thinking? Did she realise she was leaning into him—as if being drawn closer by a magnetic force? He dipped his head a little more. Far enough for his lips to be almost brushing hers.

'What's the real reason not to? Because we agreed we don't want Jenni to know anything about this?'

'She was right. It would be too weird. It might mess with our friendship.'

'And I'd feel guilty,' Jock admitted. 'Not that I made a promise that I wouldn't lay a finger on you. She just assumed I did.'

'She'd know.' Grace was decisive. 'And it might spoil her visit.'

'Not if it had stopped happening before she got here.'

'That's only a couple of weeks away.'

'More than enough time to make sure the experiment really was a success.' Jock let his lips settle on hers for just a heartbeat. It wasn't as if he was a stranger to intense but deliberately short physical relationships. 'A "use-by" date like that is perfect,' he murmured. 'By the time she gets here we can be absolutely telling the truth when we say we're just good friends. She's not going to ask too many questions, anyway. We do know when to respect each other's privacy.'

Jock reached past Grace to turn the sandwich maker off.

He didn't want the house to start burning down while he kissed her as thoroughly as he intended to.

It was a risk, of course.

The bar had been set so high the first time that Grace wasn't at all sure the sex could be anything like as good as that again. She was risking that memory, in fact. The memory she had spent today thinking she could rely on if she ever needed to feel better about herself. *Special…* Or just to feel better about the world in general. Or dream of a future, perhaps, where she wouldn't be alone.

But Jock was right. If she really was going to give that future another chance and not give up on finding a partner, then making sure that experiment had really broken through those barriers could only help.

What if the sex on the boat had only been that amazing because it was a result of not only an over-emotional day at work but the result of that dam bursting in the wake of telling Jock why it had affected her on such a personal level? A fantasy that had begun when she had accepted that she was attracted to him. That she could imagine falling in love with him, even.

It would be different this time. Her feet were back on the ground. She wasn't about to let herself fall in love with Jock McKay because the last thing she wanted was to get her heart broken. She did, however, want to have sex with him again. What woman wouldn't?

It wasn't as if she was initiating it this time either. Jock wanted this.

He wanted *her,* and that was enough to make Grace feel a little giddy.

And it *was* different. *Better…*

Because they were already more familiar with each other's bodies and Grace was learning that it was possible to relax—have *fun* in bed, even—and still feel safe. This had a 'use-by' date, after all.

Even if Jenni wasn't on her way to visit them, it would have only ever been a temporary thing. Jock never stayed in one place—or with one person—long enough for it to be anything else.

Knowing that so clearly up front meant that no one was going to get hurt here.

So maybe they should just make the most of it.

* * *

There was nothing like a ticking clock to provide focus.

Mixing in the fantasy of something that was a big step away from reality in that it wasn't a *real* relationship only increased every aspect of it—like a brief holiday on a tropical island, perhaps.

Or an intensely passionate relationship with what should have been a completely unsuitable, unavailable man.

It wasn't just the sex, despite that being the most obvious fantastical part of what was going on for Grace.

No...whatever was happening between them physically was permeating every minute of every day in the countdown to when Jock was going to drive down to Christchurch to collect Jenni from her international flight coming in from Glasgow via London and Singapore. It was there in that first sip of coffee in the morning, when she could catch Jock's gaze over the rim of her mug, and it was there last thing at night, when they had that silent conversation that could happen in a single glance.

Are you tired?

Not that tired.

Do you want to...?

Yes...oh, yes, I do...

It was there constantly at work.

If they were both involved in the same case, if felt as if there was almost an extra dimension to the passion Grace brought to her work—because she wanted Jock to be impressed with her—the way he had been when she'd been with Yvonne and David through the trauma of losing their baby.

When they *weren't* working together, there was that delicious possibility of just seeing him coming towards her down a corridor or in the café and feeling the hum of that secret between them. Perhaps it was there especially when they were not working together, with a mother and her baby that required their complete focus, because that was when she could let herself sink into that...what was it...the warmth of gratitude? Excitement? Or was it as simple as pure happiness?

Whatever it was, it felt like it was powerful enough to be spreading.

An antenatal clinic gave Grace the chance to catch up with Maureen, who was happily nesting as she got further into her final trimester and wanted to share pictures of the nursery furniture she'd ordered online that included the latest trend of a bedside crib with a detachable bassinet.

'Look, it's got see-through mesh windows and a zip-down wall. I won't even have to get out of bed to do night feeds.'

'And it gives baby a safe sleeping space instead of bed sharing,' Grace noted. 'It's a brilliant idea.'

Stella looked even happier when she came in later, having just had her anatomy scan ultrasound.

'It's a girl,' she told Grace as she lay on the bed to get her fundal height measured. 'I would have been just as happy to have another boy, as long as he was healthy, but Scott has set his heart on having a little sister to look after and I think his dad had his fingers crossed too, judging by his reaction to the picture I sent him of a pair of pink booties.'

'What did he say?' Grace turned the tape measure to eliminate any bias by being able to see the number of centimetres. With one hand, she secured the end on the point where she palpated the top of the fundus to be.

'It was a whole shower of love hearts.'

'Nice.' Grace kept the tape in contact with Stella's skin as she smoothed it down towards the symphysis pubis where the left and right sides of the lower pelvis met in the centre. 'Does Scott know yet?'

'No. I'm trying to think of a way we could do a kind of private gender reveal. Just for him.'

'Hmm…' Grace thought about that as she recorded the measurement she had just taken. 'You're nearly seventeen centimetres, Stella. Right on track.'

'The ultrasound technician, Mandy, said she'd be sending the results through to Dr McKay but it didn't matter that my appointment wasn't until next week. She said everything looks great.' Stella was smiling again. 'And she said that you don't often get such a clear view of gender at this stage but she's a hundred percent sure that it's a girl.'

'I'd love to see Scott's face when he finds out he's got a baby sister on the way.'

'He'll be more excited than he was for his own birthday celebrations.'

'There's an idea. You could get a birthday balloon and put pink glitter inside it for Scott to pop? Or buy a real pair of pink booties and leave them somewhere for him to find? Or have a pass the parcel game with something pink wrapped up in the centre?'

'I love that idea. We might keep it a secret just for a bit longer. It's kind of special having a grown-up secret that's just for the two of you, isn't it?'

'Oh, yes…' Grace's agreement was wholehearted. She knew exactly how special it was.

She got to share Stella's news with Jock later that day and a few days later she got to tell him all about her home visit to Jodie and her baby.

'She and Alec are sleep deprived and anxious like all

first-time parents, of course, but they're doing so well,' she said. 'And they're just *so* happy that everything went as well as it did at the end. They wanted me to thank you again for that.'

The smile they shared encompassed everything Grace loved about this job that she had chosen to do for the rest of her life—the joy, the tension, the drama and even panic that could be part of the miracle of bringing new lives into the world and the incredible satisfaction of beating the odds sometimes to create and share a very happy ending. Sharing it with someone she was coming to know on a very intimate level brought an entirely different dimension to every aspect of it.

Life had never been this good, in fact, and that ticking clock was making it a no-brainer to enjoy it while it lasted and not worry about any consequences. They both knew this was temporary.

Like a holiday fling on that tropical island.

And yes, they might miss it when it was over, but knowing that was coming mitigated any effects that might seriously disrupt their lives, didn't it? Jock seemed to think so and he had way more experience in playing this particular game, so Grace was perfectly happy to follow his lead.

She had the excitement of a visit from her best friend to look forward to as well.

A visit that would, hopefully, provide an easy step from fantasy back into reality.

CHAPTER ELEVEN

'I STILL CAN'T believe how different you look.'

Every time Grace had looked up since Jenni had arrived she'd found her friend staring at her. And smiling—as if Grace was radiating a contagious sort of happiness. A left-over dollop of that *joie de vivre* she'd been spreading at work in the last couple of weeks, perhaps?

'If I didn't know better,' Jenni said, shaking her head, 'I'd swear that you were madly in love with someone.'

If Grace was slightly overdoing the laughter intended to make it seem like something ridiculous had been suggested, she could at least blame it on the wine-tasting they were having in the gorgeous Tuscan-styled buildings of one of the most popular local vineyards, but she'd seen the way Jock suddenly froze with a wine glass from the middle of the array in front of him poised in mid-air.

Did he think that Jenni was picking up on something that they'd both been confident was safely buried by now? Or worse, that there might have been more going on than he would be remotely comfortable with? Jock didn't do 'falling in love' himself and it was obvious he backed off at any hint of it happening in what was supposed to be a casual relationship. How appalled would he be if he thought she'd been reading too much into what had happened between them?

'You know me better than that, Jen,' Grace said firmly.

'I'm still happily single, thank you. Maybe I'm just in love with my new life in New Zealand. Who wouldn't be, with this sort of treat on your doorstep?' She lifted the wine glass that contained the small sample of the vineyard's new rosé, but she was the designated driver today so she barely tasted it.

'That's true,' Jenni conceded. 'And we get a girls' day out tomorrow with our ferry ride and shopping trip to Wellington. Are you sure you don't want to change your mind and come with us, Jock?'

'I'm working. And I'm sure you two need some time to yourselves.' Jock finished the taste of the wine he was holding. 'I'm going to buy some of this Pinot Gris while we're here. Like drinking velvet, it is.'

His smile was the same as it had been the day Grace had arrived in New Zealand. Cheeky and warm and totally genuine. Only she could know that he was reminding her of the night they went skinny-dipping.

The night they'd made love for the first time.

Maybe he was also saluting the last time. And letting her know that he appreciated how easy she was making their transition back to being simply friends? How relieved he was that she wasn't giving it any major significance?

By mutual agreement, the experiment to see if Grace wanted to revive her sex life had been declared complete several days before Jenni had even been due to arrive in the country. It had been a complete success, it was probably well past its 'use-by' date and they could both move on with no regrets. Their new mission was to ensure that Jenni didn't guess they had strayed past the boundaries of being the good friends they would hopefully be for the rest of their lives.

Jock had given the impression that the plan was working perfectly when he'd arrived back from his trip to collect Jenni from the airport in Christchurch. They had stayed a night in Kaikōura on the way back, eaten crayfish, visited the fur seal colony to watch the babies playing in the nursery on the rocks below the main road and had been lucky enough to spot both sperm and orca whales on a boat tour. Jenni had borrowed Grace's car and gone exploring on her own when Jock and Grace were working. They were doing a tour of vineyards around the Marlborough district and tomorrow, while Jock was working, Grace was taking Jenni on the ferry over to Wellington for a day trip.

'You certainly look happier than I've ever seen you look.' Jenni was still focused on Grace. 'But I can understand why. I'm loving it here. Maybe *I* should come back to New Zealand on a more permanent basis.'

'Now *that's* a brilliant idea,' Jock said.

'We're still short-staffed.' Grace nodded. 'I'm sure you could get a job here as easily as I did. And start as soon as you wanted to.' She caught her breath, catching another shaft of that recent happiness that she'd known was too good to be true because it wasn't real. 'It would be *so* good to have you here, Jen.'

'I might actually think about it,' Jenni mused. 'I could get used to all this sunshine and the food and wine. And cooking dinner on the barbecue every night. That's something that's a rare treat in Glasgow.'

'That reminds me,' Jock said. 'I've made a booking at a Brazilian restaurant for your last night here. Then you'll know how good barbecue can really be. It's the most popular place in town—apart from the new cocktail bar that just opened near the Fisherman's Reserve. Maybe we'll go there as well and make the night one to remember.'

'A party!' Jenni grinned. 'I like that idea.'

'You'll probably meet some of the people you'd be working with if you moved here,' Grace said. 'That might help persuade you to take the plunge.'

'That's true,' Jock agreed. 'Shall we invite some people to join us, just to make sure it happens? Like Dan?'

'Who's Dan?' Jenni asked.

'An anaesthetist at the hospital. He's Jock's fishing buddy,' Grace told her. 'I think Jock entertained the idea of setting me up with him when I first arrived. And no...' she shook her head at Jenni's raised eyebrows '... I haven't been out with him. He wasn't any more interested than I was. I got the impression that he's just as much of a committed bachelor as Jock is.'

'No harm in you and this Dan getting to know each other better,' Jenni decreed. 'And Jock, maybe you could bring whoever it is you're seeing at the moment. Is that someone who works at the hospital too? Or is it still that gorgeous Swedish girl...what was her name?'

'Greta.' Jock shook his head. 'No, that was over a while ago.' He seemed to be avoiding looking at Grace. 'Have you tried this sparkling wine, Jen? It's really good.'

But Jenni wasn't going to be distracted.

'There must be someone new,' she said. 'You never stay single for long. Invite her. And find me a date for the night so I don't feel like a fifth wheel at my own party.'

'Fine...' Jock threw her a smile. 'I'll see who's around.' He glanced at his watch. 'We should get going. We don't want to be late home when you two have got an early start to catch the ferry tomorrow.'

* * *

It was a perfect morning.

Dawn was breaking as the inter-island ferry sailed through the Sounds towards the short space of open sea that would take them into the picturesque harbour of the country's capital city.

Grace and Jenni were at the back of the ship, leaning over the rail, soaking in the spectacular scenery.

'This is unbelievably beautiful,' Jenni sighed.

'I did this trip when I first arrived, sailing in from Wellington to Picton, and it felt like I was coming home,' Grace told her.

'No wonder you look so happy.'

'You could always come and live here just for a while,' Grace suggested. 'It doesn't have to be for ever. Why not put in an application form just in case? It can take up to a couple of months for applications to be processed, but then you can get a work permit and just have it ready.'

'I'll think about it,' Jenni agreed. 'But it would have to be just a long holiday. Scotland's home. I'd never want to live anywhere else for too long. Maybe I'm scared that I'll end up like Jock and never stop long enough to put down roots and feel like it *is* a real home.'

'Do you think that's why Jock keeps moving? Because he doesn't want to get attached to a place?' Grace pulled in a breath. 'Or a person? Has it come from that vow you both made to never get married or have kids?'

'Jock told you about that?' Jenni sounded surprised.

'He said it was because you got caught up in your mother going from one disaster to the next.'

'She thought that finding someone to love her would be the answer to all her problems. Apart from the ones she couldn't get rid of—the kids she'd never wanted. Somehow it was always our fault when things didn't work out.' Jenni let her breath out in a sigh. 'Maybe *she* should have gone looking for a place instead of a person. I want roots that I can trust are strong enough to hold me in one place. What we didn't have when we were kids. I think Jock's problem is that he doesn't realise that's what he's searching for too. Maybe *he* should come back to Scotland. I'd hate to think he's going to end up feeling lost. Or lonely.'

Grace opened her mouth with the intention of confessing that she had worried about exactly the same thing. That she liked Jock enough to know he didn't deserve to be lonely. She wanted to admit that they'd broken the rules and got so much closer than Jenni had thought they should, but she didn't have enough time to find the words she needed because Jenni was talking again.

'Home's the place where you feel properly safe, you know?' She shook her head. 'Of course you know. It's because you needed to feel safe that you've come twelve thousand miles to get away from your ex and start a new life.' She threw her arms around Grace and hugged her. 'And you've done that and I love that you feel at home here. That you're so happy. I'm proud of you.'

Grace let go of her intention to confess. She wasn't going to spoil this day with her best friend by telling Jenni something that could not only change their friendship but make things awkward between Jenni and her twin when they only had a small amount of time left to enjoy each other's company.

Instead, she just hugged Jenni back. 'You know that quote about today being the first day of the rest of your life?'

'The one that gets written on an inspirational picture like the view we're looking at right now?'

'Exactly... We're inside that picture. This really is the first day of the rest of our lives.'

Except that wasn't quite true for Grace, was it? The real first day of the rest of her life had been the day that Jock had reached behind her barriers and given her his hand to lead her out.

The day he'd made love to her.

'All we need now is for some dolphins to swim past,' she added, laughing.

'And to have the best day ever together. What's first when we get to Wellington?'

'We're going to take a cable car up the hill to get the best view of the city and harbour. We can visit the museum, have lunch on the waterfront somewhere, and I've been told that the best place to go shopping is in Cuba Street. We can find new dresses to wear for your farewell party tomorrow night. Oh, and we have to get a photo taken in front of the Bucket Fountain. I have no idea what that is, but it's apparently quite famous.'

How good was this?

If he'd wanted to make absolutely sure that Jenni ended the best time together they'd had in years without it being spoilt by her finding out that he'd broken the rules she'd made regarding Grace, this was the ace he hadn't known he had up his sleeve.

Inviting a few friends and colleagues to make it a really good night out had been a masterstroke. It was Saturday night, the Brazilian restaurant had a live band playing salsa music and there was great conversation and a lot of laughter and Jenni thought—as he'd intended her to—that he'd invited Mandy, the ultrasound technician, as his date. Maybe she was looking to see if she could detect any spark between Grace and Dan—who had reluctantly agreed to join this social gathering—and she was enjoying the company of Stefano, the Italian ED locum doctor who Jock had invited to keep the numbers even.

Stefano was certainly enjoying himself. He had taken charge of a platter that was part of the entrees they were all sharing. Jenni and Mandy had already taken some and he was passing it to Grace now. 'You have to try these cheese bread balls,' he told her. 'They are *così delizioso*.' He kissed his fingers like a chef. 'So delicious.'

'They are,' Mandy confirmed, smiling at Stefano. 'Can I have another one, please?'

Grace also took one and bit into it. 'Oh…you're right. How good is that? Oops…messy…' She caught the drips of melted cheese on her fingers with her tongue.

Jock knew he shouldn't be staring but, for a fraction too long, he couldn't look away. Both Jenni and Grace were wearing the new dresses they'd bought on their shopping spree in Wellington yesterday and they both looked gorgeous, but the dark blue of Grace's dress matched her eye colour and she had left her hair loose so that it fell in bouncy golden waves to her shoulders.

She was looking absolutely stunning.

And she was licking melted cheese off her fingers, dammit…

Thanks to the twist of sensation in his gut, all Jock could think of was having to turn off that sandwich maker while it was cooking cheese toasties so that he could make love to Grace without burning the house down. His entire body was reminding him of how much he'd wanted her that night.

How much he *still* wanted her, even though they had agreed that the experiment was complete and it had been a success. Jock had achieved exactly what he'd wanted and had helped Grace get past the barriers that were keeping her from living her best life and achieving her dream future of a family of her own.

He should be happy about that. So why wasn't he?

Why did he have this odd empty feeling he couldn't quite place? And why wasn't he remotely attracted to Mandy, who was supposed to be his date tonight?

Not that it mattered. Everyone was enjoying themselves as the evening went on. Mandy seemed to be getting on very well with Stefano as they all shared and enjoyed their main dishes of barbecued fish and spicy chicken and a smoky black bean stew with rice. Jock and Dan started planning their next fishing expedition and Jenni and Grace were clearly making the most of their remaining time with each other. Grace was going to miss her friend after tomorrow, wasn't she?

And that was when it hit him.

That was what that hollow feeling in his gut was about. Jock was missing Grace, even though she was right here, sitting across the table from him.

He'd been missing her for days. Ever since they'd declared the experiment over and done with before Jenni had arrived in town. Ever since he'd had to be careful not to let his gaze rest on Grace for too long or share a smile that might advertise a connection that had been far more intimate than merely friendship.

While the dishes were being cleared from the table the

band started up again after a break and Stefano looked hope-fully at the women around him.

'So…who wants to do some salsa dancing?'

'Me…' Mandy said, as both Jenni and Grace shook their heads.

Stefano held out his hand and within seconds they were both on the small floor area right in front of the band. They were both good dancers and their body language made it clear that they were increasingly enjoying each other's com-pany. Inviting Stefano to be Jenni's date tonight had clearly backfired as much as pretending he was out on a date with Mandy, but when Jock offered his sister an apologetic gri-mace, Jenni just smiled.

'You win some, you lose some,' she said. 'I won't be of-fended if you're not.'

'We're not going to let it spoil the party,' Grace said. 'Do you want to order dessert or is it time to go and check out that cocktail bar?'

'Let's give them five minutes more dancing and then go and get cocktails.' Jenni turned back to Dan. 'So how long did you say you've been living here?'

'Couple of years now.'

'What made you choose Picton?'

'Job came up. I needed a change.'

Jock hid a smile. He'd asked the same question himself and got exactly the same answer. Dan might be taciturn but he was consistent. Trustworthy. It was a shame there was no spark there between him and Grace. She wasn't even joining in the conversation at the moment because she was watching Mandy and Stefano dancing together. As if she felt Jock's gaze, however, Grace turned and there was no mistaking the invitation that lit up her eyes. She wanted to dance too.

It was more than an invitation. Maybe it was more than simply wanting to dance. It looked like...longing...

He could feel it himself. He wanted to hold Grace in his arms and feel her body close to his own. He wanted it so much, in fact, that he knew how dangerous it would be to respond to that invitation.

Worse...he didn't care. He wanted to respond. He needed to...?

Maybe it was fortunate that his phone rang to break the moment.

'Sorry... I'll have to get that. I'm second on call.' Jock got up from the table to take the call from the hospital, but he came back a short time later.

'I have to go in,' he said. 'We've got a seven months' pregnant woman who's come in via ambulance after a car accident. She's at risk of a placental abruption.'

'Someone local?' Grace was getting to her feet.

'Yes.' Jock lowered his voice. 'A Maureen Petersen—do you know her?'

'She's one of *my* mums.' Grace looked horrified. 'I should come with you.' She bit her lip, turning back to Jenni. 'This is important,' she said quietly. 'I know how much this pregnancy means to her.'

'Go,' Jenni said instantly. 'Don't worry about me. We can catch up later at the cocktail bar.'

'It might take a while,' Jock warned.

'I can find my way home in that case. I'll see you both tomorrow morning, anyway, before I get the train back to Christchurch.'

'Sorry, Jen.'

Jock *was* sorry to leave his sister on the last night of her visit but he couldn't stay. He couldn't suggest that Grace stayed either. He could see exactly how worried she was for Maureen. She looked like she had that day she'd followed Stella when she'd run away from that first antenatal appointment. And that time when she'd been such a part of the shared grief for that tiny stillborn baby, Luna. Grace cared deeply about every mother and baby she had in her care and he couldn't leave her here, not knowing what was happening.

Because he cared about *her* as well.

Dan must have picked up on the dilemma. 'Don't worry,' he said. 'I'll look after Jenni. Go. You're needed—both of you.'

CHAPTER TWELVE

'GRACE... I'M *SO* glad you're here. But how did you know I'd had an accident?'

'I was just lucky to be in the right place at the right time, Maureen.'

With Jock...

Grace had a feeling that being with Jock might always feel like she was in the right place at the right time. She had thrown a gown over her dress as they'd arrived in Picton Hospital's emergency department and then followed Jock straight to the resuscitation area, where Maureen was lying on the bed, clearly distraught.

She could hear Jock talking to the consultant on duty in Emergency behind her as a technician was positioning an ultrasound machine near the head of the bed.

'Is the speed of the vehicle known?'

'Ambulance crew said it was a low impact, single vehicle crash but the driver's front airbag deployed for some reason. There's a mild abrasion on her face.'

'Was she wearing a seatbelt?'

'Yes. And there's a mark on her shoulder but the belly's clear.'

'Any PV blood loss?'

'No.'

'Abdo pain?'

'Yes. She's complaining of abdominal discomfort.'

Maureen was terrified. 'Something like this can start labour, can't it?' she asked Grace, her voice shaking. 'Or make the placenta come away?'

'You're not bleeding,' Grace said. 'That's a good sign. Jock's going to have a look with the ultrasound now. He'll be able to see if there's any injury to the baby or hidden bleeding from any damage to the placenta. It doesn't sound like you were going very fast.'

'I wasn't. I was getting home after being out for dinner. My shoe slipped on the brake and I hit the accelerator by mistake. I drove straight into my brick fence.' Maureen pressed her hands to her face. 'I can't *believe* this has happened...'

'Hi, Maureen.' Jock was by the bedside now. He touched her arm in a gesture of both greeting and an understanding of how frightened she was. 'Take a deep breath for me, hold Grace's hand and try and slow your breathing down a little if you can. We'll see if we can find out exactly what's going on. Can I have a feel of your tummy before we do the ultrasound? Is it still sore?'

'It just feels...weird. Kind of tight.'

'Have you felt baby moving since the accident?'

'No...' Maureen was crying again. 'I've been so careful when I'm driving ever since I got pregnant. I knew to put my seat back and tilt the steering wheel up. I make sure I put the lap belt under my bump and the other one between my breasts.'

'This'll be a bit cold.' Jock squeezed gel onto Maureen's belly as he finished palpating her abdomen. He picked up the transducer and within seconds they could all hear the reassuring sound of the baby's steady, rapid heartbeat.

'There you go…' Grace squeezed Maureen's hand. 'That's exactly what we want to hear.'

Jock was focused on the screen and Grace watched as he had a quick look for anything major happening to the placenta, which was the main risk to Maureen's baby at present. Then he examined the unborn baby from head to toe for any visible injuries like fractured bones. She could feel the tension in Maureen's body. Maybe that was contributing to why her abdomen felt so tight?

'Deep breath,' she whispered. 'I know it's hard, but it's better for both you and baby if you can relax a little.' Maureen's own heart rate was too fast and her breathing still rapid and shallow, which was pushing her blood pressure higher than normal.

'But what if I go into labour? It's too soon.'

'There's nothing to suggest you will go into labour yet,' Grace said. 'But you're almost thirty weeks. Ninety-eight percent of babies born at thirty weeks survive.'

'Really?'

Grace smiled as she nodded but she gave Maureen's hand another squeeze. She totally understood how stressful this was. She could remember all too well what it was like to be wanting her baby to be safe and healthy. To be looking forward so much to its birth.

She could feel it so strongly, in fact, that it was doing something strange to her own body. Or her heart?

Something almost shocking was happening to her. Something that, only a matter of weeks ago, Grace would never have believed could ever happen again. She was feeling the longing to have a baby of her own tucked into her belly, beneath her heart. To be dreaming of what life would be like when it was born and her life changed for ever because she was a mother. She could *feel* the love she would have for that baby and child.

Jock was smiling at Maureen now. 'There's no sign of any injury to your baby,' he said. 'I'm just going to have a really good look at the placenta now, okay?'

Maureen just nodded, too emotional to speak. They both watched as he located the placenta.

'I'm looking for even a tiny tear now, where it could be coming away from the uterine wall,' he explained. 'And any blood that might be hiding between the placenta and the wall, which would mean it wasn't visible as external loss and… I can't see anything.' He smiled again. 'So far, so good, but we're going to monitor you for a while. Grace will put on the CTG machine and that way we'll know if you start getting any contractions and we'll also be able to listen to the heart rate continuously.'

Maureen nodded again. 'How long for?'

'At least six hours,' Jock said. 'But we're not going to send you home until we're quite sure nothing's going to happen.'

'But what if it does?' Maureen looked as if she was holding her breath.

'Then we'll manage it,' Jock said calmly. 'If there's a risk that you're going into premature labour, we can try and slow things down and give you medications to help the baby's lung development. If we can't stop it or there's any danger to the baby and it's going to be safer to be born, then we'll manage that too.'

'I'll stay with you,' Grace added. She caught Maureen's gaze as she wiped the gel off her skin. 'We've got this…'

The words were as much for herself as for Maureen. Her own emotional reaction to this situation was something to put aside and think about later.

Maureen's return smile was wobbly but it was there. She saw her gaze slide sideways to watch Jock as he was scribbling notes on her chart and Grace could see her finally trying to slow her breathing as Jock had advised. She was beginning to let go of at least some of her fear.

Grace could understand why. Jock had an amazing ability to demonstrate a combination of confidence and caring that would make anybody trust him completely, even with something as precious as a longed-for baby. She had seen it time and again now, with Stella and Jodie and Tessa amongst others.

She was proud of him for being so good at his job.

Grace wanted him to be proud of the way she did her job too. She placed the flat, round transducers of the cardiotocography machine on Maureen's belly, one above the foetal heart to monitor the rate and stability of the baby's heartbeat and another one at the top of the uterus to pick up any contractions that might be happening, including light ones like Braxton Hicks, explaining what she was doing and making Maureen as comfortable as possible.

When she took another set of vital signs, Maureen's heart rate and breathing were slower and she was smiling as she listened to the steady tick of her baby's heart.

'I could listen to that all night,' she said.

'That's probably just what we will be doing,' Grace said. 'But I'm hoping you'll get some sleep as well.'

'That sounds like a good plan.' Jock looked over Grace's shoulder as she wrote down her vital sign recordings. 'Try and rest, Maureen. I imagine they'll move you somewhere a bit quieter than in here, but you'll be quite safe with Grace here looking after you and I'll be hanging around for a while myself.'

Grace turned her head just enough to catch his gaze and they shared a smile. She turned back to hang the chart on the end of the bed, but she was thinking that it was Jock's care as much as the comfort of hearing the baby's heartbeat that was helping Maureen feel so much calmer. The smile on her face as she listened to Jock suggested that she knew how lucky she was to have him as her obstetrician.

Grace was even luckier because she knew was it was like to have this man as a friend. She knew what it felt like to have given this man a level of trust that she knew had changed her life for the better. A level of trust that was a form of love.

Yeah… The more she got to know Jock, the more she was coming to love him.

She loved who he was as a person and as a friend as much as how skilled and compassionate he was as a doctor.

Grace could feel herself relaxing and, as she mirrored Maureen by taking a deep breath herself and letting it out slowly, she gradually became aware of something else.

Something huge that must have been hiding in plain sight all along.

Something as shocking as realising that she could— *did?*—still want to have her own baby.

The love she was feeling for Jock wasn't simply the result of a close friendship. She was *in* love with him.

Oh, dear Lord…

When had that happened?

That night she'd overreacted to the touch of his hand on her shoulder and had smashed that plate on the kitchen floor? When he'd told her that she would always be safe with him?

Or was it when he'd apparently broken through the tangled self-protective barriers that had been holding her bound too tightly to be properly alive—when he'd offered to push her off the boat?

When he'd held her in his arms to let her cry…

No… Grace suspected it had been when he'd been floating beside her in that icy, clear water. Holding her hand like an otter, so that she wouldn't float away…

Not that it mattered.

It had happened. And it was never going to change.

Grace was in love with Jock.

And it wasn't just *a* baby she could feel herself longing for.

It was *Jock's* baby.

CHAPTER THIRTEEN

THERE WAS SOMETHING different about Grace tonight.

Was it because this was the first time they'd both responded to an after-hours call and gone into the hospital at this time of night?

Was it because he knew she had a pretty new dress on underneath that gown?

Or was it a remnant of how he'd been feeling earlier this evening—that disturbing awareness of how much he'd wanted to dance with Grace? The feeling that he was missing her even though she was right there...

While Grace went with Maureen as they shifted her into a quiet room on the maternity ward to monitor her for at least the rest of the night, Jock went to find a coffee and send Jenni a text.

Will be here for a while yet. You okay?

A response pinged back quickly. It was a photograph of a very fancy-looking cocktail in a martini glass that had a rim crusted with sugar or salt and tiny flowers floating on the top. Another one came in a moment later, of Dan looking as though the last thing he wanted was to have his photograph taken, and was followed by a happy face emoji.

Jock sent back a 'thumbs up' one.

I'll try not to wake you up when I get home. See you in the morning in time to get to the train station. Have fun.

And then he sent another one with a winking face.

Not too much fun...

He couldn't blame his sister for not responding to that one, but in the time he stared at the blank screen Jock found himself thinking about Grace.

Or, rather, he was *seeing* her—as clearly as if she was in the same space he was in.

Seeing the way she'd been looking at him earlier tonight, when it seemed obvious she was hoping he'd ask her to dance with him.

Seeing the way she'd smiled at him when they'd both been offering Maureen their care and reassurance. The kind of smile that acknowledged their shared professional anxiety for the woman who was so afraid of losing what could be her only chance of becoming a mother and their joint determination to keep both mother and baby safe.

But had there been more to that smile? Something far more personal?

Aye...that was it. There *had* been something different about that smile. Or the look in Grace's eyes. Or the alchemy of the combination.

Something that had touched Jock somewhere very deep in his chest.

In his heart...?

Oh...*help*...

Alarm bells were sounding in his head now. Loudly enough to suggest that he'd missed a chance to hear them much earlier than this.

What was even more disturbing was that he knew why those alarms had been set in the first place and what they were about.

He'd learned long ago to recognise the warning signs of getting in too deep in a relationship. The pull to get close to a particular woman, even if it was purely sexual, was a huge red flag. This was new territory because it went above and beyond anything as simple as physical desire and it was alarming because it was even further along a relationship spectrum. That hollow feeling in his gut that was the emptiness of missing something—or some*one*—important in his life was deeper now. Darker. He could fall into it if he didn't do something to protect himself.

That smile, that look, the whole *softness* about Grace in that moment, had offered him something he couldn't allow himself to even consider accepting because it would be unbearable if it was taken away. Possibly unsurvivable.

Love...

Jock was an expert in sensing the exact moment when it was time to move on in any kind of relationship, but it felt like something had gone very wrong this time.

Had he been lulled into a sense of false security because there had been a very definite 'use-by' date on the experiment? Or because, thanks to those ground rules Jenni had put in place, they'd both felt safe with each other from the moment Grace had arrived in his life?

Jock didn't feel safe now.

An unpleasant flicker of something menacing made Jock feel as if he was in danger.

No...he *knew* he was in danger.

In danger of falling in love with Grace Collins.

But maybe it wasn't too late. At least he could hear the alarm sounding now.

And if he stayed in control and moved fast enough, perhaps he could escape unscathed.

How he could manage that escape without people getting hurt in the process was another matter entirely, but at least he didn't have to think about it just yet.

Right now, he could focus on the patient he'd been called in to see this evening. And then he'd have to catch enough sleep to be able to do his job safely tomorrow, and he wanted to farewell Jenni and get her on the train in the morning to reach her flight to Australia in time without giving her any hint of undercurrents—real or threatened—due to the connection he had inadvertently allowed to go too far with Grace.

Yes…there was every reason to put off thinking about it at all until he had a safe time and space. And who knew? Maybe the universe would offer up a solution in the meantime.

It wasn't the universe that unexpectedly offered up the solution the next day. It was Jenni.

Jock was taking one last look around the station platform before his sister climbed into the train carriage. And frowning.

'Looks like Grace isn't going to get away from the hospital in time to wave you off.'

'She texted me. Her patient is getting a bit wound up about the next ultrasound she's waiting for. I told her not to worry. I'll call her when I've arrived in Melbourne. I've had the loveliest time, Jock.' Jenni threw her arms around her brother and hugged him. Hard. 'And thank you… You're doing a great job of looking after Grace. I'm so happy that *she's* so happy.'

'Me too,' Jock managed. 'You look after yourself, Jen. Have fun in Melbourne.'

'I intend to. Have you ever been?'

'No. I'd love to, though.'

And there it was… The solution.

It was time to move on to a new adventure. A new start. He could get away from any danger of things getting out of control with Grace and either of them getting hurt and he knew he could do it in a way that was kind—he was just doing what he always did, after all, and he was confident that he was good at it.

He was moving on.

Hopefully without leaving any lasting damage to what felt like the most significant friendship he'd ever had. Jock was, without doubt, closer to Grace Collins than he'd ever been to anyone other than his twin sister.

The sister who was delighted with how happy Grace was in her new life and the part Jock had been playing in looking after her best friend.

He just had to continue doing that. And it wouldn't hurt to keep his fingers crossed and hope the next step would be as easy to find as the first.

It was easy to put the issue aside when he arrived at work, especially as Grace was with the first patient he needed to see. Being in the dim light of the ultrasound room made it easy to focus completely on the screen and the relief of being able to confirm there was no sign of any damage to Maureen's baby or the placenta made it a good start to his day.

'The continuous CTG monitoring hasn't given us any grounds for concern either, Maureen,' he said. 'I'm happy to discharge you to go home, but it would be a good idea to take things easy for a day or two.'

'And call us if you're worried about anything at all,' Grace added.

He spotted Grace a short time later, on his way to get a sandwich and coffee from the café for lunch. She was walking with Maureen out of the main doors of the hospital to where a taxi was waiting. He bought an extra sandwich and presented it to Grace as she came back through the reception area.

'Ham salad on sourdough,' he said. 'I thought you might need some sustenance. You must be exhausted after being up all night with Maureen.'

'Thank you...' Grace's face looked pale but her smile reached all the way to her eyes. 'I am tired but I'm okay. And so happy that Maureen's baby is also okay. Was Jenni upset that I didn't make it to the train station?'

'Not at all. She's looking forward to telling you all about Melbourne later.'

'She loved being here, didn't she?'

'She did.'

'She'll love Melbourne too. I've heard it's an amazing place for a holiday.'

'I've heard that too.'

Jock didn't think his tone gave anything away but the look Grace gave him said otherwise.

'It's given you itchy feet, hasn't it? To go somewhere new for more than just a holiday?'

And there it was again. An offering from the universe. A signpost to his escape route. How ironic was it that it was Grace who was presenting the opportunity to take a gentle first step towards that escape and to do it in a way that could protect them both?

'You could be right about that.' Jock tried to keep his tone merely thoughtful. 'There are still so many more places in the world I haven't seen. More adventures to be had.'

Okay…he might have caught a flicker of dismay in Grace's gaze but it was hard to tell because she broke the eye contact so swiftly.

'I'd better get going,' she said. 'I've got a wee adventure myself this afternoon. I'm taking a water taxi out for a home visit to Tessa to see how she's going, setting up for the twins.'

'Remind me where she lives?'

'Kumutoto Bay. She's got a waterfront property with its own jetty.'

'Ah… I believe that's one of the arms of Double Bay in the Queen Charlotte Sound. It's a beautiful spot. Not too far away at all. No phone reception that I remember, though.'

'No. She has a five-minute climb on the hill behind the house to use her cell phone or get the internet. They've got a landline, though.'

'Tell her I'm looking forward to seeing her next week.' But Jock was frowning as he thought about the implications of an extra degree of isolation. 'I might see if I can persuade her to be admitted for a few days before her C-section is scheduled, just to be on the safe side. Maybe you could check she's got her hospital bag packed already.'

'Will do.' Grace was moving away already. 'Thanks for lunch. It must be my turn to make some dinner tonight.'

'Don't worry about me. I've heard there's a tropical low forming northeast of New Zealand in the Coral Sea that could head our way later this week and I should go and check how secure *Lassie*'s moorings are.'

Grace paused, her head turning and her expression surprised. 'But it looks as calm as a millpond out there. It's not going to get rough while I'm going out to see Tessa, is it? I'm not sure I want to be out in big waves in a small boat.'

'It never gets really rough in the Sounds. It's out in Cook Strait that you get the gnarly seas with ten metre waves. And any bad weather with wind and rain will be days away yet and it could well be downgraded before it gets here. Don't worry.' He smiled at Grace, wanting to reassure her. 'The MetService is just tracking its formation and path. It could change direction or not be as severe as they think, but it's common sense to be prepared. Even if the water's not rough, strong gusts of wind can cause boats to come loose and move enough to get damaged.'

Grace smiled back. 'Good to know. Do you need any help with *Lassie*? I could meet you at the marina after work.'

'*No...*' The word came out with both a head-shake and more emphasis than Jock had intended, but the prospect of being alone with Grace—in the very space where this had started getting out of control in the first place was something to be avoided at all costs.

'Thanks for the offer,' he added. 'But you'll be tired enough as it is after last night.' He turned away. 'It's not a problem. I can manage without you.'

Jock was running away, wasn't he?

Making sure nobody got too close to him.

Had he somehow sensed that Grace had stepped over the acceptable boundaries of friendship in how she felt about Jock?

Had it really happened that fast—in the few hours since that middle-of-the-night ultrasound on an unborn baby—or had Grace unknowingly been giving off signals earlier? Last night, perhaps, when she'd let herself think that it might be okay to join Mandy and Stefano on the dance floor and it would be acceptable to be that close to Jock? Because she'd been missing his touch so much since they'd called time on her sex-life experiment. So much that it was actually a physical pain.

No…it was more likely that he'd seen what she'd been thinking about as they'd shared a relieved smile when the ultrasound had suggested Maureen's baby wasn't in any immediate danger. Had he also seen what she hadn't quite realised herself at that point? That she could only imagine trying for another baby if it was going to be Jock's baby?

That she was head over heels in love with him?

No wonder the alarm had sounded and he was running, if that was the case. But was he so convinced that a long-term relationship and perhaps a family was the last thing he wanted that he was prepared to upend his entire life yet again and move to a new place—a new *country*—and start all over again?

She needed to fix this.

So that Jock didn't need to run away.

So that she could at least keep their friendship intact.

But, thanks to the fatigue that came from the sleepless night with Maureen, Grace couldn't think of what she should do. Did she need to step back and give Jock enough space to feel safe or would it be better to talk about it?

No…that fatigue also meant that it would be harder to avoid revealing, or even saying, something that would make things worse. Giving Jock space seemed like the only option, so Grace didn't fight the urge to crash that evening and she was sound asleep before Jock got home from checking on his boat.

She didn't see him at work at all the next day because he had a full theatre list and she had an antenatal clinic with a surprise twist when she discovered that the backache one of her mums was experiencing turned out to be the beginning of active labour. Grace was caught up with a delivery that lasted until the early hours of the next morning.

She slept late the next morning and walked to work under a moody sky that was grey with thickening clouds, responding to messages from Jenni, who was following weather reports in Australia and hoping the tropical storm that had now been upgraded to a cyclone was not going to affect her planned flight back to the UK.

She texted her back.

You'll be fine. Remember that the pilots want to get home as much as you do. They won't fly if it's not safe.

Have you heard what they've called it? Barry!!

No way!!

Grace sent a laughing face emoji, but she was starting to feel as grey as the clouds gathering above her head. Things were changing around her. Was the man who was quite possibly the love of her life moving rapidly away from her when a potentially damaging storm with the same name as her ex-husband was coming towards her?

She didn't want to be where she was right now. It felt like something was about to break.

Cyclone Barry was all everyone wanted to talk about at work that day, as they checked weather maps and forecasts. The ominous-looking circle of swirling cloud above the Tasman Sea was staying well away from the eastern coast of Australia, but it did keep tracking directly towards New Zealand and warnings were being issued about potentially very heavy rain and strong winds.

It was beginning to rain lightly that evening as Grace got home to find Jock was heading out to have a game of squash with Stefano. It was the first time they'd been face to face since he'd dropped the bombshell that he might be looking for a new life somewhere else.

'How did the visit with Tessa go yesterday?'

'Good. She's well set up with two of everything and a very supportive husband, Lawrence, who was there as well. He likes the idea of Tessa being admitted before the Caesarean. I asked if she had friends or family she could stay with in town if the weather got bad enough that it might cut them off, but she said she had too much to do at home to get ready for the babies.'

This was good, Grace thought. It was safe to talk about things like work and shared patients.

'Lawrence asked me if he should stay home himself from now on because his work takes him all over the district, but Tessa told him he'd drive her crazy if he was hanging around for more than a week watching for any signs she might be going into labour. He's taking a day off to come in for her next appointment with you, though.'

'What does he do?' Jock picked up his squash racquet that was leaning against the wall near the front door.

'I'm not sure. Something to do with the Department of Conservation, which means he spends time in the national parks.

They're both really into nature. Their house is amazing—it's in the middle of a punga fern forest with a path that goes down the hill to a tiny sandy beach and the pier. The living room opens to a big deck which has the most beautiful view I've ever seen.'

It was safe to talk about nice views too.

Would it also be safe to talk about something more personal? Jock had the perfect excuse to escape if he needed to, with his squash racquet and car keys in one hand and holding the laces of a pair of trainers in the other.

'Did you hear from Jenni? Do you know if her flight took off? Last I heard, she was really worried about the cyclone.'

'Yes. Took off right on time. I'm following the flight on a tracking app.'

Grace bit her lip. 'Did you hear that they've named it Barry? My ex's name.'

Jock's expression was a sympathetic grimace as he nodded. His gaze not only met hers directly for the first time in this conversation, he held it. He was worried about how this might be affecting her, wasn't he?

He *cared* about her…and that gave Grace a squeeze around her heart that felt a lot like hope.

'It's quite an appropriate analogy really.' Grace took a deep breath. 'He's going to blow in, might do a bit of damage and then he'll disappear, never to be seen again.'

The corners of Jock's mouth curved upwards. 'I like it,' he said quietly. 'And the sooner he's gone for good, the better.'

Grace couldn't look away as his gaze softened and then dropped to her lips. He was thinking about kissing her, wasn't he?

He *wanted* to kiss her.

She wanted him to.

She felt something else then, in the instant Jock jerked his gaze away from hers. A heartbeat of the kind of awkwardness they'd had before—after Jenni had jokingly suggested there could be something going on between them and the idea of being physically attracted to each other had been hanging in the air.

But this was worse because it was for a very different reason this time. It was because there *had* been something going on between them and...

And Grace's heart was breaking as she watched it fading into the distance because it was something Jock really, really didn't want. He couldn't get away fast enough right now, that was for sure. He muttered something about keeping Stefano waiting and then he was gone.

The first effects of Cyclone Barry began to be felt at the top of the South Island of New Zealand late the next afternoon, with heavy, squally rain showers and gusts of wind that were strong enough to be turning umbrellas inside out.

Jock was in the reception area of the labour ward when Grace went to file her patient notes.

'Sharon's ready for discharge,' she told the ward clerk. 'Baby number four has arrived with the minimum of fuss and she's keen to get back home before this weather gets any worse.'

'Aren't we all?' One of the registrars was shaking her head. 'I hear the river's rising quite fast. We might get stuck here ourselves.'

'Did you hear that the cyclone's been upgraded?' Someone else was scrolling a weather website. 'A cruise ship has cancelled a visit to Picton and there could well be disrup-

tions to ferry crossings by this evening. It could be a cat-
egory three, when or if it makes landfall.'

'When is that forecast for?' Jock was frowning. 'I hadn't
heard that update. I'd better go and check on my boat again
on my way home.'

One of the nurses shook her head. 'And this is the man
who was just talking about some idyllic job opportunity in
the Solomon Islands? You do know that's like the birthing
suite for tropical cyclones, don't you?'

Grace caught her breath. Was Jock already searching for
his next job? Talking to other people about it, but not to her?
Was he thinking of going somewhere even more remote
than Australia, like a group of islands in the South Pacific?

She handed over the patient notes. 'I need to go and help
Sharon get sorted.'

What she really needed was to get away. As fast as Jock
had when they'd been tempted to kiss each other last night.

She couldn't stop herself thinking about that the moment
she walked through the door after fighting her way home
through the wind and rain.

This wasn't going to work, was it?

The thought of being at home alone this evening while
Jock was on board *Lassie*—the place he'd first made love
to her—was almost unbearable.

He'd made it so very clear that he didn't need her. That
he didn't want her as anything more than a friend.

She could hear the echo of his voice again.

As *if*…

Grace had known how he felt about commitment from
before she'd even met Jock, so this was her problem, not his.

There might very well be no way of fixing this.

She had become everything he'd vowed to never have in

his life, hadn't she? Someone who was in love with him and would marry him in a heartbeat if he asked.

Someone who wanted to have the baby he had sworn he would never bring into the world.

She was his worst nightmare, wasn't she?

The ringtone of her phone was a welcome interruption to the negative spiral her thoughts were threatening to develop into. Until she answered the call.

'Grace…? I need you…'

'*Tessa?* What's wrong?'

'I think I'm getting contractions.'

The hairs on the back of Grace's neck prickled. 'How often?'

'I've only had two. One was about fifteen minutes ago and I just got another one while I was climbing up the hill. It doesn't hurt but… I'm scared…'

'Where's Lawrence?'

'He was at work…the Pelorus Bridge Reserve…' The phone line was crackling. Fading in and out. '…been a slip on the main road and he's stuck…'

'Is there anyone who can bring you in to the hospital?'

'No… I tried…but…' Her words were cut off. The next ones were an agonised wail. '…all my fault…'

'Go back inside and stay dry and warm.' Grace raised her voice in the hope that Tessa might still be able to hear her. 'I'm onto it. I'll get hold of the coastguard. We'll come and get you as soon as we can…'

But Tessa didn't respond.

The only thing Grace could hear was the beeping sound of a disconnected call.

CHAPTER FOURTEEN

THERE WAS SOMETHING very disquieting about having no control over what was happening around you.

Jock didn't like the creaking and cracking sounds of boats bumping and scraping against their moorings as they rocked in the unsettled water beneath them and the gusts of wind that had seagulls shrieking as they battled the air currents in the fading daylight above.

There was nothing more he could do to make sure *Lassie* was securely tied up and nothing he could do if another boat came loose and created havoc. It was time to go home. He was hungry and the only thing on board the boat that was edible was a can of beans and he didn't want to heat that up because…

Because it would only make him remember being in the limited space of this tiny galley with Grace. Reaching past her to find a can opener and his arm brushing her skin. That look in her eyes when she told him how much she trusted him. When she asked him to make love to her…

Oh…*man*…

He could almost taste that first kiss all over again.

Could almost hear her voice. Calling him.

'Jock… *Jock*…are you there?'

Wait… He *could* hear her voice.

'Grace?' He walked out of the wheelhouse to look along

the wooden pier. Yes, there she was, running towards him, a large backpack in her arms. 'What is it?'

'It's Tessa...' Grace was gasping for breath. 'She thinks she might be...going into labour. The coastguard's not... available...'

'No. I've been listening to the radio. There's a yacht in trouble at the entrance to the Sounds. And the tugboats are tied up trying to help get a ferry into port.'

'I can't find a water taxi...' Grace's gaze was fixed on his. 'I need to get to Tessa, Jock. She's all alone. And I can't get there by myself. I need *you*...'

He held his hands out. 'Give me the pack. Wait for me to help you on. There's enough of a swell to make movement unpredictable and I don't want you falling into the water.'

The pack was heavy. 'You've been *running* with this?'

'I drove to the hospital and then to the coastguard buildings. I'm parked at the marina entrance.' Grace's grasp of his hand was tight as he helped her jump over a gap that suddenly widened between the side of the boat and the pier. 'But I did take the full home birth kit, just in case. It's got an oxygen cylinder and all the resuscitation gear, including fluids.'

'Good thinking,' Jock said. 'But let's hope we won't need it. Best-case scenario, we can look after Tessa, the coastguard will be able to get there and we can get her into hospital in time for that C-section.'

He let out a sigh of relief as *Lassie*'s engine started instantly. He jumped out of the boat then, unwinding the ropes he'd tied so firmly around the bollards. Seconds later, he was focusing on manoeuvring through gaps between other boats that were rolling in the swell.

'Put a life jacket on, Grace,' he ordered. 'And throw me

one. It might be a bit gusty on the head of the arm before we turn into Kumutoto Bay. Do you think you'll be able to recognise Tessa's jetty?'

'Yes… If you can get into the bay, I can find it. The posts at the end are carved in a Māori design like a totem pole. They're very distinctive.'

The swell of the sea became more noticeable as they left the shelter of the marina. Jock could see how pale Grace's face was. Was she scared by the way the engine was surging as *Lassie* tipped and rolled in the dark sea water around them?

'We'll get there,' he promised. 'Just hang on.'

Grace nodded. 'I just know how Tessa's feeling,' she said. 'That this is *her* fault.'

'What? The cyclone? Going into labour?'

'Being trapped. Alone. Having herself and her babies in danger. She'll be thinking that she should have done something different, like coming to stay closer to the hospital. Or not talking her husband out of staying home with her. Even if it's not true, blaming yourself or someone else blaming you can destroy lives.'

Jock might be focusing on managing the roll of the boat as they sped out into the Sounds but he turned his head to give Grace an appalled look.

'Did *your* husband blame you?'

'I didn't do what he told me to do,' Grace admitted. 'I didn't stop work when he said I should. I wasn't eating the right food. I kept going to my yoga classes.'

Jock shook his head. 'He made you believe that you caused the death of your baby? He was gaslighting you, Grace—you do *know* that, don't you?'

She was staring through a windshield that had runnels of water streaming across it.

Like tears.

'I blamed myself, anyway, so what difference did it make?'

'Is that why you stayed in an abusive relationship for so long? Because you thought you deserved to be punished?' Jock's heart was breaking. 'Oh, Grace… You deserve so, so much more than that…'

He'd proved to her that she was capable of getting close enough to someone new to have an intimate relationship. But how did you make someone believe that they deserved to be loved? It would be like someone trying to tell him that he never needed to worry about not being good enough. That he would never hear anyone tell him ever again that he had ruined their life.

A larger swell brought *Lassie* down with a thump and Jock knew they were close to the head of the bay they were heading for. Grace was holding on for dear life now. She probably wouldn't even hear him if he tried to say anything more about how wrong her bastard of an ex-husband had been.

'It's okay.' He raised his voice to make sure he could be heard over the engine noise and the wind. 'I've got this. Trust me…'

Grace trusted Jock more than anyone else on earth, but that didn't stop this being beyond frightening. She could see that control of the boat wasn't easy and she was holding on for dear life as huge gusts of wind caught them before they could turn into the more sheltered area of the bay.

It was fraught trying to secure *Lassie* to Tessa's jetty as well, and Jock might have looked calm as he fought to keep the boat steady as Grace climbed off but she could tell how tense he was as her gaze caught his. They were going to need a lot more help from a team which was experienced in rescue scenarios to have any chance of getting a woman who was heavily pregnant with twins out of here and into the safe space of the hospital.

He caught Grace's hand and held it tightly to keep her upright in the wind and stinging sheets of rain as they got off the jetty and onto the steep steps that led up the hill to the house.

When they went into the house to find Tessa on her hands and knees on the floor, crying out with the pain of a contraction, it was obvious that they'd run out of time to get Tessa into hospital anyway. She was about to give birth right here.

'I can't do this,' Tessa sobbed. 'I'm too scared… What if something goes wrong? It will be all my fault…'

'That's *not* true.' Grace crouched on the floor to put her arms around Tessa. 'Don't even *think* like that.'

Jock was crouching beside her. He had the kit opened and took out a pair of sterile gloves to put on. 'I need to check what's happening down below, Tessa. Is it okay if I examine you?'

'Yes…of course.' But Tessa groaned as she lifted her head to focus on Grace. 'But this *is* my fault… If something happens to our babies, Lawrence will never forgive me… I'll never forgive *myself*…'

Grace could feel a bubble of something that felt horribly like panic developing inside her chest.

She could hear an echo of Jenni's voice in the back of her head, telling her the horror story of locked twins who'd been in the same positions as Tessa's unborn babies. Babies who could be in very real danger because of both their prematurity and their presentation.

Tessa wasn't the only one who was too scared to do this.

'You're fully dilated, Tessa,' Jock said. 'And I think we need to get ready to meet your babies.'

He looked up to meet Grace's gaze and she could see what he wasn't saying. Could he already feel the bottom of the breech twin emerging?

He knew just how emotionally involved Grace was in this case and that she understood only too well how Tessa was feeling. He held the eye contact long enough to not need any words. She could feel him gifting her his strength and the promise that he was going to do whatever he possibly could to give this dramatic birth story a happy ending.

But Tessa was sobbing. '*No*... It's not safe... Something's going to go wrong...'

'We've got this, Tessa,' Jock said calmly. 'You've instinctively chosen the best position to be in and the babies are still small enough for this to work. Grace, can you help set up?'

Moving helped. She got Tessa's clothing out of the way properly and put clean linen on the floor. Jock was getting out an infant resuscitation kit and IV gear. With another contraction starting, she rubbed Tessa's back and could feel herself tapping into Jock's confidence as she kept her voice calm and steady.

'You're doing so well, Tessa... Breathe in through your nose and out through your mouth. Keep your mouth soft and open and let the sound come out too.'

Tessa's outward sigh turned into a groan as it continued.

'I'm going to pop a wee needle in your hand when this contraction is over,' Jock told Tessa. 'Just in case we need to give you any medication or fluids.'

Grace felt the change in Jock's focus a moment later, however, before he had time to get an IV line in, and she could see why. The small buttocks of this first twin were appearing. Jock was very still, not touching the baby as he watched it appearing. Grace was watching him as she kept encouraging Tessa and breathing with her.

When the baby had appeared to the level of its umbilicus, Jock started moving. He hooked one finger under a leg and swept it sideways to bring it out. Then he swiftly did the same for the other leg. Half the baby could be seen now, dangling in mid-air. Grace reached to pass a towel to Jock and he wrapped it around the baby's lower body.

'I need to push,' Tessa groaned.

Jock was holding the baby with his thumbs on the lower back, ready to assist Tessa's pushing by applying gentle traction.

Grace was holding her breath. She tried to shut down a reminder of what could happen if the twins were caught on each other's chins, but she froze in what felt like a heart-stopping moment.

The small body slid out to the level of the shoulders and Grace watched the skill with which Jock turned the baby to deliver one arm and then rotated it gently right around to find the other shoulder and bring out the second arm. She saw him position his hands and knew he would be placing his fingers on the baby's face to tilt the head as it lay on his palm and forearm. He was using his other hand to grasp the shoulders and deliver the head and Grace couldn't let her breath out until that happened.

As she heard the first warbling cry of the tiny newborn girl, the frozen moment evaporated into a blur of movement.

'It's your first daughter,' Grace told Tessa. 'She's safe...'

'And she's perfect,' Jock added.

He was smiling at Grace. It wasn't the usual cheeky grin she'd come to love receiving from this man. This was a smile that was so soft it told her he understood how amazing this moment was. And that it was even more special to be sharing it with her?

She knew in that moment that she *was* important to Jock. That they had a connection that would be there for ever. That he might only ever love her as a friend but that love was something deep. And too precious to lose.

Grace picked up the bubble wrap and clean towels to keep the too small body warm and a suction bulb and oxygen, although the baby seemed to be breathing well and the APGAR score at five minutes was surprisingly good. Tessa turned so that she could see and touch her baby and Grace made a pile of cushions so she could lean back and hold her baby against her skin for extra warmth as they waited for the birth of the second twin.

Jock carefully palpated Tessa's abdomen to find the position the remaining baby was in. This time, when he made eye contact with Grace, he gave a single nod that came with a sigh of relief.

'Still cephalic,' he said quietly.

With more room suddenly available, the remaining baby could have moved into a different and more difficult presentation, but this second girl arrived in a textbook, headfirst delivery with even less fuss than her sister only thirty minutes later.

It took longer for the arrival of the skilled rescue teams that could get Tessa and her babies into hospital safely and the next hours were a blur of activity as they continued caring for Tessa, another rescue team was dispatched to find

Lawrence and bring him to meet his daughters and a neonatal paediatrician was called in to assess the twins and decided they didn't need to be evacuated for specialist care.

Even Mother Nature seemed to be breathing a sigh of relief at the safe creation of this new family.

'Can you hear that?' Lawrence was holding one of his twins as Grace helped Tessa with her first breastfeeding of her babies.

'I can't hear a thing.' Tessa didn't look up. She was smiling down at her tiny, perfect daughter who was latching on like a champion.

'Exactly. The wind's stopped howling.'

'Cyclone Barry has apparently decided to move back out to sea.' Jock was looking at his phone. 'He's gone. For good.'

He sent the ghost of a wink in Grace's direction. It wasn't just the cyclone with that name that would never be able to damage her life again, was it?

Thanks to Jock…

This wasn't the time to let that thought grow. It was helpful that the twin being held by her father started a shaky cry.

'Would you like to try feeding both babies at once, Tessa?'

'Oh, can I…?'

'Of course. I'll use these pillows to help support them.'

Lawrence let Grace take the second baby from his arms. 'I'm going to find my phone and get some photos of this,' he said.

'Oh…can you find those little hats my mum knitted for the girls? She'd be thrilled to see them wearing them.'

'Sure. Where's the bag with all the baby stuff in it?'

'It'll be with my bag.'

'I can't see that either.'

Grace groaned softly. 'Oh, *no*… I put those bags right by

the door but that's the last time I saw them. With so many people there and everything that was happening to get you and the babies out of the house and into the coastguard boat, they must have been forgotten.'

Lawrence's face fell. 'I'll have to go and get them,' he said. But he looked as if it was the last thing he wanted to do. 'I don't want to leave you,' he told his wife. He reached out to touch one of the babies with a gentle rub. 'Or these little miracles.'

Jock glanced out of the window. 'It's nearly light,' he said. 'And it's so much calmer out there. I need to go and collect my boat, which is hopefully still tied up at your jetty, Tessa. I can bring your bags back.'

'I'll come with you,' Grace said. 'You've got this, Tessa, and you've got all the help you need just a bell press away here. It's time we left you and Lawrence to have some time alone together with these gorgeous daughters of yours. I can make sure we cleaned up properly after your home birth. And find anything extra you might think you need. That way, Lawrence won't need to be anywhere else for a while.' She raised her eyebrows as she turned to Jock. 'If that's okay with you?'

'No worries.' He didn't meet her gaze, however. He was busy with his phone. 'Let me see how soon I can find a water taxi to get us out there.'

CHAPTER FIFTEEN

IT WAS STILL the most beautiful view Grace had ever seen in her life.

She was standing on the deck of Tessa and Lawrence's home, looking out into Kumutoto Bay. Fronds of magnificent punga fern trees framed the view to an empty sea, with bush-covered hills in the distance. The water was still ruffled with the after-effects of the cyclone, but there were patches of blue between the clouds scooting across the morning sky and they felt like the promise of everything getting better.

Or almost everything…

Jock had taken the bags Tessa had packed down to put on board *Lassie* but she was waiting for him to come and tell her it was time to head back to town. She was hanging onto the last moments of being here in this amazing place.

Hanging onto what could be some of the last moments she ever had with Jock…?

Grace didn't turn around when she heard his footsteps on the wooden deck.

'I can't imagine choosing to leave all this behind,' she said quietly. 'It's paradise.'

'You don't have to,' Jock said.

'Neither do you.'

He came to stand beside her at the edge of the deck, putting his hands on the railing. 'I *will* miss it,' he said.

'I'll miss *you*.' Grace's voice was no more than a whisper.

'You'll be fine.' She could hear the smile in Jock's voice. 'Trust me.'

That made Grace turn her head sharply. 'Do you have any idea how often you say that?' She pulled in a breath. 'Trust is important to you, isn't it?'

Jock didn't hesitate in his response. 'It's everything,' he said.

'I *have* trusted you,' Grace said. 'More than I could ever trust anyone else.'

She swallowed hard. She had to say this, while she still had the chance. 'I trusted you to touch me,' she said softly. 'And I've never properly said thank you for what you gave me.'

Jock was staring out at the bay. 'You don't need to.' He flicked her a glance. Half a smile. 'It was my pleasure, believe me.'

Grace didn't return the smile. 'You gave me back a part of my life that I never thought I'd have again. No one else could have done that. I trusted you enough to let you touch me. I trusted you enough to fall in love with you, but you know that, don't you? That's why you're leaving...'

'Oh… *Grace*...' The low rumble of Jock's voice was almost a groan.

'I know you told me not to give up on my dreams and that I just needed to find the right person, and that person could never be you but...' Grace caught and held Jock's gaze. 'It *is* you, Jock McKay. It could never be anyone else.'

Jock closed his eyes. As if her words were visible and not seeing them could make them stop. But Grace couldn't stop. She loved Jock too much not to try and help him see something else he had been shutting out his entire life.

'You and Jenni are so alike,' she told him. 'You both think home is about a place. Jenni said it's the place where you feel properly safe and I get that. It's not something either of you had when you were growing up. Jenni's trying to make it about the place you grew up, but you're still looking for a place where you can feel that safe but, you know what? Home is bigger than just a place…it might not even *be* a place.'

Grace could hear the catch in her own voice. 'What if it's a *person*? What if all you need is the ability to trust that person?' She had to swallow the lump in her throat. 'What if you can never find your home because you can't give someone your trust?'

Jock's eyes were open again. His gaze locked onto hers.

'I trusted you, Jock,' Grace whispered. 'But you can't trust me and…it breaks my heart. And you're going to leave and maybe it's because you want to trust me but you're not going to let yourself and…and you leaving might very well break my world.' Her breath came out in something like a huff of laughter. 'I know you said you could never take the risk of building your world around someone else, but what do you do if that person *is* your world? What then?'

There was nothing he could do other than fold Grace into his arms.

And hold her.

Like he had that time when she'd told him about losing her baby. When he'd offered to push her off the boat.

When he'd held her in his arms again later than night and made love to her.

Every word she'd just said to him was true, wasn't it?

She'd trusted him so completely and he'd taken that gift, but he'd never had the courage or decency to give *his* trust to her. She deserved so much more than that.

'I'm so sorry,' he murmured against Grace's ear. 'I do run. I get scared and I run. Whenever I think someone might be getting close enough to discover the truth.'

'Which is?'

'That…' Jock struggled to find the words to something he'd never confessed aloud. 'That I'm not good enough. That if they're around long enough, they're going to find that out and it might ruin their life.'

'Oh, *Jock*…' Grace pulled back far enough to be able to look at him directly. And then she took her hands and put them on his face, cupping his chin in her palms. 'You could never ruin my life. You could only make it what I always dreamed it could be like if I was very, very lucky.'

Jock could see the tears sparkle in her eyes and then escape to roll down the side of her nose. 'You could never, ever be not enough for me. You are just perfect being exactly who you are. Except for one thing…'

Jock had to clear his throat. 'What's that?'

'You can't trust me. You've given me back my life but you can't trust me with your heart. You can't love me…'

'I *do* love you…' As the words came out, Jock realised just how true they were. And it wasn't the kind of love that bonded you with a sibling or a close friend. This was bigger. So much bigger he couldn't even see the edges of where it started or finished.

He didn't need to be afraid to give this woman his heart, did he? To trust that it would always be safe with her.

'I'm scared of the wrong thing,' he said slowly. 'What I

should be scared of is waking up to find that you're not in my life. I love you, Grace Collins. I'm *in* love with you and the only thing I want right now is...*this*...'

Jock lowered his head to place his lips on hers. He hadn't kissed her since before Jenni had arrived for her visit and...

...and he was never going to leave it that long again.

How had he believed that he could protect himself by escaping this kind of love?

He was home.

Because this was where his heart was.

Grace could feel that too, couldn't she?

He could taste it on her lips. Feel it in the way her heart was beating against his own.

But he still wanted to hear the words. Even if it meant this kiss had to be broken.

'I love you, Grace.'

'I love you too, Jock.'

It was Grace who broke the next kiss. Eventually...

'We're going to have to confess, aren't we?'

'To Jenni? Aye... And she's never going to speak to me again.'

'You might be surprised. Let's call her as soon as we get home. She might be as happy as we are.'

'No.' Jock shook his head. 'Not possible.'

Grace laughed. 'No. You're right.' She wrapped her arms around his neck. 'One more kiss before we go,' she said. 'Please?'

She didn't have to ask twice...

EPILOGUE

A few months later...

FINDING HIS SISTER on his doorstep was the last thing Jock McKay had expected. As far as he'd known, she hadn't set foot outside Glasgow since her holiday in New Zealand and that was only a few short months ago so he certainly wouldn't have thought she'd make such a big trip again so soon.

Jenni had a bunch of balloons and a carry bag in one hand. She put down the suitcase so that she could throw her other arm around her brother.

'*Surprise*... Happy Birthday, Jock.'

Jock hugged her back. 'And to you... But...you haven't come all the way across the world to celebrate our birthday, have you?'

'Why not?'

'Well, it's rather a long way to come when I hadn't even planned any kind of a party. We're in a bit of mess, what with packing and stuff.'

'We can make our own party. I've got cake. And wine. Or we can go out to dinner.'

'Am I missing something?' Jock was genuinely puzzled. 'We've never made that big a deal out of our birthdays and it's not a milestone like turning forty or something.' He took

Jenni's suitcase and led the way down the hall. 'Not that Dan celebrated when he turned forty recently, but he's not really a party kind of guy, I guess.'

Was it his imagination or did Jenni have an odd look on her face at the mention of Dan's name?

'Can I have the same room I had last time I was here? You don't have a houseful of new hospital employees, do you?'

'Yes. And no. And you do realise we're about to move into the house we've bought, don't you? Our settlement date is next week.'

'I know. Grace told me. And I've seen pictures of the house, which is absolutely gorgeous. Have you really got your own jetty?'

'We do. We're right on the waterfront but we have road access as well. Best of both worlds.'

'Are there dolphins?'

Jock grinned. 'Not resident, as far as I know.'

'Grace loves dolphins.'

'I know.' Jock could feel a smile softening his lips. And his heart. 'And otters. She loves otters a lot.'

'She loves *you* a lot.' Jenni was taking her shopping bag and the balloons towards the kitchen. 'You didn't fool me, you know. I totally knew that Grace had fallen in love. I said so, didn't I?'

'You did,' Jock conceded. 'But we didn't even know ourselves at that point. So you couldn't possibly have known.'

'I so did.' Jenni took a bottle of champagne out of the bag and handed it to Jock. 'Put this in the fridge, please.'

He shook his head. 'So why did you keep speaking to me, then? When I'd broken the rules.'

Jenni shrugged. 'Grace looked too happy. I didn't want to jinx anything.'

Jock watched a box come out of the bag.

'Mud cake,' Jenni told him. 'Your favourite. I got it in Wellington.'

'Are you going to tell me the real reason you've come back here? We could have shared a cake and a glass of wine on a video call.'

'Birthdays need celebrating,' Jenni insisted. 'And so does finding love.' She turned to Jock and her smile was misty. 'I'm so happy for you,' she said softly. 'I'm so happy for both of you. The two people I love most in the world in love with each other? What could possibly be better than that?' She looked over Jock's shoulder. 'Where *is* Grace?'

'Out on a home visit. Do you remember the last night you were here on your visit? When we had to abandon you to go and see the woman who'd been in a car accident?'

'And you left me with Dan.' Jenni's laugh sounded a little off-key. 'Yes, I remember.'

'Well, that's who Grace has been visiting this afternoon. Maureen. She went to full term with no further complications and she had a little boy. Oscar, she's called him.'

'And what about the twins that got born during that cyclone?'

'They're the cutest babies ever. I saw Tessa at her final postnatal check-up recently. Grace and I have been invited to their christening.'

'That's a bit special.'

'More than you know. It was on the deck of Tessa's house that I proposed to Grace—the day after the twins were born. The day we called you and confessed.'

'A story with a happy ending all round, then.'

'You're not wrong.' Jock could hear the front door of the house opening and then closing. He heard Grace walking down the hallway and the moment she paused when she spotted the suitcase just inside the door of the spare room. Moments later, she came into the kitchen and her jaw dropped.

'*Jenni*...what on earth are *you* doing here?'

'*Surprise...*' Jenni held out her arms and Grace met her halfway across the kitchen floor.

'It's our birthday,' Jock explained. 'Apparently, Jenni decided she needed to come and celebrate.'

'I know it's your birthday, my love.' Grace extracted herself from Jenni's embrace and came close to Jock. 'I have a present for you.' She stood on tiptoes and kissed him.

Jock could feel her whispering 'Happy Birthday' against his lips before he began kissing her back. Thoroughly enough for Jenni to make a sound of protest.

'I am *here*, you know.'

Jock just grinned at Grace as he pulled back. 'Nice present,' he murmured. 'Thank you.'

'That's not your present.' Grace laughed. 'You can have that later.' She turned back to Jenni. 'I can't believe you're here. To celebrate a birthday? It's the best surprise ever.'

'And happy endings.' Jenni nodded. 'I'm all about happy endings.'

'So are we.'

Jock waited until he caught Grace's gaze again and he could fall into how much love he could see in her eyes.

He knew she would be seeing a reflection of that love.

They both knew they were at the beginning of the best happy ending ever.

* * * * *

MIRACLE TWINS
TO HEAL THEM

ALISON ROBERTS

MILLS & BOON

PROLOGUE

LIKE ANY GOOD fairy tale—or fantasy—there was a moment when everything changed.

Alice fell down the rabbit hole.

Cinderella's fairy godmother appeared.

Sleeping Beauty got kissed.

And Jenni McKay found herself unexpectedly alone with a tall, dark and very handsome stranger by the name of Daniel Walker.

Really tall. At five foot seven, Jenni had never considered herself to be short but the top of her head was barely level with Dan's shoulder.

Really dark too. He had pitch-black wavy hair and eyes as dark as sin. Even his skin was a rich, warm shade of olive brown.

And *so* handsome. It hadn't escaped Jenni's attention when she'd first clapped eyes on him earlier this evening that Dan Walker was quite possibly the most gorgeous man she'd ever seen in her life.

And the sexiest, she decided when they were well into the dinner party they were both attending.

Maybe it was those eyes.

Or the facial hair that made him look more than a little wild despite being so neatly trimmed.

It might have been, at least partly, due to his moodiness.

Judging by his reluctance to chat to a stranger even though she was his best friend's sister and currently sitting beside him at this table in the restaurant, Daniel clearly hadn't really wanted to be invited to this gathering. Jenni had done her best by breaking the silence more than once.

'So how long did you say you've been living here?' she asked.

'Couple of years now.'

'What made you choose Picton?'

'Job came up.' The succinct tone discouraged any further curiosity. 'I needed a change.'

That was intriguing. A change from what? A place? A situation? A *woman*...?

Being mysterious added another layer to that sexiness but that trait paled in comparison to something that didn't become apparent until much later that evening, when they were alone.

A connection like nothing Jenni had ever experienced before.

Ever...

Probably the last thing either of them had expected that night was to end up alone with each other.

It had been Jock's idea to have a party to celebrate the last night of Jenni's visit to New Zealand before she headed home to the other side of the world. He and Grace—who'd become Jenni's best friend when they'd done their midwifery training together in Glasgow—were trying to persuade Jenni to consider coming to work with them in the obstetric department of the local hospital and they'd thought that introducing her to some of the people she could be working with might just tip the balance.

Jenni wasn't averse to the idea of a working holiday. The

move had clearly been exactly the right thing for Grace to have done. Like Dan, her friend had been in need of a change too.

But had Dan also been attracted to this small seaside town on the tip of the South Island of New Zealand because it felt so safe?

Ironically, as it turned out, it had been Jenni who had decided Dan the anaesthetist should be invited tonight. For Grace's sake. She wanted her best friend to be as happy as possible, after all, and developing a friendship that might even turn into something more was not a bad idea. She'd also instructed Jock to invite his latest girlfriend, who turned out to be Mandy the ultrasound technician and she'd been the one to suggest that a date needed to be found for herself, so she didn't end up feeling like a fifth wheel at her own party, which was why Stefano, one of the ED doctors, had come along.

But who knew that Stefano and Mandy would be so attracted to each other? Or that this Brazilian restaurant would have a live band playing on a Saturday night and that both Stefano and Mandy were into Latin dancing? So there they were as soon as the main course was finished, slow dancing what looked like a rumba, their bodies close and gazes locked on each other's. They were already having a party all of their own.

And then the phone call came. Jock was being called back to the hospital for a woman who was seven months' pregnant and had been involved in a car accident. The serious complication of a placental abruption was a possibility and it turned out Grace was the woman's midwife so, of course, she had to go as well. They didn't know how long they might be gone but the plan became to meet up later at the cocktail bar Jenni had wanted to go to after the meal at this restaurant.

It was Dan who'd ridden in like a valiant knight on his white horse.

'Don't worry,' he said. 'I'll look after Jenni.'

It wasn't a problem.

Dan was more than happy to take responsibility for getting Jock's sister back home safely after their night out as a group fell apart at the seams.

Why wouldn't he be? Jenni McKay's fiery red hair, the freckles on her nose and her bright blue eyes made her the female version of his colleague and fishing buddy who'd become the closest friend he'd ever made as an adult. He felt almost as comfortable in Jenni's company as he would have been going out for a drink with Jock.

Except that she talked a lot more than Jock did. And Jock's hair didn't fall in shiny waves to his shoulders and he would never wear such a pretty summery dress, so this was distinctly disconcerting on more than one level.

'Have you found something you fancy?' he asked.

Jenni looked over the top of the cocktail bar's menu.

'A black margarita sounds interesting. I didn't know that black sugar even existed.'

Dan found the image of the drink. 'It's not a silly idea,' he said. 'To put something normally used to soak up toxins, like activated charcoal, into a drink that contains four different types of alcohol. It sounds lethal.'

'It looks lethal.' Jenni didn't sound unhappy about that. 'What are you going to have?'

'Espresso martini.'

'Classic.'

'There's a reason things become classics. And coffee after dinner is always good.'

'But only after dessert.' Jenni was looking at the menu again. 'I'll have one after the…tiramisu cocktail.'

A man bumped Dan's shoulder just as he was about to pick up the cocktails they'd ordered.

'Sorry, mate.'

'No problem. Didn't spill a drop.'

'Why don't you watch where you're going?' The woman with the man sounded completely fed up. 'Oh, wait…you never think about anyone other than yourself, do you?'

'Why don't you give me a break?' the man countered wearily. 'We're supposed to be celebrating our wedding anniversary.'

The woman's voice faded. 'Yeah…*right*…'

As he turned away from the bar, Dan caught the way Jenni's eyes widened. She leaned towards him. 'I'm so glad I'm single,' she whispered.

'Me too.' Dan held the glasses high to keep them out of harm's way. 'Shall we go outside into the garden? Looks quieter out there.'

They found an empty table in the corner of the courtyard. Jenni raised her glass to his.

'Here's to *never* getting married,' she said.

Her grin had the same kind of cheeky charm as Jock's. The smile that never failed to win a woman over. Who would have guessed that it could work on men as well?

Most men anyway. Dan was immune.

'Here's to never getting married *again*,' he said.

Jenni gasped. 'You've been married?'

'Just the once.'

'And you thought that was a *good* idea?'

Dan couldn't help the smile that was tilting his lips. 'It's okay. I know better now.'

He touched his glass to hers and they shared a glance as they both took their first sip.

A kindred spirit, that was what Jenni was.

An hour and a couple of cocktails later and it was becoming apparent that Jock and Grace weren't likely to join them, but it didn't matter any longer. He and Jenni were having a competition to come up with the best reason why it was so much better to be single.

'You can eat whatever you like, *when*ever you like.'

Dan had to agree. 'Reheated pizza at two o'clock in the morning can be good.'

'As much garlic as you want because nobody's going to complain about your bad breath.'

'Nobody's going to tell me off for getting home late if I happen to feel like a game of squash after work.'

'I get to choose what side of the bed I sleep on.' That wide smile was lighting up Jenni's face again. 'Sometimes, I sleep on *both* sides. Like a starfish.'

That stopped him.

Maybe those espresso martinis were stronger than usual. Because Dan was getting an image of Jenni McKay as a starfish on her bed and…it was doing strange things to his gut.

And his head. He had the odd thought that he could tell Jenni anything. Things that he'd never said to anyone else. He didn't normally say much to anyone, actually, so it was astonishing to hear the words that were coming out of his mouth right now.

'It's safer,' he said softly. 'You have to trust someone to make a relationship work, but if you trust someone who tells you lies you give them the power to destroy you.'

Jenni finished the last of her espresso martini. 'Oh, I hear you,' she said with deep feeling. 'Why is it that some people never learn that? My mother, for example, kept falling in love. Time after time. Even when we were kids, Jock and I thought it was stupid. We knew it was going to crash and burn. When we were thirteen we made a vow that we were never going to get married or have kids.'

'That one's not a problem for me,' Dan said. 'I can't have kids.'

'Why not?'

It was weird that he wasn't bothered by such a personal question. Even weirder that he didn't hesitate to respond.

'Bad case of mumps when I was kid. I got told that I had more chance of winning the lottery than getting anyone pregnant.'

Jenni had gone very still. 'I'm sorry,' she said. 'It's not fair having a choice taken away from you.'

The empathy was as disconcerting as everything else about this woman. Surprising.

Captivating…

'Nobody said life was fair,' he growled. 'But at least it should be honest.'

'I gave up believing in Santa when I was five years old,' Jenni admitted. 'And I guess I gave up believing in happy endings when I was thirteen.'

'Fool me once, shame on you,' Dan quoted. *'Fool me twice, shame on me.'*

There was no smile on Jenni's face now. Her gaze was locked on his. 'I can't abide lies,' she said softly.

Dan couldn't break that eye contact. It felt like there was an undercurrent of silent communication going on here.

Maybe it wasn't just the caffeine in his cocktails that was making every cell in his body feel so very wide awake.

'Neither can I,' he responded. 'If you can't trust someone, they're not worth knowing.'

'I *never* lie,' Jenni said.

Dan could believe that. Maybe he *wanted* to believe that? He took a sharp breath. This was getting entirely too heavy on both the obvious and the hidden levels. He needed to break what felt like a strangely intimate connection, even though he still couldn't look away from her eyes.

He smiled slowly. 'How do I know *that's* not a lie?'

'You don't.' Jenni was smiling back at him. The sexiest smile he'd ever seen. 'But does it matter?' she said softly. 'We're never going to see each other again, are we?'

That strange sensation in Dan's gut was suddenly recognisable. The magic words had been said aloud, hadn't they? The mantra that made it safe. A holiday fling. A casual encounter with someone passing through town. Someone he was never going to see again.

'That might be one of the best things about being single,' he said.

He could see the tip of Jenni's tongue as she touched it to her bottom lip. 'Are you talking about what I think you're talking about?'

Dan held her gaze but lowered his voice. 'It gets more intriguing, doesn't it? Knowing you're never going to see that person again.'

'And when it's never going to get spoiled by finding out that the second time isn't as good?'

She looked at his empty glass. 'Fancy another one?'

'No,' he said softly. He was sitting close enough to reach up and touch Jenni's cheek. To trace the line of her jaw with his forefinger until it reached her chin—ready to tilt it so that he could cover her lips with his own—because he could see the answer to his unspoken question in her eyes.

'I fancy *you*...'

Maybe Jenni hadn't recognised the significance of the moment that changed everything when she'd found herself alone with Dan.

But she couldn't miss the moment she began to fall into the sexual fantasy that was suddenly coming to life.

The moment she let Dan kiss her.

The moment she kissed him back...

CHAPTER ONE

SOMETHING HAD REALLY CHANGED.

Or was the problem that *nothing* had really changed?

Jenni McKay glanced out of the window at the view of inner-city Glasgow. A cityscape that was blurred by the rainwater streaming down the glass and dimmed by fading daylight. The grey sky was now several shades darker than the slate roofs of buildings that had been there for hundreds of years.

No changes there. In the buildings or the bad weather, but that was okay. Jenni loved this city and, unlike her brother who had taken jobs all over the world for the last ten years, she had no intention of going anywhere else for anything longer than a holiday. A place to call home had been what she'd always dreamed of every time she'd had her life packed up and moved somewhere new as a child.

The moaning sounds from the woman in the room with Jenni were as familiar as the view. Sara was bouncing on a birth ball, leaning forward against the bed, and her partner, Callum, was rubbing her lower back. Sara reached for the mask attached to the Entonox cylinder and shoved it against her face, sucking in a deep breath. And then another, before dropping the mask again.

'I need to move,' she groaned.

'What would you like to do?' Jenni asked. 'Change your position or try walking around for a wee bit? Another shower?'

'I don't know,' Sara groaned. 'I'm so tired…'

'I know…' Jenni exchanged a sympathetic glance with Callum. The labour had started in the early hours of the morning and Sara had come into hospital as Jenni's shift had begun at seven a.m. They were all tired. 'How 'bout we get you back on the bed for a rest?'

'Yes, I think I'd like that… Are you going to check me again? I *must* be more than halfway dilated by now.'

On her back on the bed, Sara reached for the Entonox again as another contraction reached its peak. They were coming thick and fast now and Callum looked worried.

'Why are her legs shaking like that?' he asked.

'She's going into transition,' Jenni told him. She pulled off her gloves. 'Sara? You're fully dilated, love. You can start pushing with every contraction from now on.'

The rhythms and sounds and emotions of a normal labour were the same as ever. Jenni had long ago lost count of how many hundreds of babies she had delivered over her years as a midwife in a busy big city hospital. Each one was different. Some were dramatic, a few sadly tragic but, overall, each arrival of a new human into the world was an emotional journey for Jenni as well as the baby's family and she wouldn't want that to change in any way.

'Keep pushing, Sara…keep it going…more, more, more. I can see baby's head. Callum…as soon as this contraction ends, you can take Sara's hand and help her feel it…'

The look on Sara's face as she touched the dark, damp whorls of hair on her baby's head was one of complete awe and then determination, as her next contraction began.

'One more push, as *hard* as you can…'

The head emerged with almost a pop, face down. Jenni supported the head as it began to turn, lifting the body to help a shoulder free itself, and then the rest of the baby's body slid out into her hands. She lifted the slippery little person carefully, moving the baby girl onto her mother's chest. Sara looked completely stunned now—overwhelmed. She reached tentatively to touch her baby with both hands as Callum watched—tears rolling unchecked down his face and his camera on the bedside table completely forgotten.

Jenni rubbed the baby with a soft towel. She hadn't made a sound yet but she was moving more and getting pinker. She wiped the face, considered reaching for a suction bulb, but then the little girl scrunched up her face with the effort of filling her lungs with enough air and opened her mouth to give her first cry—a wobbly warble that made Sara burst into tears herself.

'Oh…oh…it's okay, darling. You're here now. You're safe and…and we love you *so* much…'

Sara was cuddling the baby between her breasts now and Callum had one hand protectively covering their daughter's back and the other on Sara's head as he stroked the tangle of her hair. The expression on Sara's face as she looked up and lifted her face to meet his kiss took Jenni's breath away.

It also made her feel curiously…lonely…

And that was something she'd been aware of ever since she'd come back from her holiday in New Zealand and having time with her brother and her best friend. Back to living alone. Back to the frequent rain and greyness of Glasgow. Back to her work of helping other people achieve their dreams of families and futures.

That loneliness had been enough for her to do something that Grace had suggested during that visit and start the process of making an application to work as a midwife in New Zealand.

The motivation to go through the process was nothing more than an insurance policy, mind you. If she found herself missing her brother and her best friend too much, she could go back. For a longer, working, holiday. She would get homesick eventually and she would be only too glad to be here again and then she could finally settle, knowing that she was in the place she would always call home.

Jenni pulled a blanket over mother and baby to help keep them warm. She couldn't leave them alone in this private moment because she needed to do the APGAR scores on the baby and be there if anything unexpected happened to Sara like a post-partum haemorrhage, but she could step back enough for them to feel as if they were alone to welcome their daughter.

It would be time to clamp and cut the cord soon too, and then she could help Sara with her very first attempt to breast feed her baby—her favourite happy ending to her part in every birth.

She loved watching the baby react to the smell and touch of a mother's nipple and instinctively open their tiny mouth so wide and turn their head, ready to latch on. Sara would have her hand on the back of the head, waiting for that perfect moment to nudge it forward so that as much of the nipple as possible filled the baby's mouth before it closed and a primal instinct activated the muscles needed to suck.

And *that* was always the moment when emotion filled her like a tidal wave. When she could relax, knowing that her part in this everyday miracle was almost over and she could take a breath and simply enjoy the privilege of sharing such an intensely life-changing event for everyone involved. She'd had to blink back tears more often in recent times because the feeling had become noticeably more powerful.

Jenni knew it was the effect of her biological clock ticking more loudly as she got older, but it had never been quite like it was today. Her thirty-seventh birthday was only a few short months away and that was getting scarily close to turning forty, wasn't it?

Time was running out.

Maybe *this* was what had changed.

The familiar mix of relief and amazement expanded into the joy and palpable love in the room and exploded into a longing so intense that it felt like a vice closing over her ribcage and making it impossible to take a new breath.

She could hear an echo of her own voice in the back of her head.

'*...we made a vow that we were never going to get married or have kids...*'

She could see Dan's face as he'd listened to her saying that. She could even feel the tension that had been unleashed in the air around them—the current that was about to wash them into the most astonishing fantasy ever. The memory of which Jenni had found herself slipping back into almost every single night in the weeks since she'd arrived home. One that was never going to be tainted by reality because they were never going to see each other again so it was...perfect.

But it was also a fantasy that had absolutely no place in her head right now and had to be banished until she got home at the very least.

Was this another kind of fantasy that she should push aside? This longing to be holding her own baby like this? Skin to skin. With a tiny mouth smooshed onto her breast and the intimate sensation that sucking would create. What was it like, to know that you could give your precious newborn everything they needed to survive from your own body?

Jenni wasn't dismissing that vow completely, of course. She was never going to make the same mistakes her mother had, thinking that marriage—if only she could choose the right person—was the answer to living happily ever after. But she knew perfectly well that you didn't have to get married, or even have a long-term partner, to become a mother. She had been a midwife for many, many women who were facing parenthood alone for all sorts of reasons.

The longing that had stolen her breath so decisively morphed into something quite different. A realisation that this didn't have to be simply a fantasy. That it wasn't just feeding a baby that a mother could do entirely alone. It was a legitimate life choice these days, for a woman to have a baby and raise them alone. She didn't have to get married or have a committed partner. There were sperm banks where you got to choose the attributes you would want the father of your child to potentially provide. She'd gone online to find out more about them when she'd started having her first doubts, a year or more ago, about that vow to never have children, and had even signed up as a potential client in order to have access to more details about the donors, including their photographs, and what fishhooks might lie in wait down the track, like a child wanting information on their biological father or any half-siblings.

Jenni quietly retreated to let Callum and Sara have a few minutes alone as a brand-new family. She took the trolley with dirty linen and other used items into the sluice room. By the time she'd dealt with it all she could do a final check on Sara and her baby and it would be high time she headed home. She'd been on her feet for more than twelve hours now and she was very tired.

Maybe that was why it felt like something had changed. Why she was overreacting to seeing a newborn in her mother's arms and why the idea of going back to the sperm bank's website was refusing to get squashed. Perhaps the best way to deal with that would be to have another look?

Which was exactly what Jenni did when she arrived home to the tiny, terraced house she'd managed to buy ten years ago—about the same time that Jock had finished his training and early years as a doctor and had chosen to use the small inheritance their mother had left them to start living and working in countries increasingly far away from Scotland. Having Grace live with her as a flatmate had helped a lot with the mortgage but Jenni was still coping financially and she wasn't about to give up the security of owning her home, especially if she was thinking about becoming a single mother.

And she was, wasn't she?

Despite having decided long ago that she was never going to get married or have children, Jenni's acceptance of single mothers had grown and that unexpected desire to have a baby of her own had taken root, to the extent that it seemed to be finally overriding the long-held conviction that letting history repeat itself and allowing a child to grow up without a father in their life—as she and Jock had done—was unacceptable because it wasn't the 'perfect' family.

Somehow, she had persuaded herself that this was completely different. Because *this* baby would have a mother who wanted them. Who loved them with all her heart. She and Jock hadn't known who their father was, but they *had* known that their mother hadn't wanted them because she'd reminded them of that so frequently. That their arrival had, in fact, apparently ruined her life so it wasn't any surprise that she didn't love them.

But Jenni would love her baby so much that it would make up for what she'd missed in her own life and the desire, after the delivery of Sara and Callum's baby, was strong enough for her to realise she was seriously considering the option of using a sperm donor.

Which was why she found herself curling up on her couch with a hot cup of tea and reading the donor profiles on the sperm bank website that accompanied photos that caught her attention. She could find out the men's height, weight, ethnicity and even their skin tone and blood type.

She only skimmed the description of characteristics that told her someone was 'down-to-earth', 'patient and non-judgmental' or 'had the ability to always look on the bright side of life' because these were written by the men themselves. What was less likely to be biased were their educational qualifications and… hair colour.

Hair colour was important. Jenni needed to at least try and ensure her child didn't inherit the bright red hair that had meant she and Jock got mocked at school for being 'carrot-tops' or 'firecrackers'. A dominant colour would be needed to counteract those genes. Black would be good.

Like Dan's hair…

Jenni scrolled through the images, discounting anyone who didn't have black hair.

Having a tertiary academic qualification was obviously a good indication of intelligence, so she filtered out occupations that only needed on-the-job training. Any kind of degree was acceptable but the ones with a medical connection were more attractive to Jenni. A vet, for example, or a physiotherapist or a doctor.

Like Dan…

With a sigh, Jenni closed her laptop. The fantasy of being

a single mother at some point in the future was not nearly as compelling as letting herself drift back into the fantasy that Daniel Walker had provided in real life.

She could already feel that curl of desire, deep in her belly. She could see those sinfully dark eyes and feel the surprising softness of the waves of his hair. Memory was a wonderful thing when it could even conjure up the taste of a coffee martini flavoured kiss or the incredible heat of a tongue touching her own.

Oh...

This *had* to stop.

This fantasy might be delightful but it couldn't be allowed to influence her life going forward. How on earth was she going to be interested in ever dating anyone ever again if she let that one-night stand get entrenched as the bar for what sex should be like? It could ruin any further interactions she might have with men, which could end up being as disappointing as flying economy after being magically upgraded to first class for the first—and most likely *only*—time in one's life.

Jenni reached for her cup of tea, which would be cool enough to drink now. She took a sip but immediately screwed up her face.

'Yuck...'

It was undrinkable. The milk must have gone off.

Dan Walker moved out of the way to let his opponent try and hit the ball hard enough to bounce it off the front wall of the squash court, but Jock McKay missed the shot, which gave Dan the winning point for this game.

'Best of five?' Dan reached for his towel to mop his face in the ninety seconds' break they could have between games.

'Sure thing.' Jock picked up his water bottle. 'I'll win the next one.'

Dan grinned. 'Sure about that?'

'Aye.' Jock took another swallow of his water. 'I was distracted.'

Dan looked around the high, windowless walls of the small room they were in. 'Ah…of course you were.'

'I was thinking about a house Grace and I saw online today. Could be perfect for us. We're making a time to go and view it.'

'I guess that's the next step. Propose to a girl. Buy a house. Get married…'

'Whoa…you don't have to get married to buy a house and live together for ever, mate. And this place has got a jetty. Grace wants to know if that's the real attraction. She did suggest once that I just wanted to live happily ever after with my boat.'

'Sounds like a great idea to me.' Dan dropped his towel. He needed a mouthful of water too. Playing squash was physically demanding and he was out of shape. Jock seemed to have a lot less time for a session like this after work. Because he wanted to spend it with Grace?

Of course he did. They were head over heels in love with each other. Besotted, even…

Dan didn't want to think about what it would be like to be in that space. He picked up his racquet.

'Ready?'

'Almost.' Jock was checking his phone. And shaking his head. 'It's raining in Glasgow,' he said. 'Who knew…?'

Dan couldn't help himself, even though he knew it wasn't the best idea to let his lips form her name. 'Message from Jenni?'

'Aye…'

'How is she?'

'Okay, I think. Took her a while to get used to being back home after her trip. She loved it here. Loved Melbourne too.'

'She was visiting a friend there, wasn't she?'

Jock nodded as he swapped his phone for his racquet. 'An old boyfriend, it was. Her first, in fact. They haven't seen each other for about twenty years.'

Dan made a sound that was no more than a grunt. Almost a growl…

Good grief…was he *jealous* of an old boyfriend of a woman he was probably never going to see again?

No. This was relief, that was what it was. It would make it even easier to not be distracted by any thoughts of women, unlike Jock.

Dan picked up the ball they needed. 'My serve, I believe.'

It was. Because he'd won the last game. He might be winning every squash game with Jock for quite some time, given that he would never be in any danger of being distracted in that way himself.

He'd needed that reminder of how disruptive it could be. Because, if he was honest, he *had* found himself thinking, rather too much, about the night he'd had with Jock's sister.

Oh…*man*…

That sensation of pure…what was it? Lust? Desire? *Need*…?

Whatever it was, it was powerful enough to instantly cut through the physical—and mental—focus needed to see where that tiny rubber ball was heading at warp speed and intercept it to get it back to the front wall.

It was only there for a nanosecond. A flash sparked by the memory of the best sex he'd ever had in his life. He could almost feel his fingers buried in those waves of hair the colour of flames as he'd cradled her head to try and savour just one more kiss…

He could hear the music of the accent in her voice and smell the scent of her skin.

He could see those extraordinarily blue eyes. A gaze that held his as if there was no space between them at all and…it felt like a connection he'd never known existed. It almost felt as familiar as looking into a mirror, but this was with a perfect stranger and that made it…weird.

Dangerous, even.

Thank goodness Jenni had left the country the very next day and was now safely back home on the other side of the world.

The flash of the memory with its inherent urgent warning was over in virtually the same blink of time with which he'd registered its presence.

But it had been long enough to be disturbing.

And long enough to miss an easy shot. The first point of this game was Jock's so it was no surprise that he could see a triumphant grin in his peripheral vision.

His opponent's confidence was premature, however.

Dan knew exactly how to conquer a distraction like that.

It wasn't going to happen again.

Life was full of ironies, Jenni thought as she stared at the small window in the middle of the plastic stick she was holding.

She was a midwife. She should have recognised the signs of pregnancy long before this.

She'd been scrolling through potential candidates on a sperm donor site, for heaven's sake, when she'd been pregnant already.

She'd told herself the milk was off. That her periods were irregular anyway so it was no surprise that international travel had made them even less reliable.

So here she was, not only pregnant but probably a couple of months along.

Okay…who was she kidding? Jenni knew the *exact* date of this conception. Which meant she knew exactly who the father of this baby was.

Daniel Walker.

Her brother's best friend.

And there was another irony. She'd warned her brother not to even think about hitting on *her* best friend when Grace had decided to go and work in New Zealand, because she'd been worried that somebody would get hurt and relationships between both siblings and friends could be damaged.

Now Jock and Grace were madly in love. *Engaged* even, and had just purchased a property together.

Dan had not only made his feelings about significant relationships known but he also clearly believed he was incapable of fathering a child. How was Dan going to react when he learned that he was mistaken? How was *Jock* going to react when he discovered just how his friend had looked after his sister when they'd been left alone together on the first night they'd met?

Would the bomb that Jenni was inevitably going to have to drop be enough to destroy a friendship and make things weird between herself and her brother?

The urge to talk this through with her best friend was strong enough to make Jenni reach for her phone, but she didn't make the call. She couldn't tell Grace because she couldn't ask her to keep a secret from the person she loved enough to be planning to spend the rest of her life with him. And what if Dan had said anything to Jock about what had happened that night they'd been left alone together? It wasn't rocket science to put two and two together and guess who the father was. Letting someone else reveal this news was dodging a responsibility that was entirely her own.

Jenni didn't have to tell anybody anything just yet, though, did she? Things could go wrong in a first trimester.

And maybe she didn't want to tell anybody until she had got her own head around this. She could keep this a secret at least until she didn't feel quite so stunned.

It took another week before the shock began to wear off properly but, when it did, Jenni could feel the tendrils of quite another reaction beginning to grow. When another week passed and she saw the images on her first ultrasound examination, she knew that this was meant to be.

This was Fate giving her the gift of something she'd wanted for even longer than she had admitted to herself. Being a mother. Being able to protect and love and *want* a child. To give him, or her, the life that she wished she and Jock had been given.

No…to give *them* that life she and her brother should have had.

Was Fate pleased with herself, repeating history by doubling up on this miracle? The genetic likelihood of conceiving fraternal twins *was* hereditary, but Jenni hadn't even considered the possibility so she found she had tears rolling down her face when the ultrasound technician turned the screen and she could see the distinct shape of two babies in her womb.

This twist in just how much her life was going to change made it more complicated to figure out how to drop the bombshell news. It wasn't something to put in an email. Or a video call. Especially knowing just how shocked Dan was going to be. It didn't matter that Jenni intended to be a single parent so she wasn't expecting—and might not even welcome—any major input from the father of these babies, there was no getting away from the fact that he had the right to be a part of their lives if he chose to be.

And part of Jenni really wanted him to make that choice, because that was something else she and Jock had wished for when they were growing up without even knowing who their father was. They would be living on opposite sides of the world but that didn't necessarily mean that he couldn't be as important to his children as Jock and Grace would be. Technology made sharing lives so much easier now and Jenni loved what she'd seen of New Zealand so far. If she could afford it, she wouldn't be opposed to an annual holiday in the country that represented half the heritage of these babies.

This was going to be life-changing news for Dan. And for Jock, who was going to become an uncle. An uncle of *twins*. Jock and Jenni both knew how special that bond was.

It was news that needed to be delivered face to face, Jenni decided. But how would she explain why she was planning another visit so soon after the last when it was such a long journey and so expensive?

There was too much to think about in the next few days and while Jenni was finding it progressively easier to imagine herself as a mother, the prospect of revealing her news was daunting enough to make it preferable to put off making any decisions.

A wake-up call came with an email that arrived unexpectedly in her inbox from the New Zealand Midwifery Council to say that her application for registration had been successful. There would still be interviews and assessments to be ticked off in person but, with a work visa already added to her passport, Jenni could theoretically start looking for a job as a midwife in New Zealand. She had no intention of actually doing that, but it could be a legitimate reason for another visit to the country.

And then an even better one presented itself. Where she would be able to dodge any questions and guilt that she could be seen as deceiving the people she cared most about because she wouldn't have to tell anybody she was coming.

It could be a surprise visit. And what better reason for a surprise visit than a birthday? Jenni would be well into her second trimester by the date of her shared birthday with Jock and it might be hard to keep her secret that long, but perhaps Fate was giving her this time as well. So that she could plan and dream about the future before having to face the shock—and understandable concern—from everybody else involved. And what if Dan turned his back on acknowledging his children? Was she ready to deal with a rejection that could open old wounds for both herself and Jock?

When Jenni opened a calendar to choose a date that was early enough to allow for the international travel and time zone changes and let her arrive on the right day, she saw the note that Jock and Grace were planning to move into their new house the following week so they'd be in the middle of getting packed up, wouldn't they?

Should she change her travel plans?

No. Jenni drew a big circle around the date she'd chosen.

Having the distraction of moving might be the perfect way to demonstrate that her news wasn't going to stop the world turning and life could continue as normal. And what better time to reveal the impending birth of *her* babies than the day to celebrate the birth of their mother and uncle? With a new auntie and…maybe even Dan if he wanted to be involved in their lives in an acceptable way.

He was their father, after all.

Part of their family.

And he had the right to be part of their lives.

CHAPTER TWO

'*SURPRISE!* HAPPY BIRTHDAY, JOCK.'

Jenni put down her suitcase so that she could hug her brother with one arm.

Jock hugged her back. 'And to you… But…' He was still blinking at her in astonishment. 'You haven't come all the way across the world to celebrate our birthday, have you?'

'Why not?' Jenni tried to sound offhand. If the oversized top she was wearing wasn't doing a good enough job of hiding the newly discernible bump of her pregnancy, the bunch of balloons and carry bag she had in her other hand were an additional disguise.

'Well, it's rather a long way to come when I hadn't even planned any kind of a party,' Jock said. He waved a hand at a stack of boxes in the hallway by the front door. 'We're in a bit of a mess, what with packing and all the chaos that goes with moving house.'

'We can make our own party. I've got cake. And wine. Or we can go out to dinner.'

'Am I missing something?' Jock sounded distinctly puzzled. 'We've never made that big a deal out of our birthdays and it's not a milestone like turning forty or something.' He took Jenni's suitcase and turned to lead her into the house. 'Not that Dan celebrated when *he* turned forty recently, but he's not really a party kind of guy, I guess…'

Jenni needed to take a big breath.

Hearing Dan's name being spoken aloud suddenly made this very real. She was here. She would be seeing Dan very soon.

And she was feeling very nervous…

Jock had to be picking up on that nervousness because his tone suggested that he was sensing an undercurrent that was disturbing him. Had she made a huge mistake keeping this secret for so long? Not in giving herself time to get used to this before bringing Dan into the picture, but what if Jock and Grace were going to be angry at being excluded for so long? Or worse, hurt by having such a life-changing secret being hidden?

She opened her mouth to try and give Jock a heads-up that she did have another important reason for being here, but she couldn't think of how to broach the subject. Maybe she needed Grace here to potentially dilute the impact just a little. Or maybe she had become too good at procrastinating.

'Can I have the same room I had last time I was here?' she asked brightly instead. 'You don't have a houseful of new hospital employees, do you?'

'Yes. And no. And you do realise we're about to move into the house we've bought, don't you? Our settlement date is next week.'

'I know. Grace told me. And I've seen pictures of the house, which is absolutely gorgeous…'

Just the mention of Grace's name was enough to change Jock's characteristically cheeky grin into the soppiest smile she had ever seen on his face. This was a man who was utterly in love and while they chatted about the house as they made their way to the kitchen, Jenni had to blink back the mistiness of knowing how happy her brother was.

'Where *is* Grace?' she asked eventually.

'Out on a home visit. Do you remember the last night you were here on your visit? When we had to abandon you to go and see the woman who'd been in a car accident?'

'And you left me with Dan?' Jenni laughed but it sounded forced, even to her own ears. 'Yes, I do remember.'

The tension was escalating. She *had* to reveal her secret. Soon...

She could barely focus on what Jock was telling her about the happy aftermath of the woman from the accident that night giving birth to a healthy baby not long ago.

At least some of that tension dissipated when the wait for Grace to arrive home ended and she walked into the kitchen with an expression of complete disbelief on her face.

'*Jenni*...what on earth are *you* doing here?'

'*Surprise*...' Jenni held out her arms and Grace met her halfway across the kitchen floor.

'It's our birthday,' Jock said. 'Apparently, Jenni decided she needed to come and celebrate.'

Oh...the look of love that passed between Jock and Grace excluded Jenni completely for a moment and she got a flash-back to that odd loneliness she'd been haunted by after her return to Glasgow. She thought that had been buried the moment she knew that she was on the way to creating her own little family, but it caught her by surprise again now as she watched her brother and her best friend share a very tender kiss and it was sharp enough for her to make a sound of discomfort.

'I am *here*, you know.'

There was laughter in the room as well as all that love. A short time later, Jock was taking the bottle of champagne Jenni had brought with her from the fridge and Grace was finding glasses.

'Not for me,' Jenni said as Grace took a third champagne flute from the cupboard.

Three tiny words but they fell into the room with the effect of a match lighting a grenade fuse. The pop of the cork shooting out of the bottle Jock was holding added a rather appropriate explosion into the sudden silence.

Jenni could almost feel the pennies dropping around her. They both knew how much she loved champagne. They both believed she was here, at least in part, to celebrate a birthday.

'Aye…' She tried, and failed, to defuse the atmosphere with a smile. 'I'm pregnant.'

They were still staring at her. 'How far along?' Grace breathed.

'About seventeen weeks.'

Jock was an obstetrician. Grace was a midwife. In the time it took for them to share a glance with each other, they'd done the calculations and come up with an approximate conception date.

'It happened on your holiday?'

'Yes.'

Grace's eyes widened. 'Was it Melbourne? You and…what was his name—your first ever boyfriend? Jeremy?'

'No…' Jenni was shocked. 'We had lunch. He showed me around Melbourne. Jeremy's *married*. I met his wife and kids.' She shook her head, appalled that either of them would think that was even a possibility.

'It couldn't have been anyone here.' Jock was frowning as he thought aloud. 'You were with one of us the whole time you were in New Zealand.'

But Grace caught his gaze again. 'Not the *whole* time,' she murmured. 'We left her alone with Dan, remember? When we got called back into work.'

Jock looked as if something might be hurting him physically. 'But he said he was going to look after Jenni.'

He swallowed visibly. 'I don't believe this...'

He looked down at the bottle of champagne he was still holding. 'When I told Dan it was my birthday he said he might drop in later to have a beer. Does he know *you're* here?'

He looked up. He *was* hurt. Jenni's heart broke a little.

She shook her head. 'I decided I needed to tell him in person. I needed to be sure of how I felt about it myself and... and I wanted to wait until I was in my second trimester just in case...' She could feel tears prickling at the back of her eyes. 'And then I thought you'd guess something was up if told you I was coming back so soon and it wasn't that much longer to wait to have the excuse of coming for our birthday.' The tears were starting to spill. 'I'm sorry I didn't tell you sooner.'

'Oh... *Jenni*...'

Grace's arms were around her, but Jenni pulled back. 'There's more,' she confessed. 'It's *twins*...'

Somehow, that changed everything. This was history threatening to repeat itself and she could see Jock being dragged back in time. Remembering their childhood. The times when it felt like they only had each other in a world where no one really wanted them. Where they only had one parent—the one who hadn't been able to walk away so easily?

'I don't want my babies growing up not knowing who their father is,' Jenni said quietly. 'Like we did. Or that there's a man out there somewhere who has no idea that he is a father. What if our father had known we existed, Jock? Maybe he would have come to find us. He might have *wanted* us and... and everything would have been so different...'

It was Jock who was folding her into his arms now. 'Do you want us here when you tell Dan?'

Jenni shook her head again. 'Best I do that by myself, I think.' She made a huff of sound that was almost laughter. 'Would you believe we spent most of that night talking about how much we liked being single? I told him about our vow to never get married or have kids. He told me he *couldn't* have kids…' She let her next breath out as a sigh. 'I have a feeling he might not be too happy about getting this news.'

The last thing Dan expected when he arrived at the old villa, to see if his mate wanted that beer he'd promised, was to find Jock's sister sitting on the top of the steps that led to the veranda.

No…the *very* last thing he expected was the rush of feeling that followed the shock of recognising that it was Jenni McKay. It was, weirdly, almost relief. He couldn't deny that he'd thought about her so often he had missed her presence as almost a physical ache sometimes. Or maybe it was joy rather than relief. He'd thought he might never see Jenni again but here she was—as if someone had waved a magic wand and made his wish come true.

'Hey…' He could feel his smile stretching muscles that hadn't been used that much lately. 'When did you arrive?'

'Today.' Jenni was smiling back at him. 'Just a couple of hours ago.'

Her gaze was holding his and Dan got the impression that she was just as surprised by how she was feeling about seeing *him* again. Or was he simply seeing a reflection of how he was feeling? How *happy* he was suddenly feeling…

'And you're still awake? I'm impressed.'

'I'll crash soon. After the birthday party.'

'That's why I'm here. To wish Jock a happy birthday.'

'He'll be back soon. He and Grace have gone to the supermarket to get some more boxes for packing. And they're going to pick up Thai takeaways or fish and chips on the way home.'

There was no point going inside by himself and he'd be able to see Jock returning home from here—hopefully soon. Dan put down the chilled six-pack of lager he was carrying and sank onto the step beside Jenni.

'Fancy a beer?'

'No, thank you.'

'It didn't occur to me to pick up anything as exotic as a black margarita, sorry.'

Oh, *help*… Why on earth had he said that? It would have been far more sensible to avoid any reminders of that night. Just the mention of her choice of drink and he caught a flash of how it had felt being with her in that cocktail bar. Watching the way her face lit up as she smiled. Feeling the first spikes of a physical attraction that was…almost illicit, after promising Jock he would take care of his sister. Unwise, anyway, but that only gave it an edge he'd never had the pleasure of experiencing before.

Dan blew out a careful breath. Was Jenni remembering that evening as well? He needed to steer them back onto safe territory. Fast.

'So that's why you're here? For Jock's birthday?'

'It's my birthday too.'

'Of course it is. Sorry… I forgot about that twin thing.' He found a smile. 'Happy birthday, Jenni.'

'Thanks. I hear you had a big one recently.'

Dan shrugged. 'Age is just a number. I don't do birthday parties.' He gave Jenni a quizzical glance. 'I didn't think Jock did either.'

'Neither of us do. We were lucky anyone remembered when we were kids.'

'But you've come this far to celebrate this birthday?'

'That's one of the reasons I came, yes...' Jenni's gaze slid away from his.

A faint sensation, like a chill, ran down Dan's spine.

They both sat in silence for a long moment, staring down the street as if they were both hoping that the distraction of Jock and Grace returning would be available.

It wasn't. And Dan suddenly had a thought that might explain that odd premonition.

'You're not planning to come and live here, are you?' he asked.

'What on earth makes you say *that*?'

Her glance was startled. More than startled. It looked like a flight or fight response had just been triggered. Jenni looked... *frightened...*?

'It was something Jock said a while back. That he never wanted to move back to Scotland but that he and Grace were working on a plan to persuade you to come and live in New Zealand.'

Jenni shook her head sharply. 'Scotland is my home,' she said. 'I have no intention of living anywhere else.'

Dan could feel a wash of something like relief now. Because he'd never factored in *seeing* Jenni McKay again, let alone living in the same town. He only ever indulged in sexual encounters when there was no likelihood of that happening. Or at least no chance of being unable to escape being in close proximity unexpectedly. The sort of occasions that might occur if they had mutual friends, perhaps—or having to work together. He'd learned long ago that the ideal scenario was when he was on holiday a long way from home. Or with someone who was on holiday here and just passing through, like Jenni had been. He'd already spent far too much time thinking about that night he'd had with her.

Dreaming about it.

Coming to terms with the fact that he was probably never, ever going to experience sex like that again in his lifetime.

Oh, man…he could actually feel the pull of this woman again right now, as he sat this close to her. By some trick of the mind, he could sense the warmth and scent of her skin. He could even imagine that he could *taste* her, and in that instant he knew he was in trouble.

That pull was irresistible. If he even made eye contact with Jenni while this spear of desire was simultaneously touching every cell in his body, he could imagine it would be contagious enough to have them kissing passionately within a heartbeat and it was a no-brainer what would happen next…

So he stared down the street again. And then he cleared his throat as if that might stem that disturbing level of physical attraction he was experiencing.

'I also wanted to see you,' Jenni said into this new, slightly awkward silence.

'Oh…?' Dan risked the eye contact. Because…if Jenni was only here for a holiday again, didn't that make it just bending the rules about his sex life a little and not breaking them enough to be a problem?

'I'm pregnant, Dan…'

The words didn't make any sense. Oh, he could understand them, of course, but why was she telling *him*? He could feel himself frowning and raising his eyebrows at the same time, which made his whole face feel strangely tight.

'Ah…congratulations?' Should he say anything else? 'Are you…happy about that?'

'Yes.' The affirmation had a thoughtful tone but it was surprisingly decisive.

'Does Jock know?'

'Yes.' He could hear Jenni taking a deeper breath. 'But I had to tell you too. That's the main reason I'm here.'

That chill was back again. This time it had sharp edges—like claws. 'I don't understand…'

'You were wrong, Dan,' Jenni said quietly. 'About never being able to have kids. I'm not here to mess with your life or ask for any kind of commitment, but you have the right to know that you're going to be a father.'

It looked like an almost automatic gesture to put both her hands on her belly, smoothing out that floppy top. Dan could see the soft mound of what he could very easily remember as being a delicious area of skin between Jenni's hipbones that had been as flat as a pancake when he'd put his own hands there not that long ago.

Her words became muffled by a noise that was rather like the static that came from not being quite on an exact radio frequency. There was interference as well, that came in the form of long-buried memories suddenly escaping their prison.

'I'm pregnant, Dan.'

'No way…it's not possible.'

'It's happened. See?' His wife had held up the test stick for him to see the lines in the window.

'But they said I had far more chance of winning the lottery than getting you pregnant.'

'Are you happy?'

'I'm stunned. And…yes, of course I'm happy. Beyond happy. It's what we wanted. It's everything I've ever wanted. A family of my own…'

Dan ruthlessly slammed the door shut on the ghost of

that conversation before any more of his ex-wife's words re-appeared. Getting to his feet seemed to have helped, although he had no memory of having moved. That lack of control over his body seemed to apply to what he was saying as well.

'You don't expect me to *believe* that, do you?'

Jenni wasn't saying anything. She had wrapped her arms around her knees and her head was bent.

'You *do* remember that I told you I was infertile?'

'That's part of the reason I thought you should know.' Jenni's voice was quiet. Expressionless. 'Just in case, you know...you got carried away with someone else and thought there was no reason to worry about not having any protection available.' She wasn't looking up at him. 'And yes, I know you can have a very low sperm count after a bad dose of mumps, but it only takes one that gets to the right place at the right time.'

'Not going to happen when that "one" probably has motility and morphology issues that render it completely useless.' Dan could hear the ice in his voice. 'Why are you doing this, Jenni? Why aren't you sitting on the step of that old boyfriend of yours that you went to see in Melbourne on your way home from here?'

Or had it been before then? Had she already been pregnant when she'd come here on holiday?

He'd seen the obvious weight gain on her belly when she'd outlined it with her hands. A quick mental calculation told him it was less than four months since their night together. It wasn't normal to have that much of a bump this early in a pregnancy, was it?

'How did you know that?'

'Jock told me. He got a text message from you when we were playing a game of squash not long after you'd gone home.

I asked how you were and he said you'd loved your visit to Melbourne and that you'd had a good time catching up with someone you hadn't seen for twenty years. I've heard that you never forget your first...'

Jenni had gone very pale. He could see individual freckles dotted over the bridge of her nose and the top of her cheekbones as she finally looked up at him. She looked so shocked that Dan could feel a cloud of misgiving forming around him.

He ignored it. He was just as shocked that she would be suggesting this in the first place. 'You want me to do a DNA test to prove that I'm not the father of your baby, Jenni? Fine... bring it on.'

She still didn't say anything. And Dan finally realised that he'd probably said too much.

He didn't bother picking up the cans of lager he'd brought to share with Jock. He couldn't wait a second longer to get away from this.

From those ghosts.

From Jenni...

'Was that Dan's car I saw going past us when we came out of the chip shop?'

'Could well have been...' Jenni was still sitting on the step. 'He couldn't get away fast enough after I told him I was pregnant.'

'It will have been a massive shock,' Grace said. 'I imagine he's going to need some time to get used to the idea.'

'He's not going to get used to it.' Jenni shrugged. 'He doesn't believe it. He made it very clear that he thinks the real father is Jeremy. That I'm... I'm deliberately *lying* to him.'

The tears Jenni had been holding back were way too close to

the surface now, but there was more than disappointment causing her distress. It was beginning to feel more like…*anger*…

Jock and Grace exchanged a glance that seemed to be a whole conversation.

'I'm going to put the kettle on,' Grace said. 'And make some tea. I'll be back soon.'

She was leaving Jenni alone with Jock, wasn't she? And it was the best thing she could have done. Because Jock understood.

'I told him, that night,' Jenni said as Jock sat where Dan had been sitting only minutes before. 'I said that I can't abide lies. That I'd *never* tell them myself. You know what *he* said?'

Of course he didn't. Jock hadn't been there. If he had been, Jenni wouldn't be here now.

'He said "How do I know *that's* not a lie?" And I just smiled and said that it didn't matter because we were never going to see each other again.'

That was enough to flick the switch. Jenni burst into tears. 'It's going to be us all over again, Jock. Two little kids who are never going to have a daddy or feel like they have a real home.'

Jock put his arm over Jenni's shoulders. 'It's not going to be anything like us,' he said quietly. 'I promise. And *you* know I never make promises I can't keep.'

Jenni did know that. It was for the same reason she never lied. A broken promise was just another kind of lie, and they both knew the disappointment—despair, even—that the aftermath could bring, especially to children who had yet to learn not to hope that this time really would be different.

'Of course I'll be there to pick you up after school…'

'Yes… Father Christmas is coming this year. He won't forget again…'

'It'll be different this time. I promise… We'll be a real family…'

Jock's quiet voice dispersed the ghosts from their childhood.

'These babies are going to have a mum who's never going to let them think that she never wanted them or that they've ruined her life,' he said. 'They're going to have an uncle and auntie who will love them to bits and never break any promises. You don't need Daniel Walker in your life.'

'I know… I didn't even *want* him in my life.' Jennie sniffed hard and rubbed her nose on her sleeve. 'He told me to do a DNA test so he could prove he wasn't the father, but you know what?'

'What?'

'I'm not going to. Not before they're born, anyway. If he actually believes I'd lie about something this important, he's not someone I want in my life. I'll do it later, when I'm back on the other side of the world and these babies are safely born, but as far as I'm concerned he's just thrown away his right to know for sure that he's going to be a father and to share in this pregnancy and the birth of his children.'

'So you told him it was twins?'

Jenni's huff of laughter was anything but amused. 'Are you kidding? When he reacted like that to the idea of one baby, there was no way I was going to double up on the bad news.'

Jock squeezed her shoulders tighter for a moment. 'I'm sorry, Jen. Can't say I'm overly impressed with Dan right now.'

'Neither am I.' Grace was back with a tray that had a teapot and mugs on it. She set it down on the wrought-iron table between two chairs on the veranda. 'But I'd like to know why he's so sure he can't have kids.'

'Bad dose of mumps when he was young, apparently,' Jenni said.

'Only takes one good swimmer to do the deed,' Jock murmured. 'I've seen more than one surprise pregnancy from a dad who had a low sperm count.'

'That's what I told him,' Jenni said. 'But he just muttered something about the motility and morphology being useless.'

'That kind of makes sense.' Jock gave Jenni another squeeze and then let her go so that she could reach up to take the mug of tea Grace was offering. 'Even the success of invasive procedures like intracytoplasmic sperm injections and IVF relies on those factors. Sounds like he's been properly tested. Not that it's something I've ever talked to him about.'

'And it's not something I intend to talk to him about again,' Jenni said. 'I'm sorry, Jock. I've kind of ruined our birthday, haven't I?'

'We're not going to let it,' Jock told her. He snapped his fingers. 'I know…we're going to celebrate on UK time, which means that it will still be our birthday tomorrow. I've got an afternoon off. What are you doing, Grace?'

'I've got a home visit booked in, but it's more of a social one because it's well outside the official six-weeks' follow-up for new mums. The department's been given a sample of a new breastfeeding wraparound pillow for using with twins and I was going to take a water taxi and deliver it to Tessa so that she can try it out and give us some feedback. You remember me telling you about the twins we delivered when that cyclone hit while you were on your way back to Scotland, Jen?'

She nodded. 'I was asking Jock about them just before you got home today. He said that was when he proposed to you.'

'It was…' Grace and Jock shared a glance that looked as though it was about to turn into a kiss, but then Jock broke the eye contact.

'I've just had the best idea. Why don't Jenni and I take you over to visit Tessa? We might get lucky and see some dolphins.'

'Oh, no...' Jenni widened her eyes theatrically. 'You think I'm going to get on your boat? So you can push me off again like you did when we were kids?'

Jock was grinning at her. 'You fell off that boat,' he said. 'You were leaning over the side too far because you thought you could see a fish. I was trying to *catch* you.'

Jenni had always known that was true. She also knew that she hadn't been in any real danger in the knee-deep pond, but she'd never quite forgiven her brother for laughing at her instead of being the hero who had always been there to protect or comfort her. He was stepping up now though, wasn't he? He wanted to be here for her in a new phase in her life that was rather more serious than getting wet and muddy by falling out of a boat.

And she needed him as much as she had when she had been bullied at school, yet again, for being the new girl. Or for being one of those twins whose mother couldn't be bothered looking after them properly.

No...right now she needed him more than she ever had before.

CHAPTER THREE

IT TURNED OUT that Jock's idea to take Jenni out on his boat the next afternoon had been inspired.

It was exactly what the doctor ordered to break the re-markably unpleasant quicksand of emotions like anger and confusion, disappointment and anxiety. There were shades of betrayal that were lurking as well, after Jock and Grace had considered, however briefly, the possibility that she might have slept with Jeremy, and having someone believe that she was deliberately lying about something *this* important had deliv-ered a blow that felt as visceral as a physical attack.

The exhaustion of jetlag fortunately meant that her mis-ery didn't stop Jenni falling deeply asleep, but it coloured her dreams as she slept the clock around and then lingered to make her feet feel leaden when she woke to find she was alone in the house because Jock and Grace had already left for work. Those emotions had become even more intense as she sat out-side and relived Dan's visit last night.

Unbelievably, there was another element trying to edge its way into the anger she felt towards him.

That curl of sensation she'd experienced when she first saw him again after so many weeks, walking towards her. How *happy* she'd been to see him. Just as tall. Just as dark and, if anything, even more attractive, because she could remember—

all too well in way too intimate detail—just how amazing it had been to have this man make love to her.

Okay, so it wasn't really a *curl* of sensation, like something gentle and pleasant. No…it was more like a spear with a sharp point that caused pain as it scythed a path through the core of her body.

Sheer physical desire, that was what it was…

Unwanted.

Unacceptable. Especially now that he'd deemed her dishonest. Deceitful. Someone who wasn't worth knowing.

Could his reaction be excused by the fact that he'd had a shock? That he had genuinely believed that he wasn't capable of fathering a child?

Yes.

No…

Okay…*yes*…but Jenni wasn't ready to accept that. Perhaps because part of her wanted an excuse to pat herself on the back for having done the right thing and then disappear back into her own life, where she would have no interference in how she raised her family.

Even a walk through the pretty township of Picton hadn't really helped her internal arguments and low mood, but watching the uncoiling of the ropes that tethered Jock's lovely clinker-built cabin cruiser boat named *Lassie* to the bollards on the pier made it feel as if some of those horrible knots in Jenni's gut were also unravelling. Gliding smoothly through the still waters of the marina towards the more open sea of the Sounds increased that relief by several notches. They were leaving the town behind.

She was leaving Dan behind, along with the whole tangle of the bond that had inadvertently been created between them.

How much better was it going to be to get on a plane and

feel that distance becoming the solid barrier of thousands of miles?

No…best not to try and imagine that. Because Jenni had the sneaking suspicion that it might not be better at all and that she might be leaving behind more than she wanted to, even when she took Jock and Grace out of the equation.

The peacefulness of this stunning scenery was soothing as they motored towards the humps and peaks of forest-covered peninsulas and islands emerging from deep, clear blue water.

Jenni and Grace were sitting on either side of *Lassie*'s deck. Jock was under the canopy at the wheel but with the engine running at a gentle speed and the silence around them being broken only by the occasional cry of a seagull, it was easy to hear him when he looked over his shoulder to speak.

'Grace and I were talking about you on the way home this afternoon,' he said.

Jenni found a smile. 'I can't imagine why.' Her smile faded. 'Did you see Dan at work?'

'No.' Jock's tone was tight. 'Which is probably just as well. I'm too angry to want to talk to him right now.' He turned back to watch where he was steering the boat.

'I'm sorry, Jock…' Jenni's breath came out in a heartfelt sigh. 'Please don't let this wreck a friendship for you. Friends are important.'

'Not as important as a sister.' He turned again to throw her a smile. 'Which was what Grace and I were actually talking about. It's going to be okay, Jen.'

'It *is*,' Grace said.

Jenni swallowed hard. 'I know…'

'We're going to do whatever we can to help,' Grace added. 'We thought you might like to think about coming to live here,' Jock said. 'So we could really help with the babies, especially in the early days.'

'I can't do that.' Jenni shook her head. 'Glasgow's home. And home is as important as friends. I've got some of those there as well, you know. They'll help. And I love my wee house. I wouldn't have anywhere to live here.'

'You could live with us,' Jock said. 'We're your family.'

'You could both come and live in Scotland,' Jenni countered. 'That's your real home. And you've still got family in England, Grace, so it's close to home for you too.'

This time, when Jock turned back, it was Grace he was looking at and they shared a long glance. And a smile.

'Look around you,' Grace said. 'Why would anyone want to live anywhere else?'

Silence fell between them as Jenni did what she was told and gazed out at the scenery again.

'This is the Queen Charlotte Sound,' Jock told her a short time later. 'Which is the main drag for marine traffic into Picton. We're heading for Kumutoto Bay, which only has access by boat.'

'That would have been a challenge when Tessa was expecting twins.'

'Nobody expected a cyclone,' Grace put in. 'But yeah... there's always a risk that twins are going to arrive early.' She was holding Jenni's gaze. 'I'll be worried about you,' she added quietly. 'If you're too far away.'

'It's going to be okay...' Jenni liked the sound of her new mantra. 'You'll see.'

The water became an astonishing shade of almost emerald-green in the shallows of Kumutoto Bay and both Jock and Jenni were invited into the house for Grace's visit to Tessa and her twins. Watching this new mother handle both her babies as she tried out the new type of breastfeeding support pillow was a very welcome bonus to this outing.

Jenni felt better than she had in a long time as they motored back to the marina in Picton. Maybe since she'd acquired a very new level of anxiety after seeing those two lines in the window of that pregnancy test.

'I can't believe how easy Tessa made it look to be looking after twins on her own.'

'She's not on her own. She's got a very supportive husband.'

'She was on her own this afternoon. And she was coping just fine.' Jenni's smile was confident. 'I'm going to be like Tessa. Just minus the husband bit. Because, you know, I did make a vow that I was never going to get married.'

Jock laughed. 'That vow was about never having kids either. You're breaking that part.'

'So are you. You're engaged to be married.'

'Only to one person. You're *double* breaking the part about the kids.'

They were all laughing by now and the smile stayed with Jenni as Jock slowed *Lassie* to enter the marina.

She didn't need to upend her entire life and move to a new country.

And she didn't need Dan Walker...

That smile vanished a short time later, however, when *Lassie* bumped gently into the pier as the ripple of a swell from an outgoing boat made her rock.

'Can you get the rope, please, Grace? And throw it around the bollard?'

'Sure.'

Grace climbed up on the seat with the coil of rope in her hands. She went to step onto the pier to get close enough to the bollard just as another ripple reached *Lassie*. Jock was busy trying to keep the boat steady against the wooden pier so it was only Jenni who saw Grace's foot slip. She fell onto the pier rather than into the water, which was a good thing, but her foot ended up between the side of the boat and the wooden pole on the pier as she fell, and that was most definitely *not* a good thing. Jenni thought she could actually hear the crack of a breaking bone.

Jock certainly heard Grace cry out in pain. He cut the engine and leapt from the back of the boat to the pier. He took the rope and hastily secured *Lassie* but it was Grace he was focused on as she was dragging herself further away from the edge of the pier. It didn't need medical training in order to see how bad this was. Grace's foot was at a very odd angle to her leg. It was clearly a nasty dislocation and probable fracture of her ankle. She was as white as a ghost and Jock didn't look much better as he took his phone out.

'Don't move,' he told Grace. 'I'm calling an ambulance...'

Well...this was awkward.

Responding to a call to the emergency department, Daniel Walker found himself face to face with Jock McKay as he approached the central desk. He hadn't been this close to Jock since he'd told him he might drop in to share a birthday beer with him yesterday.

Before his sister had told him that she was pregnant.

And that he was the father of the baby.

He'd been so angry when he'd walked out on Jenni to go home. He had, in fact, changed his clothes the minute he was through the door and had gone for a very long run. Long enough to begin to succeed in burning off the anger that had scorched its way through the shock. Anger that he couldn't control this shove back into a past he'd worked so hard to get over. Anger that he had to feel the pain of his whole life imploding all over again. Burying it for so many years had, strangely, not reduced its power to hurt. If anything, that surprise ambush had made it even sharper.

Because it was history repeating itself.

And he hadn't been able to shut out the extra echoes of his ex-wife's voice after all. Those casual words that had destroyed his dreams—and his life as he'd known it then.

The words that revealed the cruellest lie he'd fallen for. The words that had haunted him for so many years.

'You didn't really think it was your baby, did you, Daniel? You're not capable of fathering a child like a normal man. We both know that...'

But Jock looked...terrible, and Dan's first thought was that something had happened to Jenni. The sudden tightness in his chest came from nowhere and it was enough to make it impossible to pull his breath in any further. Slivers of potential grief were in there somewhere. And regret...?

'What's happened, mate?'

'It's Grace... She's had a fall. Fracture dislocation of her ankle. They're taking her up to Theatre any minute. Oh...' Jock rubbed his forehead with his fingers. 'That's why you're here? Are you going to be doing the anaesthetic?'

'Yes. I had no idea it was Grace.' There was something too close to relief to be felt now, which was disloyal of him, wasn't it? In the bigger picture, he knew Grace a lot better than Jenni. But his connection to Grace was through Jock. He might have met Jenni because of *her* connection to Jock but the pull that had been there between her and Dan was very different. And disturbingly powerful.

There was no outward hesitation to reveal that Dan was

even aware of that flash of almost-relief. 'What happened?' he asked.

'She slipped getting off *Lassie*. Her foot got caught between the boat and the pier.' Jock gestured at the computer screen behind him. 'It's a Bosworth fracture. Wasn't apparent until the attempt at reduction failed and they took a new set of images.'

'That's where part of a fibular fracture is dislocated and trapped behind the tibia, yes?'

Jock nodded. 'At least the popliteal sciatic nerve block has given good pain relief.'

'How long ago was the accident?'

Jock checked his watch. 'Nearly three hours. Come on, I'll show you where she is. You'll be wanting to do a pre-anaesthetic check and get consent.'

'Yes…and Jock…?'

Jock looked back over his shoulder. 'What?'

'I'm sorry about yesterday.'

Jock dismissed the distraction with a single shake of his head. 'It's Jenni you should apologise to,' was all he said. He held Dan's gaze for a heartbeat. 'My sister doesn't lie. Ever.'

Dan could hear an echo of Jenni's voice now.

'I never lie,' she'd said.

He'd believed it. It had only been a joke when he'd asked how he could know that *that* wasn't a lie.

Jenni was standing beside Grace's bed. She seemed to be avoiding making eye contact with Dan and he got that odd tight feeling in his chest again. Jock was right. He needed to apologise. She *had* to be mistaken. Maybe her periods were irregular anyway and if she'd had a dating scan, perhaps the technician who'd done it wasn't particularly proficient at their job and he was right in thinking that Jenni had already, unknowingly, been pregnant when she had arrived in New Zealand.

Whatever the reason for the error, Jenni clearly believed that he had fathered her baby, which meant she thought he had simply denied what was the truth as far as she was concerned. He had not only not offered her any kind of support, he'd all but called her an outright liar.

There was no getting away from it. Jock was right and he needed to apologise because he'd handled the situation very badly and he needed to fix it.

But not here. And not now.

'Hi, Grace...' He stepped closer to the head of the bed. Jenni stepped back from the other side and Jock took her place as he continued talking. 'You've done a bit of damage to yourself, haven't you? I'm sorry to hear that.'

Grace grimaced. 'It was such a stupid thing to do. I can't believe I've got to have surgery. I'm going to be off work for weeks...' Her eyes filled with tears. 'I've got so many women who need me.'

'They'll be taken care of.' Jock took hold of Grace's hand. 'You don't need to worry about that right now, sweetheart.'

'But there's nobody to take on the extra workload,' Grace said. A tear escaped and rolled down her cheek. 'That's why they were so keen to employ me. We're still short of midwives.' She turned her head to look directly at Jenni. 'You could stay, couldn't you?'

'*No...*' Jenni sounded as if the notion was ridiculous. 'I'm only here for a quick visit.'

'But your application for registration was accepted ages ago. You've got a work visa. You said that you might want to have a working holiday here one day...' Grace's voice cracked. 'Why not now? I *need* you, Jen. You *can't* leave.'

Dan picked up the chart on the end of the bed. He took in the latest observations of Grace's vital signs. Her blood pressure was up a little, but that wasn't surprising with the pain she'd been in initially and how stressed she was now. Had Jenni really jumped through the administrative hoops to get a visa that would allow her to work in New Zealand? Would she *want* to?

No... Of course she wouldn't.

Because she was pregnant.

And because *he* worked here...?

He expected to hear Jenni tell Grace that she couldn't possibly stay. Part of him wanted to hear that she couldn't stay. He'd been alarmed at the idea that she might have been planning to emigrate even before he knew she was pregnant. Because he knew how hard it would be to stay away from her and he was so determined not to get emotionally involved with anyone again.

Ever...

But she didn't get a chance to say anything. They were interrupted by the return of the orthopaedic surgeon. 'We've got a theatre available. Ah, Dan...you're here. Are we good to go?'

'We will be in a minute or two. Grace, when did you last eat?'

'Lunchtime. Just a sandwich.'

'That was well over four hours ago now,' Jock added.

'Are you on any medications currently?'

'No.'

'Have you ever had a general anaesthetic before?'

'No...'

Grace had put her hand over her eyes but Jenni could see the tears leaking between her fingers. She'd never seen her friend this miserable.

Or her brother, for that matter. He was holding Grace's hand and being strong for her but Jenni could see past the outward appearance. He was worried sick. She could see the way he was gritting his teeth as he listened to Dan calmly asking questions about Grace's medical history, outlining the potential risks of anaesthesia and obtaining her consent for the procedure.

'Don't worry,' he finally told her. 'I'm going to look after you, Grace.'

Could Dan feel her staring at him? Was that what made him glance up and for their gazes to collide? Was he remembering that he'd said those same words the night they'd been left alone together, except that he had promised to look after *her*? What he had actually done was play a part in making sure her life was never going to be the same again, but now he wasn't prepared to even acknowledge that.

Except…

Was she imagining the impression, in that fleeting eye contact, that something might have changed since she'd dropped that bombshell on him yesterday? Had Grace been right in suggesting that it had been such a massive shock that Dan had simply needed time to absorb the news?

Not that it would change anything for her. The damage had been done.

It still stung that he hadn't given her a chance. That he'd decided she was lying to him and that was that. The connection she'd thought they had that night had been snapped and she'd prefer to have nothing more to do with Daniel Walker.

How could she possibly stay here, even if her brother and her best friend might desperately need her to help them through this crisis?

But she couldn't leave either.

Not immediately, anyway.

She walked behind the bed as they took Grace up to Theatre

and then waited with Jock in a staff area until the surgery was over. Jock was allowed to go and sit with Grace in Recovery.

'Stay here,' Jock told her. 'I'll come back and get you as soon as Grace is allowed to see you.'

But it was Dan who came into the lounge a short time later.

'Jock told me you were here,' he said. 'He asked me to tell you he might be a bit longer than he thought. He's going to stay with Grace until they take her up to the ward.'

Jenni nodded. Then she took a deep breath. This wasn't about her. This was about Grace. She could talk to Dan.

'How is she?'

'The surgery went well. They reduced the dislocation and the fracture and put in a plate and screws for the internal fixation. The surgeon was worried about damage to the ligaments but found they were intact when he was able to check them, so that's good.'

Jenni nodded again. She let out the breath she hadn't realised she was holding.

'She's been put in a tall immobilisation boot. One of those fancy new ones made with a rigid plastic shell and heavy-duty Velcro straps.'

'A walking boot?'

'Yes, but she's not going to be able to weight-bear for at least four weeks. Could be three months until the fracture's completely healed.'

'Oh, *no*…' The realisation that there was no way she could walk away from this and head home any time soon was enough to make Jenni do what Grace had done earlier and put her hand over her eyes.

'What's wrong?'

Jenni shook her head. 'This is a bit of a disaster all round, isn't it?'

There was a long moment of silence and then she felt the cushions of the couch move as Dan sat down beside her.

'Will you stay?' he asked quietly. 'I heard Grace say that you've already sorted registration and a work visa.'

Jenni dropped her hand but didn't look up. 'Grace will be stressed enough that she's letting all the women on her list down and she'll hate not being able to help Jock with the house moving. She might try and do more than she should and end up getting complications with that fracture healing. And if *she's* stressed, Jock will be stressed.' She finally looked up to find Dan watching her. 'We're talking about my best friend. And my brother. I can't *not* stay, can I?'

'But…' Dan's hesitation pushed a button that Jenni didn't know she had.

Was he trying to find reasons why she shouldn't stay? Because he wasn't comfortable with the idea of having her around? Well…tough… This was *her* choice. Like the way she was going to raise *her* babies would also be her choice.

'It won't be a problem for me to get leave from work for a family emergency,' she said tightly. 'I've got friends who'll be happy to look after my house. And if filling in for Grace professionally works out and it's the best way I can help, I'll do that.'

Had Dan's gaze shifted to her belly?

'Being pregnant doesn't mean I'm incapable of working,' she snapped.

'I didn't say it did.'

'Some midwives I've known have worked until they were almost full term.' Jenni's tone was still cool. 'I'm sure Grace will be back on her feet well before I'm anywhere near that stage.'

Dan was looking down at his hands. He really was struggling with the idea of her being back in town, wasn't he?

But that hadn't been the impression she'd got when he'd first seen her, sitting on that step. He'd looked as happy as she'd felt to see him again. Almost as though seeing her had been the best surprise he could imagine...

She wanted to hang on to feeling angry with him—maybe because she knew it might be harder to feel any other way—but it was proving difficult. She was starting to feel sympathy creeping in.

She could—and intended to—shut it out. She didn't want to start feeling sorry for Dan and make excuses for the way he'd reacted but she had pulled the plug on his life as he knew it, hadn't she? Not only that, she'd told him that something he believed was impossible was actually happening—that he was going to become a father.

Of course he needed time. She'd had the luxury of months to get used to all of this.

'It's okay, Dan,' she heard herself saying aloud. 'I might have come here to see you but that's not the reason I'm going to stay. I'm not going to make life difficult for you. Or ask you for anything. I'm quite prepared to be a single parent. To be honest, that's what I would prefer to be, anyway.'

Dan cleared his throat. 'I'm sorry,' he said quietly. 'About how I reacted yesterday. We should talk about that.'

Jenni could feel her lips curving into a smile, albeit a wry one. 'I suspect we'll have plenty of time,' she said.

Dan got to his feet. 'I'll go and see what's happening with Grace. I'm sure she'll be a lot happier when she knows that you'll be staying.'

Jenni watched him walk away. There was something very different about his body language from when she'd seen him walking away from her yesterday evening. When he'd looked as if he couldn't get away fast or far enough. She was getting a sense that the shock was, indeed, wearing off. And that he was grateful for the room to breathe.

Perhaps they both needed that room to breathe. Was this yet another ace Fate had found to pull out of her sleeve? One that would force Jenni to think twice about shutting the father of her babies out of her life?

What if Dan got himself tested again and discovered that it wasn't as impossible as he believed?

That her children could end up having a father?

What if, when he knew he could believe her—and trust her—*everything* could change?

CHAPTER FOUR

'SO YOU'RE JENNI...' Obstetrician Maria Gould was smiling broadly. 'I was delighted when Jock asked if I could keep an eye on you for the next few weeks. I didn't know he had a twin sister. And you're expecting twins yourself!'

'Thought I should keep up the family tradition,' Jenni joked. Maria was a senior colleague of Jock's, probably in her fifties, which gave her a rather welcome motherly vibe. 'Thank you so much for fitting me in.'

'No problem. Happy to help.' Maria opened the file of notes in front of her. 'Makes it a lot easier that you've printed off all your notes from your antenatal visits in Scotland. You've been in New Zealand for...nearly three weeks now?'

'Yes. I know I'm due for another scan and I should have come in earlier but Grace has been helping me keep an eye on my blood pressure and urine analysis and it's been crazy busy.'

'I'm sure it has. I knew Jock was due to move and then I heard about Grace's accident. I didn't realise you were visiting or that you'd come on board as a locum midwife.' Maria's eyebrows rose. 'How's that going?'

'My head's spinning,' Jenni confessed. 'The whole process was accelerated to give me a practising certificate so it felt like back-to-back interviews and assessments and orientation and... so much study. I spent several days in Wellington but I've still got online courses to finish in some areas. Midwives have more scope here than we do at home, with things like what medications can be prescribed, interpreting blood test results and making referrals and then there's all the cultural aspects that are important for Māori and Pasifika women that I need to get more familiar with. I'm loving the challenge, though.'

Because it had been demanding—and exhausting—enough to leave very little time to think about Daniel Walker. How lucky was it that she was in Wellington for her assessments at the time Dan had been helping with the house move? She'd only seen him in passing since she'd started working in the hospital, so it had been relatively easy to give him all the space and time he needed to come to terms with his impending fatherhood. To at least be prepared to find out the truth, at any rate.

What was taking him so long?

It was almost as if he still believed he couldn't be the father of these babies, which meant that he still believed Jenni was lying to him.

'Jock sounds like he's thrilled with the new house,' Maria said. 'I hear he's got a private jetty for his boat.'

'It's gorgeous. Right on the shore, but still close enough to town to be an easy commute and it has road access.'

'So you're living there with them?'

'No. I decided to stay in the hospital accommodation. Grace is doing well on her crutches now and I wanted to give them time to settle into their first home together by themselves.'

That had kept her safe from being included in any time Dan and Jock were spending together out of work hours. As far as she knew, Jock hadn't tried broaching the subject because he'd agreed with Jenni that giving Dan some time to get to grips with the situation was the best way to handle this.

He's the kind of guy who'll shut down to protect himself.

Disappear, even. I've seen him do it with women who want more from him than he's prepared to give... I suspect that getting away from something or someone was why he moved here in the first place.'

'Fair enough...' It sounded like Maria was agreeing with the echo of Jock's voice but she was actually busy scanning her notes now. 'So they're definitely non-identical fraternal DCDA twins.'

'A boy and a girl.' Jenni nodded. 'Just like me and Jock.'

'The perfect instant family.'

'Mmm...' Jenni's smile felt tight. It was probably due to the way she and Jock had been raised. Or maybe she'd read too many stories about children finding their happy ever after endings. She'd certainly been left with the image that a *perfect* family would include a father...

'It makes your multiple pregnancy lower risk, as I'm sure you know. You'll be offered a planned birth at thirty-seven weeks but there's a sixty percent chance you'll deliver before then.'

'Grace will be back on her feet well before that so I'll be back in Scotland. Most airlines have a cut-off for international travel of thirty-two weeks for multiple pregnancies.'

Maria nodded. 'Remind me to give you a cover letter when you book your flights.' Her smile was sympathetic. 'It must be difficult being this far away from home...and your partner...?'

'I'm not in a relationship,' Jenni said.

Maria nodded but Jenni knew that saying she was single wouldn't prevent the assumption being made that the father of her children was someone who lived in Scotland. She knew about hospital grapevines and she was working in a new environment where she would be a subject of interest, especially as a noticeably pregnant midwife. She could imagine how

Dan might react if any rumours got started. He'd run for the hills, wouldn't he.

That was a big part of why she wasn't about to push her way back into his space.

At some point, Dan was going to know the truth and they would have to interact in some way, even if they were living on opposite sides of the globe. How much better would it be for everyone involved if that interaction could be amicable, perhaps even friendly? However tempting it might be, burning bridges was only going to make it harder down the track.

Jenni still had what felt like plenty of time.

And she was more than busy enough during the day to make it easy to push any doubts aside and too tired at night to be kept awake.

'It's reassuring that your first trimester scan didn't show up any major anomalies. No growth discordance or markers for Down syndrome or spina bifida.' Maria's glance at the wall clock suggested she was aware of the time restraints of this appointment. 'I can't see any results for an amniocentesis or blood tests for other syndromes like Edwards' or Patau's.'

'No. I decided not to have an amniocentesis or chorionic villus sampling. Even such a small risk to the pregnancy wasn't one I was prepared to take.' She didn't need to confess how much she wanted to become a mother, did she? Or that she'd been planning to go to a sperm bank.

Maria just nodded. 'I'll schedule a second, anomaly scan for you, which should show us everything in much greater detail.' She reached for the cuff of the blood pressure monitor as she stood up. 'In the meantime, let's get on with the boxes we need to tick for today. You said you've got an outpatient antenatal clinic starting at nine o'clock and I'm due in Theatre, then for a hysterectomy.'

* * *

Dan got the call to the maternity department as he was starting to think about grabbing a quick late-morning coffee.

A woman who was thirty-seven weeks pregnant had been admitted for monitoring after having been found with markedly elevated blood pressure and higher than normal levels of protein in her urine at a routine antenatal clinic appointment. If the provisional diagnosis was confirmed to be pre-eclampsia, an early delivery was very likely to be recommended and part of the protocol was an anaesthetic consultation as soon as the patient was admitted.

Dan expected to find a registrar and/or the consultant for the obstetric team on call to be on the ward. He also expected at least one of the department's midwives to be looking after the patient.

What he didn't expect was to find Jenni McKay in the room.

Why not? He knew she'd started working as a locum to cover Grace being away with her badly broken ankle. He'd seen her more than once in the hospital over the last week or so, but he'd made no effort to have that talk he himself had said they needed to have.

Again…why not?

It wasn't as if he hadn't been thinking about how to approach what could be an awkward conversation. After Jenni had said she wasn't staying here because of him and that she wasn't going to ask him for anything, it seemed to confirm that there were options other than himself as the father of this child. If she was so sure it was him because she hadn't slept with anyone else around that time she would have had every right to ask him for financial support, at the very least. It would be stupid not to.

But did he really want to ask personal questions about

Jenni's sex life in the period of time just before or after they'd had that ill-advised one-off passionate encounter themselves?

No…he really didn't. He also didn't want to analyse *why* he didn't want to talk about it, so he'd been doing what he was good at doing when it came to dealing with uncomfortable emotional issues in his personal life.

Backing off. Procrastinating. Waiting for the right moment.

Hoping that whatever the issue was, it might somehow magically disappear before it had to faced.

Not that this was the right moment, of course, but being this close to Jenni again was a wake-up call and it had made one thing suddenly very clear in no more than the space of a heartbeat.

He was being a bastard by giving the impression that he didn't give a damn.

Okay, he'd apologised for how he'd reacted when she'd told him she believed he was the father of her baby, but that wasn't enough, was it? He owed her more than that. And he owed it to his best friend to treat his sister better than this. They might have been able to put it aside during the hectic activity of shifting house, when Dan had hired a truck and helped Jock move all the second-hand furniture he and Grace had acquired, but, inevitably, it had to affect their friendship.

For just another heartbeat, Dan wondered what might be going through Jenni's head as she glanced up to see him come through the door of this patient's room, but there was no indication that she was taken aback. Quite the opposite.

She was smiling at him.

'Hi, Dan.' She turned back to the woman in the bed. 'Ashleigh? This is Dan Walker, the anaesthetist that Jock told you would be coming to see you.'

Jenni was looking completely at home in her new workplace, in her pale green scrubs, with a stethoscope dangling around her neck as well as an official lanyard. She reached up to hang the cuff of the blood pressure monitor she was holding beneath the wall-mounted sphygmomanometer and it stretched the front of her tunic against her body. The bump of her belly was a lot more noticeable than it had been a couple of weeks ago and…yeah…she had that glow that pregnant women often had in their second trimester.

Mind you, Jenni had had that kind of a glow the first time he'd met her. It had been part of what had made her so damned attractive…

'Dan? This is Ashleigh Perrin and her partner Craig.'

'Hi.' Dan stepped closer to the CTG machine beside the bed. Ashleigh had the discs strapped onto her belly and he could hear the rapid beat of an unborn baby's heart that was reassuringly steady. He caught Jenni's gaze again briefly. 'Is Jock still around?'

'He's gone to chase up the blood test results and ultrasound report. He should be back any minute.'

Dan acknowledged the information with a brief nod. He had already shifted his attention to Ashleigh.

'How are you feeling at the moment, Ashleigh?'

'I feel fine,' she said. 'A bit of a headache, maybe, but I never expected to end up in here. I thought it was just going to be my last check-up before I went home to wait to go into labour.'

'Blood pressure's come down with the first dose of nifedipine,' Jenni said. 'Currently at one-sixty over ninety-eight.'

It was still high enough to be a concern. 'What was it initially?'

'It was one-ninety over one-oh-five when I took it in the

clinic earlier.' Jenni's voice sounded commendably calm but Dan knew how alarming that reading would have been.

'Any visual disturbances?' Dan asked Ashleigh. 'Like blurred vision or bright flashes?'

'No.'

'Any abdominal or back pain?'

'No.'

'Any nausea or vomiting?'

'No…honestly, I feel fine, apart from this headache. I'm probably wasting your time. I'm not going to need an anaesthetic, am I, Jenni?'

'It's something to be prepared for,' Jenni said. 'As Jock said, we need to keep a close eye on your blood pressure, which is why I'm checking it every thirty minutes. We need to see what's happening with your blood tests and the ultrasound, but you're at a stage of your pregnancy where it's perfectly safe for you to deliver and, if that's going to be safer for you and baby, the best option will be to induce you. That's where Dan comes in. He'll be the one to give you an epidural anaesthetic.'

'But what if I don't want that kind of pain relief?' Ashleigh's expression was dismayed. 'We were planning to have a natural birth. In water. With the lights dimmed. We've got our playlist ready with all the music we've chosen and essential oils to burn.'

It was Jenni who caught Dan's gaze this time. She was wondering whether she should say any more or did he want to step in?

There was a lot he could say, but scaring someone when the objective was to try and lower their blood pressure was not going to be helpful. On the other hand, if this was severe pre-eclampsia, which could compromise the safety of both mother and baby, an urgent delivery would be the only option and that could end up being a Caesarean section.

Dan got the impression that Jenni was aware of the complications that could arise from the blood-clotting abnormalities caused by pre-eclampsia. A general anaesthetic was riskier because swelling of the airway could make intubation more difficult and the body's response to having a tube inserted could potentially be severe enough to cause a cerebral haemorrhage or pulmonary oedema. A neuraxial anaesthetic like an epidural was preferable but there might only be a limited window of time to place a catheter in the space around the spinal cord before platelet levels became too low and the risk of haemorrhage too great.

He held her gaze a heartbeat longer as he hesitated. Dan knew he was more than competent clinically at his job, but his now well-honed ability to keep a safe distance from other people—including his patients—meant that he was less capable of sensing emotional boundaries and danger zones. There was another level of discomfort trying to edge in here as well. An unprofessional one. He knew he could prevent himself from letting it affect him but the connection he had with Jenni McKay, along with all its emotional implications, was noticeably there.

Waiting in the wings...

To his relief, a split second later, he found he didn't have to say anything and that slightly disturbing eye contact was broken when Jock came into the room. He greeted Dan with a nod and then perched on the end of the bed, case notes open in his hands, to talk to Ashleigh and Craig.

Jock had a natural, almost cheeky charm that made him very easy to be around and Dan could understand why both Ashleigh and Craig had visibly relaxed in his presence. He also had no difficulty being empathetic but conveying all the information they needed to have. He was very good with people in both a professional and personal arena. He was, in fact, the best friend Dan had ever had and Jenni was so like her brother it was really no surprise that the connection he'd felt with her had been so instant. So powerful. He'd felt like he'd already known her for ever, hadn't he?

'So…' Jock was flicking through a swatch of test result papers. 'I'm not too concerned with the results of your blood tests although they need watching, especially your liver function and platelet levels. We'll repeat the tests later today. Your ultrasound examination shows that baby is fine at the moment but the rate of growth has slowed since your last scan and that could be due to the blood flow from the placenta to the uterus being a bit lower than we'd like.'

'What does that mean? Is it dangerous?'

'There's no danger at the moment but it could mean that it will be better for baby to be born sooner rather than later. That will certainly be the case if we can't get good control of your blood pressure. I'll be back to check on you a wee bit later, but Jenni's going to take good care of you till then.'

Ashleigh was smiling at Jock. 'It's really cute that you and Jenni are twins.'

Jock grinned. 'The red hair is a dead giveaway, isn't it? Or is it our accent?'

Craig laughed. 'Jenni told us.'

'We were talking babies…' Jenni patted her belly.

'And she told us she's expecting twins.' Ashleigh nodded. 'And how happy she is about that because she knows how great it is to *be* a twin.'

Dan had the odd sensation that he could feel his blood draining out of his brain, making it difficult to join thoughts together.

Jenni was pregnant with *twins*? It shouldn't be that much of a surprise, given that fraternal twins ran in families, but it had just pulled the rug out from under some mental feet. That first impression that Jenni was far enough along in her pregnancy to make it obvious he couldn't be the father had just been blown out of the water.

It was instinctive to look at Jenni. To make eye contact to see if it was true. To try and make sense of the scramble of thoughts in his head.

Her gaze was so steady.

Calm.

Yes…her gaze told him. It's twins. And yes…she believed she had told him the truth when she'd told him he was going to be a father.

She'd just left out the bit about there being more than one baby.

That she was carrying what pretty much amounted to a small but perfectly formed family.

If only…

In that moment, before Dan took a deep breath and excused himself from the room for long enough to follow Jock and discuss this case in more detail, he was aware of how much he would have loved it to be true.

But it never could have been.

Because it might be an old-fashioned concept, but a *perfect* family had two parents. Two people who loved each other. And one of those people would never be Daniel Walker. He simply wasn't capable of loving someone like that again, so there was no point even thinking about it.

Oops…

It hadn't occurred to Jenni that a friendly chat with Ashleigh might lead to another bombshell revelation as far as Dan was concerned. Although, if he was so convinced she was lying and he wasn't the father, why would the fact that it was twins make so much of a difference?

But there'd been no mistaking the shock she'd seen in his eyes.

Distress even, and that had given her a strange squeeze in her chest that was definitely more than a stronger frisson of the sympathy she'd felt when she'd acknowledged her part in turning his world upside down.

Being angry with him and so disappointed in his reaction to her telling him she was pregnant had buried it, but it was peeping out again.

That extraordinary connection she'd felt with this man that had culminated in love-making that had felt like her soul was being touched as much as her body had been.

A fantasy of a relationship that could never be real because it was too intense…too *good*…to be true.

But Jenni could actually feel that distress she could see in Dan's eyes right now, and that was making her chest feel tight enough to be painful.

Did he still believe that she wasn't being completely honest with him? That the truth was an impossibility? There had to be a reason why he couldn't or *wouldn't* let himself be persuaded that he could be wrong, and it was bigger than simply dismissing her as being a liar.

Much bigger?

And something he would prefer to keep private?

Thank goodness she had given him space since she'd announced she wasn't going home in a hurry. And that she hadn't tried pushing him when she clearly didn't know what else might be going on, because that might have guaranteed that she would never find out.

She wanted to find out.

Because that feeling of connection stayed with Jenni as the day wore on and there was only one reason why she was feeling so curious about what was going on in Dan's head.

Quite apart from him being the babies' father, she cared about him.

Ashleigh's blood pressure dropped a little further, stayed steady for a couple of hours but then, despite the medication, it began to rise again. Not only that, but Ashleigh began to experience more symptoms that were concerning enough for Jenni to call Jock.

'She's got epigastric pain that's new and she's feeling short of breath.'

'What's her blood pressure?'

'Rising. Five minutes ago it was one-sixty-five on a hundred.' Jenni could hear Jock whistle silently.

'Oxygen saturation?'

'Ninety-six on room air. Up to ninety-eight with some low-flow oxygen.'

'Are the latest blood results back?'

'I was just about to go and check.'

'I'll do that. I need to come and see her, anyway. We're going to need another IV line in and start some magnesium to prevent seizures.'

Things began to speed up after that and both Ashleigh and Craig quickly became alarmed enough at what was going on around them to discard their birthing plan in favour of getting their baby born as soon and as safely as possible. They agreed to induction and consented to a C-section if necessary. When the latest blood test results came back with elevated liver enzymes and a falling level of platelets the management of Ashleigh's labour stepped up another notch and Dan was called back.

'I know it's early in your labour and an epidural wasn't something you wanted but if we don't do it now, it may not be possible later on.'

'But what if I do need to have a Caesarean?'

'You'd have to have a general anaesthetic.'

'But then I wouldn't be awake for the birth…'

'No. And it's also safer for both you and the baby to have a spinal anaesthetic for a Caesarean.'

'Do it…' Craig sounded adamant. 'Whatever's the safest—that's what we want, isn't it, Ash?'

Ashleigh was crying. Her voice was muffled behind the oxygen mask that had replaced the nasal tubing. 'I'm scared…'

'We've got you.' Jenni moved in. 'We're all going to look after you, okay? Let's get you ready for the anaesthetic while Dan's getting scrubbed. We need you sitting sideways with your bottom right in the middle of the bed. I'm going to stand in front of you to help you stay in the right position.'

Seeing Dan gowned, masked and gloved for the sterile procedure made it easier to be this close to him as she stayed in front of Ashleigh with both hands on her shoulders to keep her still and hunched into a forward leaning position. It steered this further into professional rather than personal territory.

'This will be the worst bit, Ashleigh,' Dan warned. 'It's just the sting of the local going in. Count to ten and it will be fading.'

Ashleigh was hunched forward, her gown open to expose her spine, stained brown with the antiseptic it had been swabbed with. She had her head bowed so low her chin was touching her chest so it was easy for Jenni to watch Dan at work. He palpated the iliac crests on either side of Ashleigh's pelvis, with his hand outstretched so that his fingers were on the crests and his thumbs were feeling for the space between the lower lumbar vertebrae.

For just a nanosecond, things flicked for Jenni from being professional to being extremely personal.

Because she knew what it felt like to have Dan's fingers on her body and it was impossible to prevent the spear of sensation that seared her own nether regions. It didn't help that she had no part in this procedure other than to hold Ashleigh's shoulders and prevent any movement at critical moments.

'Stay still,' she reminded her. 'The sting should be starting to fade now.'

Jenni was hoping the sensation she was experiencing herself would also start to fade very soon but, if anything, as she watched Dan's deft movements as he discarded the syringe and needle he'd used for the local anaesthetic onto the sterile draped trolley and picked the specialised needle he needed to administer a combination spinal and epidural anaesthetic—the best option in case a Caesarean was needed—it seemed to be getting more intense.

Jenni knew what this was about. She'd talked to pregnant women for years now and she had listened to many confessions about the increased libido that could happen in the second trimester of pregnancy. She could explain why it happened, with the different levels of hormones circulating and the increased blood flow that was focused on supplying the uterus, that meant that the whole lower area of a woman's body could be more sensitive. Having your breasts get bigger, along with the rounded belly, could make you feel sexier too. It was one thing to share a conversation with other women, a giggle about an increased desire for sex and the shenanigans that were sometimes undertaken to satisfy it and even advice on the best positions to try when the bump was big enough to get in the way, but it was a very different matter to be experiencing it herself.

For someone with whom it had been a big mistake to have sex in the first place.

Even if it had been the best sex she'd ever had…

With an enormous effort, Jenni focused hard on the procedure and not the man doing it with such skill and efficiency.

She watched Dan insert the much larger hollow needle into the now anaesthetised gap between the vertebrae. She could feel his concentration as he carefully felt his way to the resistance that would let him know he'd reached the ligament just before the epidural space. He attached a syringe with saline in it, tapping it gently each time he advanced the needle a little further, until it emptied easily and let him know he was exactly where he needed to be. A long, thin spinal needle went in next, to administer drugs to a deeper level that would work fast and be effective for hours, and then it got swapped for a flexible catheter that would stay in the epidural space and could deliver medication via the port at the other end to keep the anaesthetic going as long as it was needed.

An adhesive sterile dressing went over the catheter on Ashleigh's back and the procedure was complete, fast enough to fit seamlessly between contractions. Not that Dan was going anywhere else in a hurry. He was drawing up more drugs as Jenni helped Ashleigh into a more comfortable position on the bed to breathe through her contraction and then took another set of vital signs.

It was much easier now to dismiss that unwelcome intrusion of something unacceptably personal that had happened only minutes ago. So recently that Jenni could still feel a twinge of it remaining.

That…*desire*…

For sex.

Not just sex.

Sex with Daniel Walker.

Something that should be the last thing she'd want to do with someone she had been so angry and disappointed with only a matter of days ago.

But there it was.

There was no way around the fact that she wanted him. Just as much—no, probably *more*—than she had that first time.

Maybe it was just as well that it would be the last thing Dan would want to do with *her*.

Jenni had to reach past where Dan was beside his trolley with the syringes he was filling with medications and carefully labelling. He had taken off the gown over his scrubs so his arms were bare again and Jenni could actually feel the warmth of his skin as her own arm came too close to touching his.

Startled, she glanced sideways to find Dan had looked up from his task.

Just for a heartbeat.

But it was long enough for Jenni to feel a much sharper echo of that unacceptable sensation.

It was also long enough to see what looked disconcertingly like a reflection of what she was feeling in Dan's eyes.

Oh, dear Lord...

That connection was still there, wasn't it?

And, at a visceral level, it wasn't affected by anything else that was going on between them.

Because this was all about sex...

CHAPTER FIVE

THE PRIMAL GROAN was an indication of how much effort was being put into this push to help deliver a baby, but there was enough pain mixed in with the sound to be an indication that a top-up was required for Ashleigh's epidural anaesthetic.

It also felt weirdly like an echo of the way Daniel Walker was feeling at having to come back into this room. A few hours' respite hadn't really blunted the shock of the revelation that Jenni was pregnant with twins.

It wasn't so much the fact that she was carrying two babies that was messing with his head, though. It was that he'd been so prepared to use his observation that she had a bit more of a bump than he would have expected as confirmation that she was lying to him.

He felt ashamed of himself, to be honest. Part of that initial intense connection he'd felt with Jenni had been down to feeling safe with her. Knowing instinctively that she could be trusted as much as he trusted her brother.

But in the end he hadn't trusted her, had he?

So this felt awkward, especially when it was added to his avoidance of that conversation that was still hanging in the air as unfinished business between himself and Jenni. A perfect time to have that conversation was never going to turn up, so he was going to have to take advantage of the first private time that appeared.

Which wasn't going to be any time soon. They both had work to do.

Dan swiftly drew up and administered the drugs into the port on the end of the catheter and then found a spot where he could stay out of the way but keep an eye on his patient's vital signs every five minutes for the next half an hour or so.

Not that it was likely to take that long for the birth to occur as Ashleigh was well into the second stage of her labour. Dan would need to stay longer than that, however. Active management of the third stage in a woman with pre-eclampsia was important because there was an increased risk of a postpartum haemorrhage. Adjusting the anaesthetic for surgical intervention would be his responsibility if an urgent trip to Theatre became necessary.

In the meantime, he could see a monitor screen that gave him the figures for Ashleigh's heart rate and the automatic cuff was supplying a blood pressure recording every few minutes. He could count her respirations between contractions at least, and noting a sedation score was purely observation.

He could also watch Jenni McKay at work for the first time and she was so intensely involved with what she was doing she had no idea that she was also under observation.

'Breathe in deeply now, Ashleigh. Try and feel your tummy expanding. I'm just going to get another pillow between your legs, okay?'

Ashleigh made no response. She had dropped her head to lean into the crook of Craig's arm. She was lying on her side, her upper leg already supported by one pillow. Jock, gowned and gloved, was at the foot of the bed. Dan knew that the nearby covered trolley would have sterile kits available with equipment like forceps and vacuum cups for assisted delivery.

Jenni was rubbing Ashleigh's lower back after positioning the pillow and Dan saw her take a deep breath.

'Here we go…you've got another contraction starting. Keep your tummy out, breathe out really slowly through pursed lips and push down into your bottom. As hard as you can…that's great…you're doing *so* well… Keep it up, Ashleigh… Push and push and *push…*'

The broad Glaswegian accent was very familiar, thanks to having spent so much time with Jock since he'd arrived in Picton, and because of the friendship between the two men it also made him feel as if he was in good company.

Safe company…

There was more to listening to Jenni, however. The focus she had on Ashleigh—the encouragement and caring in her tone—was so compelling to listen to. Dan found himself unconsciously copying the breathing instructions. Watching the expressions on Jenni's face was just as compelling. She was demonstrating the breathing techniques, pursing her lips or taking a new breath, screwing up her face to mirror the strain of pushing and then her features would relax into a smile as she praised the efforts.

A look and then a swift nod passed between Jock and Jenni and Dan knew that the arrival of this baby was imminent.

'Don't push with this breath, Ashleigh. I want you to pant. Short breaths, like you're blowing out the candles on the biggest birthday cake in the world. Good girl…that's perfect… your baby's almost here…'

Dan couldn't look away. Everyone else in this room was watching this baby crowning and then sliding into the world but Dan hadn't shifted his gaze.

Jenni McKay was…

Stunning, that was what she was.

Not only physically beautiful, with that fiery red hair and pale, perfect skin and the brightest blue eyes he'd ever seen. She had this...glow...that came from within. Something fierce but gentle at the same time. Clever but still eager to learn.

Confident but vulnerable.

Things that should have been contradictions but seemed absolutely compatible.

She was intriguing.

So damned attractive it was dangerous.

The cry of the baby finally broke the moment, but not until he saw the huge smile that lit up Jenni's face even more and the sparkle in her eyes that could well have been caused by tears. She had a towel in her hands to take the slippery baby from Jock.

'He's gorgeous,' Jenni pronounced, smiling down at the baby as she held him for a moment to wipe his face with a corner of the towel. 'Such a bonny wee lad...'

She glanced up as she lifted the baby to put it on Ashleigh's chest, skin to skin, and caught Dan's gaze. She was still smiling. The kind of smile that went with the joy of witnessing the arrival of new life and the magic of a new family being created. Dan had seen it many times, of course, but he'd always managed to stay detached.

It had never felt like this.

He'd never thought he would feel this again, in fact. This... bone-deep yearning to have that family bond. To be a father.

He could imagine Jenni holding up one of her own babies like this. One of the babies that she said he was the father of.

He could imagine being that father. Feeling the relief of his son's safe arrival, the astonishment of this miracle of life happening before his eyes and...all the hope for a future that he'd only dreamed of having.

If only what Jenni believed to be the truth actually *was* the truth.

Dan had to stamp on that flash of a thought. It couldn't be allowed. He wasn't going to be sucked back into even hoping there was any possibility of it being true because that was the portal into a world that could feel so solid and secure and then simply disintegrate and mix your soul into the broken shards.

Jock was busy actively managing the third stage of labour. He had no idea he was handing Dan a lifeline when he handed him a labelled syringe to administer into the IV line he was about to flush to make sure it was still patent.

'This is some oxytocin we're giving you,' Jock told Ashleigh. 'It'll help with the delivery of the placenta and things should start to settle down for you after that.'

Dan let a long breath out as he slowly injected the medication. He could only hope that things might start to settle down for him as well.

Jenni was in no rush to go home, even though her shift had finished some time ago.

It had been a pleasure to be there to help Ashleigh and Craig with the first breastfeeding of their son and then catch up on what was some very detailed paperwork for a birth that needed careful medical management. Ashleigh was still receiving medication by IV infusion to control her blood pressure and prevent seizures so intensive observation was in place for the next twenty-four hours and a hospital stay of at least three days was recommended. It had taken some time for Jenni to provide a thorough handover for the nursing staff who would continue Ashleigh's care overnight and she finished up by calling Jock, who'd gone home over an hour ago. He was more than happy with the report on his most recent patient.

'You should go home and get some rest, Jen. It's been a long day.'

'I'm going now.'

'You're welcome to come here for dinner. Grace would love to see you. She's hanging out to hear how your appointment went with Maria this morning.'

'I've got a day off tomorrow. Tell her I'll bring some lunch and bore her with all the details. Right now, all I want to do is go home, have a long shower and blob out on the couch.'

Jock laughed. 'Fair play... See you later...'

Jenni left the birthing suite and maternity ward and headed for the corridor on the other side of the central space with the lifts and stairwell and a wall of windows that looked down on the gardens between the hospital buildings and the main road. Consultants' offices and on-call rooms were tucked into this space, along with the staff locker room, where Jenni had left her bag and clothes, including the comfortable trainers she needed to walk home in.

She was at the entrance to that corridor when she heard her name being called and she turned her head in surprise.

'*Dan*... You haven't been called to see Ashleigh, have you?' The beat of concern was for a complication from the epidural or spinal anaesthetic.

'No...'

'Have you got someone else in labour who needs an epidural?'

'No... I...was hoping to find you, actually.'

'Oh...' Jenni felt the thump of a missed heartbeat. Had Dan seen something in her expression earlier today? Had he felt the strength of those totally inappropriate thoughts about his body? She had to look away from him now, to make sure he didn't catch any lingering guilt about that. Or maybe to stop them coming back with renewed potency due to there not being any need to focus on professional responsibilities. There was no one else to hide any previous personal connection from either.

But Dan's expression was apologetic rather than accusatory. 'I keep waiting for the right time to talk to you,' he said. 'But I realised today that it's not going to magically happen unless I do something to *make* it happen.' His face softened into something close to a smile. 'So here I am, making it happen. Unless you need to be somewhere?'

Aye... Jenni needed to be standing in a long, hot shower, washing away the fatigue of a long day. Or lying on the couch with her feet up because she knew her ankles would be puffy by now after so much time on her feet with the extra weight she was now carrying. But this was important. And if she tried to walk away from Dan, Jenni suspected that her body would refuse the command.

The pull was astonishingly powerful. Magnetic...

'I'm done for the day,' she told Dan, letting her gaze flick back to catch his. 'I'm totally available.'

Oh, help...why on earth had she said something as ambiguous as that? She broke the eye contact and her line of vision shifted to the grouping of couches and chairs beside the windows. There was no one else taking advantage of the seating space or the view at the moment and Jenni would love to take the weight off her feet, but did she want to sit down next to Dan? What if her hormonally disrupted libido got even more out of control and he could see a thought bubble over her head that contained images rather than any words?

The kind of images that Jenni had deliberately kept fresh in her memory ever since that night...

She wasn't looking directly at Dan but she could feel *his* gaze. She needed to escape, she decided. But she'd just told him she was totally available and with that instant of hesitation it became too late to change her mind.

'I wish you'd told me,' he said quietly. 'That it's twins.'

One set of lift doors slid open behind Dan and a kitchen staff member pushed one of the big stainless-steel trolleys that contained in-patient meals into the foyer, coming closer to Jenni and Dan as she turned it to head towards the maternity ward.

Jenni stepped further into the corridor to give them the privacy that this conversation suddenly needed and Dan followed her lead. The open door beside her showed an on-call room that was unoccupied. Perfect. She went inside and then turned to face Dan, catching her bottom lip between her teeth.

'I thought that you finding out that there's one baby on the way would be enough of a shock to start with.'

'I did think your bump might have been a bit bigger than normal.' Dan cleared his throat. 'But then I thought you might have put on a bit of weight so I couldn't say anything or that… or…'

'That I was further along in my pregnancy than I said I was?' Jenni lifted an eyebrow. 'Of course you did. You thought I was lying anyway, didn't you?'

Dan looked totally lost for words. Guilty. Confused, even?

'You still think I'm lying, don't you?'

'No.' Dan's head shake was sharp. 'I don't.'

He was saying something else, about Jock telling him that she never lied or that she'd said that herself, but the words were blurring for Jenni.

He believed that what she'd told him was true and that was all that mattered, wasn't it?

Except that she could hear the note of doubt in his tone. As if it was still too much of a stretch to really believe that he'd beaten the odds and been able to father a child. She could understand how difficult that would be to get his head around. Jenni was more than happy to do a non-invasive prenatal paternity test. It only needed a blood sample from her and a cheek swab from him and the comparison of DNA had an accuracy of nearly a hundred percent.

Or was that pushing Dan too fast and too far?

There was time to do this with more consideration, wasn't there? With some empathy for how huge this was for Dan.

'I know how unbelievable this must seem,' she said. 'But… people do beat the odds. Some people even win the lottery. It might help if you got yourself tested again, Dan. Maybe the initial results weren't that accurate?'

He didn't believe any of that, she could see it in his eyes. But she could also see that doubt. The lack of comprehension and a good dollop of confusion. And…maybe even a little bit of hope?

It made him seem vulnerable.

It made her want to give him a hug.

To tell him that everything was going to be okay.

That she was happy to be having these babies and quite prepared to raise them herself. He wasn't going to have to do anything he really didn't want to do.

But then he surprised her. He was holding her gaze and his tone was as serious as his expression.

'A repeat test is worth considering,' he said. 'I'll make some enquiries about arranging one.'

It felt like a huge step had just been taken. Jenni found she couldn't look away from him. A wash of warmth that was a mix of relief and gratitude hit her like a small tsunami. She wanted to smile, but something was stopping her.

Another wave of sensation that had nothing to do with what they'd just been talking about.

It had nothing to do with anything that was going on with either of their lives outside of this room, in fact.

They'd both stepped back in time.

Oddly enough, it was back to that moment when Jenni had told him she never told lies. To that first moment when the connection between them had become something intimate and then overpowered everything else.

To that first kiss…

Maybe she did have a thought bubble that was visible and Dan could see the replay of that kiss that was filling her mind and fuelling the flames of desire flickering through her entire body.

Except he wasn't looking at the air over her head. His gaze hadn't shifted from hers and it felt as if Jenni was watching a replay of a whole lot more than that kiss in the depths of those sinfully dark eyes.

Not a word was spoken.

Dan used his foot to push the door of the room shut behind him and it closed with a definitive click that suggested the snib lock had fallen into place. And then he reached out with one hand as he stepped closer to Jenni, sliding his fingers around the back of her head to cradle it as he bent to cover her lips with his own.

Jenni heard herself make a sound like nothing she'd ever heard herself make before.

A sound of pure need.

She reached up with both arms to lock them around Dan's neck and stood up on tiptoes to press her body closer to his, not letting this kiss finish any time too soon.

She didn't want this to stop.

She wanted more. And she wanted it more than she'd ever wanted anything before in her entire life...

This really wasn't a good idea.

But Daniel Walker's body was having no trouble whatsoever in squashing that small voice in the back of his head that was issuing the warning.

He could even sidestep the pull into a part of his past he would never choose to revisit with the knowledge that he was making love to a woman who was carrying new life. It simply became part of a fantasy.

The perfect woman.

The perfect life.

The perfect sex...

Ultimately sensuous. Silent because there was nothing they needed to say aloud. They could communicate much more effectively with their bodies.

He hadn't forgotten the taste of Jenni's mouth, the heat of her tongue, the tendrils of fire her fingers created against his skin. What had dimmed, however, was just how explosive his reactions were and the difference in clarity was between memories and the real thing.

He had forgotten the tiny sounds she made as he touched *her* that made him feel as if he was giving her the world. As if she wanted him more than she could ever want anything.

As much as he wanted her in this moment.

The single bed in this on-call room was far from ideal, but it didn't matter. The loose scrubs they were wearing were too easy to slip out of and...dear Lord, that roundness of Jenni's belly was the sexiest thing Dan had ever seen. Or felt...but it also generated a new kind of protectiveness that had never been a part of physical intimacy for him before.

Did Jenni sense that beat of pulling back as he tried to control the fall into the climax neither of them could resist? Maybe that was why she took the initiative and chose a position that would put no weight on her belly. On top of Dan, where he could hold her hips in both hands and watch her face as *she* fell…

And that was as perfect as everything else about this.

He had no idea how long it took to come back to earth. For his heart to stop pounding and his breathing to return to normal. About as long as it took for Jenni, it seemed, because he could feel her heartbeat as he lay behind her, spooning her with one arm over her body. It was only then that he realised he was holding her hand.

Or she was holding his?

It didn't matter who had initiated the hand holding. What did matter was that Dan had broken one of his golden rules that he could only indulge in sexual encounters when there was no risk of seeing each other again.

Living in the same place was enough of a red flag. Working in the same place was totally unacceptable.

Except…this still felt safe.

Was that because Jenni was still only here for a short time? That she was on holiday, albeit a working one?

Like the holiday she'd been on the first time they'd met?

She would be heading back to Scotland again soon.

So, yeah…this did still feel safe…

It was Jenni who broke the silence. With two simple words.

'Thank you,' she whispered.

Dan smiled. His fingers tightened around hers.

'You have no idea how good that was,' she added.

His smile widened. 'Oh, I think I do.'

Jenni broke their hand hold as she rolled to face him. She was shaking her head. 'No…you're not the one tormented by pregnancy hormones,' she said. 'It's astonishing what it can do to a woman's libido.'

Dan blinked. Was that what this had been about? Just the sex, rather than anything to do with him?

Would it bother him if it was?

Yes…

No…

Who was he kidding? No man on earth would decline fantasy sex like that because someone was only interested in his body.

If anything, it only made it more perfect.

Even safer…

He cleared his throat. 'I hadn't realised that,' he said.

'It's not the same for everyone. I think I must have a bad dose.'

Dan could feel the breath of her sigh against his skin. 'Is it a problem?'

'It'll wear off. Give me another few weeks and it'll probably be the last thing I feel like.' Jenni's smile was pure mischief. 'Maybe I should make the most of it while it lasts.'

Dan was genuinely shocked, until he saw the gleam in her eyes that told him that this was an invitation.

A party that only he was going to be invited to.

They had been avoiding each other for weeks, thanks to the gulf of being blindsided and the swirling accusation and anger on both sides that made it impossible to find a way of closing that distance between them.

Well, they'd closed it now, hadn't they?

He'd only been planning to talk to Jenni. To try and suggest, politely, that a mistake had somehow been made.

What had made things change in such a dramatic fashion? Was it simply because they'd been alone and close enough for that overwhelming physical attraction to explode?

No. Of course it wasn't.

Dan knew perfectly well what had made that change. He could hear the echo of their earlier conversation.

'You still think I'm lying, don't you?'

'No... I don't.'

Should he have said more? That he believed *she* believed she wasn't lying?

Jenni had taken it to mean that he believed he was the father of her babies but he didn't believe that, did he? How could he?

She wouldn't either, if he went ahead and got that test and she could see the current results there in black and white.

In the meantime, was there any harm in being closer?

This close...?

Building a friendship, perhaps, that might mean they could part ways in the near future with no hard feelings on either side?

The internal discussion had happened in the space of no more than a heartbeat. Jenni was still giving him that look. Her naughty suggestion of making the most of her libido was still hanging in the air between them.

And Dan was smiling again.

'Let me know if I can help with that,' he murmured.

The soft gurgle of Jenni's laughter was as captivating as everything else about this woman.

'Mmm...' The sound suggested that the invitation might be rather tempting. 'I'll keep that in mind...'

CHAPTER SIX

'I'M PAST THE point of no return.'

'I suspect you were past that the moment you hooked up with Dan Walker.'

Jenni avoided meeting Grace's gaze. She hadn't guessed that something was going on again between herself and Dan, had she?

But Grace was smiling. 'You were definitely past it when you found out you were pregnant, weren't you?'

'That's true.' Jenni let out a relieved breath and opened the car's passenger door. 'I should have said I'm past the half-way point.'

'Well past, I would hope.' Grace laughed. 'You're nearly twenty-three weeks and twice that would be a ridiculous gestation even for a singleton.'

'I keep thinking of this as the twenty-week anomaly scan so it's usually halfway. I know I'm late but apparently it's helpful to leave the anomaly scan a bit longer for multiples. You can see more.' Jenni bit her lip. 'You don't mind coming with me, do you?'

'Are you kidding?' Grace handed her crutches to Jenni to stow in the back hatch. 'It's a treat to get out of the house and I can't wait to see the new members of the family.' But her smile was sympathetic. 'And I know it's a bit nerve-racking.'

'I just want them to be healthy. What if they've got congenital heart defects? That's the most common abnormality that gets picked up.' Jenni was watching Grace lift her injured foot into the car and got distracted as she saw her friend flinch. 'Your ankle's hurting, isn't it?'

'A bit. Maybe I was moving around too much yesterday. I got bored and sorted the kitchen boxes. And then I went down the steps to the jetty to have a look. Jock's been fixing it up ready to move *Lassie* from the marina to her new home.'

'Steps were not sensible.' Jenni shook her head as she peered at the parts of Grace's foot visible between the straps and casing of her walking boot. 'Aye...your toes look swollen. I think you need to get it checked out while we're at the hospital.'

'I'll see what Jock thinks. He's coming to the scan too, isn't he?'

'My instructions from the radiography department said I was allowed one relative or friend in the room.'

'You're a staff member. You can have anyone you want in there.' Grace waited until Jenni had done up her seatbelt and started the car before she spoke again. 'Maybe it'll be Mandy doing it. You met her, remember? The night before you went back to Scotland.'

'How could I forget? Last time I saw her she was on the dance floor, joined at the hip and dancing with that Italian doctor who was supposed to be my date for the night.'

Aye...and Daniel Walker had been invited as a potential date for Grace. Talk about Fate having a bit of a laugh.

The beat of something awkward told her that Grace was remembering how that had worked out as well. She sounded slightly hesitant when she spoke again.

'Did you ask Dan if he wanted to come to the ultrasound?'

'*No...*' The suggestion was unexpected. 'I haven't even asked if he's booked another sperm test yet. I can't push him,

Grace. He might believe I'm telling the truth but he obviously needs time to get used to the idea of being a father.'

'I reckon seeing his babies on the screen might be just the push he needs in the right direction. You're being too nice to him.' Grace's tone became puzzled. 'You've changed your mind about him completely, haven't you? You *like* him again…'

Jenni could feel the weight of the glance she was getting. She kept her eyes firmly on the road as she started driving. She knew that 'like' wasn't the word Grace would have chosen if she'd known what had happened in the on-call room the other day but Jenni had only revealed that she'd talked to Dan—that he'd told her he now believed she hadn't been lying to him and that he had agreed to have another fertility test.

She'd told herself she was keeping the rest of that encounter a secret because things were complicated enough already, but maybe the truth was that she was being sucked into a fantasy world again.

A different one, this time. This wasn't about amazing sex with a gorgeous stranger she was never going to see again. This was about a fairy tale family, complete with a mother and a father and children who were the centre of their world, coming together and living happily ever after. She could almost imagine the tears of joy on Dan's face when they opened the envelope together that would give them the results of the DNA test with the truth there in black and white for the whole world to see.

It wasn't going to happen like that, of course. Jenni knew that. This was real life, with all the complications and emotional baggage that had the potential to cloud any major life event. Even if Dan did accept that he was the father of her children and decided that he wanted an active part in their lives, it wasn't going to lead to any kind of committed relationship.

Jenni might have changed her mind about becoming a mother but the aversion to getting married was still very much intact, thanks to the legacy her mother had left behind. She'd always found it so easy to fall head over heels in love and she'd always been so convinced that this man was 'the one'. That she was always going to be this happy and that life would finally be as perfect as she had dreamed it could be. Jenni and Jock had been only too happy to believe it too. Because life had been so much better when their mother was happy. Because what they'd wanted more than anything was a real family. To be loved and cared for. To be wanted.

It had always fallen apart, of course. And it had always been their fault. Jenni was never going to risk her babies believing they were responsible for their mother's bad choices and failed relationships.

Believing in the dreams of a 'real' family might be long gone, but indulging in them a little could be like a mood-enhancing drug and there could be a happi*er* ending than she'd been beginning to expect. To have Dan acknowledge paternity and want to be part of his children's lives was worth being open to. Hoping for, even. To have him as part of her life, even if it was temporary, was...

Well...it was irresistible, to be honest.

That sex had been the best ever and, with the memory of the first time they'd made love, that was saying something...

It had been too long since he'd had an afternoon off.

So long, it seemed like the last time he and Jock had been out fishing together was only a distant memory. Dan glanced at the clock in the locker room as he finished changing into his civvies, wondering what time Jock might be finishing work today. Hadn't he said something, during the chaos of moving house and dealing with Grace's injury, about there being a few rotten boards on the jetty at his new place that needed fixing before he moved his boat? Dan could help with that. It might be a good way to check that their friendship wasn't being irreparably undermined by what was happening between himself and Jenni.

On the other hand, it might be better if Jock didn't know what had happened most recently between them.

Oh, man…

The *sex*…

Every man's dream. An unexpected sexual encounter that had been hot enough to smelt iron into steel. With a woman who was going to be out of the country in a matter of a few weeks, which made it almost possible to ignore the obvious strings attached.

For the moment, anyway.

Dan coiled his stethoscope, put it inside his battered leather satchel and hung the strap over his shoulder. He was ready to head home.

Except that he was still thinking about the sex and he certainly wasn't ignoring those strings. Because they'd added a whole new dimension to the experience. The physical things like the rounded belly and breasts that had such a delicious fullness to them were gorgeous but superficial. What was staying even longer in Dan's mind was the appreciation of something different about Jenni. A confidence, perhaps? Or a contentment? Whatever it was, she was in a space where she was in charge of her life and that was damned sexy all by itself.

She'd kind of been in charge of the sex too, choosing positions that were the most comfortable and some of those had been off-the-charts sexy.

Dan shut the door of his locker with a deliberate slam.

Was he hoping the jarring sound would distract him before he needed to take a cold shower? It would definitely be a good idea to avoid Jock's company right now, he decided.

He should have known he was tempting fate.

He could almost hear a faint suggestion of cosmic laughter when he walked into the hospital's foyer to get to the main doors and found Jock, Jenni and Grace in front of the corridor that led to the radiology department. Dan wondered if it might be possible to pretend he hadn't seen them and keep heading outside, but Jenni's head was turning in that instant—as if she could feel his presence even though he was too far away to even call out a greeting.

And her face lit up as if she was delighted to see him.

Jock had seen that change in his sister's face as well and he turned his head to spot Dan, so there was no chance to side-step this encounter. He needed to draw on his considerable ability to hide any inappropriate emotional reaction to anything around him. Like he did with every professional inter-action he had. Yes…that was the way to go. Dan would act as if these people were a patient's family.

Or was one of them an actual patient?

Grace wasn't looking very happy at all She was pale and tired-looking and leaning heavily on her crutches. He could hear that she sounded upset as he got closer.

'I don't need a wheelchair, Jock.'

'You shouldn't be on your feet. Not until we know what's going on. You need an X-ray. Hi, Dan…' Jock was frowning. 'What do *you* think?'

'About…?'

'Grace's toes.'

Dan dropped his gaze but it was an effort when what he really wanted to do was make eye contact with Jenni. He wanted to know if it had been his imagination that made it look as though she was so pleased to see him. If it wasn't, he wanted to know if there was any chance she would like to see him alone.

And *when*…

It was a good thing that he needed to look at Grace's toes.

'They look like sausages,' he said.

Jock huffed with laughter. 'That's your professional opinion, is it, mate?'

'What are the limb baselines like?'

'Haven't had a chance to find out.' Jock glared at Grace. 'I was about to take Grace into Emergency and get someone to page whoever's on call for Orthopaedics.'

'I'll do it later,' Grace said. 'I'm not going to miss going to Jenni's scan with her. She's nervous enough as it is.'

Something dropped in the pit of Dan's stomach. He caught Jenni's gaze but any questions he might have wanted answers to had evaporated completely.

'Is something wrong?'

She shook her head. 'Not at all. I'm just here for the twenty-week anomaly scan. A belated one,' she added hurriedly, as if she knew Dan was trying to make sense of conflicting information on the stage of her pregnancy.

'But you're nervous?'

She shrugged, her smile a little embarrassed. 'There are times when ignorance is definitely bliss. I seem to have a long list of birth defects and genetic abnormalities that are chasing each other around in my brain.' She turned back to Grace. 'You should absolutely go and get your ankle checked.'

'I can do it later, after your appointment.'

'What if it's a blood clot? You're not going to collapse with a pulmonary embolism in the middle of my scan, thanks very much.'

Grace looked torn. 'Jock can go with you, then. I don't want you doing this alone.'

But Jock was also looking torn. And slightly paler at Jenni's suggestion of a serious complication with Grace's ankle fracture.

'*I* could go with you.'

The words were out of Dan's mouth before he could stop them and they fell into a silence that was sudden enough to make it very clear that they were all aware of the significant undercurrents here.

What had he done?

Wow…

For a heartbeat, Jenni was completely shocked. Was this it? Dan stepping up to acknowledge that he was the father of these babies? That he was invested in their wellbeing and he wanted to be a part of their lives?

Why else would he want to see them before they were born?

Jock and Grace were looking a wee bit stunned as well.

Even Dan looked as if he couldn't quite believe what he'd just said.

But the moment passed almost as instantly as it had arrived as Jock's lips curved into a smile that suggested the perfect solution had been found.

'Good on you, mate,' he said quietly. Then he turned back to Grace. 'Don't move,' he ordered. 'I'm going to get a wheelchair from Reception.'

Movement helped dilute the undercurrents. Jenni helped get Grace settled into the wheelchair and then the small group broke up. Jock wheeled Grace towards the emergency department and Jenni and Dan walked into Radiology.

'I'm Jenni McKay,' Jenni told the receptionist. 'I've got an appointment for an ultrasound.'

'Ah...yes. You're with Mandy. She told us you were coming. You're Jock McKay's sister, aren't you?'

'I am.'

The receptionist shifted her gaze to Dan. Jenni's heart sank as the young woman's eyebrows rose. Dan must have known he would be recognised in his workplace. He'd also know how fast a rumour would get around a hospital. Jenni felt suddenly protective. Dan was taking a huge step here. He didn't deserve to be the subject of generalised gossip at the same time.

'Jock was going to come with me,' she told the receptionist. 'But he's caught up. Dan offered to come instead—as a friend. My instructions did say I could bring a family member *or* a friend.'

'Okay...yes, that's fine...' The slightly disappointed tone told Jenni that she'd been successful in diverting attention from Dan. 'Take a seat and you'll be called soon.'

The receptionist might be disappointed but the glance from Dan told Jenni that he appreciated his privacy being respected.

As much as Jenni appreciated that he was here with her?

Two parents, about to get a peek at their unborn children?

She didn't mind keeping it a secret at all. They both knew the truth and that was what really mattered.

The ultrasound technician, Mandy, accepted the same story that Dan was just filling in for Jenni's friend and brother to keep her company.

'I get it.' She nodded. 'Everybody's nervous of this scan so it's good to have someone with you.' She smiled at Jenni. 'Must be hard doing this bit alone—so far from home. I'll get lots of pictures for you so you can share them with everyone.'

'Thanks so much...that will be great.'

Jenni was settling back on the pillows. The big screen on top of the ultrasound machine was tilted in her direction. Mandy sat in front of it with another screen amongst all the controls, squeezed some gel onto Jenni's abdomen and then picked up the transducer. She grinned at Dan.

'You don't have to stand in the corner,' she said. 'Come and sit down. It's not that scary. You might be doing this for real one day, you know.'

Dan said nothing, but sat down on the chair on the other side of the bed, which put him right beside Jenni's head. It was a position that made it easy for the extra person to see the screen clearly. It was close enough for it to be easy for the father of the baby to hold the hand of the mother-to-be.

This was as close as he was ever going to get to doing this 'for real'. If he let himself, just for a few minutes, he could pretend it *was* real, but he wasn't about to do that.

No way…

For a while, it was easy. Fascinating, in fact, as Mandy expertly manoeuvred the transducer until she got the view she wanted and then froze images on her screen for a few seconds, swiftly shifting cursors to mark points and measure parameters. She was good at her job and gave them as much information as she could—probably a lot more than she would have with patients who weren't medical colleagues.

'They probably used the crown to rump length of the smaller twin to establish gestational age in your first trimester scan, but it's less accurate in the second trimester. The measurements are still within an acceptable range for variation, though. You don't have an accurate date of your last menstrual period, do you?'

'No. I've never been that regular and I think that international travel and jetlag might have disrupted things even further.'

'Jetlag is horrible,' Mandy said. 'Must have been worth it for such an amazing trip, though, right?'

'It was a memorable trip,' Jenni agreed.

'And you're back again already. Can't keep away from us, huh?'

'Something like that, aye…'

Jenni had her lips pressed together as she let her gaze slide sideways to Dan in a brief flicker of eye contact. It looked as though she was trying not to smile—with that hint of a suggestion that making love with him again might be too tempting to resist. The same kind of smile she'd given him in the on-call room when he'd offered to help her with her out-of-control libido.

Dan felt one of his eyebrows flicker as he tried to send back a silent message.

Just say the word, babe… I won't say no…

Why would he? In the big picture of his life, this was just a few pixels. A few weeks and then it would be nothing more than a very pleasant memory.

The perfect kind of relationship as far as Daniel Walker was concerned.

The only kind, in fact.

And he'd regained his normal level of emotional control. Look at him now—keeping a safe, clinical kind of distance even while negotiating an emotional minefield of disturbing memories, broken dreams, accusations and mistakes.

Mandy was back in clinical mode too.

'Okay…look…this is a four-chamber view of Twin A's heart. We can see normal anatomical structure and ventricular function. Heart rate's also normal at one forty beats per minute. Looking good…'

No abnormalities were seen with either twin's heart. Or

their brains. They both had two kidneys and no hint of mal-alignment or other issues with their spines. Minutes ticked past to become an hour and kept going. The position of the placentas had been confirmed, and the gender of the babies.

'One of each.' Mandy nodded. 'Perfect.'

Twin B made it difficult for Mandy to locate a view to measure the length of both a femur and a humerus. She focused on the screen as she repeatedly shifted the transducer and the silence grew until it was uncomfortable.

Dan was starting to wonder if he could slip away at some point soon. Maybe Jock, with or without Grace, would turn up and be able to take over keeping Jenni company? He wasn't really paying attention to the blobs on the screen when they shifted and morphed into something new so he certainly wasn't expecting to have one of those emotional mines detonate right in front of him but…there it was…

A tiny hand that was moving as though it was waving at him. He could see the miniature fingers clearly enough to count them. He could almost feel what it would be like to have them closing around his own finger and the curl of sensation that speared his chest took his breath away.

This was the tiny hand of a real person and suddenly this became a fantasy moment—a glimpse into what his life could have been like if it hadn't fallen apart in such a spectacular fashion.

He must have made a sound. Or perhaps Jenni had the ability to sense his emotions even when she wasn't looking at him, because she turned her head in that split second and caught his gaze. Just for a heartbeat before she was drawn back to that screen, but it was long enough for it to become part of the fantasy—as if they were both looking at the hand of one of their own babies.

Except that this crossed the boundary between fantasy and reality, didn't it? Because Jenni actually believed this *was* his baby's hand that he was seeing for the first time. If Dan wanted to, he could step into that space and be the father he'd always dreamed of being. He could decide not to get himself tested and, as infinitesimal as the possibility was, he could let himself believe that a miracle *had* happened. He could suggest to Jenni that no DNA tests really needed to be done. He could become a part of her life and help her raise the twins— as their father. Perhaps they could even get married and live happily ever after?

Except they would all be living a lie, and that would be unacceptable for everybody involved.

But…and the thought came so unexpectedly it stole Dan's breath.

What if they didn't have to lie?

What if it was all out in the open right from the start?

If it didn't actually matter that he wasn't the father?

People had found ways around their inability to have their own children for ever. Babies were adopted. Surrogates could be used. Assisted fertility with sperm or egg donations if necessary were commonplace these days. If his marriage hadn't imploded perhaps that was how Dan would have achieved his own family in the end. But he'd felt betrayed enough to never let anyone close enough again to form the kind of relationship that would be a strong foundation to share parenthood.

Did he feel safe enough to let Jenni that close?

Maybe…

Could he be a father to children that weren't biologically related to himself? Love them as if they *were* his own? Judging by the way he'd felt when he'd seen that tiny hand on the ultrasound screen, the answer to that question was a resounding 'yes'.

The prospect of his life changing to that degree was everything he could have dreamed of.

But the prospect of it all going horribly wrong was scary enough that it would make it easy to back away.

The scales were tipping. One way and then the other. With fear on one side and a bone-deep yearning on the other.

Dan pulled in a deep breath that felt shaky.

Jenni must have heard—or felt—that wobble. When she glanced up at Dan, this time, she had tears in her eyes. That she was as overcome with emotion as he was created an astonishingly powerful connection.

He hadn't realised that he had his hand resting on the side of the bed until Jenni's fingers touched his. She had already turned back to the screen but she didn't take her hand away. Her fingers curled around his to cup them gently and Dan didn't take his hand away as he also shifted his gaze back to the screen. He could see the rest of the arm now and the image stilled as Mandy clicked to measure the bone length between the elbow and shoulder. He could see the baby's head in profile, with a tiny button of a nose and a mouth that he could imagine was smiling.

Dan could feel his own lips curving and he had to swallow a lump in his throat. He closed his fingers around Jenni's so that he was holding her hand properly.

Those scales had stopped rocking.

Yearning had won, at least for now. Maybe that was because there was nothing permanent about this. The clock was ticking and it was only a matter of time before everything changed again. This window was the only time that Dan would ever have to be this close to the dream.

And that was huge.

The fear had simply been outweighed.

CHAPTER SEVEN

'YOU'RE GETTING STARED AT. *We're* getting stared at.'

'People find obvious pregnancy fascinating for some reason. Maybe they think there's a chance I could go into labour or even give birth in a public playground.' Jenni offered Dan a slightly apologetic smile. 'And I guess they assume we're a couple so we're walking around advertising the fact that we have sex occasionally.'

Dan laughed. 'Want to sit down for a minute?' He gestured towards park bench that was currently empty. 'We're going to be too early for dinner even if we take a detour to the beach on the way.'

Jenni was quite happy to sit and rest. She loved this area of Picton with its majestic palm trees on the edge of an area that was a community magnet on a sunny late Sunday afternoon. People walked dogs or pushed prams on the pathways, sat on the grass in the sun to read a book or have a picnic and, most popular—there was a children's playground that even included a huge pirates' ship to climb on and play inside.

'Playgrounds have changed since I was a kid,' Dan said. 'We were lucky to have a row of swings, a slide and a seesaw.'

'Did you have those witch's hat things in New Zealand? Where you sat or stood on a narrow wooden edge and hung onto the spokes and it whirled around and went up and down at the same time.' Jenni blew out a breath. 'I was terrified of them.'

'I remember an iron horse,' Dan told her. 'With bars to hang onto in front of all the metal saddles in a row. It was on springs and you could make it rock hard enough for someone to lose their grip and go flying. All good fun—unless you were the one who got bucked off.'

'Did you have brothers and sisters to go on the horse with you?'

Jenni felt almost shy asking the question. There was too much she didn't know about the father of her children so it was lovely to be getting into the habit of spending more time with just the two of them. Getting to know each other better as Dan began to let his guard down and talk more. Right now, they were on their way to the Brazilian barbecue restaurant that had been where they'd met for the very first time. Just them. They hadn't invited Jock or Grace.

Dan didn't seem to mind the personal question. 'No,' he said. 'But I had lots of cousins. I got brought up by an aunt on my mother's side of the family, after my parents died in a car crash. Big Pasifika families always seem to have room for one more...' He hesitated for a moment. 'But I was just one in a crowd. It wasn't quite *mine*, you know...?'

'I do know,' Jenni said quietly. 'It must be a bit like being in a foster home. Even if the families we went to seemed like they genuinely wanted me and Jock to be there, we never felt like we really belonged.'

Dan nodded. 'That's why I wanted to get married and have a bunch of kids. A big family that was all mine.'

'And I went in the opposite direction and decided to never even try to have a family.' Jenni laughed. 'Look at us now.' She put her hands on the mound of her belly. 'They're having a bit of a party in here.' She reached out and caught Dan's hand and put it where her hand had just been. 'Can you feel that?'

Dan's face went very still and then his lips curved in a gentle smile as he spread his fingers to feel the ripples of the baby moving beneath them. The first time he'd done this had been when they were in bed together, just after Dan had come to that ultrasound scan with her. When things had changed between them.

This wasn't simply about the sex any longer. Maybe it was because her pregnancy hormones were changing and that flush of libido was fading. Or—and Jenni suspected this was the real reason—it was the feeling that they were becoming a real couple. That the relationship they were forming between each other was just as important as the bond Jenni was hoping would form between her babies and their father.

Not a real couple in the sense of it being a permanent relationship, of course—like a marriage—but still a couple.

Two people who had created children together.

Parents that would have a bond that would last for a lifetime.

Friends…?

A woman walked past the bench and noticed Dan's hand on her belly. Her smile suggested that she knew they were a lot more than friends and Jenni felt herself catch her breath. They weren't a *real* couple. She knew what happened when you believed that a perfect future depended on being a real couple.

Dan's hand slipped off her belly as she got to her feet.

'I'm starving,' she announced. 'If we turn up, I'm sure they'll let us have our table a bit early. I don't want to be out late, anyway. Early start tomorrow. Grace is coming in to do her first antenatal clinic since the accident.'

'Grace…you're back! I'm so happy to see you.'

'My first day. And I'm just very part-time for a while. I'm

testing my ankle by helping Jenni with the clinic this morning. How are you, Lynn?'

Lynn handed her urine sample to Jenni. 'Counting the days.
I told Chris this morning that he gets to have the next kid in
this family.'

'He's not with you today? It's been too long since I last
saw you both.'

'I know. We were so disappointed when we heard about
your accident and that you might not be with us for the birth.
No offence, Jenni.'

'None taken.' Jenni was unscrewing a jar to get a dipstick.

'He couldn't make it today—urgent appointment with one
of his clients. I told him he didn't need to come. This is the
perfect pregnancy and nothing is going to go wrong.' Lynn
beamed at Grace. 'Do you think you'll be properly back on
deck for our big day? Will four weeks or so be enough time?'

Jenni gave Grace a stern look. 'Only if she follows the rules.
She overdid it a while back and ended up in Emergency with
a foot that looked more like a foot*ball*.'

'Oh, *no*... Ankles can be tricky, can't they?'

'It's fine,' Grace said. 'They had to check that the align-
ment of the fracture repair was still okay, but it came right
after I kept my weight off it for a few days. I'm walking well
now, but I can only increase the time on my feet gradually.
With a bit of luck, I'll be able to be with you and Chris when
your baby arrives.'

'And if you're not? Will you still be here, Jenni?'

'I'll keep my fingers crossed, but it might be cutting it a bit
fine. I haven't booked my tickets yet, but I'm almost twenty-
eight weeks now and the cut-off for flying when you're carrying multiples is thirty-two weeks.'

'You're nearly as big as me.'

'I'm starting to feel it,' Jenni said. 'Not that I'm ready to slow down yet, but my ankles can be very puffy by the end of the day. It's probably a good thing I'll be job sharing with Grace from now on. Now...let's get you up on the bed and Grace can do your tummy check.'

Jenni took the opportunity to sit down for a moment then, noting the normal result of the urine analysis in Lynn's notes. Unconsciously, she found herself feeling for the upper border of her own uterus when Grace was doing the same on Lynn's exposed belly as she began the abdominal examination.

The strong kick and then another from the small feet beneath Jenni's hand made her smile.

It had made Dan smile yesterday too, hadn't it? And not just at the playground.

Jenni closed her eyes as she let out a slow breath, letting herself sink back into the pleasure of their time together after they'd been out to dinner.

The sex had been very gentle.

Very slow.

Unbelievably delicious...

He had spooned her for a while afterwards, with his arms around her, both hands cradling her bump in the hope of feeling the babies moving again, but he hadn't stayed the night.

He never did.

Because they weren't a real couple. Neither of them wanted to be.

And Jenni would be going home to Scotland very soon.

She still felt safe.

When she opened her eyes again, pulling herself back into the present, Grace was lifting the tape measure she had stretched across Lynn's belly and swapping it for the foetal Doppler to check the heart rate.

'Fundal height thirty-seven centimetres and heart rate is one-seventy,' she told Jenni, who noted it. 'Your baby's following every rule in the book,' she told Lynn.

The rest of the antenatal visit went just as smoothly and then Grace took a seat at the desk and put her foot up on another chair.

'You should have your feet up too,' she told Jenni.

Jenni laughed. 'We'd look a right pair if someone came into the room, wouldn't we?' She picked up her pen. 'Let's get these notes sorted. I think you've been here long enough for your first day back.'

'Ooh… I like having a secretary.' Grace leaned back in her chair. 'Lynn Grimshaw, primigravida, thirty-seven weeks. On examination, abdomen gravid, appropriate for dates, linea nigra present. On palpation—a singleton foetus, longitudinal lie and cephalic presentation.' She was smiling. 'I've missed this.'

'What—all the paperwork? Or being at work?'

'Being at work with *you*.' Grace held Jenni's gaze. 'I don't want you to go back to Glasgow, Jen.'

'But I have to.'

'Why?'

Jenni blinked. Surely the answer was obvious? 'Because it's home.'

'But isn't home where the heart is?'

'And my heart's in Scotland,' Jenni said. 'Where I grew up. Where Jock and I both grew up knowing what it was like to never feel like we had a real home. I'm not going to let my kids feel like that. Ever. And I don't have to. I've got a house there. I've got a job to go back to.'

'But you've got family here. Your brother. And *me*…'

'You guys might decide to come back to the UK one day.'

Grace shook her head. 'We love it here. We're actually going to go and talk to someone about applying for permanent residency and, hopefully, citizenship down the track.'

Jenni's heart sank. She'd be living on the other side of the world from the only real family that her children had, apart from their mother. If she added their father into the lineup, it was starting to feel…wrong…?

'You're going to need all the help you can get when these babies turn up.' Grace's tone held a plea. 'Who better to do that than their uncle and auntie?'

'I can't stay here to give *birth*…' Jenni shook her head to underline how unacceptable the suggestion was. 'I've got to get home well before they're due. I've got a lot of organising to do. Bassinets and nappies and clothes and goodness only knows how many other things.' She blew out a breath. 'I'd better start making some proper lists. And book my tickets home. How did I think that I had plenty of time and I could just ignore it all?'

Because she'd been floating along in the very unexpected new relationship kind of bubble she'd found herself in with Dan?

Aye…doing something as practical as booking her flights home would have burst that bubble in a hurry.

They'd both known that it was temporary, of course—that was part of the reason they had allowed themselves to indulge in the pleasure of their attraction to each other, wasn't it? But the reminder of the cut-off point for international travel for pregnant women this morning had been a wake-up call that the end was rapidly approaching.

The clock was ticking quite loudly, in fact.

And that was a bit of a shock, to be honest.

Grace must have seen how disconcerted Jenni suddenly was.

'Sorry, I didn't mean to stress you out.' Grace made a face. 'Hey… I've got lists that we give to first time mums on their initial antenatal visit. I'll print you a copy.'

'Thanks. Are you coming in tomorrow?'

'Yes. I'd like to come with you for the home visits you've got scheduled and see how well I do with different houses and steps and so on.'

'Good plan. But you need to be honest if it gets too much for your ankle and I'll drop you home. Overdoing it at this stage would be silly.'

Grace made a face but nodded her agreement and then smiled. 'And you're coming to dinner, remember? Jock and Dan have a day off and they're fixing the last bit of the jetty and then they're going to go and get *Lassie* and bring her home. If the weather stays this nice, we might have a picnic on the beach.' She was watching Jenni carefully. 'That's not a problem, is it? Having an evening with Dan?'

'Um…no…' Jenni cleared her throat. 'We've actually been getting on quite well recently…'

Perhaps it was the tone of her voice. Or the certain type of smile she couldn't suppress. Or maybe her friend just knew her too well, because Grace's eyebrows rose sharply.

'*How* well?' She was still staring at Jenni. 'Oh, my God… are you *blushing*, Jenni McKay?'

'I never blush.'

'You blush all the time. You're a redhead.'

'So's Jock. I've never seen *him* blush.'

'He's a boy.' Grace was still smiling. 'I wonder if Dan's going to tell him what's been going on?'

'I doubt it. It's not as though it's anything significant. We're just…friends, I guess.'

Grace's smile faded. 'You're a bit more than friends.'

Jenni broke the eye contact. 'Aye, well…we've got a bond that's going to be there for the rest of our lives. It will be better if our relationship is amicable.'

Amicable…? That was a bit of a joke, given how close they'd been—again—only last night.

But Grace didn't pick her up on her word choice. Her brow was furrowed now, as though she was worried about something.

'Maybe that's the best reason of all to have your babies here,' she said quietly. 'To let their father bond with them.'

Oh, *help*…

Jenni could feel a prickle of sensation on her skin right now—as if Dan's hands were on her belly again, the way they had been last night. She could feel his pleasure in feeling the ripples and bulges of the movement of the tiny bodies beneath her skin. How much more intense would it be for him to be actually touching—and holding—his babies in their first moments of life?

She would be denying him that experience.

And that was definitely something she could start feeling guilty about.

This was like old times.

Before life had been tipped upside down.

To one side, Daniel Walker could see the white-tipped ripples of the wake Jock's boat was making as they left the marina behind and gained some speed. If he turned his head, he could see Jock at *Lassie*'s wheel, focused on the route he was taking to get his boat home to tie up at his own jetty.

They'd spent all day working on the jetty. They'd removed some decking boards to replace the last rotten beam and rafters beneath, replaced the decking boards and then finished with a coat of timber stain. They'd carried the portable barbecue and a chilly bin full of beers down the steps to the small private beach and then set off to collect *Lassie*. The jetty would be dry and the beers still cold by the time they got back to enjoy the picnic dinner planned for later.

'Have we got time to stop and catch a snapper to go on that barbecue?'

Jock threw a look over his shoulder. 'Sadly, no. But Grace has got some fancy sausages from that gourmet butcher in town for us tonight.' Jock grinned. 'It's one of our favourite dinners. I reckon she started falling in love with me when I fed her their traditional British bangers.' He was looking straight ahead of the boat again now but Dan could still hear him clearly. 'Jenni's coming over. She'll be there by now...'

Something tightened in Dan's gut with an extremely pleasurably twinge. Okay, maybe this wasn't really like old times, when he and Jock would spend a day out fishing and then share a dinner at the old villa that was the hospital accommodation for temporary or new staff members. Jock was engaged to the love of his life and Dan was helping him sail his beloved boat to the property of his dreams, where he was going to live happily ever after.

And Dan was having a fling with Jock's sister, for heaven's sake. Getting steadily closer to a woman who was pregnant with twins that she believed were his own children.

He was being offered the opportunity of getting as close as he'd ever dreamed of getting to living happily ever after himself. And the time together last night, when he'd felt the movement of the babies as clearly as if the barrier of Jenni's skin had evaporated, had stayed with him today. He could still feel the tingle of it in his hands.

So life couldn't be any more different really, could it?

Not that he was committing to anything yet. He was taking one day at a time. One magic night with Jenni at a time, because that was all that he could allow himself to do. What would make it perfect, of course, would be if they fell in love with each other, but how likely was that to happen? Jenni had told him she was quite prepared to be a single parent—that she would, in fact, prefer it. And for himself, well…the kind of trust you needed to fall in love had been so broken for him, it could never be the same. It might not even be a possibility.

But that didn't necessarily mean it was impossible to find something you could trust enough to rest a future on, though.

Did it?

It felt like that question was being answered only a short time later, when Jock slowed *Lassie*'s engine and Dan got ready with the ropes to tie the boat up as they came into the jetty and he could see Jenni and Grace waiting for them.

When the smile on Jenni's face gave him that spear of sensation in his gut again, and this time it spread its warmth right through his body.

Yeah…it felt like he could trust someone who smiled at him like that.

Life was different all right.

Better…

So much better…

The small beach was framed by Pohutukawa trees that had low horizontal branches that, along with some big boulders, made natural seating so that they could admire the jetty and how it looked with Jock's pretty boat tied up to it and the stunning backdrop of the water view and islands not too far away.

It was a perfect evening for a picnic too—a simple meal of sausages, grilled until their skins were crispy, wrapped in soft white bread with a liberal garnish of tomato sauce and a token lettuce leaf or two so that they could pretend it wasn't such an unhealthy meal. There was ginger beer for Jenni and lager with wedges of lime stuffed into the bottles for everyone else and there was the sound of animated conversation and frequent laughter and the feeling of...well, it felt more like family than friendship.

Dan hadn't felt like this in a group of people for so many years. Not since he'd walked away from the ruins of his marriage and members of his extended family, quite a few of whom had simply shaken their heads.

What did you expect, man? Get over it... She wanted kids and you weren't up to the job, were you?

The echo of the past was so faint it was more than easy to ignore—it was just a part of some life baggage that no longer seemed nearly as important. He had moved on and life was so much better.

He raised the bottle of lager he was holding. 'Here's to *Lassie*,' he said. 'She's found her new home and I hope she remains here for many years to come.'

Jock and Grace exchanged a glance. And a look so full of love that Dan's breath caught in his chest.

'Like us...' Grace smiled.

'Just like us,' Jock agreed. His smile became his trademark cheeky grin. 'We've decided to get married,' he announced.

'That's old news,' Jenni said. 'You've been engaged for months.'

'No...we want to get *married*,' Grace said. 'Soon. Before you go home, Jen, so that you can be my bridesmaid. Will you...?'

Jenni had her hand pressed against her mouth. She looked as if she could start crying at any moment.

'Of course I will,' she said. 'I'd love to.'

Jock caught Dan's gaze and his grin faded to make his face unusually serious. 'I'm hoping you might be my best man,' he said.

Dan got why Jenni had looked so misty. He had a lump in his own throat now.

'Sure...' was the only response he managed, but Jock didn't seem to mind. He was smiling again and he reached out to clink his bottle against Dan's.

'We only need two witnesses,' Grace added. 'And an approved celebrant. And we can get married anywhere we want to as long as we specify the place on our application.'

'What about here?' Jock suggested. 'On our own beach?'

'That would be perfect...' Grace leaned her head against Jock's shoulder. They were sharing that look again. The one that gave Dan the kind of poignant sensation that he recognised because he'd experienced it quite recently. When he'd been with Jenni at that ultrasound scan and he'd seen the baby's hand on the screen.

Yearning, that was what it was.

For things he'd believed he could never have.

Children.

Love.

A family of his own...

He had to make an effort to tune back into the conversation around him.

'So we submit the application and see a registrar to sign a statutory declaration that we're not already married, et cetera, pay a fee and have to wait three days and that's it. We could do late next week?'

Dan's jaw dropped. 'Next *week*?'

'It'll have to be soon.' Grace nodded. 'Jenni's planning to go back to Scotland and the cut-off point for flying when you're pregnant is a lot sooner when you're carrying twins. She's only got a few weeks to play with here.'

Okay… Dan had known that his time with Jenni was only temporary. That she had every intention of returning to Scotland to have her babies, but…a couple of weeks? It felt like a ripple of sensation had just run down his spine and was now sending out tendrils of something cold and unpleasant. Had he really thought he had the chance of a future that included being a parent and a partner—to have a family of his own? How was that supposed to work when he would be living eighteen thousand kilometres away in an opposite time zone?

'Unless…'

Dan's voice sounded oddly raw. 'Unless what…?'

Grace glanced at Jenni, who shook her head firmly but it didn't stop her. 'I've been trying to persuade Jen that it might be a good idea for her to have the babies here in New Zealand,' she said. 'So that we could help out for the first few months, at least. She's got a year's maternity leave to play with, after all.'

This felt like a reprieve.

'Sounds like a good idea to me,' he said.

Grace and Jenni exchanged another glance that was very brief but seemed oddly significant. As if he'd said more than he realised? And then she looked back at Jock with her eyebrows raised as if she was encouraging him to say something.

Jock cleared his throat. 'We discovered something else when we were online finding out about the requirements for getting married in New Zealand,' he said. 'You don't have to be residents to get married here but we wanted to know how to go about applying for permanent residency and citizenship and we stumbled on something that we thought you should know about, Jen.'

'But I'm not going to emigrate,' Jenni said firmly. 'Scotland's home for me. You both *know* that.'

'Yes, but this isn't about you,' Jock said. 'Your children might want to live here one day. They're half Kiwis, after all.'

Dan closed his eyes for a heartbeat. Jock and Grace both believed he was the father of these babies.

Oh, man…he should have got on with it and had the repeat fertility test done long ago, shouldn't he? Jock was a medic. He'd be able to see those results and know just how likely it was that Jenni had to have made a mistake.

Why *hadn't* he got on with it?

He could have just excused himself by how busy he had been. Or how he might not want such a personal test being done in his place of work. But Dan knew it went a lot deeper than that. Maybe, on some level, he didn't want Jenni to know he wasn't the biological father of her babies because then she might not want to share the kinds of magic that Dan had never thought he could be part of. A scan to see the images of an unborn child. Permission to rest his hands on Jenni's belly to feel those babies moving with nothing more than a layer of skin between them.

And maybe…just maybe…there was that tiny hope that he could be wrong. That something might have changed. That perhaps, by some miracle, he really was the twins' father.

He didn't want to have to wake up from the dream just yet, that was what it was.

But he could hear the alarm sounding now. Loud and clear.

'We'll all be visiting as they grow up—especially if you and Jock are going to be here for ever,' Jenni added quietly. 'They can make their own choices about where to live when they're old enough.'

She looked disconcerted, Dan thought. Maybe she didn't

want to think that far into the future. Or maybe she was regretting coming here to tell him that he was going to be a father and involving other people in decisions about her children's future.

It had been a brave thing to do, hadn't it?

But she had believed she was doing the right thing.

He felt proud of her for having that strength.

'But what we found out,' Jock said, 'was that if you have your babies in New Zealand and can prove that the father is a New Zealander, that makes them automatically citizens. They could hold two passports.'

Dan swallowed hard. Taking that fertility test had just become a priority. Along with a DNA test. They all had to know the truth. To see it there, in black and white on an official document.

'Does that not happen if they're not born in New Zealand?'

'They can apply but who knows? The rules might change by then.'

There was a moment's silence, broken by a sigh from Grace. 'Sorry... I didn't mean to spoil our picnic.' She looked as though she was pasting a smile onto her face. 'Where you have your babies is your decision, Jen. If you change your mind and stay for longer that will be fabulous, but we want to get married soon anyway. Don't we, Jock?'

'The sooner the better,' Jock agreed softly. He bent his head to plant a tender kiss on Grace's lips.

Dan found his own gaze seeking Jenni's and there it was, as if she'd already been looking at him. For a heartbeat, and then another, they held that gaze and it felt as if they were kissing each other with as much of a tender connection as Jock and Grace were enjoying.

He wanted, more than anything, to be alone with Jenni right now.

But that wasn't a good idea…because that would lead to physical intimacy, which made it so easy to ignore other things.

Important things, like the future.

And being completely honest with each other.

The moment was gone, in any case. Jock was getting to his feet.

'I'd better check *Lassie*'s moorings and get her secure for her first night in her new home.' He looked over his shoulder. 'Want to give me a hand, Dan?'

'Sure…'

Behind him, Grace and Jenni were starting to clear up the picnic leftovers and he could hear them talking about wedding plans.

Dan was making plans of his own. At the top of that list was to get a copy of his medical records and then to get on with repeating that test. But something else came a close second.

He wanted to talk to Jenni. To see if he might be able to persuade her to stay here to have the babies.

To give them more time to build the kind of trust that could provide a foundation for a future that Jenni might not have considered yet.

A future with *him*…

CHAPTER EIGHT

JENNI AND GRACE were both watching—and listening to—the drop in the baby's heart rate on the CTG machine.

As the contraction faded, the baby's heart rate increased again rapidly and then settled to a normal baseline rate. Jenni shared a glance with Grace, who was taking the lead in her first delivery since she'd started back at work part-time.

Both midwives had been in agreement that continuous CTG monitoring was a good idea when they'd noticed the variation of the baby's heart rate from intermittent monitoring as the first stage of labour progressed and it was reassuring that the baby was not showing any warning signs of distress, but Jules was getting tired. She'd been labouring for many hours overnight before Jenni and Grace had taken over her care when they came on duty at the hospital this morning. She was coping less well with the pain too, with only gas and air to help after a dose of intravenous analgesia had worn off some time ago. She reached for the mask Nathan was holding and jammed it against her face as each new contraction started.

Nathan was looking anxious. 'Is it normal for it to be taking this long?'

'Absolutely. Especially with a first baby.'

'I feel like I want to push,' Jules said.

'Let me check,' Grace told her. 'We don't want you to start pushing unless you're ready.'

There was a new energy in the room when Jules started pushing a short time later, leaning back against Nathan, putting her chin down on her chest to increase her efforts.

'You're doing it, Jules…' Nathan sounded as if he was imitating her pushing. 'Go, go, go…'

'Keep it going, Jules,' Grace encouraged. 'Keep pushing—as long as you can.'

Jules was giving it everything she had but, thirty minutes later, as the contractions continued relentlessly, Jenni looked up from the CTG screen to catch Grace's gaze.

'Variable decelerations,' she said, keeping her tone calm. She noted the W shape on the graph. 'And they're biphasic.'

'Shouldering?'

'No.' The spikes of a heart rate going high and then settling to a normal baseline again, known as 'shouldering', were absent. These were all signs of umbilical cord compression and a baby that was getting distressed through lack of oxygen.

'Can you give Jock a bell?'

Jenni stopped the printout of the screen and ripped off the trace. 'I'll be back in a minute.'

Jock's examination of Jules when he arrived was brief but thorough. 'Baby's getting tired,' he told Jules and Nathan. 'I think you're going to need some help.'

'I've changed my mind about having an epidural,' Jules said. 'But it's too late now, isn't it?'

'No. That's going to be our first step in helping to get your baby born as soon as possible.'

'Will I have to have a Caesarean?'

'That is an option,' Jock agreed, 'but we'll keep it up our sleeve for now. We have other things we can try first. Given where baby's head is now, the best option for you is for an assisted delivery—with forceps—as soon as your anaesthetic has taken effect.'

Jenni knew that Jock was also choosing forceps because it would be the fastest option to get this baby out safely. Given the changes they could see happening to the baby's condition, this could become a matter of life or death all too soon.

'I'm going to go over it all with you and Nathan and then we'll move you to Theatre,' Jock said. 'I can answer any more questions you have then, but I'd rather you were in the right place if it does become necessary for you to have a C-section.'

Both Grace and Jenni went to Theatre with Jules. It was Dan who was there to administer the spinal anaesthetic and, for just a very brief but rather unprofessional moment, Grace's glance was checking to see how pleased Jenni might be to see him.

And yes…the physical reaction to being this close to Daniel Walker—the way her heart rate picked up and that curl of sensation in her belly—was not something Jenni could control. Judging by the way Dan's gaze caught on hers for an instant longer than it needed to, it seemed that he was just as pleased to see her, which only intensified her reaction, but neither of them were about to let anything so personal interfere in any way with the job they were here to do.

The anaesthetic had taken effect by the time they had Nathan in his gown and mask and hat and Jock was scrubbed and ready for the instrumental delivery. Grace stood in position where she would be able to support Jules and coach her with her pushing and also to take the baby as soon as it was born if it wasn't in need of resuscitation. Jenni stood back, a little to one side of where Dan was at the head of the bed, monitoring Jules's vital signs. He could top up the drugs being administered for the spinal block if needed, or move to a general anaesthetic in the event of an emergency complication.

There was nothing for Jenni to do other than watch, which she was more than happy to do. Not just because she could steal the occasional peek at Dan as he worked but this was, in fact, the first time she'd seen her brother performing a forceps delivery and...she was impressed.

An episiotomy was needed to allow enough room to position the forceps correctly and then, between contractions, Jock gently slipped one handle into place for the curved blade to cradle one side of the baby's head. With the second handle positioned and the two locked together, they waited for the next contraction and for Jules to push as Jock applied pressure to pull.

'Here we go, Jules,' Grace told her. 'I know you can't feel it but bear down and push. Keep it going...'

'Good...' Jock was completely focused on his task. 'Try and get another push in for this contraction. We're almost there...'

'*Oh...*' Nathan was mesmerised by what he was seeing. 'I can see something,' he breathed. 'I can see her...what *is* that?'

'It's her hair.' It sounded like Jock was smiling beneath his mask. 'I'm going to take the forceps out now, Jules. You can push your baby out all by yourself with your next contraction.'

Which was exactly what Jules did. It wasn't the birth that Jenni was watching, though. She wasn't watching Jock any longer either. Because Dan was clearly as captivated as Nathan as he watched this baby girl being born and...watching *him* was making Jenni feel something new. An oddly intense but very real connection to this man. When you knew you were going to become a parent yourself in the very near future, it completely changed how it felt to witness a birth, didn't it?

It was even more intense for Jules and Nathan, of course. As Grace took the baby from Jock to put her skin to skin with Jules, both the young parents had tears streaming down their faces. When Nathan was given the task of cutting the umbilical cord the young couple shared a look of absolute pride— and wonder—with each other.

Grace looked after the delivery of the placenta and it was Jock who stitched up the episiotomy. Dan was continuing to monitor Jules as he shut off the anaesthetic and tidied up, but Jenni stayed where she was, blinking back a tear or two herself as she watched Nathan and Jules, blissfully unaware of what was happening around them. They were both gazing at their newborn daughter, who lay quietly cradled in her mother's arms, clearly falling totally and utterly in love with the infant.

Jenni tried to swallow the lump in her throat as she shifted her gaze towards Dan. He was replacing a bag of saline and adjusting the drip level to keep a vein open for Jules in case any other medication was needed so he didn't see her looking at him, but making eye contact wouldn't have changed anything. Jenni had made up her mind.

She couldn't do it.

She couldn't go back to the other side of the world and steal what was almost certainly the only opportunity Dan would ever have to be present at the birth of his own children. She couldn't steal the magic of these first minutes of being a parent and being able to experience this kind of falling in love that would be there for the rest of your life, no matter what.

It might be within her rights to do that.

But that didn't make it the right thing to do.

For a long, long moment Dan simply stood on the footpath without going through the gate to the old villa that was the hospital accommodation. He was staring at the steps to the veranda and thinking just how much his life had changed since he'd come here on the night of Jock's birthday to find Jenni sitting on those steps.

His life was about to change again—possibly not in a good way.

The dream was over.

Folded up in the back pocket of his jeans were the results from his semen analysis test. The results that could make Jenni realise she'd made a mistake. That she might need to search elsewhere to find the real father of her babies.

He took a deep breath and opened the gate but, just as he did so, the front door of the villa opened and Jenni came out. Her smile told him how pleased she was to see him and his heart sank a little bit further.

He loved that smile…

'Dan…just the person I need,' Jenni said. 'I've got Grace's car stuffed to the gills. Can you help me unload it, please?'

'Sure.' It was a relief to be able to put off the reason for his visit. 'What is it? Groceries?'

'No…baby stuff.' Jenni had reached the gate and she stood on tiptoes to give him a brief kiss. She was still smiling. 'Two bassinets. Two car seats. I found this online marketplace that sells all kinds of second-hand baby things.'

Dan blinked. And then he stared into the back hatch of Grace's car. Why on earth was Jenni buying ridiculously bulky items of baby gear when it would be far more practical to wait until she got back to Scotland before making such purchases?

He turned his head to find Jenni watching him. When she spoke, it felt like she was reading his mind as well.

'I'm not going back to Scotland,' she told him. 'Not yet, anyway. I'm going to stay here to have the babies.'

Dan simply stared at her. He could actually feel that folded piece of paper in his pocket, but how could he pull it out or even think of revealing its contents when Jenni was looking at him like *this*?

Did she have tears in her eyes?

'I can't do it, Dan.' Jenni spoke so softly it was little more than a whisper. 'I can't take away what could be the only chance you'll get to see your children being born. To see them take their first breaths. To hold them in the first minutes of their lives.'

Oh…*man*…

There was no way on earth that Dan could pull that paper out of his pocket now. He opened his mouth to say something but then simply closed it again. He had no words…

Jenni didn't seem to mind. 'I can manage the bassinets,' she said. 'But two car seats are quite heavy. Could you carry those?'

Moving physically was a good thing. At least his legs still knew what to do despite his brain being mush.

'So I'm going to have the babies here and stay for a few months,' Jenni told him. 'Grace was right. It's a much better idea to have family around to help for a while.'

Yeah…he remembered that conversation on the beach. He'd thought it was a great idea that Jenni stayed longer. To give them time to build a relationship that would mean he could live his dream of having a family of his own. But what if those results changed everything? Created another twist in the story that took him further away from a happy ending?

Maybe Jenni sensed that Dan needed some time to get his head around this twist in the story that the two of them were creating. Was that why she was changing the subject?

'We're going shopping tomorrow,' she was saying. 'Getting up at the crack of dawn to get the early ferry, like we did the first time I was here and she took me sightseeing. This time we're going hunting for wedding things.' Her smile was even brighter than it had been when he'd arrived. 'It's going to be such fun.'

It also provided a means for Dan to escape before he ruined how happy Jenni was right now. He wouldn't stay, he said. She needed an early night because it was going to be a big day tomorrow.

He kissed her goodbye but he could still feel that folded paper in his pocket. So hot now if felt like it was burning his skin.

He knew he had to tell her.

He just couldn't do it right now.

'I'm so happy...'

'Of course you are. We're about to go shopping for your wedding dress.'

'I still think I could wear that dress I bought for your farewell party.'

Jenni laughed and patted her bump. 'I can't wear mine, that's for sure. And yes, that dress is very pretty but fuchsia pink doesn't exactly scream "bride", does it? You're only allowed to do this once—seeing as it's my brother you're getting married to.'

Grace gave a huff of laughter as if that warning was too ridiculous to merit a response. But then she tilted her head.

'We'd decided that all we needed was a simple family ceremony. No big deal, you know? I had no intention of screaming bride at all, but now...' Her smile wobbled a little. 'This is a big deal, isn't it? And I know it's the only time I'll ever want to do it. I think I *would* like to look like a bride and have flowers and fairy lights, maybe even a garter.'

'*Yes*...' Jenni was nodding enthusiastically. 'Let's do this properly. Those bridal boutiques won't know what's hit them. This is going to be so much fun...'

Jenni and Grace were at the back of the inter-island ferry, leaning over the rail, captivated by the stunning scenery of the Sounds they were sailing through as the sun rose. They were also hoping they might be a bit luckier than last time and get to spot a pod of dolphins.

'It's not just that I'm getting married,' Grace said then. 'I'm this happy that you've decided to have the babies here. Can I be your midwife?'

'Yes. But Jock can't be my obstetrician, even if something happens so that Maria can't be there. I'm not having my brother looking at bits of me I haven't even seen myself.'

Grace laughed. 'Fair enough.'

Jenni let her breath out in a sigh. 'Do you remember what we were talking about the last time we did this?'

'About your mother?' Grace sounded serious now. 'And how you and Jock never felt like you had a proper home?'

'Aye... I was worried that Jock was never going to stay in one place long enough to put down roots and he'd never feel like he had a real home and he'd never be truly happy.' She stopped for a moment and then threw her arms around Grace. 'I can't believe I'm so lucky that I'm going to get my best friend as my sister-in-law. And I've never seen Jock this happy. Ever. He adores you.'

'I feel the same way about him.' But Grace wriggled free of the embrace. 'We'll both be bawling our eyes out in a minute if we keep this up. Let's talk about something else. Have you heard back from the friend that's renting your house in Glasgow?'

'Yes. And she's more than happy to stay there for as long

as she can, so her rent will cover what I'll be paying for somewhere here.'

'It's a shame you can't stay in the hospital accommodation.'

'I won't be a hospital employee by then. You'll be back full-time. Besides, it would hardly be fair to be keeping any new staff members awake all night with crying babies.'

'You know you can stay with us. We won't mind being kept awake.'

'Be good practice for the future, I guess.' Jenni smiled. 'But no... I really do need my own place. I'm going to have to learn to manage by myself before I head home. Not that it won't be fabulous to have you and Jock on hand to rescue me to start with.'

'And Dan...'

'Aye...and Dan...'

'Have you told him yet? That the babies are going to be born in New Zealand?'

'Only last night. I've hardly seen him in the last few days. He came around when I got back from collecting that second-hand baby gear I found online. It was fairly obvious I wasn't going to be putting things like bassinets and car seats in my suitcase to go home.'

'What did he say when he knew you were staying?'

'He went a bit quiet, to be honest.' Jenni bit her lip. She really wasn't that sure how thrilled Dan had been at her news.

He hadn't even stayed to have a meal with her, saying that Jenni needed to get up so early to catch the ferry that he didn't want her to lose any more sleep.

He had kissed her, but even that had felt...different? As if his mind was somewhere else entirely.

'It must be overwhelming,' Grace said. 'Being present at

the birth is a pretty emotional thing.' She hesitated for a beat. 'Will you let him be there the whole time?'

'Yes… If that's what he wants. That was the main reason I decided to stay here. I didn't think it would be fair to take away an experience he might never get the chance to have, otherwise.'

Grace nodded. 'It's all about bonding, isn't it? And that's going to underpin his involvement with the twins for the rest of his life.'

And with her for the rest of *her* life…?

Okay, maybe it wasn't surprising that he'd needed some space to get used to the idea. This was huge. Not as life-changing as becoming a mother, but it was still huge.

It wasn't something Jenni had ever planned—to have a particular man as a significant part of her life. It should be a disturbing concept but…this was Dan, wasn't it?

He was a friend.

More than a friend. She couldn't say they were lovers because she wasn't *in* love with Dan and this physical relationship was only ever going to be temporary—maybe it was already fading, in fact—but…she cared about him.

As a friend.

As the father of her children.

And that was definitely a form of love.

So…aye…she loved Daniel Walker.

The swift mental gymnastics that had allowed this conclusion to surface with such conviction hadn't changed anything.

This still felt safe.

It still felt that she had done the right thing to come here and tell Dan the truth face to face. It didn't feel dangerous that they had become a lot closer than either of them might have predicted and it didn't feel like a mistake to have made the decision to stay a few months longer.

It wasn't going to change the big picture. She and Dan were totally on the same page. He was just as happy as she was to stay away from a committed relationship with a partner. It wasn't as if they were planning to get married. Or even live in the same country in the near future. It would, however, make their connection as co-parents stronger and that had to be a good thing.

They could remain the best of friends for the rest of their lives. They could love and care about each other as well as loving and caring for the children they shared. It could possibly work better than most marriages, in fact.

It would definitely work better than any of her mother's marriages or relationships, that was for sure.

'Hey...' Grace broke into her thoughts. 'You never told me what the results were of that fertility test Dan was going to get done?'

'I don't know myself. I don't think the results have come back yet.'

'But he did that test well over a week ago, didn't he? Right after that night when we were talking about how it would be a good idea for the twins to be born here.'

'A few days later. He had to...you know...abstain from sex for at least three days.'

'Oh...guess it might take a bit longer, then.'

'Mmm...' Jenni tried to make it sound unimportant but that abstinence hadn't been broken yet, had it? Was that why she was starting to think the attraction might be wearing off? Maybe Dan had actually come around the other night to tell her it was over and, if it was, she would be okay with that.

But was it a coincidence that the last time they'd made love had been before the night of the beach picnic? When they'd talked about the potential rights of the twins to become New Zealand citizens.

Jenni could feel herself frowning and deliberately pushed away whatever doubts were trying to sneak up on her. This was going to be a happy day that she and Grace would be able to remember for ever. They were going to shop till they dropped for dresses and other bridal necessities like flowers to wear in their hair and possibly a veil and garter and pretty underwear for Grace. They would be more than ready for a late lunch and then a dash back to catch the ferry home. And there were so many other things to talk about. Even though this was going to be a very small and simple ceremony, there was still a lot of planning and organisation to be done and that had to be Jenni's priority for the next couple of days.

If banishing doubts about how Dan had reacted to knowing he could be present at the birth of his children was going to contribute to making this special day as perfect as possible for both her best friend and her brother, then that was exactly what Jenni was going to do.

She wasn't about to let anything spoil such a special day.

'Oh, *look*, Grace...' Jenni pointed at the splash she had just seen not far from the ship. Graceful grey shapes could be seen taking turns to arc over the calm water and then dive to speed through the sea, still visible just under the surface. *'Dolphins...'*

She could feel her smile stretching right across her face.

This was a sign, wasn't it?

This wedding *was* going to be perfect.

It was about as perfect as it could be, Dan decided.

The autumn weather was lovely, warm enough for the summery kind of dresses both Grace and Jenni were wearing, and there was not a breath of wind. The tree-covered islands in the distance, a fishing boat that was anchored not far out from the beach and even the jetty and *Lassie* were being perfectly reflected in the mirror-calm surface of the clear, dark sea water.

It was too light for the fairy lights that had been strung in the Pohutukawa trees overhanging the beach but they would come into their own later, when a few close friends had been invited to join them all on the beach for an epic evening barbecue. This part of the day, however, was intimate. Right now, the only people standing in silence broken occasionally by birdsong were himself, an uncharacteristically nervous-looking Jock and the celebrant, a local woman called Aroha who might be well into her sixties but her delight in her job hadn't dimmed. She knew how to use technology too, and had the music that had been chosen loaded onto her phone, which was connected to a Bluetooth speaker hidden between rocks.

At the appointed time she started the music that was Grace's cue to come down the path to the beach, so he was listening to John Legend's romantic song when he saw Jenni for the first time in days.

Since the evening when she'd told him about her decision to stay here to give birth.

When she'd invited him to be present at the birth of the children she was so confident were his.

The same day he'd received the semen analysis test results that confirmed just how impossible that was, because the figures were even worse than they had been when he'd been tested the first time.

He'd gone to see her to show her the report because she needed to know the truth. Good grief...she had decided to stay here for the twins' birth after that conversation with Jock and Grace about them having automatic citizenship if they were born in their father's country. They all thought his name was going to be recorded on their birth certificates. They all needed to know the truth.

But then Jenni had blindsided him with her invitation to include him in the birth and early months of the twins' lives—and that was another layer to the fantasy of parenthood that he had been allowing himself to indulge in ever since he'd been present at that scan.

It was going too far, though, being present at something as intimate as the birth if he wasn't the biological father. If Jenni still wanted him to be there when she knew the truth then he would embrace the experience, but it could only happen on a foundation of honesty and he just hadn't been able to find the right words that night.

And then she'd been away with Grace to go shopping in Wellington, work had been frantically busy yesterday and she'd disappeared with Grace today to go to a hairdresser and florist and then hide themselves in the house to get ready. Not that he could say anything today, of course. This was Jock and Grace's day, and the expression on his best mate's face as he watched the woman he loved walk onto the beach brought a lump to Dan's throat.

The bride walked between the boulders onto the small sandy beach and…she looked stunning. Her lacy dress wasn't blindingly white—more of an ivory shade. The top fitted her like a glove but the skirt swirled with every step. She had tiny daisy-like flowers woven into her long blonde hair that was hanging in loose waves and she carried a simple bouquet of long-stemmed blooms that matched the ones in her hair.

No wonder Jock was looking like all his dreams were coming true. Grace was looking at him in exactly the same way and the love between these two people was enough to light up the whole beach. That lump in Dan's throat suddenly grew jagged edges.

This was what was missing from his own life.

And always would be…

Oh, help… Dan had to make sure that the shaft of pain—and loss—he was feeling wasn't showing on his face during this happiest of occasions. He shifted his gaze from the bride and, just as the song was soaring into its chorus about all of him loving all of her, he saw Jenni come through the boulders and onto the sand.

For Dan, she looked even more stunning than the bride.

Jenni was wearing a dress in a shade of bluey green that looked like sea water. It fitted snugly over her breasts and there was a knot beneath them in the centre of the dress that cleverly allowed for extra fabric to fall elegantly over the bump of her belly. Her arms were bare and her hair was also loose—fiery auburn waves that were catching the last of the day's sunlight.

She was smiling. Of course she was. Her best friend was getting married to her brother and she couldn't be happier about it. Except that it wasn't Jock or Grace that she was smiling at.

It was him.

As he held her gaze and smiled back, Dan could feel something in his chest that he'd thought he would never feel again. A feeling of warmth and softness that was expanding at a rate that threatened to break something.

Like his heart…?

It was love, that was what it was. Maybe it was an echo of the energy that Jock and Grace were creating.

Or maybe Dan had just woken up to the fact that he was in this a whole lot deeper than he'd realised.

He had fallen in love with Jenni McKay.

Jenni had to wipe tears away more than once during the ceremony.

Jock and Grace had written their vows themselves and it felt like she and Dan were privileged to be included in something that was a very private part of the love between them.

They held both of each other's hands as they stood in front of the celebrant, with Dan and Jenni on either side.

Grace had spoken first. 'We're all searching for a place to call home,' she said softly. 'But we both know now that home is bigger than just a place. That it might not *be* a place at all. That it might be a person…' She had to catch her breath and brush away a tear. 'Because home *is* where the heart is. You're my home, Jock McKay. You're my heart. I will love you for as long as I live…'

Jock had cleared his throat, blinked back tears and then taken a deep breath. 'When otters are sleeping they hold hands so they don't float away from each other. We did that once in the sea, not very far from where we are right now. I held your hand and you held mine and…and that's what I will always do for you, Grace Collins, because I love you and always will. It doesn't matter whether I'm actually touching you or not, I'll be holding your hand—so you don't float away…'

Oh, *my*… The tears were gathering yet again. Enough to make Jenni's vision more than slightly blurry even after a couple had escaped. Had it been the way she'd touched her face to brush them away that had caught Dan's attention? Was that why she could feel the intensity of the way he was looking at her? She couldn't stop her gaze slipping sideways to catch his.

Was it the blurriness that made it seem like he was looking at her as if he didn't want *her* to float away?

As if…

As if he loved her?

As if he was *in* love with her?

Was it contagious? Weddings were notorious for making guests realise how they felt about life and love and each other. Was that what was happening here?

Did Jenni want it to be what was happening?

Jock and Grace were exchanging their formal vows now and Jenni could feel the words resonating as if she was speaking them herself.

I do…

CHAPTER NINE

THAT FEELING—that glow of hope and longing and a kind of joy she'd never felt before—stayed with Jenni for the rest of that magical day when her beloved twin brother got married to her best friend.

It was still there the next day and the day after that, and that was when she began to wonder if it was more than simply an echo of the wedding joy she'd been immersed in. If it could possibly be...*real*...?

Not that she'd had the chance to spend any time with Dan after the wedding. With a run of split shifts to cover, he seemed as absent from work as Grace and Jock, who had taken some annual leave to fly down to Queenstown for a brief honeymoon. Without Grace, Jenni was kept busier at work, which was getting more and more tiring, but she was busy out of work hours too. New staff members were due to move into the hospital accommodation, which was the push Jenni needed to make a serious effort to find her own house to rent in Picton.

She was online as soon as she got home, searching for any new rental properties that had become available, preferably immediately available. She wanted to move as soon as possible so that she could stop working in a week or two and put all her energy into getting ready for the birth of her babies.

Nesting...

It was something Jenny had imagined doing ever since she

knew she was pregnant. She could see bassinets made up with snowy white sheets and soft blankets with colourful mobiles hanging over them. A baby's bath and piles of nappies. Tiny clothes neatly stacked on shelves and cute cuddly toys on a windowsill waiting for their turn to be useful. She'd just never imagined she would be doing it on this side of the world.

But being displaced wasn't as daunting as it could have been, thanks to Jock and Grace's wedding. Echoes of the vows they had exchanged had stayed with Jenni as strongly as that feeling of wanting Dan as an integral part of her future.

The idea that *home* could come in the shape of a person rather than a place.

Could love really be trusted that much? Could it be as solid as the ground beneath your feet and the walls and roof of a house to shelter you?

Her brother—who'd grown up with exactly the same reasons not to trust the people who claimed to love you—was prepared to believe it was. Enough to let him risk giving his heart to someone.

Jenni wanted to believe it was but…it would be the biggest step she had ever taken.

Because if she could believe it, she might—finally—be able to let go of what she'd believed with such certainty all her life—that you couldn't trust everybody to be telling the truth and that offering someone else your heart was quite likely to be the fastest road to broken dreams and a miserable life.

But now there was that glow that wasn't fading into oblivion and perhaps it was a good thing that she hadn't seen Dan since the wedding because it wouldn't take much for it to be snuffed out. She would only need to see something in his face or hear a note in his tone that tickled one of those doubts she'd managed to bury and she'd be running, wouldn't she?

She might remember the way he'd reacted when she'd told him she was going to stay for the birth of the twins. Or that the last time he'd held her or had his hands on her belly to wait for the movement of the babies had been the night of the picnic, when Jock and Grace had shared their plans to get married. Now they were away on their honeymoon, so it had been... oh, *help*...more than two weeks ago?

The reminder of Jock and Grace being away was timely. Jenni shut her laptop and hauled herself to her feet. She had promised to go and water Grace's indoor pot plants while she was away and she'd completely forgotten about it until now. Going out again was the last thing her sore feet and tired body would have chosen after a long day at work, but how guilty would she feel if they came back to find their plants dying? And, on the bright side, she could pick up a takeaway on the way back and that would save her having to cook anything for her dinner.

There was an even brighter side that was totally unexpected. Having watered the plants and locked the front door of the house behind her, Jenni was startled to find Dan arriving.

'I promised Jock I'd look in and check on *Lassie*,' he said.

'I've just been watering the plants.' Jenni could feel her heart beating against her ribs. She was searching Dan's face for signs that the surprise of finding her here might not be a pleasant one but she couldn't see any.

He was smiling.

There was a softness in his face and in those gorgeous brown eyes that reminded her of the way he'd been looking at her during that emotional moment of the vows that Jock and Grace had been making to each other.

And if her brain was still trying to come up with a reason

not to trust what she thought she was seeing, it was silenced completely as Dan stepped closer.

Close enough to touch her face. To let his hand slip behind her neck and then let his fingers thread themselves into her hair to cradle the back of her head.

To kiss her.

Slowly.

Tenderly.

In a way that made that glow become so bright that, even though Jenni had her eyes firmly closed, it felt bright enough to blind her.

'It feels like ages since I've seen you,' Dan said softly when he finally raised his head. 'I've missed you, Jen.'

'Mmm…' Jenni felt completely out of breath. 'Same…'

'Come down to the beach with me while I check *Lassie*'s moorings? Then, maybe I could take you out to dinner? I'm doing a night shift tonight and I don't have to be at work until ten p.m.'

Miraculously, Jenni's fatigue seemed to be evaporating. 'Sounds wonderful,' she said.

Dan took her hand as they reached the steps that led down to the beach and he didn't let go even when they reached the safety of soft, flat sand. They walked through the boulders to have that beautiful backdrop to the wedding in front of them again. Jenni could feel the warmth of Dan's hand holding hers and could hear the echo of Jock's oh, so loving words to Grace about being her otter and always holding her hand so she wouldn't float away and…

And she knew *she* could trust *this*.

She could feel Dan's gaze resting on her and she looked up, knowing that making eye contact with him would make this absolutely real.

And it did.

'I love you, Jenni,' Dan said—so softly his words were no more than a whisper.

'I love you too,' Jenni whispered back.

'I never thought I'd ever feel like this again. Or be able to trust it.'

Jenni's nod was almost shy. 'Same…'

'I want to be with you for the twins' birth. I want to be a part of their lives—a part of *your* life, Jenni McKay.' She could hear the way Dan sucked in a deep breath.

Okay…that glow was definitely blinding now. So bright it was painful. It was more like the light of an explosion than something warm and comfortable. Was it too much, too soon?

Dan was still talking. Jenni forced herself to focus. Had he just said *'But'*…?

'It wouldn't make any difference at all. I'll love the twins as if they *were* my own children.'

Wait…

What…?

Jenni felt her body moving backwards as if Dan had just forcefully pushed her away from him. She took another step more slowly and then sank onto one of the larger boulders because it didn't feel as if her legs wanted to hold her upright any longer.

'What did you just say?' Her words emerged sounding bewildered, as if she couldn't possibly have heard him correctly.

'That I want us to live together.' Dan's tone had changed as well. There was a puzzled note in it. 'To be a family…'

'A family with children that you don't believe are yours?'

'They can't be.' Dan crouched in front of the boulder Jenni was sitting on, so that his face was closer to hers. 'I'm really sorry…but the odds of that being the case are astronomically small. My test results are worse than they were when I first got tested more than ten years ago.'

It sounded as if Dan's voice was coming from much further away than it was.

'In a healthy male there should be twenty million sperm in every millilitre of semen. Mine doesn't even crack one million. And yeah…it does only take one sperm, but with numbers like that the only way it has even a remote chance of being successful is for it to be injected directly into an egg. Intracytoplasmic technology.'

His voice was clearer now. The shock of what he'd said was finally wearing off. What was taking its place was a disappointment that was so bitter it instantly morphed into overwhelming anger.

Jenni's voice was even clearer than Dan's. And much, much colder. As cold as ice.

'I asked you whether you still thought I was lying and you said "no". I *believed* you.'

It had been the moment that changed everything, hadn't it? The memory of that intimate connection they'd discovered with each other had grown and pulled them back together with a force she'd never known could exist between two people. Her breath came out in an incredulous huff of sound.

'It was enough to persuade me to trust you enough to have *sex* with you again, for God's sake. And now you're saying I *was* lying all along?'

'No…' Dan's hand covered one of Jenni's that was lying protectively on the top of her bump. 'I did say I didn't think you were lying because I knew *you* believed you weren't lying. It's just a mistake, that's all. There's a window of time on either side of an estimated conception date. You were on holiday…'

His voice trailed off, as if he realised that what he was suggesting was humiliating. To be fair, he only had his own experience to have based his reasoning on.

'So...what you're really saying is that I spent my holiday having one-night stands with any man I met along the way?' She pulled her hand out from beneath Dan's.

He stood up again and used that hand to rub his forehead. 'No,' he said. 'That's not what I'm suggesting at all. But you did go from here to visit your old boyfriend in Melbourne, didn't you?'

'Jeremy.' Jenni's voice was still icy. 'Who's now married. Happily married. With kids.' She pushed herself to her feet. 'So, no... I didn't jump into bed with him for old time's sake.'

She turned towards the path and steps that led back to the house. And to where she'd parked Grace's car. She had to escape.

Now...

'This was never going to work,' she said, without looking at Dan. 'I thought I was doing the right thing, but it's clearly been the biggest mistake I've ever made and there's no point in dragging this out any longer. Hopefully, it's not too late to change my arrangements and get on the first plane I can back to Scotland.' She lifted her chin and turned her head just far enough to catch his gaze. 'I don't want you in my life, Daniel Walker.'

Jenni started walking away. 'I don't want you in the lives of my children either.'

CHAPTER TEN

OBSTETRIC CONSULTANT MARIA GOULD looked up from the report she was reading and the expression on her face made Jenni McKay's heart skip a beat.

'There's something wrong, isn't there? Something that showed up on the biophysical profile ultrasound?' Jenni found she was holding her breath.

She had taken the test yesterday afternoon, where sensors had been strapped to her belly to record the heart rates of each twin and individual ultrasounds done to measure and score their body movements, muscle tone, breathing movements and the amount of amniotic fluid around them.

She had not invited Dan to attend the appointment.

Despite her best efforts, however, she'd thought about him the whole time it was happening but she had refused to let herself feel guilty. He didn't believe these twins were his babies. He didn't deserve to be there.

He had tried to call her more than once after she'd walked out on him the night before last. She hadn't picked up and then she had blocked his number. When she'd seen him at a distance at work yesterday, she'd turned and walked in the other direction without making eye contact. Luckily, no one in her care had been in need of any kind of anaesthetic.

Jenni was still angry.

Deeply disappointed.

Hurt beyond measure.

She didn't want to talk to the man who only believed she wasn't lying to him because he believed that she'd been having sex with other men. Besides, she'd been ridiculously busy, both at work and at home. She had handed in her resignation to take effect almost immediately—as soon as Grace got back from her honeymoon in a day or two and could take back her caseload. She'd made the appointment with Maria and persuaded Mandy to fit her in for the extra ultrasound test. She'd pored over flight itineraries, booked and paid for airline tickets. She'd started packing...

Jenni couldn't let go of that breath that had caught deep in her chest until Maria smiled. 'Nothing wrong showed up on the profile,' she said. 'Quite the contrary. The twins both scored nine—normal is eight to ten. They're a good weight. Twin A is one point two kilos and Twin B is one point four. That's about three pounds and three point two pounds. I'm happy to stay with the estimated delivery date we came up with originally, but that means you're getting close to thirty-two weeks.'

Jenni nodded, pulling in a new, deeper breath with relief.

'You're pushing it.' Maria's tone was worried. 'For international travel.' She picked up another piece of paper from her desk. 'You're planning to fly from Blenheim to Auckland, connect with an international flight to London via Singapore and then take a domestic flight from London to Glasgow. Total travel time of nearly *thirty-five* hours?'

Jenni bit her lip. 'I know...it's horrible.'

'The airline requires a clearance from me. I have to sign my name to information about this being a multiple pregnancy, whether there are any complications, the EDD and whether I think you're fit to travel.'

'I am fit to travel,' Jenni assured her. 'And I haven't crossed the thirty-two-week barrier yet.'

'That could well be debated. Especially if anything went wrong—like delivering premature twins at thirty thousand feet. Or a pilot having to divert the plane to get you to a hospital. Have you got travel insurance?'

'That needs a clearance from you as well,' Jenni admitted. 'I *have* to travel...' She could feel her eyes filling with tears. 'It's...to do with the babies' father,' she added, her voice cracking. 'I have to get back home and if I don't go now it'll be too late...'

Too late for her to escape, but she couldn't tell Maria that. Jenni might prefer to never have to see Daniel Walker again in her life but she still wasn't going to risk making his involvement in her pregnancy public. One day, in a future so far away she didn't need to think about it right now, her children might want to find their biological father. It would be best if he was prepared to make that easy and that would be a lot less likely if he'd been subjected to widespread judgement or disapproval of the way he had denied paternity. He was probably going to get enough shade from Jock and Grace anyway, when they found out what was going on.

Maria had made the assumption, at her first appointment, that the twins' father lived in Scotland. Now she was probably thinking that her relationship was in jeopardy or that her partner was desperately ill. She certainly looked torn.

'How are *you* feeling?' she queried. 'Be honest, please...'

'I'm a bit short of breath sometimes,' Jenni responded. 'I get some backache, I need to pee frequently, and I'm not sleeping that well. The usual stuff for this stage of pregnancy. Better than usual for a multiple pregnancy.'

Any physical symptoms were compounded by feeling more

utterly miserable than she had ever felt in her life, of course, but she couldn't tell Maria that either. She had to be strong. This was about her future. And the future of her children. They deserved to grow up with a mother who respected herself enough to know that she couldn't be with someone who didn't believe in her integrity.

Maria was silent for a long moment and then she sighed as she picked up her pen. 'Okay... I'll sign you off, but you've still got forty-eight hours before your first flight. If *anything* changes, I want to know about it.'

Jenni nodded. 'I won't go anywhere if I think there's any danger to these babies,' she said quietly. 'They're my absolute priority.'

'Are you working today?'

'It's my last full day. I'll be tying up loose ends tomorrow, ready to hand everything back to Grace.' Jenni got to her feet. 'I might even get most of that done today.'

'Don't tempt fate,' Maria warned but she was smiling. 'Best of luck.' She handed over the sheet of paper that was her clearance for Jenni to travel. 'It's been a pleasure meeting you.' She raised an eyebrow. 'Does Jock know that you're rushing back to Scotland?'

'Not yet. I didn't want to tell him while he's on his honeymoon.' Jenni folded the paper carefully, trying—and failing—to squash another pang of guilt. 'Thanks so much for all your help, Maria.'

Jenni remembered Maria's warning about tempting fate the moment she walked back to the maternity ward to find that Lynn Grimshaw had arrived with her partner, Chris. She was in established labour, with strong, regular contractions and already five centimetres dilated.

She remembered it again several hours later, when she

had to call for the obstetrician on duty—who happened to be Maria—when the labour had failed to progress despite trying everything Jenni suggested, like walking around, changing positions, bouncing on a birth ball, a hot shower... Lynn was getting tired, her contractions were getting weaker and there were some decelerations happening with the baby's heart rate. A decision was made to start an oxytocin infusion to augment labour, to do a bedside ultrasound to check the position of the foetal head in relation to the pelvis and Lynn asked to have an epidural as well.

Fate—having been tempted—apparently had one last ace up her sleeve when it came to the anaesthetist on duty because it was Daniel Walker who walked into the room a short time later as Mandy was doing the ultrasound examination.

For a horrible moment Jenni actually wondered if she could do this. If she could be totally professional and not let anything to do with her personal life affect her professional abilities. Emotions were threatening to overwhelm her. The anger was still there but the hurt was far more powerful.

Thank goodness Maria had stayed to observe the ultrasound and the initial effects of the infusion. She introduced Dan to their patient and her partner and gave him all the medical information he needed and that gave Jenni a good couple of minutes to centre herself and get into a space where nothing personal could interfere in any way with her part in something that was a critical time in the life of both a mother and a baby.

This was her last day at work here.

The last time she would ever have to be in the room with the man who'd broken her heart so badly.

She could do this.

She *had* to be able to do this...

* * *

Good grief…she looked so pale…

Unwell, even.

And it was his fault, wasn't it?

For the space of a heartbeat and then another, Dan actually wondered if he could be in this room and give a hundred per-cent to the woman who needed his medical care.

Maria was filling him in. 'Lynn Grimshaw is a thirty-eight-year-old primigravida, full-term, textbook pregnancy with no known issues. Foetal lie is longitudinal with a cephalic pre-sentation.'

Dan nodded but it was an effort to focus. If he couldn't… if too much of his mind—and heart—were on the care that another woman in this room needed—the woman he loved, he would have to excuse himself somehow from this patient and find someone else to administer this epidural anaesthetic.

'Lynn went into spontaneous labour fourteen hours ago. She came in this morning at five centimetres dilated but has failed to progress past six centimetres for more than four hours. Decelerations of the foetal heart rate have been noted so we started an oxytocin infusion nearly an hour ago. Contraction strength has improved and she's currently at seven centime-tres dilated.'

Maybe it was the way Dan saw Jenni's shoulders move, as if she was straightening her back to face whatever she had to deal with, that suddenly brought everything into sharp focus for himself.

This wasn't about them. It was about a tired mother, her anxious partner and a baby that was in increasingly urgent need of a safe arrival. Jenni was handling this like a profes-sional and so could he.

He picked up Lynn's chart and noted the last vital sign recordings. 'She tachycardic,' he murmured. 'Heart rate of one fifteen. Her blood pressure's a bit low at ninety-six over fifty-five.' He looked at the screen of the ultrasound machine and lowered his voice. 'There's no indications of placental abruption or bleeding, is there?'

'No, but the sensitivity for picking it up on ultrasound can be as low as twenty-five percent. There's no visible bleeding.' Maria was also looking at the screen. 'I'm happy with the foetal head position too, if we need to go for an instrumental delivery.'

'The sooner we get the epidural in the better, then.' Dan stepped towards Lynn. 'I'm going to get you to sit with your legs over the edge of the bed,' he told her. 'Jenni will help you lean forward and stay as still as possible. This won't take long…'

Fifteen minutes later, the epidural had taken full effect but the pain relief hadn't reduced Lynn's rapid heart rate or breathing. Dan made the decision to stay in the room a while longer. It was probably because Jenni was here that the atmosphere felt so tense but instinct was telling him that something else was contributing to this feeling of unease. Lynn was his patient now as well. He wasn't going to leave until he was confident there was nothing to worry about.

Was Jenni feeling that frisson of concern too? Or was she concentrating on the screen of the CTG machine in order to avoid catching his gaze?

'You're doing well,' Jenni told Lynn. 'Your contractions are still strong and they're lasting well.'

'I feel weird.' Lynn reached for her partner's hand. 'Something's wrong, Chris…'

Maria straightened up from doing an internal examination. 'You're in transition, Lynn,' she said. 'That can make you feel anxious. You're at least eight centimetres now. You'll be able to start pushing very soon.'

'No...' Lynn's head rolled from side to side on her pillow. 'I feel...sick...'

'That's normal,' Jenni assured her, but her gaze flicked past Dan and he could feel something change in the room again.

Concern was growing...

'What's happening...?' Lynn sounded frightened now.

'Your waters have finally broken,' Jenni responded. 'It's okay, Lynn...'

Except it wasn't. Dan could see that the fluid had a green stain that meant it contained meconium.

'I want to get up,' Lynn said. 'Please... Chris... I have to go home...'

Chris looked at Jenni, his eyes wide with alarm.

'It hurts,' Lynn cried.

'What hurts?' Dan's heart rate picked up. Was the epidural infusion failing?

'My chest...' Lynn was gasping now. 'I can't breathe...' She fell back against her pillows.

'Foetal heart rate's dropping,' Jenni warned as an alarm sounded on the CTG machine.

Maria was moving fast. 'She's fully dilated,' she said moments later, turning to her registrar. 'Open that forceps kit for me, please. We need to get this baby out.'

'Lynn...?' Dan was at the head of the bed. He gripped her shoulder. 'Can you hear me? Open your eyes...'

Dan was removing the pillows from behind Lynn so that he could tilt her head back and open her airway.

Because she wasn't breathing...

He had to ask Chris to step back so that he could get to the bag mask and put it over Lynn's face to help her breathe.

'Sorry, mate…we need a bit of space…'

But Chris wasn't moving. He was standing, stunned, as though he couldn't understand what was happening. Jenni moved swiftly and took hold of his arm.

'Come over here, Chris. Look…your baby's being born…'

She had to leave Chris standing by himself seconds later, as a limp-looking baby emerged and was put into the towel Jenni grabbed. The registrar headed for the phone, presumably to summon the assistance of neonatal paediatrics. Maria was dealing with what looked like a significant postpartum haemorrhage and Dan…

Dan couldn't find a pulse.

'Someone push the cardiac arrest button,' he shouted. 'I'm starting CPR.'

Dear *Lord*…

Jenni had to think faster and focus harder than she ever had or she might have become as frozen as poor Chris was right now. She'd stand there watching the controlled chaos of the response to an emergency situation and listen to directions being called and alarms sounding and all she'd be thinking about was how could this have gone so horribly wrong?

At least she had something to do that needed all her concentration. This baby girl was scarily pale and limp. Jenni put her down on the waterproof mattress of the resuscitation table, beneath the radiant heat source. Using a soft towel, she began drying the baby with firm stroking movements—on her head, her body and her legs to provide stimulation as well as removing the moisture that would be sucking away body heat. She looked up as she wrapped another dry towel around the infant to see the registrar standing, hands poised above Lynn's chest to restart the chest compressions as soon as she was intubated. Maria was doing bimanual compression, clearly trying to control the amount of blood Lynn was losing. Dan was bent over Lynn's head, his concentration fierce enough to be palpable. He had a laryngoscope blade in her mouth and was slipping an endotracheal tube into place to secure her airway for ventilation.

The baby was gasping rather than breathing well herself so Jenni positioned her head to open her airway before she placed the disc of a stethoscope on the small chest. The heart rate was less than a hundred—too slow. She picked up one of the small, round masks to check that it was the right size to make a good seal over the tiny mouth and nose. Then she attached it to an Ambu bag and gave five slow, gentle breaths, watching the small chest to make sure the lungs were being inflated.

The baby's colour was improving. Jenni was about to re-check the heart rate when the first of the extra medical teams summoned burst into the room. The cardiac arrest crew on call surrounded the bed but somehow, a few seconds later, Dan slipped through the tight group of people to appear beside the resuscitation table. He caught Jenni's gaze.

'What can I do?'

It was only then that Jenni realised how alone she'd been, looking after this newborn. How *scared* she'd been…

And that tone in Dan's voice. The focus. The offer of support. The caring… It was enough to bring the prickle of tears to the back of Jenni's eyes. But it was the baby who began to cry. She was getting rapidly pinker too, and starting to move her arms and legs.

'I think we're okay,' Jenni told Dan. She caught his gaze again for a heartbeat. 'But…thank you.'

She picked up the baby girl and took her to Chris, who was still standing to one side. His view of what was being done to help Lynn was almost totally obstructed by so many people but that was probably a good thing because, from what Jenni could hear, the resuscitation was not going well.

Chris began crying as he saw the baby. Silently, with the tears rolling unchecked down his face. His hands were shaking as he reached out to touch her.

'Is she okay...?'

'She's good. She needed a wee bit of help, but now she's doing well.'

'Can I hold her?' Chris asked, his voice breaking. 'Please...?'

He needed something to hold onto, didn't he? As the world as he knew it was apparently disintegrating.

'Come and sit down,' Jenni said gently, her heart breaking for him. 'I think being held by her daddy is exactly what your daughter needs.'

What both father and baby needed.

The paediatric team arrived but didn't immediately take the baby from her father's arms. Bags of blood and IV fluids were being delivered. More and different drugs were being administered and there was a discussion about taking Lynn to Theatre to try and get control of the bleeding but, in the end, they had to admit defeat.

Someone looked up at the clock on the wall. 'Time of death,' they said quietly. 'Sixteen forty-three...'

Lynn Grimshaw had tragically become one of the very rare cases of a woman dying during childbirth even in a well-equipped hospital setting.

The silence that followed the announcement of the time of death only lasted a few seconds but it was one of the most profound silences Jenni had ever experienced.

Even the tiny baby in the room was quiet. And still.

Everyone was still. Maybe that was why Jenni was suddenly aware of her own babies moving.

It was then that a new fear was born.

What if something terrible happened when *she* was giving birth?

Alone…?

What if her babies survived but there was no one there to hold them?

Like…their *father*…?

CHAPTER ELEVEN

BETWEEN THE INTERNAL hospital driveway and the main road leading into the centre of the town there was a garden that was the pride and joy of the Picton Hospital groundsmen.

There was a central fountain, neatly clipped hedges, rose gardens bursting with colour in the summer, shelter from the huge horse chestnut trees and plenty of rustic wooden benches to provide seating. It was popular with staff members, visitors and patients who were mobile enough to escape outside for a break and a bit of fresh air on fine days.

It was usually easy to find an empty bench that afforded privacy, which meant it was also a refuge for people who needed time and space alone to deal with the unimaginable, and when Dan went looking for Jenni as the traumatic aftermath of a totally unexpected patient death was finally ebbing, someone told him that they'd seen her going into the garden a short time ago.

It was dark outside now and while there were antique-style streetlamps that provided plenty of light, it didn't seem a safe place for a woman to be alone. It would also be cold. Dan picked up one of the hospital's bright red woollen blankets before he went out to see if Jenni was still there. If she wasn't, he was going to find her.

He'd seen the fear in her eyes when the call had been made to stop Lynn's resuscitation and her time of death had been recorded.

She was due to give birth herself in a matter of weeks and she'd just witnessed the worst possible outcome.

She couldn't be alone.

She might not want his company but Dan knew that Jock and Grace were still out of town and…he couldn't let her be alone…

Because he loved her.

He found her, sitting alone near the very centre of the garden. She wasn't crying but she looked so forlorn that Dan could actually feel his heart cracking. She was also shivering so, without saying anything, Dan wrapped her in the fuzzy red blanket.

And then he sat down beside her and wrapped her in his arms.

Oh…

Grace had been so right, hadn't she?

Home *could* be a person and not a place.

She should have known that all along. Jenni hadn't felt this afraid since she was a child, and in those days it had been Jock who could make her feel safe.

She was grown up now and confident enough in her independence that she'd been more than happy to plan on being a single parent. But she couldn't make herself feel quite *this* safe. Because the love that wrapped around you from the outside was so very powerful—if you could trust it.

But how could you trust anything when it felt like everything that mattered the most was teetering on the edge of a cliff?

'I'm scared,' she whispered against his chest. 'I'm *so* scared, Dan.'

'I know.' He held her tighter. 'It's not going to happen to you, Jen.'

'It happened to Lynn.' Jenni could feel tears that had been caught by the ache in her chest for hours and hours beginning to escape. 'Why...? *How* did that happen? Did I miss something that could have stopped it happening?'

'No.' The word was certain. 'There were discussions about it when you went with Chris and the baby to NICU for her neonatal check. The general consensus is that it was most likely an amniotic fluid embolism. She had all the features, with an acute maternal collapse and foetal compromise during labour or immediately after the birth. She had the respiratory symptoms, hypotension, confusion, agitation...'

'But the bleeding... Did we miss an abruption?'

'They think the bleeding was caused by coagulopathy. Clotting issues also fit the preliminary diagnosis. We'll know more after the post-mortem.' Dan's breath came out in a sigh. 'You and Maria did as well as you could have done. I hear the baby's doing well. They're only going to keep her under observation in NICU overnight.'

'Chris isn't leaving her side. He even took her with him when he was taken to see Lynn.' The tears were flowing faster now. 'I went with him. He told her that he was going to look after their daughter for the rest of his life. That he would always love her...twice as much as he would have because he'd make sure she had her mother's love as well. That he was going to love her as much as he's always loved Lynn...'

Jenni's voice broke completely. Dan tried to say something but the words were too strangled so Jenni scrubbed at her face and tried again.

'I was going to go back to Scotland the day after tomorrow,' she confessed. 'I've got the tickets and everything.'

'*No...*' The word was almost a plea. 'Please don't do that, Jen. I don't want to lose you...'

'I'm not going to do it,' she said. 'I knew I couldn't the moment Lynn died. When I saw her baby in her father's arms. You have to be there, Dan...in case something bad happens to me...'

'Nothing bad is going to happen.' Dan had his cheek pressed against Jenni's hair. 'I won't let it. I'll keep you safe... I'll keep you *all* safe...'

They both knew that was a promise that couldn't be made, but it was what Jenni needed to hear.

'Even if you don't believe that you're their father?'

'But I do,' Dan said.

Jenni shifted in his arms, sitting up enough to be able to see his face properly. 'But...'

'I said it badly,' Dan said quietly. 'What I meant was that even if I wasn't their father biologically, I would still feel like I am.' Jenni could hear him pulling in a deep breath. 'And that's been the hardest thing for me—a risk I never thought I could ever take again. To have the dream of being a father come true and then to lose it.'

'*Again...?*' Jenni felt a shiver run down her spine. 'I knew you'd been married but you never said you'd lost a child. You said you *couldn't* have kids...'

Her brain was trying—and failing—to fit puzzle pieces together.

'I believed I was going to become a father.' Dan was speaking slowly, his tone bleak. 'My wife found out she was pregnant, ironically not long after we'd had the results of my first fertility test, when we were just starting to gather information about using technology to try and help us start a family.'

'So you knew it wasn't impossible...' Jenni wasn't sure

if she'd spoken those words aloud but Dan seemed to be responding to them.

'She let me believe I'd beaten those astronomical odds for months but then I found out about the affair she'd been having for the last year. That the father of her baby was actually the man that she ended up leaving me to be with.'

The puzzle pieces were falling into place with painful precision.

Jenni could hear echoes of things that Dan had said on the evening they'd met for the first time.

'If you trust someone who tells you lies, you give them the power to destroy you...'

'Fool me once, shame on you. Fool me twice, shame on me...'

Jenni sat up straighter. She lifted her hand to place it on Dan's cheek. 'I get it,' she said softly. 'And I'm sorry. I was asking too much.'

She could feel Dan shaking his head beneath her hand. He opened his mouth to say something, but Jenni shifted her hand so that her fingers were on his lips to prevent any words escaping. She had more she wanted to say first.

'I expected you to believe me simply because I knew I was telling the truth. I wish I'd known what you just told me because then I would have known that you didn't have that kind of trust any longer, and I *know* what that's like. Do you remember me telling you that Jock and I made a vow when we were thirteen that we'd never get married because we saw our mother bounce from one marriage or relationship to the next and they never turned out well?'

This time Jenni could feel the nod beneath her hand but she still didn't move her fingers.

'There's something I didn't tell you, though. I didn't tell

you that Jock and I learned that it was better not to trust even the people that said they loved you—maybe *especially* those people—because they made you hope that things would be different, but it never lasted. We learned not to trust before we even understood what trust was.' She swallowed hard. 'And we learned that it was always our fault. That just being born had ruined our mum's life, so it wasn't her fault that she never kept her promises. The ones about Father Christmas bringing presents or that she'd be there to see our school play didn't matter so much. The worst were the ones she made when she'd fallen in love—yet again—and promised us that everything was going to be wonderful because we'd be a real family this time. Years before we made the vow about not getting married or having kids, Jock told me he was never, ever going to make a promise he couldn't keep and I said I was never going to tell lies. Jock said that a broken promise was a kind of lie, but it felt bigger to me.'

Jenni was trying to smile but her lips wouldn't cooperate. 'Do you remember when I told you, that night we first met, that I never lie and you asked how you could know whether that was a lie?'

Her fingers had slipped away from Dan's lips now but he didn't say anything. He just gave a slow single nod.

'*That's* why,' Jenni said. 'I can't deliberately lie because I know how much it can hurt. That's why I understand why it's been so hard for you to trust—in me, in relationships… in a universe that's made something happen that's magic because you never thought it could happen. But it's the truth, Dan, and…and so is this…' Jenni took a very deep breath. 'Up until now in my life, Jock's been the only person I've trusted enough to love with all my heart. I never thought I'd trust anyone else that much. Or love anyone else this much, but I love you, Daniel Walker. That much and more. And I love our babies. *Our* babies…' She found the smile she'd lost. 'You're the only person I've slept with in more than a year.' Her voice dropped to a whisper. 'You're the only person I *want* to sleep with for the rest of my life…'

'That's exactly how long I want you in my bed,' Dan said softly. 'How good is that?' He bent his head to brush her lips with his own. 'I thought I couldn't believe in miracles any longer. That I couldn't even believe in love. But you've changed everything. And we've been reminded today that life can change in a heartbeat. *This* is what really matters.'

He pressed a real kiss onto Jenni's lips this time and then rested his forehead against hers. 'I love you,' he said. 'I think I fell in love with you that first night. When you told me you can sleep like a starfish. I just didn't realise that it had happened—until the day of Jock and Grace's wedding. It took me a few days to find the courage to tell you and…well…that didn't turn out so well, did it?'

'That was my fault more than yours. I'm sorry…'

'I get it. And I was asking too much from you, wasn't I? That I could tell you that I love you but, at the same time, tell you that I still couldn't believe the impossible had happened and I was the babies' father.'

The echo of her own words about asking too much just made this soul-deep connection between them stronger.

And she could hear another echo. The question of whether she could trust the love she could feel all around her.

The love that was coming from Dan.

That was the moment she knew she *could* trust it. It felt like she had no choice because she loved Dan. She had already given him her heart.

And he was still holding her as if that was exactly what he wanted. As if he loved *her* that much.

Maybe he could feel what she was thinking.

'I love you,' Dan told her again, softly. 'I need to be this close to you…for ever…' But he broke the contact of their skin a moment later. 'Come home with me now,' he said. 'I want to take care of you and it's too cold out here.'

It *was* cold. Jenni's legs felt stiff as she got to her feet. Her whole body felt stiff, in fact. And sore enough to make her groan.

'What's wrong?'

'I think I've done something to my back. It's really sore…'

Dan put one hand on her lower back. 'Here?'

'Yes.'

Dan's other hand was on her belly. 'Can you feel that?'

Of course she could. The tightening was like a vice being wound up. 'It's a contraction,' she said. 'I've had Braxton Hicks contractions before. It'll go in a few seconds.'

Except it didn't.

Her belly had never become this hard before. Hard enough to make the pain in her back become more intense.

The fear and distress that had brought Jenni into the sanctuary of this garden in the first place had begun to fade the moment Dan had taken her into his arms. As they'd opened their hearts to each other the connection between them had felt strong enough to conquer anything.

But the fear was crowding in again.

The fear that something terrible was going to happen and all the love in the world couldn't prevent it.

'I think this is a *real* contraction.' Jenni's voice was hollow. 'And it's too early.' She met Dan's gaze. She didn't need to tell him how scared she was. She could see a reflection of her own fear in his eyes.

He pulled the fuzzy red blanket around her more tightly and then lifted her into his arms as if she wasn't such an awkward, heavy shape with her huge belly.

'I've got you,' he said as he began to walk back towards the hospital. 'We've got this... Just hang on.'

Jenni wrapped her arms around his neck and held on.

As tightly as she could.

Maria Gould was still the obstetrician on call for Picton Hospital that evening and she arrived in a commendably short period of time after Dan strode into the emergency department with Jenni in his arms.

'How long have you been getting the contractions?'

'I'm not sure. I've had a few Braxton Hicks contractions over the last week or two but I wasn't really paying much attention earlier.'

Maria nodded. She knew exactly why. 'It's been a very stressful day,' she said quietly. 'And you've been on your feet for a long time.'

Jenni tried to hold back the wave of fear. 'Severe stress is a known cause for preterm labour, isn't it? And carrying twins is another.'

Had Dan sensed how frightened she was? Was that why he took hold of her hand? Maria wasn't the only staff member in this resuscitation room she'd been put in. The news that they were in a relationship was going to spread like wildfire, but maybe Dan sensed that thought as well and that was why he gave her hand a reassuring squeeze.

He wasn't going to let anything stop him staying this close to her.

'This is only a suspected PTL,' Maria said calmly. 'It's not established yet. Have your waters broken?'

'No.'

'Any bleeding or discharge?'

'No. But I've had a sore back for a while.'

'Yes, I remember you saying this morning that you were getting backache quite often.' If this experienced consultant was feeling justified in having been reluctant to give Jenni clearance to take an international flight back to Scotland she was professional enough not to let it show. 'Is this pain different? Worse?'

'It gets more intense when I'm getting a contraction.'

'How often are they happening?'

Jenni looked up at Dan, who was standing right beside her bed. 'She's had two in the last ten minutes or so.'

Maria nodded. 'We'll get continuous CTG monitoring on for you and see what the frequency and duration of these contractions are. Stress is a known trigger for increased Braxton Hicks activity. I'm going to do an ultrasound to have a look at your cervix to see if there's any indication of thinning or dilating and we'll go from there.'

Jenni nodded but it was Dan's gaze she sought as the anchor she needed.

'We've got this, darling,' he said.

Both his tone and the endearment made it clear that he wasn't simply holding Jenni's hand as a friend. Maria had a little more difficulty in hiding her reaction this time. A hint of a smile was there now.

'We *have* got this,' she said. 'I'm going to get some air transport on standby just in case we do need to transfer you to a facility with a higher level of neonatal intensive care available, like Wellington or Christchurch. We can give you tocolytic drugs to slow or stop a premature labour if that's what's actually happening and we'd also give you steroids to lower the risks for the babies of any complications for preterm birth.'

A portable ultrasound machine was being wheeled into the room. The CTG machine was right behind it.

'Has someone let Jock know what's going on?' Maria asked as the technician got ready to place transducers on Jenni's belly.

'I can do that,' Dan offered.

This time Maria let herself smile warmly. 'No. Don't move,' she said. 'I think you're in exactly the right place at the moment. I'll go and give Jock a quick call before I do the ultrasound.'

Jock and Grace were in the room when Maria visited the maternity ward later the next day.

'How did you get back so fast?' she asked them.

'We were already on the way,' Jock said. 'That's why I didn't pick up your message for a while.' He was smiling at his twin sister. 'Talk about coming down to earth with a bump. The honeymoon is definitely over.'

'Sorry about that,' Maria said. 'I should have waited before calling anyway. I hear things have settled nicely overnight, so it seems that this has been a false alarm and the combination of Braxton Hicks, backache and the involvement in a traumatic case was enough to give us all a fright.'

'I heard about Lynn…' Grace had tears in her eyes. 'It's so awful…'

Jock put his arm around Grace's shoulders but it was Jenni whose gaze he was holding. 'A once in a lifetime event in your career, I hope,' he said. 'But the worst time it could have happened. I'm sorry I wasn't here.'

'You're here now,' Jenni said. 'And…it was okay because… Dan was here.'

Dan reached for her hand but spoke to Jock and Grace. 'I've been up to NICU this morning. The baby's fine. The dad, Chris, has a hugely supportive family, including his in-laws, who are surrounding him. He's still in shock, of course, but he told me that this is the way he can honour his wife—by protecting their child—and he's not going to let either of them down.'

They were all quiet for a long moment, which made it easy to hear the sound of two strong foetal hearts beating in the background.

'I think we can take those transducers off,' Maria said. 'And let you go home to rest properly. As long as you've got some-one keeping a close eye on you?'

'I'll be doing that,' Dan said.

'So will we,' Grace added, sharing a glance with Jock.

Maria was giving Jenni a stern look now. 'I'll want to see you every few days from now on. We'll be doing a biophysi-cal profile ultrasound at least once a week. You do realise there's absolutely no chance of you getting on any interna-tional flights now, don't you?'

'What?' Grace and Jock spoke together.

'Long story,' Jenni told them. 'I'll tell you later.' She smiled at Maria. 'It's okay, I'm not planning to go anywhere. I'll be cancelling my tickets first thing in the morning.'

'You're coming home with us,' Jock said. 'I'm not having you alone in that hospital accommodation.'

'No…' Dan shook his head. 'She's coming home with me.'

Everybody was looking at Jenni.

She was looking at Dan.

'I will come home with you, please,' she said softly. Her

smile was wry. 'Good thing I have all my things pretty much packed already.'

Maria was looking from Jenni to Dan and back to Jenni. 'When did this all start?' she asked. 'When you stepped in for Grace and began working here?'

'Um…' Jenni shared a glance with Dan. Asking permission to share something private? The smile she received looked like permission. 'We actually met a while ago,' she told Maria. 'Around the time I got pregnant.'

'At exactly the time she got pregnant,' Dan added. 'I'm the father of these babies.'

Maria's jaw dropped.

'That reminds me,' Jenni said. 'I need to get some blood taken for a DNA test. We might need to provide proof of Dan's paternity for the twins' birth certificates. The powers-that-be might be justified in being a bit suspicious of someone arriving in the country already pregnant and then claiming citizenship for their kids.'

'Well, I never…' Maria seemed lost for words. She looked at Dan and then at Jock. She shook her head. 'I should have known that things were going to change around here when your twin arrived. Double trouble…' She gave Jenni another stern look but she was smiling at the same time. 'No more trouble with this pregnancy, though, thank you. You go home and take it easy. Your job is to keep those babies inside for as long as you can. Two or three weeks would be ideal.'

It was exactly three weeks later when Dan arrived home from work to find Jenni slowly pacing the floor, her hand pressed against her back.

'Backache again?'

She nodded.

'Any contractions?'

'Just the usual Braxton Hicks. I'm counting. I've only had two in the last thirty minutes.'

Dan shrugged off his jacket and hooked it over a chair beside the dining table. He put his phone down on the table and picked up an envelope lying beside a bowl of fruit. 'What's this?'

'It came today.'

'Looks official.' Dan scanned the return address and his jaw dropped as his gaze locked with Jenni's. 'It's from the laboratory in Wellington. It's the DNA test results.'

'I know…'

'You haven't opened it.'

'I thought we should do that together.'

Dan nodded but his mouth had gone very dry and his fingers wouldn't move. And then the envelope slipped from his fingers to land back on the table and become irrelevant for the moment because Jenni had suddenly wrapped her arms around her belly and was leaning forward. Fluid was running down her legs to puddle on the wooden floor.

'My waters have broken.' Her announcement was redundant. 'Or one of them, at least. Maybe they're not just Braxton Hicks.' Her eyes were wide. 'They're not painful but we'd better start timing them.'

'Maria wants you in hospital at the first sign of labour.' Dan's heart rate had picked up noticeably. 'As far as I'm concerned, your waters breaking is right up near the top of that list.'

'Ooh…' Jenni was hanging on to the back of the couch now. 'Okay… I can feel this one…'

'I'll get your bag. Are you all right there for a sec?'

'Yes. Can you get a towel for the car too?'

'Don't move. I'll be right back.'

Jenni had packed her hospital bag ages ago—during the first days after she'd been released from monitoring the premature labour scare they'd had. When she had moved in with Dan and they were sharing the bubble of being openly in love and totally committed to each other.

Those days had passed in a dreamy blur for Dan.

There was, of course, no hint of anything sexual in their relationship currently but, strangely, that had made it deeper and so much more intense. They had lain in bed together, holding hands and...talking. Talking for hours and hours, night after night. They'd shared memories of their childhoods, the minefield of being teenagers, tales of failed relationships and the passion of training and working in their chosen careers. They knew each other's favourite foods and music and movies, books they'd choose to read again and places they'd love to travel to.

They knew each other now—it was as simple as that.

They loved each other—it was as significant as that.

And they were about to become parents together—and it was as life-changing as that.

Dan had the handles of a soft bag over his shoulder and those of a larger bag in his hand as he got back to the open-plan living area. Jenni had ignored his instruction to not move and was heading for the door. Dan increased his stride to catch up, but had to pause as he noticed his phone on the table. He reached to pick it up and for some reason he also picked up the envelope beside it that he'd dropped only minutes ago. He stuffed both items into the side pocket of the bag over his shoulder.

'Wait for me,' he called as Jenni disappeared through the door. 'Don't go trying to get down those stairs by yourself.'

* * *

It was only a fifteen-minute drive to get to the hospital but Jenni had to cope with five contractions, each of them lasting forty-five to sixty seconds. Dan was trying to hold Jenni's hand when she reached for him and at the same time trying to drive safely and swiftly with only one hand on the wheel. It was a relief for both of them when he turned into the ambulance bay and abandoned the car to run inside and grab a wheelchair. Other staff members rushed to help and Jenni saw Dan throw his car keys towards an orderly so that someone else could sort shifting the vehicle.

It wasn't just Maria waiting for them in the labour suite. As her midwife, Grace was there and either she or Dan must have called Jock because he was there as well. Looking excited but nervous.

'You can't come in,' Jenni told her brother.

'No, you can't.' Grace backed her up. 'You'll have to wait outside because Jenni doesn't want you to see her lady bits.'

'But I see them all the time,' Jock protested.

'Not mine, you don't.'

'Sorry, mate.' Dan threw a look over his shoulder as he pushed Jenni's wheelchair into the room. 'I'll keep you posted, I promise.'

'Oh, I've got the penthouse suite,' Jenni said. 'How did you manage that, Grace?'

'Pure luck it wasn't occupied when Dan rang,' Grace said. 'I ran up and put dibs on it for you. I've even started filling the pool.'

Jenni felt the wheelchair stop but she couldn't move to get out of it. She was gripped by a new contraction and the increase in intensity—and pain—had, quite literally, stolen her breath away.

'Remember to breathe...' Grace's calm voice was close to her ear. 'You've got this, Jen.'

Jenni managed to blow out a breath.

'Forty-five seconds.' Grace clicked a stopwatch. 'Can we get you on the bed so that Maria can give you the once-over and see how far along you are?'

Jenni wasn't at all sure she wanted to stay on the bed, however, especially when Maria told her she was six centimetres dilated and in active labour. Another contraction had started only two minutes after the last and this one was painful enough to make her groan.

'Have you changed your mind about preferences for pain relief?' Maria asked. 'Are you still wanting to avoid an epidural?'

'Not unless it's needed for a Caesarean,' Jenni said. 'Can I try a hot shower first, Grace?'

'Of course. The pool's nearly ready too, if you still fancy being in water.'

The shower helped but it was sinking into the warmth of the deep water in the birthing pool later that made a real difference.

'This feels amazing,' Jenni sighed. She knelt in the pool, her arms hooked over the side. Dan knelt on the floor in front of her, his hands on her arms.

Her contractions were speeding up and getting longer. When she felt ready to push, Maria put on long plastic gloves that went up to her elbows so that she could check on how dilated her cervix was.

'You're good to go,' she told Jenni. Then she turned to Dan. 'Do you want to get in the pool with her?'

'Can I?'

'Yes.'

'I put boxer shorts in the bag for you,' Jenni told him. 'In case you wanted to.'

'Do you want me to?'

'Yes… I need you closer.'

She sat back in the pool as soon as Dan climbed in, so that she could lean against him within the circle of his arms. She could push back on him to brace herself and he could push back against her for more support and it felt as if they were both bringing this first baby into the world.

Grace was on one side of the pool and Maria on the other.

'You're doing so well, Jen,' Grace said. 'Keep pushing. Gentle pushes now…keep going…that's it…and breathe…'

'Baby's head's out,' Maria said. 'Wait for the next contraction…'

It came within seconds. Jenni barely had time to reach down to feel her baby's head.

'Big push…' Grace sounded breathless herself. 'Keep it up…there we are…'

Twin A—their baby boy—was lifted from the water to be put on Jenni's chest, still within the circle of Dan's arms. For a long, long moment, it felt like it was just the three of them because Grace and Maria somehow managed to fade into the background. Jenni had done that herself, so many times, as she'd witnessed this magic time when a new family was born, but she'd had no idea how powerful it actually was until she was holding her own infant and looked up to see her own emotions reflected in the eyes of the man she loved.

But the water was getting cold now and she shivered.

'The cord's stopped pulsing,' Maria said. 'Would you like to cut it, Dan?'

'Yes…' Dan took the scissors after the clamps were in place. Jenni was still shivering and had goosebumps on her arms.

'We need to get you out of the pool,' Grace said. 'It's too cold.'

Jenni squeezed her eyes shut. 'I'm not sure I want to do this again.'

She could hear the smile in her best friend's voice. 'You're already doing it,' Grace said.

Dan climbed out first and Grace wrapped the baby for him to hold but then, as Jenni was helped to climb onto the bed, she got the most intense contraction yet and cried out for him.

'Your waters have just broken for Baby B,' Grace said.

'And she's managed to turn herself around,' Maria added. 'I can see her foot.'

Jenni was shocked. Their baby girl was now a footling breech and she felt a flash of fear. 'I need you, Dan,' she called. 'I need you to hold me again…'

'But…'

Dan was torn. He looked down at the tiny face of his oh, so vulnerable premature newborn son. Then he looked at the face of the woman he loved, twisted by pain and fear, and the decision was a no-brainer. He made an executive decision and he opened the door of the birthing suite.

'Jock? Get in here. You need to hold your nephew for a minute or two.'

A minute was pretty much all it took for Twin B's somewhat dramatic entrance into the world to be completed and this time the parents were dry and warm as they cuddled their daughter and waited to cut the cord.

Jock brought the little boy back to join his family. 'I didn't see a thing,' he assured Jenni.

She smiled but there were tears lurking. Such happy tears.

She had her entire family here. Jock and Grace, Dan and

these two beautiful, healthy babies. They would need a thorough paediatric check very soon and would probably need to spend a day or two in the NICU, but they were doing well enough for Maria to deem the parents could have a few minutes to themselves when it was all over and there were no signs of any problems with either Jenni or the babies.

Everyone else left the room.

Dan adjusted the pillows on either side of Jenni so that she had a baby in the crook of each arm.

'Look at them,' he said softly. 'They're perfect...just like you... I love you, Jenni McKay. Too much to be able to find the words. Mind you, I've never been that great at finding words...'

He leaned closer to kiss her, so tenderly it made her heart ache.

'You found some pretty good words,' she murmured. 'I love you too, Daniel Walker.' She looked from one baby to the other. 'And you're right...these guys *are* perfect.'

'I'll just get my phone,' Dan said. 'I need a picture of this.'

He delved into the pocket of the bag to find his phone and Jenni saw an envelope fall to the floor at the same time.

'What's that?'

'Nothing...' Dan snatched it up and went to put it back into the bag. 'I don't know why I even picked it up when we left home.'

'It's the DNA paternity test results, isn't it?'

'Yes.'

'Bring it here.'

'Why?'

'I want to see it.'

'I don't,' Dan said.

'Don't you?'

'No.'

'Why not?'

'Because I don't need to,' Dan said quietly. 'I already know I'm the twins' father.'

Jenni knew exactly what would be on that result sheet but she still wanted to see it—in black and white—officially recorded for ever.

'Humour me.' Jenni smiled. 'I've just given birth.'

Dan had to open the envelope and pull out the sheet of paper to give to Jenni because she could only use one hand. He kept his eyes on the twins as she scanned the contents. The silence finally made him look up. He swallowed hard as he saw the tears in Jenni's eyes.

'Do I want to know?' he asked softly.

This time, her smile was so full of love it lit up the whole room.

'You were right,' she whispered. 'You already know.'

EPILOGUE

Two years later...

THE BRIDESMAID WAS heavily pregnant.

'I'm so happy that my bridesmaid's dress is getting a second outing,' Jenni said.

Grace patted her belly. 'I'm so happy that I've only got one baby in here. I don't know how you've coped so well with twins. There... I think we're finished here.' She used a final hairpin to secure the half-updo she'd given Jenni that left a tumble of red curls to tickle the bare top of her back. 'You look absolutely gorgeous.'

Jenni stood up and did a twirl in the living area of the small cottage they were in, getting ready for this wedding. 'I can't believe I found the perfect dress in a shop in Blenheim. A vintage nineteen-forties dress, even.'

The pale mushroom silk and lace dress had a fitted bodice with a sweetheart neckline, tiny cap sleeves and a swing skirt that had a ballerina length hem. Like Grace had done when she'd married Jock more than two years earlier, she was wearing only flowers in her hair for this intimate wedding ceremony that they'd chosen to have at Furneaux Lodge, a beautiful historic homestead at the head of Endeavor Inlet in the Marlborough Sounds that had a backdrop of native bush and only well-kept lawns between the homestead and the beach.

Just out of sight, moored on glassy smooth water, was Jock's boat *Lassie* that had brought them all out into the Sounds a couple of days ago.

Jock and Grace were in one of the resort's self-contained cottages—right beside the one that Jenni and Dan and the twins were in. Both cottages had a view across the lawns to the beach and the two friends took a moment to look out and soak in the blues and greens of a perfect New Zealand summer's afternoon.

'Brilliant idea, this,' Grace said. 'To have your wedding and honeymoon in the same place.' Then she laughed. 'And to invite the rest of your family to stay as well.'

'You need a babymoon,' Jenni told her. 'You won't have any time for much of a holiday for ages after that baby of yours turns up.'

'You got to go to Scotland. How old were the twins then? Nine months?'

'Aye…but I wouldn't recommend international travel with two babies. We only did that because I needed to sort all the legal stuff to sell my house and tie up all the loose ends so we could get on with finding our new house in Picton.'

They didn't have a private beach and a jetty like Jock and Grace did. They'd found an old villa on the hill, very like the hospital accommodation that had been a part of both Jenni and Grace's journey to finding the men they would be spending the rest of their lives with.

Their loves…

'Oh, look…' Grace was shading her eyes as she peered down at the beach.

'Are they building sandcastles?'

There were two tall men on the beach already, their trouser legs and the sleeves of their white shirts rolled up as they did their best to keep two excited toddlers entertained until the bride arrived. Their celebrant, Aroha, was waiting patiently near an archway that had been positioned on the beach, ready to frame the bride and groom as they exchanged vows against the stunning backdrop of one of the most beautiful places in the world.

'That'll be Dan's idea. I would have gone for collecting some shells myself.' But Jenni's smile was misty. 'He's the best dad ever. I'm so lucky…'

'He thinks he's even luckier. I heard him tell Jock that the other night when they were having that two-man stag party at our place. I'm just surprised it took him more than two years to propose to you.'

'He didn't,' Jenni confessed. 'I proposed to *him*.'

'Really?' Grace blinked.

'Really. I don't think he would ever have proposed. He knew I had no intention of ever getting married and he said it didn't matter—that all he wanted was for us to be together. For ever…'

'Oh…that's so romantic.'

'I had the feeling that he wanted to be married, though. Deep down. When you and Jock told us you were having a baby, he made a joke about Jock breaking both the vows we'd made when we were teenagers. Up to then we'd only broken half of them—one each—with him getting married and me having kids. There was something in his voice that caught me…here…' Jenni touched the skin over her heart. 'So that's when I proposed. I said I wanted to tell the world how much I love him and what an incredible father he is…to wear his ring for the rest of my life and to see him wearing mine.'

Grace was looking misty herself now. 'Come on…let's get down there. I want to hear these vows and see you both putting those rings on each other's fingers. And I want to see Sophie and Noah throwing rose petals at their parents—if they're not building sandcastles again by then.'

Jenni swallowed back tears of joy that might well ruin her eye make-up. There would be time for those later, perhaps, when she was folded into Dan's arms much later tonight. For now, there were declarations of love and promises to share with the people that mattered the most in the world.

With her family...

And, most of all, with the love of her life.

He was waiting for her on the beach. She saw him look up, as if he was wondering how soon he might see her.

Jenni gathered the ripples of her skirt in her hands and looked over her shoulder at Grace. 'Come on... I can't wait any longer...'

* * * * *

If you missed the previous story in the
A Tale of Two Midwives duet,
then check out

Falling for Her Forbidden Flatmate

And if you enjoyed this story,
check out these other great reads
from Alison Roberts

Therapy Pup to Heal the Surgeon
Forbidden Nights with the Paramedic
Rebel Doctor's Baby Surprise

All available now!

COMING SOON!

We really hope you enjoyed reading this book.
If you're looking for more romance
be sure to head to the shops when
new books are available on

Thursday 24th October

To see which titles are coming soon, please visit
millsandboon.co.uk/nextmonth

MILLS & BOON®

Coming next month

FESTIVE FLING WITH THE SURGEON
Karin Baine

'You don't want me to talk? I thought some women liked that sort of thing?' he teased her, whispering low in her ear, knowing the effect it had on her.

Her knees buckling, goosebumps rippling over her skin and a little gasp emitting from her lips were all things he remembered from their last time together, and he wasn't disappointed.

'Hmm, I'm of the opinion your mouth could be put to better use…'

The growl that came from deep inside his chest spoke of those caveman urges Tamsin appeared to waken in him. He'd never let himself get so wrapped up in thoughts of a woman that he'd brush aside all of his long-held reasons for avoiding commitment for something as basic as sex. Yet that was exactly what Tamsin did to him. All he could hope for now that he was lost to this chemistry was that things between them remained strictly physical. With any luck, a short fling over Christmas would give them both what they needed and they could move on in the New Year without fear of recriminations.

The knowledge that he didn't have to curtail his needs, that they'd gone into this together, eyes wide open, unleashed a part of Max he usually held back. Tamsin was getting more of him than anyone ever had.

Don't miss
FESTIVE FLING WITH THE SURGEON
Karin Baine

Available next month
millsandboon.co.uk

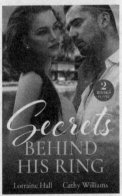

LET'S TALK

Romance

For exclusive extracts, competitions and special offers, find us online:

f MillsandBoon

X @MillsandBoon

⊙ @MillsandBoonUK

♪ @MillsandBoonUK

Get in touch on 01413 063 232

afterglow BOOKS

 Sports romance

 Sports romance

 Workplace romance

 Workplace romance

 One night

 Spicy

OUT NOW

Two stories published every month. Discover more at:
Afterglowbooks.co.uk

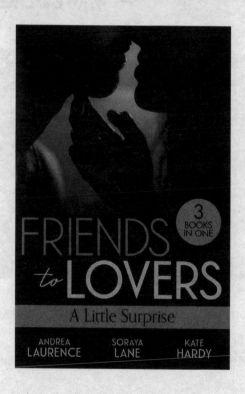

MILLS & BOON

THE HEART OF ROMANCE

A ROMANCE FOR EVERY READER

MODERN

Prepare to be swept off your feet by sophisticated, sexy and seductive heroes, in some of the world's most glamourous and romantic locations, where power and passion collide.

HISTORICAL

Escape with historical heroes from time gone by. Whether your passion is for wicked Regency Rakes, muscled Vikings or rugged Highlanders, awaken the romance of the past.

MEDICAL

Set your pulse racing with dedicated, delectable doctors in the high-pressure world of medicine, where emotions run high and passion, comfort and love are the best medicine.

True Love

Celebrate true love with tender stories of heartfelt romance, from the rush of falling in love to the joy a new baby can bring, and a focus on the emotional heart of a relationship.

HEROES

The excitement of a gripping thriller, with intense romance at its heart. Resourceful, true-to-life women and strong, fearless men face danger and desire - a killer combination!

From showing up to glowing up, these characters are on the path to leading their best lives and finding romance along the way – with plenty of sizzling spice!

To see which titles are coming soon, please visit

millsandboon.co.uk/nextmonth

GET YOUR ROMANCE FIX!

Get the latest romance news,
exclusive author interviews, story
extracts and much more!

blog.millsandboon.co.uk